SINGLE DAD

Elle M Thomas

Cover design and editing by Bookfully Yours
Formatting by Lia V Dias

This is an Elle M Thomas mature, contemporary romance. Anyone who has read my work before will know what that means, but if you're new to me then let me explain.
This book includes adult situations including, but not limited to adult characters that swear, a lot. A leading man who talks dirty, really, really dirty. Sex, lots and lots of hot, steamy, sheet gripping and toe-curling sex. Due to the dark and explicit nature of this book, it is recommended for mature audiences only.
If this is not what you want to read about then this might not be the book for you, but if it is then sit back, buckle up and enjoy the ride.

Other titles by Elle M Thomas:

Disaster-in-Waiting
Revealing His Prize
One Night Or Forever

Love in Vegas Series (to be read in order)
Lucky Seven (Book 1)
Pushing His Luck (Book 2)
Lucking Out (Book 3)

Falling Series (to be read in order)
New Beginnings (Book 1)
Still Falling (Book 2)

The Nanny Chronicles (to be read in order)
Single Dad (Gabe and Carrie)
Pinky Promise (Seb and Bea)

DEDICATION

For the book boyfriends
and those of us that love them

Chapter One

Carrie

Sitting before Mr Caldwell, I felt nervous.

Gabriel Caldwell was an imposing figure, easily six feet tall and broad, and with his dark hair and eyes he certainly fitted tall, dark and handsome down to a tee. Unlike the archetypal tall, dark and handsome he was also cold, brusque and oozed a strange darkness I couldn't name or identify.

"Miss Webber." His voice caused me to straighten in the chair with a start. "If you could remain focused that would help."

With a silent sigh and a mental note to concentrate on the matter in hand rather than my potential new boss' good looks and personality short comings, I offered a passive, "Sorry."

He frowned. "Quite. If we could get on then."

For the next hour I managed to remain focused and attentive to everything Mr Caldwell was saying until he got to his feet and gestured to the door. "Shall we go and meet her then? Assuming she approves, we can finalise the details of your employment and I will show you to what will be your accommodation."

The question and statement offered no opportunity for discussion or debate leaving me with very little option but to obediently comply. I followed him through the house, remaining on the ground floor, bypassing a lounge, dining room, and study until we reached a large, sunny conservatory where a woman in her fifties sat holding a book in one hand and a cup of something steaming in the other. Her gaze lifted as we entered the room and her face broke into a warm and genuine smile as she looked directly at Mr Caldwell, then me, over her glasses that were perched on the end of her nose.

"Hello, dear," she said before looking back at the man beside her, "Gabriel, darling."

"Sorry, this is my mother, Christine Caldwell. Mother, this is Miss Webber, Charlotte's new nanny."

Both Mrs Caldwell and I seemed taken aback by the announcement. He'd stressed several times during the interview that any appointment would be determined by his daughter and whether she liked me and now the job had been offered before we'd met.

"Christine, please," she offered along with an outstretched hand after removing her reading glasses having already put her cup and book down.

"Carrie." I reciprocated with a warm smile to match the other woman's as I accepted the hand I hoped was of friendship.

"Charlotte?" asked Gabriel.

"She got fed up of waiting, she's in the garden." She smiled before getting up to lead us into the room further.

The silence was broken by a little girl bounding in from the back garden, her braided brown hair bouncing as she ran.

"Daddy, can you push me on the swing now?" she asked as her father scooped her up into his arms.

"Maybe later, or Grandma can. There's someone I'd like you to meet, this is Carrie, Carrie this is Charlotte."

I held my hand out towards the little girl, unsure whether that was an appropriate way to greet a little girl of three or not. The little girl stared up at me intently, Charlotte's dark eyes seemed to stare through me until her lips curled slightly, meaning an outstretched hand was clearly the way to go.

"Could you push me on the swing, Carrie, please?" the little girl asked and looking into her pleading eyes I wondered how anyone could ever say no to her.

Before I could say anything, Mr Caldwell spoke. "Sweetie, Carrie can't push you right now, but maybe another time. Miss Webber, let me show you the rest of the house."

With a short nod from me, Mr Caldwell reached forward and

his fingers skimmed my elbow. An innocent touch that saw me pulling back as if I'd been scorched, a move he mirrored and then we left the conservatory behind.

"Assuming you plan on accepting the job, Miss Webber, I'll show you to your accommodation." My new boss turned so abruptly I almost collided with him.

"Yes, of course, thank you." I babbled, entirely unsure exactly what I was accepting.

I found myself almost walking to heel like an obedient dog as we made our way back through the house until we eventually found ourselves on the second floor of the property where I was shown to my room. Upon entering it I could see why Mr Caldwell, Gabriel, had called it my accommodation because it really was so much more than a room. I was essentially entering a self-contained flat, my own place and space.

"Wow," I said, almost speechless as I walked through the open plan lounge that also housed a small kitchen area.

"I'm glad you like it. There's a bathroom and a bedroom over there," he told me from his position still in the doorway where he pointed to two other doors.

"I just expected a bedroom," I admitted.

"Well, everyone needs their own space and I'm sure you'll have no desire to spend your spare time in mine, my mother's or Charlotte's company," he said flatly causing a frown to crease my brow, but he was right. I didn't know any of them and this was a job. These people were not my friends or family. "I can leave you for a while…"

"No, it's fine…where is Charlotte's room?"

"Downstairs, next to mine. She does have a nursery next door. When I decided to employ a live-in nanny, my mother suggested that you might want to spend time up here during the day so the only other room on this floor is a nursery, just a small one.

"Thank you." I felt unsure just what I was grateful for, but my own confusion blurred as I wondered what his bedroom would look like.

A flush crept up my neck and face as I questioned why I should care what his room might look like. He was not my date;

he was going to be my boss. He was older, a little, and he was also the scariest man I'd ever met and that was saying something because all men scared me.

"Miss Webber, shall we finish the tour?"

"Of course. Charlotte is a lovely little girl and very beautiful."

"Thank you," Gabriel said, freely and with acceptance as a smile tugged at his lips. They were possibly the first words he'd uttered that didn't feel forced or pained.

****

It was a week later when I boarded the train to make the journey back to the Caldwell's house. The decision to apply for a job that would take me away from home had been an easy one.

As the train pulled out of the station, I allowed a ghost of a smile to curl my lips with thoughts of a new life, the start of one at least.

When I'd applied for the job I was able to think of at least three reasons against it for every one for it, moreover, I could think of countless against me rather than in my favour but he, Gabriel, I smirked as I thought of him in such familial terms as his first name, he had seen the pros of employing me rather than the cons. At the very least he had seen more pros than cons.

The countryside was passing by while I continued to think of Gabriel, the man rather than just my employer. He was undoubtedly handsome, rich and smart, but I was uninterested in those things as I considered him now. My focus was on the person, the father, the son, the lover, the husband, the widower.

Chapter Two

Gabriel

I sat in the conservatory with the doors into the garden open. Charlotte lay on the sofa next to me, snoring gently. I smiled down at her. I had no idea I could love another person as much as I loved my daughter. She was the one person in this world I would literally kill for. She muttered something in her sleep and then giggled, making me laugh out loud as she rolled over and settled fully into her afternoon nap.

With my gaze diverted to the garden I watched a couple of squirrels playing together, chasing, teasing, wrestling each other as they competed for a nut or some such thing. I didn't know why, but as I continued to observe them with amusement, my thoughts drifted to Miss Webber.

"Miss Webber. Carrie." It almost felt as though I could taste her on my tongue when I said her name out loud. Was Carrie short for anything, not that I could think of anything that would logically be the full name equivalent.

I glanced down at my watch, briefly losing focus on the squirrels who were running up the old oak tree at the bottom of the garden. Two o'clock. An hour and a half until she arrived. Why the hell had I employed her? I didn't really want a nanny for Charlotte, but when my mother pointed out that the care of an increasingly lively three-year-old was becoming too much for her, I didn't have much choice.

When I placed the ad, I had an extremely specific image in my mind of what *nanny* would look like. I laughed again as I imagined anyone calling Miss Webber *nanny*. I assumed the person I employed would be female, physically capable of keeping up with Charlotte, maybe late twenties, certainly no younger, someone lively, with a good sense of humour, but also serious, educated, possibly bi-lingual and able to discuss topics that may be considered highbrow like art, classical music, literature.

And what did I get?

"Miss Webber." I savoured every sound of her name on my tongue.

She was female, of that there was no doubt…she was all *woman*. I shook those thoughts from my head and went back to my candidate specification list. So, yes, female. I didn't doubt she'd be able to keep up with Charlotte physically. Late twenties, hmmm…twenty-three so more early than late twenties. Lively, there were times when she'd barely seemed to be listening to me during her interview so the jury was out on lively, same with the good sense of humour, although, before she left here she managed to laugh at a couple of things my mother said. Again, jury was out. Educated? I knew she had qualifications, but bi-lingual? Maybe not, well, not beyond GCSE level French, or Spanish or whatever her school had delivered. Serious might prove difficult, same with highbrow topics of conversation considering I heard her asking my mother if she'd been watching the most recent run of some reality show I had no knowledge or understanding of. And then, when her text alert sounded in her bag she shouted, making me jump, something about, *I've got a text*! I mean, what the fuck does that mean and who in their right mind would announce it? My mother smiled, probably mainly at my discomfort and startled expression.

And still I offered her the job, and despite my reservations I hadn't withdrawn the offer. Why was that? I refused to be drawn on it, even when my memory reminded me of the shock of electricity I felt when we touched, albeit innocently, yet still, the feel of her skin against mine scorched, shocking me as if a thousand volts had been put through me.

"Fuck," I muttered, pushing my hand through my hair. "She

is the nanny, staff, and totally out of bounds." I turned my attention back to the squirrels who I was sure were humping. "Bollocks." With a shake of my head I then laughed at the ridiculousness of the whole situation.

I got up and closed the door and when I turned back towards my daughter, I caught sight of myself in the mirror. "Because clearly she's going to fall at your feet." I laughed again, but before I could ponder the likelihood of Miss Webber having any interest in or attraction to me, Charlotte appeared, standing on the sofa, her arms thrown up towards me. "Hey, baby girl, how's my princess?" I picked her up, hugging her to me.

She immediately pulled me in for a kiss.

"I don't need any girl other than you, do I?"

My daughter's response to my question was to cup my face to kiss my lips.

"Yeah, Daddy is a one-woman guy," I told her and myself and I was more than happy with that.

****

I checked the time on the large clock that hung on the kitchen wall. Half-past-four. She should have been here by now, but I had seen no sign. Charlotte was happily sitting at the table with some paper and crayons, drawing.

"Daddy...Grandma...Grandad...Charlotte." She pointed to each coloured blob in turn.

I smiled at my beautiful, clever little girl who had now added legs and arms to the blobs that represented faces. Granted the legs and arms were coming out of the faces, but still. I was about to bestow compliments on her, wanting, needing her to never doubt how amazing and wonderful she was in my mind when a huge crash sounded above us.

"What the fu—" I cut myself off. The last thing I needed was for my kid to be the one that effed and jeffed at pre-school. She didn't start there for a few more weeks, but that would not be the ideal start for either of us, especially when I would be charged handsomely for the privilege of her attending.

With my attention returned to the crash from upstairs and my daughter's eyes cast to the heavens, I leapt into action. I grabbed Charlotte and headed for the stairs, taking them two at a time. I followed the continued sounds of disturbance and came to a standstill on Miss Webber's landing where a suitcase lay, open and empty, things strewn across the floor, leaving a trail into her accommodation. A trail I followed; t-shirts, sweaters, jeans, socks, yoga pants, those tight figure hugging things that should be illegal because they leave nothing to the imagination and that tended to be really bad or really, really good, dependent upon the woman filling them.

"Stop!" My mind ignored my word as my glance returned to the floor to be greeted by small, pretty, lacy things; pants, teeny tiny scraps of fabric that would cover very little and bras, many matching the tiny scraps I'd already seen. For no reason I could offer, I reached down and picked up a black lacy thing. As it dangled from my finger, I realised that it shouldn't even qualify as a pair of pants. It was a thong, a miniscule thing that surely served no real purpose other than to be removed by someone's teeth. Mine. "Fuck!" I cried, somehow incapable of containing the expletive or the image in my head of Miss Webber in black lace as my mouth made its way over her body.

"Fuck!"

The sound of my sweet, beautiful daughter uttering that one word broke my dirty thoughts. The sight of Miss Webber standing before me, abject horror on her face, me with her thong still on my finger, holding it out as if it was an offering or worse still a trophy had those same dirty thoughts racing back to the forefront of my mind.

The stiffening in my trousers as her mouth moved into a perfect 'O' as she uttered a whispered, "Oh no," only served to increase the filth in the thoughts.

"What the hell!" I recovered quickly, maintaining eye contact as I held her thong out, forcing her to accept it from me, knowing I now knew what she was packing beneath her innocent jeans and sweater.

"Sorry—my case broke—the lock—hence my clothes—my pants."

Her voice was no more than a whisper. Her cheeks were red with embarrassment and her eyes looked sorrowful, maybe even ashamed as she accepted her underwear, our fingers briefly touching as the prickling sensation I'd previously felt returned. She slipped her pants into her back pocket. I felt sorry for her, a little, but then wished I'd slipped them into my own pocket…

"You said I should use the side entrance to get up here," she said as if in explanation for her being here.

"I did?" I'd meant once she'd moved in. For her privacy and to ensure she could lead a life independent of her job and duties, not that she couldn't use the front door. As if she was only the hired help. I stopped myself from saying any of that because for all intents and purposes, that's what she was, the hired help and although she was pretty, beautiful, wore sexy little pants and had a curvy and soft body that would undoubtedly offer comfort and so much more, a body my own responded to on a very basic level, I needed to keep a professional distance.

"You did," she confirmed. "So, I did, but my case…"

"I see." I frowned at her, unsure why, but I did. "Well, if you could tidy up the mess." I gestured once more to her personal items, her intimate wear.

Her face fell at my tone and choice of words. She probably thought I was a complete and utter tool, a dick, and I was when I needed to be, and with her, I needed to be.

"Half an hour and I will see you downstairs."

Her response was a short nod before she turned to Charlotte who I had almost forgotten was still there, in my arms. "Hey, Charlotte." She smiled so sweetly I almost offered her tea and cake as an incentive to come downstairs sooner.

"Hey," Charlotte replied, her smile as sweet as her nanny's but bigger and more confident. "Fuck!" she repeated.

I had never sworn in front of Charlotte before today. It had happened once and now it was stuck on repeat in her fucking head. Fuck my life!

The sound of Miss Webber's laughter broke my wallowing thoughts and as much as it warmed me, it pissed me right off because somehow it was condoning my daughter's swearing, or at least that's what I told myself. The truth was something very, very different.

I scowled in her direction. "Ten minutes, downstairs," I barked and then turned my attention and much softer tone to my daughter. "Don't say that, baby, it's a bad word."

"Sorry, Daddy," she replied as we began our descent of the stairs leaving nanny behind, for now.

Chapter Three

Carrie

I watched Mr Caldwell's back get farther and farther away when he headed downstairs. Charlotte looked over his shoulder and smiled at me. She might just be the cutest thing I had ever seen. I laughed out loud as I remembered her saying fuck, twice, and then laughed louder at just how outraged and horrified her father appeared to be.

"Dick." I muttered that one word and as much as his touch sent me into girly overdrive; giggling, panicking, saying stupid things as my skin flushed and tingled, I totally believed that the man was a twat of the highest order, but he really did make very cute babies. "No." My chastisement for myself was in vain because I was already thinking about making babies, the physical act, imagining my new boss naked and sweaty as he stripped me bare and devoured me—

"Miss Webber, those ten minutes are now down to four."

I shook all thoughts, good, sexy thoughts from my mind and refocused on my boss, the dickhead.

With my belongings literally thrown in a heap on my bed I made my way downstairs, as commanded. I followed the sounds of Charlotte's laughter and the rumbling of her father's voice to the kitchen. The sight that greeted me was one of ovary bursting proportions. He, Mr Caldwell, Gabriel, was singing and dancing to a popular song about a shark family with his daughter. Charlotte's giggles that I was sure were being pulled up from her boots echoed around the room. She joined in with all the actions and the repetitive parts of the song between peals of laughter, laughter her father joined in with as the song came to an end on the TV screen hanging on the kitchen wall.

"Again, again," she squealed, excitement rolling off her.

Mr Caldwell laughed at her demands before hitting play again. I was unsure whether I should have announced my arrival but with the singing and dancing in full flow once more I was incapable of doing anything other than watch on.

Charlotte was giving her father a round of applause as he threw in some impromptu moves that I was sure weren't part of the *official* dance when he spun around and came to a dead stop at the image of me grinning inanely.

"Erm, I, Miss Webber…you're here, at last…come in."

I bit back a smirk at his discomfort at having been discovered but also at his attempt to somehow move past his song and dance routine and refocus on my arrival with the inference that I was late.

"Yes. I'd have come down much sooner had I known there was a party."

He laughed and blushed a little at the same time and oh my good lord, if he wasn't even more gorgeous than ever. Don't think that way about him, he's a dickhead, remember, I told myself.

I clearly wasn't listening because my mouth opened again, and I continued to speak before he could respond. "And you're light on your feet for a big man."

He stared at me as a *what the fuck* rang around my head. I needed to get a grip here because I was at risk of, well, I had no clue what I was at risk of. He was gorgeous and I found him attractive, but he was my boss, no more, plus, it was quite clear that he barely tolerated me.

"No party…" He coughed, clearing his throat before reverting to type after the barriers shot back up. "I don't appreciate lateness." He looked across at the clock. "And I'm not good with mess and clutter." His eyebrows raised and he glanced towards the ceiling, presumably that was a reference to my belongings strewn across the landing.

"Of course." I still stood in the doorway, unsure what to say or do.

"Good. Well, a cup of tea maybe?"

"Thank you." I nodded.

"I will make the tea, maybe you'd like to take Charlotte into the garden, get to know one another and then after tea we will arrange a mutually convenient time for us to get together and lay down a few ground rules."

"Of course, yes, thank you." I had no idea why I had added the thank you, or indeed what I was thankful for, but I'd said it and before I could change it or attempt to understand it, Charlotte was heading towards me in the doorway, excited at the prospect of going into the garden with me.

It was a few minutes later when Mr Caldwell appeared in the open doorway of the conservatory. Charlotte saw him first and ran to him, excitedly chatting about how high I'd pushed her on her swing. I panicked slightly in case that was wrong, but he just smiled down at her and enthusiastically encouraged her to talk more.

Okay, so he was a dickhead still, but he was attractive, and more than that he was a good father. Briefly, my mind went to Mrs Caldwell, Charlotte's mother, not his. I wondered if he'd been different when she was alive. Had he laughed and been more relaxed, more at ease or was the uptight, slightly serious and disapproving man I had seen on every occasion we'd met, always been there? I had no way of knowing and despite my own warnings to myself, I really, really wanted to get the lowdown on my new boss.

"Let's take Miss Webber in for her tea," he said to his daughter, but had already scooped her up in his arms and was heading back inside.

I obediently followed him and sat when and where directed to. His phone sounded an alert and once he'd checked the screen he turned to Charlotte. "Grandma says hello and sends you lots of love."

The little girl smiled as she pulled some toy food from a toy chest.

"And she says she can't wait to see you in the morning."

"The morning?" I asked, wondering why his mother was

coming around when I would have officially started work.

"Yes, the morning. We, she, thought it would be nice for you to have her around to lean on until Charlotte gets used to you."

I nodded, unsure if I should speak, apologise maybe.

He didn't seem to need any input from me as he cocked his head slightly and arched an eyebrow. "Good. I'm sure she'll be thrilled to know that her plans meet with your approval."

My mouth opened several times, but no words came out.

"Miss Webber, drink your tea."

I felt as though he had just given me a direct order, so I sipped at the hot liquid in the cup I held. "You can call me Carrie," I said for no reason beyond the fact that Miss Webber sounded overly formal considering I would be living in this man's house.

He stared at me, studied me then shook his head and adopted a sour expression, as if he was shaking thoughts from his mind or removing a bad taste from his mouth.

"Drink your tea," he repeated, "Miss Webber."

The mutually convenient time came around half past eight. After our tea I had returned to my room and tidied up a little. I checked out my social media and flicked around the TV before my rumbling belly alerted me to the fact that I hadn't eaten that day. Unfortunately, there wasn't time to right that as I was due to meet with my new boss.

I made my way downstairs and found Mr Caldwell wearing a pair of track bottoms and a formfitting white t-shirt that was a little damp and clung to every ripple and curve of his chest, arms and abdomen.

"Am I early?" I asked, knowing full well that I wasn't but felt uncomfortable in catching him less than prepared to meet with me, or so I thought.

"No, you're spot on. Shall we?" He gestured towards his office, where he'd interviewed me.

I took the seat I was offered and sat and listened as Mr Caldwell discussed details; mealtimes, Charlotte's schedule and routine, his mother's role and her potential to take over, the nursery Charlotte would be attending and what he expected from a nanny, from me. I nodded, a lot.

At no point did he discuss Charlotte's mother or her maternal family. He referred to his work several times and as much as I wanted to know what he did, I stopped myself from asking, in case that was overstepping some mark I wasn't yet aware of.

"Do you have any questions?"

I had dozens but tried to ask the most important. I failed. "What should I call you?" That is what I came up with and could have kicked myself. Judging by Mr Caldwell's face I reckon he could've happily kicked me too.

"Mr Caldwell. You should call me Mr Caldwell, Miss Webber."

"Oh. I don't mind you calling me Carrie," I told him, repeating my earlier offer.

"Next question, Miss Webber."

Okay, clearly, we weren't ready for first names.

"Charlotte can call me Carrie though?"

"Of course. Anything else, aside from names?"

"No," I almost whispered, feeling more ridiculous for not having anything else to add.

My stomach chose this moment to growl loudly, causing us both to look down at it.

"Have you eaten?" he asked.

I shook my head, confirming my lack of food. He returned the shake of his head, but his was more disapproving than anything.

"You are welcome to eat anything from the kitchen. The cupboards and fridge are well stocked. Obviously if you'd prefer to eat breakfast and dinner alone in your rooms, I have no objection."

I exchanged my earlier shake of the head with a nod.

"Speaking of your rooms...erm, visitors, guests." He looked a little awkward as he spoke.

"Guests?" I thought I knew what he was saying, insinuating...boys, men, but just in case I'd misread things I allowed him to uncomfortably explain further.

"Yes, guests...erm, friends, liaisons, boyfriends..."

I stifled a smirk at his use of the word *liaison*. "Ah. I don't have a boyfriend."

"I see. Then even more reason to clarify. Your rooms are your domain. I don't need to know what happens in your personal life and I would never judge your choices morally, but Charlotte… she doesn't need to be exposed to a string of men, or women passing through."

My hard stare was one of shock and irritation. "I have never had a string of men passing through anywhere so that won't be an issue. If we're done here?"

How dare he? Sanctimonious, judgemental twat! Maybe I'd find a string of hot and available men just to piss him off. I obviously wouldn't. That wasn't me, never had been.

I was dismissed with a nod. My phone sounded a text alert as I got to my feet. I pulled it from my back pocket, still annoyed with my new boss. I wondered if I could ask the same of him, for the benefit of his daughter—no beautiful and willing women passing through. "Goodnight, Mr Caldwell."

"Goodnight," he called after me. "Eat something," he added, sounding firm and determined.

Chapter Four

Gabriel

"Eat something." That was the best I could come up with as I watched her leave. "Idiot," I muttered to myself. I was unsure what I should have said to her beyond extending the use of my house and consumption of the food in it.

She looked seriously pissed off by my words. Not the offer of food but the inference that she was likely to have man after man passing through my house, passing through her bedroom, through her. In fairness to myself I reasoned that she could be sexually promiscuous. I didn't know her, and no number of references were going to divulge her sexual appetite or moral compass. I didn't care what she got up to or who with. I only cared about the impact of that on my daughter. Or at least that's what I told myself because she was the nanny, no more, couldn't be, and whilst I found her attractive that is where it started and ended. Briefly, I questioned the sizzle between us and fireworks of pyrotechnic proportions that went off every time we touched or held each other's gaze for a second too long. It was nothing, I replied to my own question.

"Fuck!" I muttered as I got to my feet and paced a little, coming to a stop in front of the seat she'd occupied earlier. "What the—"

I reached down. She'd left something behind, maybe when she retrieved her phone from her pocket. As I stood to my full height again, I smiled, rubbed the item between my fingers, teased the fabric I held. I just about managed to resist the temptation to lift the item higher, to inhale them, rub them against my face. Her underwear, the skimpy item I'd returned to her after finding it on her landing and here they were again, in my hand.

"Destiny, it has to be," I said, unsure if it was me or her underwear I was speaking to, but either way I accepted this as fate. With the tiny scrap of material being pushed into my pocket, I understood that this was like no fate any rational person would acknowledge never mind embrace. I roughly rubbed my hands over my face, desperate for some clarity or a revelation, but I got neither. With my hand finding its own way into my pocket where it caressed the soft fabric of Miss Webber's, Carrie's, tiny scrap of underwear, I felt myself stiffen. "Shit. I need to get laid, quickly."

****

I turned my alarm off forty minutes before it was due to go off. The truth was that I could have turned it off an hour before I did because I hadn't been asleep for hours, had barely slept with thoughts of Miss Webber keeping me from slumber.

"Get a bloody grip, Gabriel," I told myself as I immediately sprang from my bed and headed straight to the shower where I was determined to think of anything other than my nanny or her pants that were currently nestled beneath my pillow.

I failed miserably on both counts, and by the time she appeared in the kitchen wearing a pair of shorts and a vest top, my mood had darkened to a new low with everything and everyone, mainly her.

"Good morning," she chirped as she leaned in and smiled at Charlotte who was eating her breakfast of cereal and juice.

Her smile for my daughter was full, warm and totally fucking gorgeous. So much so that I found myself smiling at the sight of it. I really wished she smiled at me the same way. I shook that final thought from my mind because I swear to all I held dear that if she ever fucking smiled at me that way I would be powerless to do anything other than pull her to me, hold her and kiss her.

"Morning," called my mother, her over the top greeting breaking all thoughts of holding, kissing and Carrie bloody

Webber, full stop. "How are we all?" she asked, already leaning down to kiss Charlotte's cheek and then mine. "Have you settled in, Carrie?"

"Getting there."

My mother and Carrie laughed together, Charlotte joined in, not really knowing what she was even laughing at but the sound of it filled the room and somehow seemed contagious judging by the smile that briefly curled my lips, especially at the notion that she might have thought she'd almost settled in but I knew full well that she was missing a pair of pants.

"I should be going. Have a good day, all of you."

Mother offered me a nod as her response, Charlotte squealed a *bye Daddy* before pursing her lips, inviting me in for a kiss while Miss Webber nervously shuffled from one foot to the other, drawing my attention to her feet, from her pink painted toes to her slender ankles and well-toned legs before my eyes landed on her behind.

"Bye then," she almost whispered, then offered me a little wave, her fingers flexed and curled making me think immoral thoughts involving those fingers wrapped around my dick.

Shit! I wondered if I should go out after work and hook up with someone willing and able. Anyone who wasn't my nanny… maybe someone the opposite of her.

By the time I arrived at my office my equilibrium had been restored. Everything was as it should be, and all thoughts of home and my nanny were out of my mind. After all, people paid good money to have my attention and they deserved for it to be focused and undivided.

My first few clients came and went, nothing remarkable occurred. I felt better, more centred, and then a message alert on my phone drew my attention. The message was from my mother with photos attached.

My receptionist had just entered my office with a bundle of files and a cup of coffee as I opened the message to see the photos and the simple message of, *I think Charlotte has a new favourite person* :-D

Laughter rang around the office as I noticed her use of keyboard characters to make a smiley face rather than an emoji.

The laughter stopped just as quickly when I saw the images from that morning.

The photos began around my kitchen table where Charlotte held pencils and crayons, drawing pictures with Carrie, then she put shoes on, with Carrie, ran to the park, with Carrie, played on the swings and slide, with Carrie and finally ate ice-cream, with Carrie. The image of them both in each shot showed them happily laughing and clearly enjoying each other's company, which was good, amazing as Miss Webber was her nanny and Charlotte could be a little reluctant to warm to new people...she got that from me.

"Is everything okay?" asked my receptionist, Shelley.

"What? Yes! Sorry." My mood was in no way her fault, so I felt genuinely apologetic for snapping at her. "Thanks for the coffee. You can take lunch whenever you fancy."

"No problem." She offered me a small smile as she left me alone with my furrowed brow, sour mood and photos.

Receiving photos from my mother wasn't unusual but them including the new nanny was and it threw me. Or at least that's what I told myself was at the root of my sudden change in mood. The truth was that I couldn't stop looking at them, and as much as I loved seeing my baby happy and having fun, it was the images of Miss Webber I was incapable of dragging my glance from. The last one, her licking her ice-cream called to me on an extremely basic level but the one on the slide where she was laughing and racing Charlotte to the bottom tugged on something deeper. Fuck! She was gorgeous, no denying it and in a different world, a different time or circumstance...but it wasn't, so no dwelling.

With the photos closed I called up another number, Seb, my oldest and best friend. "Hey, how's things?" I asked when he answered.

"Shit if you really want to know. This fucking sex free life is not for me." He at least laughed at his final comment, as did I.

"Yeah, tell me about it. So, how about you and me, tomorrow night, drink, more drink, maybe some pretty and uncomplicated ladies? What do you say?"

"Fuck, yes is what I say. Shall I come to you and then I can at least say hi to Charlotte?"

"Yes, sounds like a plan. You know she loves you and your storytelling, so I'll see you about seven."

"Cool and then you can tell Uncle Seb all about it."

Nobody knew me quite like Seb and I should probably have known he'd figure there was more to this than a simple catch-up.

"Whatever. Don't be late and keep my girl waiting."

Operation *Get Carrie Webber out of my head* had commenced.

Chapter Five

Carrie

Christine was amazing. My first day couldn't have gone better and that was because of her. She took us, me and Charlotte, to the park and then to a playgroup, a stay and play thing at a nearby community centre. She introduced me to some of the parents there and for the most part they were friendly, although a couple of them treated me with suspicion, but I kind of understood that, they don't know me. I was the newbie in town, and they were there with their kids and they all seemed pretty well off. The truth was that I felt more comfortable with the other nannies that she introduced me to; they were closer to my age and treated me like one of them straight away. I'd agreed to meet a couple of them on Saturday night for a few drinks and some dinner which I was really looking forward to as I had no friends here, well, the truth was that I didn't really have any friends full stop.

Gabriel called to say he'd be late home. I couldn't imagine calling him anything other than Mr Caldwell, but in my head, I'd begun to think of him in more familiar terms. We shared a home after all. Well, I shared his home, but you know. So, by the time he returned home I had bathed Charlotte and put her pyjamas on, she looked adorable in her mermaid covered nightwear.

Christine was still there and had made dinner for her granddaughter, dinner she wolfed down and there was some food left for her son. She offered to feed me too, but I politely refused as I planned to eat once I returned to my own accommodation. Christine offered to bathe Charlotte, but I did it and the little girl seemed keen for me to be the one doing bath time followed by a story. I agreed to story time on the understanding that if her father was home first, he would do it, which is how he liked it according to his mother.

I had just tucked Charlotte into bed and was reading a story involving a princess who was having a shitty time in her shitty life and a charming prince who was clearly going to rescue her.

The words *and they all lived happily* ever *after* had just left my lips and I had closed the book. I looked down at the cover, a beautiful woman; young, happy, flawless skin, perfect hair and a body shape to die for. She stood alongside her Prince Charming; tall, dark, handsome, stand out eyes, perfect hair and teeth, kind, muscular, loving and loyal. Why did we do this to children, specifically to little girls? We built up this myth that all we needed to do was wait and struggle, maybe suffer a little, but it didn't matter, it would be okay because one day our prince would arrive and rescue us, save us and then we would live happily ever after.

"As if!" I muttered aloud. Kids really should be able to sue their parents for selling them this crazy shit that never, ever happened.

I got to my feet, placed the book down and as I prepared to leave, I suddenly felt the presence of someone behind me, Gabriel. Mr Caldwell. Turning slowly, I saw him standing before me, leaning against the door jamb, watching me. Just how long had he been there? His gaze flitted to his daughter then straight back to me before moving again to the book I had just read and once more his eyes landed on me.

"Not a fan of the fairy-tale?"

I frowned, unsure what he was asking or referring to.

He smirked as if he was in on some great secret.

My frown deepened.

"As if?" he said, repeating my own words to me. "And they all lived happily ever after?"

He'd been there that long.

I shook my head, confirming my disbelief in the fairy-tale

myth. "How many people do you know who have that life? Have ever had that life or are likely to?"

I sounded cold and cynical to my own ears so goodness knows how I must have sounded to him.

His shrug was his only immediate response, somehow forcing me to continue.

"You can't pin all of your hopes and dreams on someone else. If you want something from life, then there is only really you that has enough of a vested interest to make it happen."

He nodded at me, looking thoughtful. "Maybe." He turned slightly and with an outstretched arm indicated that I should leave. With his other hand gently closing the door of his daughter's bedroom he faced me. "Is that what you do, Miss Webber? Do you make your own dreams and hopes come true?"

My mouth dried and I was unsure if I could respond. Even more so when I noticed the gap between us had closed. We were virtually toe to toe. My heart had sped up, my pulse raced, and my palms had grown clammy…all of me had grown clammy.

Without waiting for an actual response from me, he continued, "And I can't help but wonder what your hopes are, and your dreams…what precisely occupies your mind when you're sleeping? What is it that you subconsciously want, hmmm?"

What the actual fuck was happening here? His head moved even closer and he leaned in a little as if he was going to kiss me and God knows, I wouldn't resist him. It didn't even happen in my dreams, ones which had been filled with this complicated, confusing and mercurial man who excited me and petrified me in equal parts.

My lips parted as if in preparation to speak, but even my inner self wasn't buying that. I knew that I wanted to feel his lips on mine, to be kissed by him and then whatever else he might offer.

"If that's true, that you make your own hopes and dreams come true then I encourage you to continue to do so."

I knew I was staring but was incapable of blinking at that precise moment. Was he saying what I thought he was? Did he mean him, kissing, that I should make it come true?

"I mean, if you see something you want, you should grab it

with both hands."

The arch of his brows confirmed that he was goading me to do exactly that and his suggestive smirk told me I might need to grab him with both hands. Shit! How did I manage to find myself in this situation with a man that petrified me, fascinated me, and had my whole body quivering and quaking? I closed my eyes, well, blinked, a long blink until I felt his breath dance across my lips causing a low moan to escape me and then the bedroom door swung open revealing Charlotte, covered in sick.

"Daddy," she cried.

"Oh, baby." He bent down and immediately picked her up and began to comfort and soothe her. "Goodnight, Miss Webber."

"I could help," I offered, my suggestion a genuine one, although judging by the scowl being levelled at me, he didn't look convinced of that.

"That won't be necessary. I've got this. Charlotte is my responsibility and you are off the clock. Goodnight."

"Daddy." Charlotte sounded tearful again as she suddenly began to heave.

He immediately and rightfully so, gave her his undivided attention. Leading her into the bathroom he shut the door behind him, shutting me out.

I stood, more confused than ever for a matter of seconds wondering what the fuck had happened before uttering two words. "As if."

Chapter Six

Gabriel

What the actual fuck was I thinking of last night? I had barely slept between checking on Charlotte and replaying events with Carrie bloody Webber, and therefore I was grouchy when I arrived at work early, incredibly early. The truth was that I wasn't thinking at all when I came within a hairs breadth of kissing her and Lord knows what else.

I came home and my mother told me how amazing her day with Carrie and Charlotte had been. She told me all about their time together and how everyone had loved Carrie at stay and play, how she'd made friends and how much the children had all loved her, especially Charlotte.

With a smile, I listened because I did want Miss Webber to be settled and happy here. It was in mine and specifically my daughter's best interests for her to be that way if we wanted her to stay here. Well, that's what I told myself, but it ran deeper. Her experience and qualifications were all satisfactory and her references were excellent. She seemed happy, but beneath the façade she looked sad, jaded, disappointed by life, so I'd offered her the job and now, even in this weird predicament of her permanently being on my mind, I still couldn't bring myself to regret employing her.

Once my mother had finished raving about the nanny, she made her excuses and left. I knew that Carrie had agreed to do bath time and story time with Charlotte so I made my way upstairs, to allow her to clock off for the night and do whatever it was she did once she was alone. God! The things I imagined her doing. Anyway, I went upstairs and could hear her before I saw her; her soft voice reading about a poor princess who had been treated badly by life, only to be rescued by a dashing prince who loved her and only wanted to care for her and make their happy ending a reality. *And they all lived happily ever after,* that's what she'd said and I'm sure she couldn't have sounded more disgusted in those seven words had she tried. Her *as if* confirmed that. She sounded as though she didn't believe in fairy-tales or true love, and whilst I was inclined to agree with her, she should believe and want it all.

My phone vibrated on my desk. Glancing down I saw a message from Seb, confirming our plans for the night. I shook all thoughts of my nanny, our strange, almost kiss on the landing from my mind because none of those things had a right to be there and every time I thought of her and happy ever after, I ultimately ended up thinking of a very different kind of happy ending. I wondered if she'd missed her pants yet.

"For fuck's sake, stop it!" I shouted at myself. "Get your head in the game," I added. I made myself think about the night out with my friend and all that would entail, beer, laughter and pretty ladies.

****

"Are you sure you don't mind watching her tonight?" I asked my mother for possibly the tenth time.

"Of course not. You have fun, although not too much fun with Seb." She grinned, knowing exactly just how much fun could be had with my friend. She'd had me come home very late and very drunk after many a night out with him.

"You know Seb." I grinned back before leaning down to kiss my mother, preparing to leave when I remembered my watch.

I dashed back up to my bedroom, having checked on Charlotte on the way. After being sick once last night she was fine and by all accounts had been her usual self all day, but I checked on her anyway.

I fastened my watch and checked my appearance in the mirror, dark jeans, white button-down shirt, casual but not too casual. I turned to leave and then spotted those little pants of

Miss Webber's, peeking out from the drawer. I pulled them out, teasing the fabric between my fingers, imagining my fingers being as close to her body as this item had been. What I wouldn't give to touch her—

"Mr Caldwell."

"Fuck!" I leapt away from the sound of her voice, quickly shoving her underwear into my back pocket, hoping she hadn't busted me. "Miss Webber, what are you doing here?"

She was on the threshold of my room and that is where she needed to stay because if she crossed it, I was unsure if I'd be able to control myself...God knows I was struggling as it was.

"I wanted to speak to you. I've missed you all day."

We both stared at one another, both of us hearing the words she'd uttered.

"No, not missed you, not like that. I mean I missed you."

"Miss Webber, I have no clue what you're talking about." I felt the smile tugging at my lips as I watched her nervously shuffling from one foot to the other, her cheeks flushed, the repeated words she somehow expected me to understand with their different meaning, her eyes darted between me and the floor and her hands rubbed down her thighs, presumably drying her sweaty palms.

"I meant I had missed you—"

"You said." I interrupted, my smile unmistakable now, as was her scowl that suggested she thought I was an arsehole. I was.

"As in I haven't seen you, not that I *missed,* missed you."

"Oh." I know I shouldn't have felt anything by that, but I did, I was disappointed.

She continued, "And I wondered if we should talk about last night."

She was a nice shade of crimson now and rather than reassure or ease her embarrassment I went full out arsehole, leaving her in no doubt that I was one. "Last night, I see. Well, Charlotte was sick just the once so it may just be that she'd overindulged in ice-cream and the park."

Her glare suggested my arsehole was coming through loud and clear.

"She went back to sleep once she was clean and settled,

unlike me who was up most of the night checking on her." My accusatory tone didn't go unnoticed by her. "The sheets and bed cover seem to have recovered along with my daughter though."

Her glare had turned quite murderous. The fact that I had a near overbearing urge to drag her inside to kiss her breathless and fuck her until she couldn't walk for that look alone, confirmed I was doing the right thing here. I needed her not to think about our almost kiss because if she did, that would complicate things even more than the *almost* kiss itself.

"And thank you for reading Charlotte a story. I'll be sure to add the overtime to your wages."

That was the killer blow. The way her eyes turned cold and her posture became one of stone, broke me a little, but this was for her own good, and mine.

"Good night."

I watched her back disappear and then heard her steps ascend the stairs to her own space. I wanted to follow her, but that would be a bad move, so, I took a deep breath and made my way downstairs for a night with Seb.

****

"So, let me just get this straight; you have hired a hot nanny for Charlotte who is amazing, Charlotte loves her, Christine loves her, you fancy the pants off her, literally." Seb sniggered. I didn't. I shouldn't have told him about the pants. "She is neither looking for or believes in the bullshit fairy-tale, you almost kissed last night and only didn't because Charlotte was unwell, and when she tried to discuss it you were a dickhead and pretended like it didn't happen?"

"Yes." I offered no further words. He'd summed it up pretty well.

"And now you are looking for alcohol and maybe a different woman to scratch your itch?"

"Yes."

"Right, then let's get this show on the road." Seb was already heading to two women who sat alone, nursing their drinks.

We pulled alongside them and took the available seats at their table and immediately began to chat and offered them a drink. They were both nice; friendly, funny, attractive and had very good figures that were being shown off in their short and tight dresses.

We danced, drank some more, chatted and arranged another night out, Saturday. My mum usually came over on a Saturday or took Charlotte to hers if I went out, so I knew that wouldn't be a problem.

My date for Saturday, Leigh, was a leggy blonde with a full and genuine smile, sparkly blue eyes and really big boobs. Seb kept getting distracted by them and every time he did, I laughed. Leigh's friend, and Seb's date, was Lorna, a shorter redhead with freckles and big brown eyes. They were both lovely ladies and there was no reason to think we wouldn't have a blast on Saturday because tonight had been fun, even without getting laid, but that was okay.

Seb and I walked the girls out to the taxi rank and after a kiss goodnight we made sure they were safely on their way home before we said our own goodnights then headed home with calls of *see you Saturday.*

Chapter Seven

Carrie

I heard Mr Caldwell's car drive away and safe in the knowledge that he was gone, I popped downstairs to see Christine. Maybe she'd like some company. Charlotte was already in bed and presumably sleeping soundly.

Christine was sat in front of the TV that was tuned to some soap opera she seemed less than interested in.

"Hi," I called as I entered the room. "If I'm interrupting…" I began to stammer thinking that if it had been Mr Caldwell down here, I wouldn't have dreamt of coming down like this.

"Carrie, come in, please. I watch this from time to time but it's a bit farfetched," she said, pointing towards the TV. "He's having an affair with his teenage daughter's friend, she is pregnant, he's gay but nobody knows yet and her dad is about to come back from the dead."

We both laughed at her synopsis.

"Just a regular day with regular people in a regular street in a regular town then?"

"Absolutely." She grinned and held a half bottle of wine up. "Can I tempt you? I'm driving so it will only be the one for me, but I am more than happy to share if you grab yourself a glass."

We sat for an hour or so and chatted about everything and nothing, mainly safe topics like books, music, films and Charlotte, then Christine turned conversation to my new nanny friends.

"They're nice girls from what I've seen. You should go out

with them sometime, the pictures or a meal and drinks. You're young and pretty and should be out there dancing with good looking men."

We both laughed, but I nodded, she had a point, about the nanny friends. "I'll call later, when I go up."

"Good, and don't worry about Gabriel."

"Gabriel?" I asked, wondering why she thought I would worry about him and specifically how those worries might relate to my new friends and socialising.

"Yes, Gabriel. He's not as grouchy as he sometimes appears, and I am sure he'd want you to settle in here and have a life and friends of your own. I mean, you have your own entrance to your rooms and what he doesn't know won't hurt him." She finished with a suggestive wink for me.

I laughed, despite the inference, got to my feet and headed back to my room to contact my new friends.

By the time I put my phone on charge, I was in a group chat with the nannies I'd met and some associated friends of theirs. What's more, I had been invited and had accepted their invitation to join them for a night of eating, drinking, fun and dancing on Saturday and I couldn't wait.

Lying in bed, I tossed and turned, going over that evening with Gabriel 'I am an arsehole' Caldwell. What a complete and utter dickhead move to make out that nothing had or was possibly going to happen between us before Charlotte interrupted the previous night. I mean, what was I expecting? I didn't really know, but I hadn't expected him to pretend like it had never happened. I could have kicked myself for allowing our near miss kiss to even be a thing and I could have kicked myself a little harder when I recalled how I had blurted out that I'd missed him, even if I hadn't meant it that way. Dickhead, arsehole, twat—

The closing of a car door broke my chain of expletives for him. I climbed out of bed and looked from my window to see his car was back. I stared for a few minutes, at his car, the stars and the moon and then another car door closing gained my attention. Christine's car had pulled out and was driving away. I laughed thinking about the conversation I'd had with her earlier. I really

Single Dad

liked her, although I figured, as his mother, she might be the only one who would suggest her son was less grouchy than he acted or that he wanted me to in any way be happy and settled. Her leaving meant he was downstairs alone. Maybe I should go and tell him just what I thought of his idiot move earlier. Leave him in no doubt that we were going to kiss whether he wanted to admit it or not.

I was already heading for my door, ready to rush downstairs and confront him when I paused. I could hear something, his footsteps coming up the stairs. I move closer to the bannister along my landing that overlooked the stairs and floors below, glancing over it to see Mr Caldwell arriving on his landing. I watched as he entered Charlotte's room, checking on her. A smile spread across my face. I still considered the man a dickhead and every other expletive I could think of, but he was a good dad, a great one even. He left her room and glanced up at me. We stared at one another, neither of us speaking for long, long seconds, the air between us thickening. I was confused as to what I should do, what I wanted him to do. God, I had even forgotten what I'd planned to do.

"Goodnight, Miss Webber."

I still stared down at him as he dropped his gaze.

"Call me Carrie, please." I had no clue why this was becoming increasingly important to me, for us to be more familiar, for him to be more familiar with me.

Without lifting his gaze, he began to ascend the stairs to my floor while my breathing hitched, almost stopping as I nervously awaited his arrival.

"I can't do that, Miss Webber," he told me, having come to a standstill just a few inches away from me.

"Why? I wouldn't mind."

"Why do you think?" His eyes were fixed on mine as he waited for a response.

"I have no idea."

"Of course, you do. We both know what will happen with this tension between us if we don't keep some distance. You have hit it off with my mother and most importantly, my daughter. I think you could give Charlotte the young, carefree, fun input that she needs and deserves as a little girl, and I don't know why I trust you to keep her safe, but I do."

"Like last night?" My voice was barely a whisper. "The tension?"

"Yes." He reached up and brushed the loose hair back off my face, pushing it behind my ear.

"But my name." I had no idea why the name thing was such a thing for me, but somehow, I couldn't seem to move past it.

"If I say it, to you, if I call you Carrie…" He winced as if in pain when he uttered my name. "Then it makes this personal and I won't stop."

"Stop?"

"I will kiss you until you're gasping for breath. I will pull you into my arms and hold you there, adjusting your position so I can completely consume you and then I will remove every scrap of clothing and devour you from head to toe. I will feast on you until you are begging me to make the ache go away. Until the burn you feel has you pleading in breathy gasps for me to take you, to fuck you hard and make you come all over my dick."

"Oh." One word I opted for, one bloody word and that word was oh.

"Precisely. So…" His hand that had tucked my hair behind my ear moved through my locks so he could cup my head, gently tilting it, pulling me closer, almost close enough to taste.

"So…" One word responses were clearly my thing now.

He grinned, cocky and self-assured. "So…" He leaned in for a split second and I felt his warm breath dance across my ear before he whispered, "Goodnight, Miss Webber."

And just like that he was gone, and I was even more confused than ever and that ache and burn he spoke of? Yeah, well, that was aching and burning in the extreme.

Chapter Eight

Gabriel

She was my fucking kryptonite. That was the only reasonable explanation for my ridiculous behaviour around her. The urge to touch her, kiss her, tell her the things I wanted to do to her. Every time we were alone together the air crackled until it felt like a bomb was likely to go off and that bomb involved me and her getting naked, the two of us hot and very sweaty.

"Gabriel." My mother called my name, possibly not for the first time judging by her tone and expression.

"Yes, sorry."

"I was asking about your plans for this evening with Seb."

"Dinner, drinks and a club I believe. I've left the details to Seb, so who knows."

We both laughed, with Seb at the helm anything really was possible.

"Just the two of you?" She smirked, taking her seat opposite me in the conservatory while Charlotte played outside on the enclosed trampoline I didn't want, but she loved.

"We are meeting two ladies we met the other night—"

"Oh."

"No '*oh*', Mother. It is one night out, so don't get carried away."

"Of course."

I watched as my mother sipped her tea, a small smile curled her lips, like I had just confirmed some deep, dark secret.

Charlotte all but ended conversation when we were both

drawn to her excited squeals outside. She was bouncing up and down on the trampoline, waving and shouting as she looked to the heavens.

"Carrie," she called, revealing exactly what had got her all riled up and excited. I could relate to that for sure.

"She is smitten for sure."

"What?" My mother's statement threw me...I had kind of heard her but had no clue who she was speaking about or the context.

"Are you having some issues with your hearing, dear?" She smirked while I frowned. "Just asking as I seem to need to keep repeating myself today."

I huffed. I actually fucking huffed at my mother. I was supposedly an adult. I didn't think I was much of a huffer or pouter when I was an adolescent and yet now, under the heady influence of Miss Webber, and the way she messed with my head, I had become one. I swore if I stropped off and slammed a door then I might need to book myself in for some kind of intervention.

"I said, she is smitten for sure. Charlotte, with Carrie. She is a lovely girl though and a natural with children. She had all of the children at stay and play eating out of her hand." My mother suddenly laughed. "There was one little boy who sat on her lap and looked up and stared for about half an hour. Charlotte soon ousted him once she was ready for cuddles."

I smiled when I thought of my daughter liking Carrie, being comfortable enough with her to stake her claim, but more than that I grinned at her ousting the poor boy who was simply content to gaze at her, and why wouldn't he be? She was beautiful. I wish I could be content enough to look and not touch.

"Come and bounce with me," Charlotte called.

My eyes were out on stalks, drying at the image in my mind of Carrie bouncing, possibly not on a trampoline and certainly not with my daughter.

"Daddy," Charlotte called, summoning me from my X-rated thoughts of her nanny.

I got to my feet and entered the garden, then standing next to the trampoline, beneath the sun that warmed my skin I glanced up to see Carrie leaning out of her window smiling down at my daughter.

"Hi," I muttered, taking in her appearance. Her hair was up in a towel and her shoulders and upper chest was bare. Presumably she had a towel wrapped around her, meaning she was naked beneath it.

"Hi," she replied and offered me a little wave. "Sugar!" she cried as she disappeared from view, managing not to swear in front of Charlotte, returning to the window with her head towel dishevelled while she appeared to be securing the towel around her body meaning she'd lost her towel when she waved, leaving her naked.

"Shit!" Apparently, I was less capable of swearing in front of my daughter who turned to me, considering repeating it. "Sorry," I rambled quickly. "How's the bouncing, baby?"

"Look how high I can go," she squealed. "Carrie, come and bounce with me."

I looked up and waited for Carrie to respond, unsure whether her coming down to bounce would be the worst idea ever or my every living dream.

"Sorry, Charlotte. I can't today. I have to go and meet my friends but next week, I promise."

"Yay." Charlotte gave a little cheer as she almost knocked me over in her hurry to go and report back to her grandmother.

Carrie and I stared at each other for a moment and then her words resonated in my mind. She was going out with friends. I was unsure how I felt about that…Conflicted? See, my kryptonite. I had no clue where she was going or who with or what her plans were and the truth was, they were none of my business and I hated that, all of it, however I was pleased she was making friends because that maximised the possibility of her staying around for Charlotte. Just Charlotte.

"Well, I will see you on Monday, Miss Webber. Enjoy your night out and your Sunday tomorrow." I walked away, incapable of trusting myself to say more. I left her behind, let her watch me leave and entered the house with the sound of her window closing.

"Right then my little cupcake," I said to Charlotte, and chased her until I caught her and scooped her up in my arms. "Let's get you ready for your sleepover with grandma." I cheered, exciting her with my enthusiasm for her night with my mother and my own excitement for my own night out. Both Charlotte and my mother joined in with my cheers as we made our way upstairs to gather an overnight bag.

****

"Leigh is seriously into you, buddy. You could get seriously lucky tonight. In fact, you'd have to seriously fuck it up not to find yourself not nestled between those thighs."

I laughed at Seb, his desperation for me to get laid and his enthusiasm for the woman who was more than willing to facilitate that. "And Lorna?"

He crinkled his nose, not quite frowning. "She's nice, but she might be too nice for me."

I studied him for a few seconds. "Too nice?"

"Yeah. Her ex was a complete douche and treated her badly and she really wants her faith in mankind restored, and yes, I could do that, but only for tonight and then tomorrow when I don't call and don't give her my number she is going to feel like shit and her faith in men will be further diminished."

"What the fuck has happened to you? Have you been reading the women's magazines in waiting rooms again? I can't dispute what you're saying, but fuck me, I never thought I'd hear those words leave your mouth."

He flipped me off as he ordered more drinks at the bar we stood at before we returned to the ladies. The ladies were giggling and had clearly discussed how they planned on moving the night forward. We'd met in a bar, had a few drinks and then moved into town where we had dinner before hitting a club. I thought my clubbing days might be behind me but occasionally I could manage the thumping music and the need to shout to be heard. God, I felt old.

The ladies wanted to dance. Seb and I, we didn't really dance, but we were happy to keep the table while the ladies did their thing. We watched them begin to move and it was clear that both had rhythm and knew how to work their bodies to the music.

There was no denying that they looked very sexy. Seb was reconsidering damaging Lorna's view on mankind forever more and as I watched Leigh, I thought that one night of uncomplicated sex with her would be a really good idea. It would be the perfect way to put Miss Webber out of my mind and when I jacked off in the shower I'd be able to replace the images of her and her sexy little pants, her smell, the way her breathing hitched when I got near, well, I'd be able to put that from my head and replace it with Leigh.

My plan was hatched, and I was all ready to set it in motion. I got to my feet, prepared to step onto the dancefloor behind Leigh when I looked further afield, and there she was, all of my wet dreams poured into a tiny black lace dress, my daughter's nanny, Miss Carrie Fucking Webber. And like the snap of fingers, my plan with Leigh died a quick death. As I glared across at Carrie, tipping her head back in laughter at something a young, tall, dark fuckboy had said, nobody else existed, and I'd be fucked if whoever that was, was going to gain entry to my house, or my nanny.

Chapter Nine

Carrie

I couldn't believe I'd dropped my towel. Thank goodness he couldn't see, although I think he knew what I'd done. I loved my job and Charlotte was absolutely bloody adorable. It was her father who was proving to be my biggest concern. I couldn't stop thinking about him and I dreamt of us being alone together, but then every time we were it got heated and to be honest, what might happen fucking petrified me.

With my hair dried into its natural kink and curls and my minimal look make-up on, I set about finding something to wear. I skimmed through the limited options I had. Drinks and dinner, my new friend, Bea, had told me, but then she'd text about an hour ago to add a nightclub to the plans. That was fine, I liked to dance, so long as it wasn't too sleazy or crowded. I only really had one dress that was dressy but still nightclub appropriate. I pulled the short and tight black lace dress off its hanger and put it on. It was very tight and clung to every part of my body, finishing just below my thighs, emphasising my boobs and arse, but covered them with its round neck and tiny collar detail along with three-quarter sleeves. I opted for bare legs and a plain pair of black heels.

I left the house via my own exit and entry point and jumped into the cab that waited there for me. I had no idea where Mr Caldwell was, but I knew that Charlotte was staying over at her grandma's, by all accounts that was not unusual. I loved that the little girl had a female role model in her life that was positive and who adored her, an adoration that was totally reciprocated.

****

Bea was already in the bar where we'd arranged to meet. There was quite a group assembled, far more than I had anticipated, but everyone was friendly, and most seemed to be nannies or old friends of Bea or the others. There were young men and women and one, Toby, seemed very friendly, even going so far as to buy me a drink and then attempted to pay for my dinner, an offer I refused. He was tall, dark and quite good looking in a young kind of way. His skin and expression were soft and full rather than being defined by a little maturity and life. Immediately my mind wondered, as it so often did, to Mr Caldwell, Gabriel. There was nothing soft and full about him. He was the total opposite; hard and lean, mature, a man rather than a boy and clearly confident and knowledgeable of the world. The way he looked at me, the way my body came to life when he touched me and the things he had said. I shuddered.

"Are you cold?" Toby asked as we walked along the road, heading for some club the others knew. Apparently, it was popular with all age groups, except for the very young ones, meaning it had a more relaxed vibe that made for a good night out.

"No, I'm fine, really." Despite my words I pulled my leather jacket closer as we joined the queue to the club.

Once inside we found a space near the bar with a high table and several high stools. The place was busy without being crowded and the music was a good mixture of contemporary and classics that allowed dancing and some conversation. There was a rail framing the dance floor that was bigger than I imagined it might be and it was pretty full, mainly with women dancing and just a few guys dotted in here and there.

I was beginning to loosen up, but wasn't drunk, maybe just a little merry. Toby leaned in and made some really lame joke about the barman and his likeness to a cartoon character. I laughed, then laughed louder when he did a decent impression of the character. I threw my head back and released quite a throaty laugh. Maybe I was more than a little merry, but still not drunk. Toby helped me to my feet and led me to the dance floor.

Once in the middle of the dance floor we began to move to the music. Toby was quite a good dancer. A little animated and over the top in his moves, but still rather good and some of those moves made me laugh. We danced together for a couple of numbers before the rest of the group joined us. Bea brought my drink with her and we all moved to the beat and rhythm of the music. I was enjoying myself and I really thought I could be genuinely happy here with my new friends and job, maybe even with Mr Caldwell. I giggled as I thought his name and could have sworn I saw him on the other side of the dance floor making my giggle turn into loud laughter that I was now imagining his presence even when awake.

"You okay?" Toby whispered in my ear.

I nodded and moved to dance in front of him, a little closer. A lot closer. Very soon I found I had one arm around his neck while I held my drink in the other and he had an arm draped around my middle, his fingers sitting incredibly low and close to my behind. I made a mental note to ensure his hand didn't drop any lower.

"Shall we ditch this place?" Toby asked, a look of optimism and hope in his eyes.

I shook my head. "I like it here. I'm having fun."

He smiled but somehow it looked a little forced. Then he took my almost empty glass from me, spun me around and headed off to the bar taking my glass with him.

"He likes you," Bea told me, although I was beginning to see that. She looked a little nervous. "He's okay, Toby, but be careful."

I frowned. "Of what?"

"Just generally, be careful. He can be a little persistent."

Someone else spoke to her, gaining her attention and ending our conversation. I wasn't sure what her words meant. Were they a warning? I noticed he didn't look entirely happy that I'd turned down his suggestion for us to leave, alone, but he'd soon recovered so maybe I was reading too much into her words.

Before I had any time to ponder those thoughts Toby had returned with a fresh drink and resumed his dancing with big, exaggerated movements that saw me giggling again, but also dancing big and dramatically along with him.

I was in the middle of a move that resembled a baby giraffe standing for the first time crossed with a wind turbine, all arms, legs and wobbling when I laughed, at myself. I threw in some kind of spin for good measure, making my friends laugh too, but then my laughter died in an instant. There, across the dance floor, was none other than Mr Gabriel Caldwell and he was staring across at me, glaring. He almost seemed to be coming in and out of focus as I attempted to fix my gaze on him and then I realised he was, because he was moving closer.

"Fuck," I muttered, unsure why I was as nervous as I was and what I thought he would or could do. But taking in his dark and stony expression my nervousness increased because he had only one destination in mind. Me.

Chapter Ten

Gabriel

"Hey, Gabe, what's up? You look like you've seen a ghost." Seb placed a reassuring hand on my shoulder as I prepared to make my way to put a stop to any plans that fuckboy had. Precisely the ones involving my nanny.

"Carrie fucking Webber." That was my reply, and immediately Seb followed my gaze.

"That's her? Carrie, the nanny?"

"Yup."

He pulled me back to our table where we sat in silence for a few seconds as we both stared across to where fuckboy had now pulled Carrie to her feet and led her to the dance floor.

"What the fuck is going on with you and her?" Seb knew who she was and that she was permanently in my head and probably now suspected that she was in my dreams too.

"Nothing."

He arched a questioning brow.

I felt obliged to continue. "We kissed, almost, a couple of times and I can't stop thinking about her. About fucking her."

"I certainly understand that better now that I've seen her. She is a fucking delight, mate."

"Are you thinking about her naked?" I asked and could already tell that he was.

He laughed.

"Don't. Ever."

"Wow, you have it bad my old friend."

"More than you know."

"I'm guessing me thinking about fucking her and imagining her sitting on my face is a no go if naked is a no."

Seb laughed at my murderous expression, laughter I joined in with.

"Yes, it fucking is, even as a joke."

"Okay. Tell me what I don't know about how bad you have it."

Somehow it seemed easy and natural to open up to Seb about just how adolescent my infatuation was. "This is just between us. She can't ever know, and I'd say you can't use it to take the piss out of me, but you will anyway. Fuck knows I take the piss out of myself for it. I told you when she first moved in and dropped her stuff everywhere."

Seb laughed. "The day of my sweet Charlotte's introduction to the curse that is fuck."

"Yes. Well, the pants I made a point of returning to her?"

"I remember, but these details aren't conducive to me not thinking about her in naked, writhing terms."

"Fuck off!" I hissed but continued. "She must have shoved them in her pocket and left them there because when we met later for a chat, they somehow ended up being left behind and I might have hung on to them."

"Might have?"

"As in I definitely have and I look at them, touch them, imagine them and her in and out of them when I have some alone time."

"Alone time?"

"Yeah…as in me, the shower and a wet soapy hand."

Seb howled and even slapped his own leg at my pathetic revelations.

"But what the fuck do I do about it?"

"Fuck her," replied Seb flatly. "Get it out of your system and return to normal."

"What if it ruins things? Charlotte really likes her, and my mother."

"I can't tell you it won't ruin things but as things stand you and she can't continue like this. I mean, there is a guy over there who appears to be considering grabbing a handful of her arse."

"Over my dead body."

"Exactly, mate. Fuck her and put everyone out of their misery, otherwise you are going to need psychiatric help. Do you know of anyone to take you on?"

"Fuck off, Seb! And why would I pay someone within our chosen field when I have you at my disposal."

"Quite. And I doubt I'd be able to suggest fucking her if you were paying me and this is your friend speaking, not a doctor. He's definitely considering an arse grab."

I looked back across the dance floor and found fuckboy with his hand dangerously close to her arse, Seb was right, he was considering making his move, and then he leaned down and whispered in her ear. Yes, he was going in for the kill. Again, over my dead body.

"Go get her, tiger," I heard Seb say, but before I could do precisely that, Leigh appeared in front of me.

"Hey, I'm feeling a little neglected here." She pouted.

I didn't want to brush her off, nor be an arsehole, but if I didn't get rid of her I was quite possibly going to lose track of Miss Webber, her tiny black dress and that prat who was chasing her. Fuck, he might even catch her if I took my eye off the ball for long.

"Sorry. Look, something has come up. I don't want to be a knob, but I need to put the brakes on tonight. I'll call you in the week and apologise properly. Seb is hanging around though."

She was a good sport about it and didn't cause a scene. She nodded and even offered me a smile before returning to her friend and Seb on the dance floor. The latter offered me a wink as I returned my full attention to the woman on the other side of the room. She was dancing again, if you could call it that; arms and legs were all over the shop. She laughed as did her friends, including fuckboy, who at least no longer had his hands or mouth anywhere near her. I paused to watch her laughing and if she wasn't even more fucking gorgeous with her genuinely happy face and having fun. I swear she was lighting up the whole place. She did a very strange little twirl that saw her facing me. Then she noticed me and came to a standstill, her smile and laughter ending as she took in my expression and posture that told her I was far from happy.

I continued walking with only one destination in mind. When I came to a standstill before her, she really did look like a rabbit caught in the headlights. With no plan on what I was going to say I just opened my mouth. "We're leaving, now."

She stared at me confused, and why wouldn't she be? I was confused too, maybe more so than her.

"What?" she stammered nervously.

Shit! Had I frightened her? I really hoped not. I could be an arsehole, but I'd never want her to genuinely fear me. Before I had the chance to in any way soften my words, fuckboy interjected.

"Who are you?"

That's what he asked, *who are you?* Never mind who I was. Who the fuck was he?

"None of your business, that's who." I ignored him and turned to Miss Webber. "We need to leave, together. Please."

She nodded and leaned in towards her friends before turning to one of them. "I'll call you tomorrow, Bea. I need to go."

I stepped closer and with a hand against her back led her towards the exit, giving fuckboy a death glare as we passed him. We were almost at the exit when she shook me free and stormed out. Within a couple of strides, I'd caught up with her and pulled her to face me.

"What the fuck was that about?" she asked, pointing back towards the club.

She stood with one hand resting on her hip, her leg kicked out slightly and looked like sin in stilettos. Her head still shook slightly as she stared at me, waiting for a response. My response came in a rush that saw me pushing her back until she was pressed against the wall in an alley at the side of the club. My body held her captive and as her eyes widened, lit up with desire and her lips gaped slightly.

"Carrie." I uttered just one word then lowered my lips towards hers.

Chapter Eleven

Carrie

His mouth on mine felt better than I had ever imagined. It was soft and powerful, leaving me in no doubt that he was in the driving seat and yet he managed to encourage me to respond. The sensation of his tongue licking against my lips saw my mouth open, granting him access, and how he accepted the invitation. His tongue rubbed and tangled with mine until I could barely see or think.

A low gasp left my lips when I realised that while we'd been kissing, I had wrapped my arms around him, and somehow his leg had made its way between my thighs and I was rubbing myself against him. His arms had wrapped around me, one hand had laced through my hair while the other one had settled on my behind, the flesh of one cheek overflowing his hand.

"And this is why I should never call you Carrie." His lips had left mine, just the tiniest of spaces between us now.

I was clueless as to what to say in response. He smiled. I returned the curl of his lips as a group walked past the entrance to the alley. Their catcalls were full of encouragement and suggestions making Mr Caldwell laugh and me cringe and flush in embarrassment. Maybe under the circumstances I should have been thinking of him in Gabriel terms rather than Mr Caldwell.

"Let me take you home." His words were ridiculous to an extent as I lived in his house, so obviously we were going back to the same place, and yet, they were sweet and considerate because this was him asking if he could take me home, escort me and presumably pick things up where we'd just left them.

I nodded, confirming my consent as he led me from the alley towards a nearby taxi rank. There was a bit of a queue that we joined to wait for a taxi and his arm around my middle felt like the most natural thing in the world. I leaned into him, my head coming to rest on his chest where the smell of his clothes, his aftershave and his body assaulted my senses. He pulled me in tighter, leaving nothing between us. I wanted him so badly and just hoped we wouldn't have to wait much longer for a taxi to take us home.

Just a few more minutes passed before we were almost at the front of the line when a woman's voice interrupted us.

"Gabriel." Her use of his first name in isolation was something between a question, a statement and an accusation.

"Leigh," he replied, sounding a little nervous as he turned to face this woman, another woman and a man.

"Hi. Seb. Pleased to meet you, Nanny," the man said with a huge grin on his face that immediately made me want to smile, but Gabriel cut him off.

"You, my friend, are an arsehole. Carrie, this is a very old friend of mine, Seb."

He took my hand and kissed the back of it making me laugh.

"Correction, you are a complete arsehole," Gabriel told him, but laughed too.

"You're welcome, Gabe."

Gabe was clearly how he was known amongst his friends. I smiled as I thought myself to be quite adventurous in referring to him as Gabriel, if only in my head.

We were next in line for a taxi and as it pulled up to the front of the rank, I prepared to say goodbye to Seb and the two women. One had remained silent until that point but chose now to speak.

"Hi, Lorna." She held her hand out. As I shook it, she spoke again, "At least we know why Leigh's date was cut short now. Have a good night."

I said nothing but turned and glared at Gabriel. I dunno about Seb being a complete arsehole because from where I was standing the only arsehole in this whole situation was Mr fucking Caldwell.

Without risking any words or further interactions I climbed into the back of the cab and took a seat. Gabriel quickly joined me and gave the driver the address. I stared out of the window in silence. This really wasn't the journey home I had imagined when he suggested leaving together. I didn't know if it was the recent revelation, Gabriel's interruption of my evening out, our connection in the alley or the drink I'd consumed, not that I'd drunk that much, but suddenly I felt dizzy, hot and quite queasy.

Gabriel reached across and attempted to take my hand in his. I pulled my hand farther away until it sat with the other one, wrapped tightly together in my lap between my crossed legs.

When the taxi pulled up outside of the house, I exited first, and on wobbly legs, headed for the entrance to my own accommodation, not that I got far.

"Where are you going?" Gabriel asked when he caught up with me.

"Home," I replied with an immature pout.

"Come home with me."

I glared up at him as he stepped closer, standing over me.

"Fuck you!"

"I was hoping that might be part of the plan."

"Go home. Whatever we started back there, at the club, was a mistake," I told him, meaning it, but wanting him to prove me wrong.

"No, it wasn't. Come home with me or let me come home with you, let me explain what you think I did back there."

I fixed him with a cold stare, considered my options then turned and continued heading for my part of the house. After about ten steps I turned, and found he was still where I'd left him, looking confused and a little uncertain.

"Are you coming then, to explain?" I asked, deciding to put him out of his misery.

With my back to him again, I smiled a very self-satisfied grin that he was now rushing to catch up with me.

We soon found ourselves on my landing and as I fumbled with the key to my accommodation, I felt Gabriel step closer, his front almost close enough to heat my back. His hand stretched around my body, steadying my hand, assisting me in my attempts to unlock the door.

I stepped inside and he followed, this time as I turned his front was almost flush with mine.

"You need to explain," I stammered.

"Nothing to explain, not really. I met Leigh when I went out with Seb the other night. She was out with Lorna. Seb and I chatted with them and arranged to see them tonight."

"A date?" I already knew it was but somehow needed to hear it from him, but more than that I wanted him to deny it or explain it away.

"Yeah, I suppose. A double date if you will."

"How marvellous!" I snapped.

"Are you jealous, Miss Webber?"

"Miss Webber?" I wondered if his more formal term of address was indicative of a change between us.

"Carrie…"

I smiled.

"So, are you jealous?"

"No. Why would I be?"

"Because you don't like the idea of me being out on a date with someone else. But more than that, you don't like to think of me dancing, kissing, touching another woman."

We stared at each other and as much as I willed myself to deny it or to come up with some witty comeback, I didn't, I just nodded my head.

"As soon as I saw you, I was ready to flip. I told Seb who you were and when I saw that fuckboy whispering to you, making you laugh and then touching you, considering touching your arse, a switch went off."

"But Leigh?" I didn't really care about her, but I needed to know that he wouldn't be running back to her tomorrow.

He shook his head. "She was nice, but the truth is that when I met her, I was just trying to get you out of my head."

"Really?" I grinned and wobbled slightly feeling increasingly drunk.

"Really. I'm guessing by your smile that you're happy with my explanation?"

I nodded because I was more than happy with it.

"And I told her I was putting the brakes on it before I came over to you tonight. So…"

A sharp intake of breath caught me unawares as I anticipated what would follow his so.

"Yes, that, whatever you're thinking, all of it."

He was in front of me before I knew it and with one arm wrapped around my middle and the other between my shoulders, he pulled me closer. He leaned down and closed his mouth over mine. My lips softened and parted, inviting him in, desperate to feel the earlier sensations he'd triggered in me.

"Yes," I whispered when he came up for breath. My back was pressed against the wall and he was between my thighs that had opened to accommodate him and his hands had moved too; one was in the small of my back while the other had begun to trace a path under my dress and was stroking my inner thigh.

I was virtually panting. My arms were wrapped around him, pulling him in, begging for more while my sex was softening and moistening with arousal like I had never known before. It squeezed and clenched against nothing, causing more impatience and frustration from me.

Gabriel returned his mouth to my face, but this time he littered a path of tiny kisses along my jaw until he was teasing my ear as the hand in the small of my back found my behind that he rubbed, caressed and squeezed.

"I was ready to kill that fuckboy when I saw his hand getting closer to your arse."

"Fuckboy?" I laughed.

"Yes, but that's not important. He's not important."

His other hand crept higher, reaching my silky pants that were very damp. Expertly, he passed the barrier of them until his fingers were tracing the length of my seam. Instinctively, my legs spread, pleading with him to delve deeper. He did. His fingers now moved through the moisture of my arousal, dragging it forward until he was circling the nub of nerve endings that had me choking and throwing my head back.

Every part of my body pulsed and ached. I saw blackness and stars as his fingers travelled lower until they were buried inside me. My body clenched, gripping them, drawing them in. He continued to move them, slowly at first, but as his thumb stretched up, returning attention to my clitoris I was in heaven and hell at the same time. Garbled words and sounds could be heard getting louder around us. Words and sounds that were all mine. I felt like I was about to choke as my throat tightened.

"Oh God, Gabriel—"

"The sound of my name coming from your mouth makes me want to fuck you senseless all night."

My body responded to his words immediately, moving closer to release but the choking sensation increased and then it happened."

"Gabe—" It was never my intention to abbreviate his name. The full name I was attempting to say, in warning rather than encouragement, got cut off as the choking sensation progressed.

What followed my *Gabe* was something of an extreme tale of a bad date. I was scared, horrified, and embarrassed beyond belief as I, instead of coming, vomited. The world was spinning, and the sound of Gabriel's voice was getting farther and farther away as I watched, as if in flashback as he leapt back, still not avoiding the spray of my sick, looking beyond concerned, dismayed and shocked. I had actually vomited in the middle of what had been promising to be the most amazing night of my life.

And then there was nothing.

Chapter Twelve

Gabriel

I had seriously underestimated just how good kissing and touching her would feel. When I reached her in the club, and she agreed to leave with me, my heart was thumping so hard in my chest I had visions of finding it on the floor. By the time we got outside it was all I could do not to fucking consume her there and then, but somehow, I managed to wait until we were in that alley. God! How old was I? Kissing and holding a girl in an alley on a Saturday night, Sunday morning, whatever it was. The way her lips parted for me and allowed me to enter her mouth to kiss her had my already hard dick lurching against my trousers. She was the perfect combination of nervous and innocent mixed with confident and hot as fuck.

Everything was back on track and all indications were that it was only going to get better and better. She'd seemed a little tipsy at times, but she hadn't been drunk, and she was more than capable of giving consent, we both were. We'd kissed, a lot. She held me tight, as if she was scared to let me go and my hands were all fucking over her and I had never been happier. She called my name, Gabe, or so I'd thought, but it turned out that was as much as she could say without vomiting, all over the floor, herself and me, which made me question if she had been drunk after all.

Now I was sitting in a chair in Carrie's bedroom watching her sleep, ensuring she didn't choke on her own vomit. After she vomited, she seemed to pass out. I took off my shoes that were vomit splattered, along with my shirt and trousers, and picked her up, carrying her to her bathroom where I wiped her face with a flannel then took her to her bedroom where I placed her on her bed which I had imagined doing earlier but not quite in this way. Rather than rummage through her drawers and wardrobe I ran down to my own bedroom and grabbed a t-shirt of my own to put on her after removing her dress. I'd tried not to notice her gorgeous silky, black underwear. Once she was under the covers, seemingly settled in sleep, I dashed back to my own room, changed into clean shorts and a t-shirt before returning to her.

I watched over her for an hour or so, trying my damnedest not to fall asleep in case she woke up and was still unwell. *Unwell.* I couldn't quite shake the feeling that whilst she clearly wasn't well, the term *unwell* didn't quite fit. I mean, I didn't know Carrie well in a social way, but she in no way seemed drunk. She'd obviously had a couple of drinks and from what I saw of her night out she wasn't throwing anything and everything alcoholic down her throat. Indeed, when she left the club with me, she wasn't staggering or slurring, and yet when she got back here and ended up covering us both in vomit it was as if she'd downed twenty pints and had been totally legless.

She let out a little groan as she fidgeted beneath the covers when my text alert sounded. Seb.

<Holy fucking shit! You missed a real treat with Leigh. She is wild. And her and Lorna together, man! I really hope Nanny was worth it.>

I let out a short laugh as I realised that Seb had ended up in a three-way with both of our dates. At least three out of the four of us got lucky tonight. I replayed Seb's words, *I really hope Nanny was worth it.* I cast my eyes back across the sleeping shape of Carrie and considered it...was she worth it...worth missing out on getting well and truly laid by the sounds of it? I had a horrible feeling that she might just be.

Suddenly, Carrie leapt up, crying and thrashing around as if waking from a nightmare. I moved to the bed, pulled her to me, held her and rocked her, trying to calm her. After a minute or so she quieted and looked up at me.

"Mr Caldwell," she stammered.

"What happened to Gabriel?" I asked, hoping she hadn't suffered some kind of amnesia and was thinking I was a weirdo or pervert who made a habit of watching her sleep.

"What happened?" she asked, shuffling up the bed slightly. "Fuck, my head hurts." She held her head and looked to be in significant pain. "It's spinning."

"What happened when?" I wasn't sure what she remembered, if anything of what we'd shared.

"We left the club...we kissed." She blushed, but smiled, making me smile back.

"We did."

"You were there with that other woman and your friends." She scowled. I still smiled.

"We came home in a taxi and kissed again, and stuff." Her blush deepened.

She was fucking adorable. I bit back a grin.

"I was going to co—"

Okay so she remembered how far we'd got.

"You know...and then I felt ill and I was...fuck...I was sick, sorry." She looked mortified as she leapt from the bed for some reason. Once standing at the side of her bed she looked down at herself and then took in my clothes.

Her expression changed to one of fear.

"Did we, you know?"

"No, God, no. What do you take me for?" I sounded offended, well, I was. "If, when we have sex, you'll be conscious and more than capable of being participant and remembering it."

"Sorry."

She looked confused and then began to cry. I moved over to her, opened my arms, offering her a safe space. I really was becoming concerned because this wasn't normal behaviour and the truth was, I still couldn't shake the feeling that there was something more.

"I don't really drink very often, and everyone was drinking different things so I think I must have mixed things up too much."

I nodded; it was a logical explanation. She stepped into my still open arms and allowed me to hold and comfort her.

"Get back into bed, sleep," I added, hoping to reassure her of my motives.

"I'm sorry. We can just forget last night—"

"No!" I snapped out my interruption making her pull back from me. "What I mean is that I don't want to forget it, what we did, were going to do, but maybe some sleep and not focussing on the vomiting thing I can agree to."

"Thank you." She smiled. "Were you watching over me?"

I nodded.

"Thank you," she repeated.

"No problem."

"You can go back to your own room if you want to."

"And if I don't?" I asked because I had no desire to leave her, and not just because of concern for her.

She climbed back into bed, shuffling over to one side then threw the covers back, inviting me in. "You need to sleep too."

"Two minutes," I said before getting her a glass of water and a couple of painkillers for her head that she was still holding and rubbing.

Once she'd taken them, I climbed in beside her and pulled her close, held her and then together we went to sleep.

Chapter Thirteen

Carrie

When I woke up, it all came flooding back to me. Shit. An arm suddenly draped across my middle, startling me slightly until I remembered that I'd woken in the night and Mr Caldwell and I had agreed to sleep together. God, why was I still calling him that? He really had been very sweet and considerate in his attempts to take care of me. I softened into his hold and considered dozing for a while longer when he spoke.

"Morning, how do you feel?"

"Okay," I replied, although that wasn't entirely true. "Bit of a thick head and slightly woozy but okay, thanks. Thank you for last night."

"No problem."

I felt the bed move beneath me and his arm around me move slightly. His face appeared over mine.

"Would you like a drink, tea, coffee?"

I nodded, "Tea, please."

I watched him get up and disappear from my room. I followed, expecting to find a dirty, sick covered hallway, but there was no sign of it.

Returning towards the bedroom, Gabriel offered me a cup. "I was bringing this back to bed for you."

"No need. I thought I should come and clean up, but the cleaning fairies appear to have beaten me to it."

He smiled. "Never been called a fairy before, not to my face, but I'll take it. I have some pain killers for you."

"Thank you, for being a fairy, the tea and the tablets."

He smiled at me, a little awkwardly. "I should go and get a shower." He pointed towards the door, reiterating his need and intention to leave.

"Okay. Thank you." I said the last two words for what felt like the umpteenth time.

He smiled.

"Gabriel," I called, causing him to turn back to face me. "You could use my shower, if you want to." I felt the colour creep up my face and the associated heat burned me, making my embarrassment at such an obvious offer clear to us both.

"But, if I do that, I'm going to end up calling you Carrie, a lot."

"And you don't want to…call me Carrie?" I was unsure when calling me Carrie became a euphemism for sex.

He laughed and shook his head. "There might not be anything I've ever wanted to do more, but you still seem a little below par."

I was disappointed and presumably my expression portrayed that by his look of sympathy.

"How about you shower up here, I'll shower in my bathroom and we could have breakfast together and talk."

I nodded, happy to accept his offer, already looking forward to it and yet, I still couldn't shake the feeling that he was rethinking what should have happened the night before.

I showered quickly and feeling a lot better and slightly refreshed, I threw on my robe and wondered where Gabriel planned for us to have breakfast, downstairs in his kitchen or upstairs in mine. More than that I wondered who was expected to cook breakfast, not that I minded cooking for him, assuming I had enough food in the fridge to make a meal. Maybe I should just go and find him, check where he was, what he was doing and that would probably give some answers to my questions.

Plodding down the stairs, I found myself on the landing outside Mr Caldwell's room. The door was ajar, and I could hear him, not what he was saying, just the sound of his voice.

"Hi," I called, gently tapping on the door. "Mr—Gabriel."

Nothing.

I stepped further into the room. I could hear his shower. The words in my head were telling me to go away, to call him again, louder, maybe even knock on the bathroom door and ask where he wanted to have breakfast, but did I do that? No, none of it. Rather than move away, I stepped closer until I was pushing the door open and entering the confines of his bathroom.

Although unsure what I was likely to find, I was still surprised to find him in the shower cubicle, gloriously naked. His dark hair had been washed and was pushed back. The rivulets of water ran down him; his neck, chest, abs, then lower still, across the v that led to the thatch of groomed dark hair that housed—a very large erection, but more than that, he was holding it, touching himself, like in a sexy way.

I should have left, quietly stepped away and reverted to knocking louder and calling his name to check on the details of breakfast. That is what I should have done, but I didn't. Instead, I stood there, transfixed. I swallowed hard and even licked my lips as I watched him stroke along his own length that I swear was getting even bigger.

"I was just thinking about you."

His voice startled me so much that I jumped. He laughed, drawing my eyes to move higher, to his eyes from his still moving hand.

"I—erm—breakfast—sorry."

If he could decipher what the hell I was trying to say or indeed had said, then he was a linguistic genius because I had no clue what any of those words meant.

He grinned, cockily, no pun intended. "How are you feeling now?"

"Better, much better. Thank you, and for the tea." I was panicking. My flustering confirmed that.

"You're welcome, to everything."

I swear the air was thickening and the tension between us was going to end up sending us flying across the room like a scene from *Harry Potter* if the charge of electricity we shared didn't calm itself.

"I should leave you to it," I said and actually waved my hand in the direction of his hand that remained wrapped around his penis.

"If that's what you want."

This was his invitation for me to stay. Presumably staying would involve us getting close and intimate again, not that I objected to that. It was just that without the alcohol and circumstances of the previous night I didn't feel quite so brave.

"Is it what you want, Carrie?" He cocked his head slightly and drew a short breath in as he gazed down at his own arousal.

And there it was, the offer of sex in his use of my name. I smiled across at him, suddenly with bolstered confidence, knowing he wasn't regretting what could have, should have happened last night. Indeed, it would have happened had I not vomited over us both.

"Well, in that case." I had no idea where this sexy, self-assured and confident woman was coming from, but she was well and truly in the zone now as I undid the belt of my robe and pushed it off my otherwise naked body.

"Get your arse in here now," Gabriel commanded as he slid open the shower enclosure door and looked as though if I didn't get there soon enough, he would literally drag me in by my hair.

As I carefully stepped in, he held my wrist and roughly pulled me to him. There was no mistaking or avoiding his erection that dug into my front as his lips found mine and his body pressed me between him and the tiled wall.

All too soon I felt bereaved when his lips left mine, but I really needn't have worried because his lips soon returned to me, but lower this time, much, much lower.

He had dropped to his knees until his face was in front of my sex. He leaned in and kissed me there and immediately I spread my legs, inviting him in. A finger ran along my length, then back until a first and then a second finger entered me. I gripped them tightly. He looked up at me, watching my expression as his fingers began to move and his thumb reached for my clitoris.

"Oh, yes," I whimpered. That is when his mouth moved closer until it began to lick, lap and flick against my nub of nerve endings that almost saw me going off like a bloody firework. In what seemed like seconds I was ready to explode; I was burning inside and out, and my breathing was beginning to resemble a series of puffs and pants.

His eyes glanced up, knowing I was close and clearly wanting eye contact when I came undone completely, and how I fell apart. I clung to his shoulders, my eyes never leaving his as I quivered from the inside and out until I was essentially riding his hand and face as I called to God and my own choice of deity, Gabriel.

He rose to his feet wearing a large smile. "You taste fucking divine," he told me, already sucking one digit clean before smearing the shimmery coating of his other finger across my lips. Eagerly, I reached up, grabbed his shoulders and pulled his lips back to mine where we kissed, still under the spray of the shower. Briefly, very briefly, I hoped he wasn't on a water meter! What the fuck was wrong with me?

"Your turn," I said, ending our kiss.

He frowned in confusion as to exactly what I meant.

I grabbed his hand, the one he'd been using to pleasure himself, and placed it back on his groin, urging him to grip himself which he did. Then I placed my hand over his larger one.

"Show me. What you like. Show me how to please you, Gabe."

Chapter Fourteen

Gabriel

Show me how to please you, Gabe. That's what she'd said, and I wasn't sure I wouldn't blow my load there and then with her offer, inference and deference, and fuck, don't get me started on her use of Gabe. Well, I'm only human and was totally incapable of turning down an offer like that.

My hand that had been on my own dick was quickly reaching for hers and covering it, then together, my hand over and guiding hers to my erection that really was all for her. Slowly, I moved her hand along my solid length and once we'd found a rhythm, I squeezed her hand, encouraging her to tighten her grip, which she did. With every stroke her confidence grew, as did my proximity to orgasm.

"Fuck, yeah, like that. It feels so good, Carrie," I told her, although the feelings her touch was inciting made the words *so good* seem awfully inadequate.

Still guiding the speed of her strokes, I moved her hand more quickly, seriously chasing the release I was closer to with every second that passed.

"Keep up that speed, okay? Don't stop."

"Okay," she replied, her voice husky with desire.

With a nervous nibble of her lip she set about keeping the pace I'd set while I removed my hand from hers. After a couple of hesitant strokes along my length that had me gritting my teeth and breathing heavily, she gained some confidence, spurred on by my obvious pleasure.

I slid my hands through her hair, tilting her head so I could kiss her. My lips lowered to hers, moulding them to fit mine which they did perfectly. Fuck me! Kissing her was the best thing in the world. I almost forgot that her hand was wrapped around my dick, driving me on to what I knew would be an intense orgasm of almost catastrophic proportions, but not quite. The warm tingle and burn I felt deep inside started in my balls that were tightening with every passing second and pulsed through my whole body as I headed to the point of no return.

"Shit!" I hissed, returning my hand to cover hers once more, controlling the pace and speed again, biting and sucking against the flesh of her neck as the first creamy white spurt of cum left my body. Streak after streak of my release covered our hands and our stomachs.

Eventually, when our breathing slowed and I could think, speak and function we kissed again, gentler this time, tenderly.

"Was it okay?" she asked, nervousness returning to her voice.

"If absolutely fucking phenomenal is considered okay, then yes, very much so." I grinned down at her. "How about we get clean and then have that breakfast?"

She looked disappointed by my suggestion.

"What?" I asked, not really understanding why she seemed so bothered.

"I thought, you know, we, erm." She coughed, as if considering whether she should say what was on her mind. "You know...have sex."

"Oh—"

She cut me off. "But if you don't want to—"

It was my turn to cut her off now. "Of course, I want to, Carrie. Nothing I want more, but I need to collect Charlotte in about an hour."

"Oh." Disbelief clouded her eyes.

I chuckled and shook my head. "Maybe we should go out, when we're both free, or have dinner."

"Like a date?" she asked.

I wasn't sure what her meaning of *a date* was. Did she imagine that a date made us boyfriend and girlfriend? Or maybe she thought that it would be a date in the singular. Perhaps she was using the word date to convey us having sex. I had no clue what she meant, but then, I had no idea what I thought this date would mean or involve, never mind her.

"Yes, I guess, like a date."

"I'd like that." She grinned like the proverbial Cheshire cat and that in turn made me return my own.

"Then let's get clean and eat breakfast, Miss Webber."

Her grin broadened until I was almost blinded by it at my use of Miss Webber, both of us knowing that if I called her Carrie we'd never make it to the date because it was either used in foreplay or within a sexual context.

The atmosphere in the kitchen was a little awkward as we each moved around the room, her making coffee while I made us eggs, bacon and toast. It was as though once we were out of the shower and our bodies were covered, a barrier settled between us. Conversation was limited to breakfast until we sat together at the table. She had offered to cook in her kitchen and I'd considered it briefly, but then she began waffling about the food she didn't have in her fridge so we came down here, plus, I didn't want her to think I wasn't prepared for her to share my part of the house.

We sat and ate with the radio on in the background for a few minutes and then the conversation began to flow a little. We talked about music tastes, favourite movies, easy, getting to know you topics of conversation.

Her phone sounded and without hesitation she checked it. She smiled a little awkwardly and quickly typed out a response. I looked across at her expectantly. I wanted to know who it was that had messaged her and more than that I wanted to know what they'd said to make her smile. This was not me. I didn't do the chest beating, *my woman* routine and yet I desperately wanted to. It wasn't that I wasn't possessive or jealous in a relationship, I was, but I didn't need to know everything and I certainly didn't need to check phones and yet, with her, I was pissed off that I didn't know the details.

"Everything okay?" I asked, clearly fishing.

"Yes, fine."

She was going to piss me off if she didn't give a little here. I stared at her like an expectant teacher, waiting for someone who'd been talking to give the correct answer to a question they hadn't heard.

"It was just Bea, filling me in on events after I left and asking about you."

I arched a brow, wondering what that meant, *asking about you*. She sighed, an actual sigh at my need to know more.

"They had a great night, in case you're interested," she snapped.

I wasn't and her snarky tone irritated me further.

With a pout, she continued, "She wanted to know who you were, how we knew each other, and I quote, *if we had banged each other's brains out last night.*"

I said nothing as I considered banging her fucking brains out across the breakfast table.

"Oh, and Toby would like my number. He liked me and was genuinely concerned when you removed me from the club. He has called Bea this morning to see if she'd heard from me because he was worried for my safety." She laughed. I didn't. "That was nice of him, wasn't it?"

I scowled until my creased brow felt like a headache.

"Toby is a dog's name." I was the one pouting now.

She laughed, at me and my jealousy.

"I wasn't joking and why would fuckboy be worried for your safety?

"Fuckboy?" She shook her head, but smiled, a mischievous twinkle in her eyes as she got up and moved until she was straddling my lap, rubbing herself against me as she settled there. "Are you jealous, Mr Caldwell?"

"No, I am fucking not!" I was, and I was fucking fuming about it and him.

She linked her arms around my neck, her grin broadening. My hands naturally came to rest on her hips.

"It won't bother you that I am meeting some of last night's gang for lunch then, will it?"

My grip on her tightened, my fingers digging into the soft flesh beneath my hands until she pulled back and got to her feet. My mouth opened several times, but no words came out as I watched her clearing the table. Her arse that was encased in tight denim tormented me. It called for me to grab it, hold it while I fucked her or to be spanked, maybe all three, although I wasn't entirely sure in which order.

I was beyond bothered by the idea of her meeting some of the gang full stop if part of the gang included Toby the fuckboy. With actual words formed in my mind I prepared to speak when my own phone sounded, a text from my mother, confirming the time I was going to collect Charlotte. I made a quick reply and got to my feet, coming to a standstill behind Miss Webber.

"I'm going to collect Charlotte. Don't worry about the breakfast things, I'll do them when I get back."

She nodded, turning so that she faced me. With my arms on either side of her body, gripping the worktop I had her caged.

"Have a good weekend, Miss Webber. I'll see you Monday." My voice was flat and just like that my game face was reinstated.

Her face fell in disappointment, at my words and the resumption of our roles. I liked that she was disappointed, especially with fuckboy back on the scene and her earlier amusement at my jealousy. I turned and grabbed my keys, needing to leave before I ended up fucking her seven ways to Sunday, if only to mark her as mine.

Chapter Fifteen

Carrie

I was confused. Mr Caldwell and his hot and cold routine was difficult to keep up with.

I got that he needed to collect Charlotte, and of course she should be the priority, his priority, collecting her, bringing her home and not abusing his mother's kindness in taking care of her. However, he didn't need to turn so quickly, and his dismissal was completely unnecessary. Arsehole.

The sound of my laughter rang around my bedroom where I was just adding a denim jacket to my outfit of boyfriend fit jeans, a t-shirt emblazoned with the name of an old rock band and flat casual pumps, at the memory of him getting all jealous and shirty when I got the message inviting me for lunch. I laughed even louder when I recalled him referring to Toby as fuckboy. He was jealous. I shook Toby from my mind as anything other than an associate, a friend maybe, but no more. The idea of Gabriel being jealous of anyone seemed ridiculous because he was the perfect specimen of a man, even with his hot and cold routine that pissed me off and left me feeling uncertain and insecure. Although, Gabriel didn't know yet that Toby held no attraction for me. Maybe it could prove to be fun, a little teasing and tormenting of him, especially when he shut everything down and went back to his, Miss Webber routine.

"Shit," I muttered. I had potentially risked my job by crossing those lines.

Maybe I shouldn't have come home with him last night and

did the things we did. The lines of him being my boss and my… my what? I had no idea, but whatever label his other relationship to me might be, the lines between that and being my boss had blurred.

Briefly, I glanced at the clock and saw that I was at risk of being late for lunch so grabbed my bag and headed outside via my own exit to wait for my taxi. I was just circling the building, coming to the front of the house when my feet almost screeched to a halt at the sight of Gabriel standing on the doorstep with Charlotte, greeting his friend, Seb. There was no way of avoiding them, of them seeing me, but it was Charlotte who spotted me first.

"Carrie." She squealed excitedly. "Come and play. You can come and bounce with me and Uncle Seb and Daddy."

I swear, Seb nearly choked as he bit back his laughter at the little girl's suggestion and muttered something that sounded a lot like, *Gabe, you wanna bounce with Nanny?*

"Not today, Potty Lottie," I replied, using one of my pet names for her, hoping to soften my rebuttal.

She pouted.

"We could bounce tomorrow—" I held back my own laughter when I saw Gabriel arch a brow at me. "Just the two of us," I clarified, addressing Charlotte.

"Okay," she agreed a little begrudgingly before Uncle Seb picked her up, threw her around and prepared to take her indoors.

"Say bye to Nanny," he called.

She giggled at his use of the name Nanny. "Bye, Carrie," she called behind her as Seb threw her over his shoulder.

"Bye, Nanny," he said to me with a cheeky grin and a wink for good measure.

I was incapable of keeping my amusement at bay. After a single peal of laughter, I replied, "Bye, Seb."

Suddenly, the atmosphere changed. It was just me and Gabriel again, staring at each other. Neither of us spoke, we simply stared at one another, waiting, but neither of us seemed to know what we were waiting for.

The taxi pulling up behind me gained my attention so that it was me who broke the gaze.

"My taxi," I said, turning back. I at least had the decency to feel embarrassed by such a ridiculous response.

"Then you should probably go," he snapped slightly.

"My friends will be waiting."

The slight snap increased until it was a snarl with his next words. "Then you'd better not keep them waiting, had you. Enjoy your *lunch*."

The final word was a full-on sneer he did nothing to hide. I blanched at the loaded inference in such an innocent word as *lunch*, but it did piss me off enough that I decided to fight fire with fire.

"Oh, I fully intend to. Have a good weekend, Mr Caldwell. I'll see you on Monday."

I didn't wait for any further interaction and hoped he recognised the recycled words he'd offered me earlier that day.

****

I arrived at the pub where I was meeting my new friends to find them already seated. We all ordered the speciality carvery and soft drinks, although Bea did order a bottle of wine to accompany lunch. The other girls were happy to get back on the alcohol bus but remembering my hangover and the still slightly fuzzy head I was sporting I was less keen.

"So, who was the guy last night?" asked Nicole with a cheeky grin that made me laugh.

I explained that he was Mr Caldwell, my boss, but for whatever reason I didn't share any more than that. Maybe because beyond that I had no idea what or who he was.

Sasha sat next to Nicole and shook her head. "I'd have handed my notice in after the way he behaved last night. He had no right to interfere with your time off. Toby was well pissed off. I think he likes you, Carrie."

The other two nodded, but Bea, who was my main friend in this little group said nothing.

I didn't want them to think badly of Gabriel or to judge him harshly. "He was concerned about me. He wasn't aware that I knew anyone and thought I may have had too much to drink." The lies came easily and even I kind of believed them. The comment about Toby, *fuckboy*, I ignored.

The girls all nodded.

"And to be honest he may have had a point. I got home and was really out of it, like totally drunk and then this morning I had the hangover from hell."

"But you didn't even drink that much," Sasha said. "Although, sometimes it's when the cold air hits you. Do you remember that time you did that?" She turned to Nicole.

"Well, not all that well, but I get what you mean."

Sasha began to explain. "So, one time we had all been out. Nicole had been out for a cigarette with some of the boys and not long after she came back in, she was totally plastered."

"I was so ill." Nicole winced at the memory. "And the morning after! The hangover was horrendous, and I couldn't really remember much of the night before. Awful."

"If it hadn't been for Toby taking you home, I doubt you'd have ever got there," Sasha said seriously but then laughed.

"My mum was so grateful to him."

"I remember. Didn't she send him a cake or something?" Bea asked, entering the conversation again.

"Yeah, well cakes and biscuits, homemade." She looked at me. "She phoned me the next day and I was still out of sorts, so I told her about Toby taking me home and staying with me to take care of me and she was very grateful."

"That was nice." I smiled, but it wasn't Toby I was thinking of, it was Gabriel and how he'd taken care of me the night before.

"Hmmm." Sasha laughed while Nicole shook her head. "Our Nic liked Toby and had just started getting somewhere with him before that night."

"And after that night he lost all interest in me beyond friendship," Nicole explained.

I briefly questioned if that's what had happened between me and Gabriel but reasoned that we had been closest after he'd taken care of me.

"Fuck," muttered Bea. "Speak of the devil."

I turned to see Toby and a couple of other lads heading for us.

"Hey," the lads called.

Toby squeezed into the booth next to me. "I text you earlier," he told me.

I reached for my bag and looked for my phone, nothing. I checked my pockets, nothing. Shit! I must have left it at home somewhere. I couldn't really remember the last time I'd had it, but I was unlikely to need it as I was only out for lunch.

****

A second and then third bottle of wine had been consumed, but that was the last thing on my mind. The truth was a cup of tea would have held more appeal at that moment. The others were all discussing moving on, maybe into town for a bit of an early evening session, but not me, I was going home.

I excused myself and popped to the ladies. As I left the cubicle I stood at the sink and looked at myself in the mirror as I washed my hands. Even with make-up on I looked tired and a little peaky. Yes, I needed to go home, have a cup of tea and maybe a little nap.

When I pulled open the door to leave, I jumped back at the sight of Toby standing there, waiting for me. I thought back to the comment about him being pissed off with Gabriel and wondered if he did like me, properly like me. He was fun but he really wasn't for me.

"I was worried about you last night," he said.

"I was fine." My reply was short, and I hoped it might end the conversation. It didn't.

"So, who was he? The arsehole who dragged you out."

I shook my head. I refused to have Gabriel painted as a villain here. "He didn't drag me out. He's my boss and was worried about me being new in town and stuff."

He looked at me, deliberating a response. I hadn't gone so far as to defend Gabriel about the arsehole accusation. He was an arsehole, but I'd be damned if anyone else was going to call him one.

"In case you were wondering I text to ask you out. Lunch, dinner, breakfast?" He smiled, moving on from Gabriel, and added a wink that made me smile back.

"I've had lunch, I may be in bed before dinner and the only person I share breakfast with is a three-year-old little girl." I was

75

trying to give him the brush off in the nicest way possible but wanted to leave him in no doubt that I wasn't interested.

"Dinner it is then."

I replayed my words and remembered that dinner and bed had been one and the same. Giving him the brush off was not working.

"Toby—" I began.

"It was a joke," he interrupted and although he wore a smile it didn't seem entirely intended. "You're coming into town though."

"No. I need some recovery time before the new week starts."

"It wasn't really a question," he snapped, making me aware of how isolated we were in this corridor with nobody else around.

Before anything else could be said, Bea burst into the corridor. "I'm off. Town and a session are a no from me and if you're not doing it, Carrie, I thought we could walk back together via the coffee shop by the canal for cake." She smiled at me then turned to look at Toby. "You are not invited. You always take too long to choose your cake and then complain that you chose the wrong one."

He shrugged, then turned to face me. "Another time, Carrie, again."

Chapter Sixteen

Gabriel

"So, you and Nanny didn't shag then?"

I glared across at Seb while we sat in the garden watching Charlotte running around.

"Why the fuck not? She's gorgeous and that arse in those jeans was a vision!" he said, then hissed between gritted teeth before rolling his eyes and whistling.

"I thought we'd established that you shouldn't think of her naked."

Seb laughed and shook his head. "Me thinking of her naked is the least of your worries if you don't shag her soon."

"And what's that supposed to mean?" Pissed off was becoming my default mode with Seb when he insisted on thinking of Carrie naked. He wasn't wrong about her arse in those jeans.

"It means that she is gorgeous and if you don't act on your attraction to her, someone else will. Maybe even her dance partner from last night." Seb laughed.

I scowled at his reference to fuckboy...Toby. "And what the fuck does that mean?"

"You know what I mean, but I'll explain if you really need me to."

I said nothing.

"Right then, if you're sitting comfortably, I'll begin; whether you like it or not, you like her, a lot and there's a lot to like. She is very pretty, and she cares for Charlotte making her even more attractive. She's kind, sweet, funny and has just enough innocence about her to make men like us want to protect her and dirty her at the same time…anyway, I digress…"

Seb's smirk and arched brow amused me but the fact that he was thinking of her in a sexual way pissed me off. "Fuck off!" Not a mature response but the only one I had.

He full-on grinned at that. "There seem to be no negatives about Nanny and whilst I am giving the full picture, others will only see the face and the body, and maybe even the innocent side they want to pervert."

The words hung between us. My friend was right, and I hated it.

"Like him from last night," Seb added, totally unnecessarily.

"Toby," I sneered. "Fuckboy!"

Seb laughed. "Buddy, she likes you, but if you don't want that then tell her and let her get it on with Toby or whoever without interfering."

I sighed. "She drives me fucking crazy."

Seb shook his head. "Really? I had no idea."

"Fuck off!" I told my best friend again who just laughed. "She's all the things you said and more."

Seb stared across at me, no smirk, no quip, nothing. He'd stated his case and the rest was down to me.

"Uncle Seb, come and bounce," called Charlotte, breaking the ice and thawing my dark and cold feelings slightly.

"On my way, chicken," he replied before turning to me. "Maybe I should invite Nanny to bounce if you're not going to."

****

Charlotte and I were sitting together in the kitchen, eating an early dinner. We chatted, well, she chatted, and I listened. She really was the sweetest little girl in the world. I was biased, obviously, but God, she was my whole world.

"Daddy, can I have some more juice, please?"

I got up to get her another drink while she chatted about how much fun she'd had with Seb and how she wished Carrie had been able to stay. Her and me both. I shook that thought from my head, then thought about Seb's advice. I gave Charlotte her drink and pulled my phone from my pocket and composed a text, several times before hitting send.

<Hi. Sorry about earlier...this morning and when you were leaving. This is weird, us, for me...you're not weird and if you are, I seem to like your weird. Charlotte missed you this afternoon...I missed you too. I enjoyed last night, not the bit where you were unwell, you know, and this morning, I enjoyed that too, thank you. I hope you enjoyed your lunch>

I reread the message, slightly embarrassed by how pathetic it was...I was, especially as this was my *best* attempt. Fuck it! I hit send and less than a second later spun around at the sound of a text alert, not mine. There was another phone in here and remembering Carrie having hers earlier, I knew it would be hers. I went to the chair she'd sat on and sure enough, slightly under the seat cushion was her phone. So much for sending a message, offering an olive branch of sorts. I picked her phone up and as I placed it on the table, my excuse to go upstairs and see her later, I touched the screen where unread messages were displayed, mine, and several others, all from fuckboy.

I should have walked away, but of course I didn't. I did what any normal, rational man would do, I picked the phone up and read the messages on the screen. I would never have gone into her messages, but like this, on her home screen was not an invasion of her privacy I told myself. Plus, fuckboy gave me a bad feeling.

After checking that Charlotte had all she needed I moved away slightly so I could read the screen without my daughter seeing the myriad of moods and emotions the messages were likely to trigger.

<Morning. I got your number off Nic, hope you don't mind. I've been thinking about you all night. I was worried about you. Who was the dickhead who came and manhandled you out of the club last night? He seemed pretty rough with you. I just hope you're okay. Maybe we could meet, alone, lunch or dinner? x>

Rereading those words did not make them any easier to swallow, if anything they just made me angrier. Not while there was a breath in my body would they be meeting alone. This fucking idiot needed to keep his lips and his x to himself where my nanny was concerned.

Next message:
<You looked amazing today. I wish Bea hadn't interrupted us x>

What was it Bea had interrupted? My blood was boiling and all Seb's words of warning were swimming around my head until I thought it might explode. Where had they been? There was one more message and I hoped against all hopes that it wasn't from him and if it was that it wasn't more of the same shit I'd been subjected to already. I ignored the fact that I was reading Carrie's messages on her phone, so I was actually subjecting myself to this.

<Dinner in bed sounds like a perfect first date...I look forward to it. x>

This fucking idiot would be eating dinner through a straw if he carried on like this.

My anger at Toby the fuckboy grew and as I slammed the phone down on the countertop my annoyance began to shift to Miss fucking Webber. She and I would be having words.

As jealous as I'd felt earlier, it was nothing compared to the rage burning me from the inside out, and she was mine, only mine so what the fuck was she doing discussing dinner in bed or anything else with him? She didn't seem the sort to come back here with me last night, allow my hands to roam all over her or join me in the shower and share what we had, only to find someone new later that day. So, what was she playing at? Well, whatever it was, much like her earlier tormenting of me in the kitchen I stood in, it would have to stop, I'd make sure of it.

Chapter Seventeen

Carrie

My bath was run, and the smell of lavender and vanilla wafted around the whole of my home. I stood in just pants and a bra with my hands on my hips, scanning the lounge again.

"Where the hell is it?"

I'd been out that afternoon without my phone and assumed it was back here, but as of yet there was no sign of it anywhere. I had turned the place upside down and had run out of places to look...I'd had it that morning when Bea had messaged, and I'd tormented Gabriel with it... "Shit!"

Had I left it down there, in the kitchen? Possibly. Probably as that was the last place I had used it. "Bollocks!" At least I knew it was safe and not lost and I was only going to play music on it whilst in the bath so it wasn't the end of the world.

I marched back to my bedroom and with a longing look at the bed I had shared with Gabriel, I grabbed a book from the shelf and headed for the bath. I would relax in the water with a book.

I had only read a couple of pages when my mind wondered to the afternoon. Lunch had been nice and listening to Nicole's experience with a hangover from hell had reassured me that mine hadn't been any more than that. Bea had been quiet, especially when the boys arrived. Maybe she fancied one of them or was shy in front of men, although she hadn't seemed that way in the club, so she was probably just tired or hanging a little herself.

I remembered finding Toby waiting for me when I came out

of the toilet. Was that weird? I shook my head. He was just checking on me. The girls had already told me how worried he'd been about me after I'd left the club with Gabriel. I felt uncomfortable for a second when I thought about his comment, the one about dinner in bed. Again, I told myself off. He was friendly, a joker. His lines were banter, no more, I was sure. Plus, he wasn't my type. If he had been, I would have gone into town rather than the coffee shop with Bea. My belly rumbled a little at the memory of the home made strawberry and clotted cream cheesecake I'd devoured.

My shoulders relaxed as I lowered myself into the water. Just my head was exposed as I attempted to keep my hair, that was up in a bundled bun, dry. I could feel everything softening as the water and the fragranced bubbles did their job and then there was a bang that had me jumping up, splashing water over the sides of the bath.

I leapt out of the water, grabbed a fluffy towel that I wrapped around me and went to the door. There was only one person it could be, couldn't it? When I pulled the door open my question was answered.

"Miss Webber, your phone."

Gabriel's hand was outstretched and sitting in the palm of it was my phone.

"Thank you," I stammered as I took in his clearly angry face that seemed to grow angrier as he dragged his eyes down my body and back up again.

At that second, when his furious eyes found mine again, I saw something else there. Arousal and desire glistened too. It was at that time that I also became aware of my near nakedness. Whilst the towel covered my body it left the length of my legs bare along with my neck and chest, not to mention my boobs that peeped over the top of it.

"I was in the bath," I told him, although I'm sure my state of undress must have suggested that.

He said nothing, he simply stared. Glared.

"Lavender and vanilla."

Still nothing, but then what could you say to that? Not much unless you wanted to sound as ridiculous answering it as I must have sounded asking it.

"Bubbles."

What the fuck was the matter with me? Why couldn't I shut up and leave silence between us?

"I didn't want to get wet...my hair...not my body...I am wet..."

His eyes widened but still he said nothing, unlike me.

"From the bath, not like wet, fuck!"

I saw the ghost of a smile curve his lips but after blinking it was gone again.

"Can I get you something?"

He quirked a brow at me now. And still I rambled.

"Come."

He nearly choked on his own saliva while I simply coloured up and burnt as he watched.

"In me—no—I mean inside me—no—tea, coffee, wine."

Had I just invited him to come inside me? This man flustered me every time we spoke. My inner voice reminded me that when he kissed me and touched me, or I touched him I wasn't flustered like this. My body knew how to respond to him in a way my mouth and brain didn't when we weren't touching.

There was no mistaking his grin now. He enjoyed this far too much. In the blink of an eye his grin disappeared at the second his eyes returned to my hand that held my phone.

"You should reply to your messages."

He turned away. Didn't look back and then he was gone again.

"What the fuck," I muttered and tapped the screen of my phone. "Bollocks!" At least I knew what had him so riled and angry now.

I closed the door and threw my phone onto the sofa before pulling the plug on my bath. All the tension was back, and then some. With my towel still wrapped around me I went through the messages starting with Toby's. The first one checking how I was, probably shouldn't have bothered Gabriel, but the references to his treatment of me and him being a dickhead may have done and the suggestion of a date definitely would have irritated him.

The next message about me looking good and us being interrupted would have pissed Gabriel off and why wouldn't it? I'd immediately want to know what had been interrupted and my mind would have run wild, like his clearly had.

"No!" I cried when I saw the message about dinner in bed. I had no desire to go on a date with Toby.

Then I saw the message from Gabriel.

<Hi. Sorry about earlier...this morning and when you were leaving. This is weird, us, for me...you're not weird and if you are, I seem to like your weird. Charlotte missed you this afternoon...I missed you too. I enjoyed last night, not the bit where you were unwell, you know, and this morning, I enjoyed that too, thank you. I hope you enjoyed your lunch>

"Bloody hell."

He was apologising and acknowledging his hot and cold thing. I let out a little chuckle at his own rambling. I appreciated him sharing his feelings with me. I laughed again at his flustered words, not that his ability to be flustered was even close to mine. I felt sure he hadn't hoped I'd had an enjoyable lunch, although maybe he didn't know Toby was there when he'd sent his message.

"Bollocks!" I needed to think of something more articulate to say in these circumstances.

I rolled my phone in my hand and considered my next move. I could leave things until tomorrow and aim to clear things up then, but what if he went to work early or had plans. Also, I couldn't clear things up if Charlotte or Christine were there, could I?

After rereading his message, I composed a reply.

<Hi, I've checked my messages. There is no need for you to be angry with me. I have done nothing wrong. Toby is nothing to me...he's a joker, no more. He thinks his banter is funnier than it is. I don't care about his messages...I care about yours.

I like that you're weird too, if you are weird. We make good weird together, don't we? I missed you too, you and Charlotte. I think about you, a lot. Still mortified about me vomiting last night, but I enjoyed last night and this morning with you. My lunch was okay. Would have preferred lunch with you>

I hit send and immediately felt sick. My eyes were glued to my screen, waiting for a response, something, anything, anything at all, I was willing to take any crumb he threw me right now.

The sound of a bang had me jumping again. I rushed to the door and flung it open to find a slightly happier Gabriel.

"Carrie."

One word, that's all he said and suddenly, he rushed me, pinning me to the wall, his lips closing over mine.

Chapter Eighteen

Gabriel

A glass of whiskey sat on the counter top in the kitchen, looking at me, taunting me, inviting me in, but I knew that one would lead to another and then another and then I would have no choice but to go and find fuckboy Toby and punch him, hard.

I laughed, suddenly remembering Carrie's flustered rambling. It was obvious she'd just got out of the bath or the shower, but her garbled explanation was fucking hilarious, especially the bit where she inadvertently invited me to come inside her. I could think of nothing better and nowhere else I'd rather be than buried inside her.

My dick was hard before I went upstairs, but once I saw her all but naked it had doubled in size, well, it felt as though it had. I should never have employed her. By doing so I'd begun to drive myself towards insanity, so much so that I felt sure Seb would have me sectioned at some point. And with all of that on my mind, I still couldn't bring myself to regret it.

My phone vibrated with a low hum as a text message landed. I closed my eyes and sent a wish to the heavens. Fuck me, destiny, fate, and now wishes being sent above.

<Hi, I've checked my messages. There is no need for you to be angry with me. I have done nothing wrong. Toby is nothing to me...he's a joker, no more. He thinks his banter is funnier than it is. I don't care about his messages...I care about yours. I like your weird too, if you are weird. We make good weird

together, don't we? I missed you too, you and Charlotte. I think about you, a lot. Still mortified about me vomiting last night, but I enjoyed last night and this morning with you. My lunch was okay. Would have preferred lunch with you>

Her words about it being banter made me think back to what Seb had said about her innocence. I wondered if she really believed that. I smiled again, knowing his messages weren't the ones she cared about...mine were.

I didn't even remember the trip upstairs. The next thing I knew I was standing at her door again, knocking on it. I couldn't have dared dream that she'd still be wrapped in just a towel, but when she opened the door she was.

We kissed for seconds, minutes, hours. Who knew? I had no idea if time had stood still, gone backwards or tripped into the future. I had one hand holding her neck and the other had wrapped around her and rested on her behind. The towel was still in place, for now. Her arms had wrapped around my neck, her hands ran across my shoulders and skimmed up into my hair, gently holding my head, as if she needed to keep my mouth on hers. The only destination any of me had was on or in her.

She tasted divine, better than I remembered which was saying something. As our kiss deepened and our tongues brushed and danced together, her moans got louder and as they did my dick got ever harder. I had never felt this way before, never, not about anyone and I loved and loathed it in equal parts.

The hand I'd had on her arse moved up her body, moving up and across until it reached the top of her towel that I quickly pulled loose, not content until I heard it drop on the floor. That is when I broke our kiss, to look down and take in the sight of her.

"Fuck, you're beautiful," I told her and smiled as I watched the flush creep up her cheeks.

She seemed to be having an internal battle, her hands that now hung at her side were flexing, as if she was considering using them to cover herself. Suddenly, she was nervous and less certain than her kiss had suggested.

"Absolutely gorgeous," I added and leaned in to land a series of gentle kisses from the corner of her mouth to her ear where I paused and whispered to her. "You are all I can think about; holding you, touching you, kissing you, fucking you until you're coming and calling my name."

Her little mewl told me her nerves were lifting and desire was taking control again. "I can't get last night and this morning out of my head. The way you felt, smelled, tasted...everything. You are a witch and more than a little beguiling, Miss Webber."

I felt her tense when I called her Miss Webber. That was the last thing I wanted, and I hadn't said it to be an arsehole, it had just come out. Maybe I should call her Miss Webber when I came inside her or as I made her come, just to add a positive spin to her more formal title.

"Have you been thinking about it, Carrie? About the way it felt as you came on my tongue, or how you saw me coming undone until my cum covered our hands and bodies?"

"Gabe," she cried, her hands already reaching for me again and her legs somehow moving so they were wrapped around one of my legs, her hot and wet sex pressed firmly against me.

My lips moved back to her mouth and we kissed again. While the kiss deepened one hand found one of her perfect breasts. I held it, cupped it and allowed my thumb to brush across the stiffened peak of her nipple. A low groan left her mouth but only got as far as my mouth that was happy to capture it.

I felt her hips begin to rock as my brushing of her nipple turned firmer until I rolled and then pinched it. Oh, she liked a firmer touch if the increase in her hip thrusting was anything to go by, and it was. With our kiss now broken I dropped my head to the nipple I had previously teased with my finger and thumb. I gave it a single lick before circling it with my tongue and then I drew it into the wet warmth of my mouth and fuck, if it didn't send her libido soaring.

Carrie was essentially rubbing herself against me and it was as hot as hell. I could feel her moisture escaping from her and coating my jeans. Shit, she was naked, and I was still fully dressed. I couldn't wait much longer to be naked and buried inside her, but I also wanted to explore her and pleasure her before then.

The sounds of her moans and panting broke my thoughts. Fuck! She was well on her way to coming, just from rubbing herself against me and whilst that was hot and I would have a ringside seat at seeing her fall apart for me, this wasn't quite how I imagined it and I was hoping to be a little more involved in that moment, so, I removed my leg from between her thighs.

A low moan of disappointment left her lips before her face registered what she'd been doing. The flush of embarrassment crept up her face again, but this one wasn't in any way good, she looked ashamed.

"Hey." I stood to my full height and gazed down at her. "Do you have any idea just how much I want you right now."

She smiled, a small, slightly disbelieving smile. I took her hand and placed it on my still covered erection.

"Oh."

"Yeah, oh." I grinned. "And we still need to arrange our date."

It was her turn to grin now.

"You still want to take me out."

"More than ever; take you out, keep you in, yes."

"Gabriel, kiss me…" her voice trailed off. "Touch me, please."

I wasn't sure I wouldn't come in my pants with those words leaving her mouth. The pleading in her tone, the glint shimmering in her eyes and her please. Yeah, those things would be my undoing.

"With fucking pleasure. Let me take you to bed."

She smiled, then reached for my hand, and with my hand in hers she began to lead us to her bedroom. "Let me take you."

Chapter Nineteen

Carrie

I was the least confident person I knew, especially sexually, and yet, with Gabriel and his desire for me, I felt able to be self-assured.

Butterflies still flipped and flew in my stomach and chest, but in a good way. I was excited to be doing this, desperate to share this moment with Gabe.

"You're sure?" he asked as we paused at my bedroom door.

"Never been surer of anything in my life."

He grinned down at me, my certainty in doing this acted as some kind of aphrodisiac. His lips were heading for mine again and then a phone rang.

"Shit!" Gabriel cursed, pulling his phone from his back pocket. "My mother, two minutes and then I am all yours." He winked as he connected his call. "Mum."

I gazed up at him and licked my lips at his words, his promise, *then I am all yours.*

He arched a brow, leaned down as he covered the mouthpiece on his phone and whispered to me. "You bet, baby."

I flushed but thought it might be more to do with arousal than anything else this time. His use of baby sounded better than it probably should.

"What? When? No, of course not. I'll ask Carrie if she can look after Charlotte and come now." He was already withdrawing. He mouthed a simple sorry and looked as disappointed as I felt.

I opened my bedroom door and made my way in to find some clothes. There was a clean t-shirt on my bed that I slipped over my head before pulling open my underwear drawer and grabbed the first pair of pants I found. Gabriel watched as I slipped them on, his eyes widening at the sight of my comfy pants that were covered in pouting lips.

"Okay, I'll meet you at the hospital, and don't worry. I'm sure she'll be fine."

By the time I returned to him he had hung up and looked awkward.

"Sorry. My grandma has had a fall and is on her way to hospital. I need to meet my mum there…she's worried about her. She has dementia, so…"

I shook my head. "It's fine. You should go and I'll take care of Charlotte."

"Thank you." His words were barely a whisper as he turned to leave and then he spun back to face me and pulled me to him.

In a split second, his lips were back on mine and he was kissing me as if his life depended on it. All too soon the kiss ended, but I was happy because that kiss meant he didn't regret what almost happened again. His kiss reassured me of that.

"We need a date night with no phones and no child or friends or anything else that is going to ruin the night again."

"Yes."

"Good. Let me make sure my mum and grandma are okay and then we can find a date. Sleep well." His lips gently brushed mine again before he rushed through the door and left.

I moved to my bedroom window and watched him drive away before going to check on Charlotte with the biggest and soppiest grin on my face.

****

I slept restlessly, waiting for any sounds or signs of Gabriel's return and finally gave up at five o'clock. I added a pair of pyjama shorts to my pants and t-shirt before I went to check on Charlotte again. Fast asleep. I smiled down at her then headed to the kitchen where I prepared her things for stay and play that morning and breakfast.

The kettle had just boiled when I felt hands slide around my middle.

"You're up early." Gabriel's breath danced across my neck as he leaned in and kissed the skin there.

"Couldn't sleep," I replied honestly.

"Hmmm, I wonder why?" he asked with a chuckle.

I said nothing, a little embarrassed to admit that he was the reason behind my lack of sleep.

"I promise you, Carrie, last night won't be the last night you lose sleep because of me."

I turned in his arms so that I was looking up at him.

He pushed some loose hair back off my face and smiled. "I like your shorts."

I laughed at his seemingly random and slightly cheesy comment.

"Oh, Miss Webber, did you just laugh at me?"

I panicked a little at his Miss Webber but seeing his grin I immediately relaxed.

"And if I did?" I teased.

"Then I might just have to take you to task." He held me against him. His hands that were on my hips pulled me closer until I felt the stiff length of him digging into my belly.

"I might like to be taken to task by you." I flushed at such a brazen reference to sex. I needed to find my confident self again.

"I fucking guarantee it. I need to take a shower. Want to join me?"

I thought back to our previous shower and could think of no better way to start the day.

"Can I go outside and bounce?" came a little voice behind us.

We both leapt away, flustered from our encounter and more flustered to have been busted by Charlotte.

"Later," Gabriel told her. "It's still early."

She brokered no argument.

"I'm going to grab a shower and get ready for work," Gabriel said, already heading for the hall.

"How are things?" I asked, suddenly thinking about his grandma. "With your trip out last night." I thought my code was adequate to keep Charlotte in the dark.

"Okay, thanks..." He paused. "Shower."

****

By the time Charlotte got her bounce time it was late afternoon. We'd spent the morning at the stay and play before heading to the park then walked home via the canal side coffee shop for lunch. Once home she'd had a little nap and I'd cleaned the kitchen and tidied around. Technically that wasn't part of my job description but in Christine's absence and with nothing else to do it seemed ridiculous not to do it. I deliberated whether I should cook some dinner for Gabriel and Charlotte as I thought Christine was responsible for that too but decided that might be a step too far.

We sat in the garden with a drink and some fruit, chatting between her bouncing. Charlotte was very animated and articulate as she told me about her favourite movie. I laughed at her wide-eyed expression at the exciting parts and gave her the biggest round of applause as she sang the songs from it.

"Can I dress-up, please?" Charlotte asked, and on the back of our conversation I assumed I would be joined by Elsa upon her return.

"Sure," I replied, and prepared to escort her back in doors, a move she halted.

"I'm a big girl now. I can dress myself," she told me.

I loved this kid's confidence.

"You could bounce while I'm gone and then we can bounce together."

I nodded. It seemed as though Charlotte had thought of everything. She ran indoors while I drank my squash and then kicked my shoes off, all ready to bounce.

The trampoline was small, plenty big enough for Charlotte but a little compact for me. I tentatively began to bounce on the balls of my feet whilst calling to Charlotte. With my movements getting faster and higher I started to bounce around, moving in a circle. I didn't have the biggest boobs, but the truth was that a better bra would have been more appropriate for this. In fairness, a better outfit would have been a good choice; the vest top I was wearing rode up from the bottom while the straps kept slipping off my shoulders and my shorts somehow managed to drop off my waist whilst getting further and further wedged up my bottom.

"Come on, my bouncing partner. If you don't get back soon, I will be all bounced out and you'll have to bounce on your own."

I laughed at the lack of a response and imagined Charlotte adding a crown, cape, wand and glittery shoes to her outfit.

"Charlotte!" I shouted in an overexaggerated dramatic tone, almost singing her name in an operatic fashion.

I spun to face the door, expecting Charlotte to be there, smiling, laughing or preparing to respond in her own dramatic way. I stopped bouncing the second my eyes landed on the doorway. I probably shouldn't have stopped dead because somehow that resulted in my legs buckling beneath me until I ended up kneeling on the trampoline, still staring at the doorway and the man filling it, looking absolutely divine, Gabriel.

"Mr Caldwell," I managed to stammer, unsure what else to say or what the hell I must have looked like.

The quirk of his brow suggested he hadn't expected me to call him Mr Caldwell. His reply confirmed it. "Miss Webber. Good bounce?"

He smirked and despite my embarrassment, I laughed.

"Hmmm."

He took in my whole appearance, his eyes skimmed from my breasts that were protruding from my vest top and bra beneath, then as I struggled to get to my feet he drank in the length of my legs. I grabbed at the netting, finding the opening, which is where I found Gabriel, an outstretched hand offered to help me down.

"Thank you."

We shared a smile as I accepted his hand and his help.

"Bouncing suits you," he said, both of us knowing exactly what that meant.

"You should join me some time, bouncing," I replied, nervously nibbling the corner of my mouth.

"Hmmm," Gabriel said before we both spun around at the sound of Let It Go being sung from the doorway by Charlotte who was likely to insist on being called Elsa from this point until bedtime.

Chapter Twenty

Gabriel

Today had been a long day, not hard, just long and that was down to lack of sleep rather than the time I'd spent at work. With everything done, I decided to call it a day. Maybe I could get home and spend some time with Charlotte before an early bedtime for her and me. I also needed to check on my mum and grandma. Ideas of bedtime sent my mind straight to Carrie, but after our last couple of attempts at sharing a bedtime I decided we might have to wait for our date, unfortunately.

I said goodbye to Shelley and left the office for the short journey home. When I arrived home the house was quiet, then I heard the sound of the trampoline bouncing and felt the breeze wafting through from the back garden. I made my way out there, expecting to see Charlotte bouncing around, maybe even trying to tempt Carrie to join her, but what I found left me speechless.

Carrie.

Fuck!

She was bouncing alone on the trampoline and called to Charlotte who was nowhere to be seen. I assumed she'd dashed inside, maybe to use the toilet. I couldn't take my eyes off her; she was wearing a little vest thing, the straps kept falling off and she kept pulling them back up. And her shorts? Fuck me! The shorts had more arse hanging out of them than safely tucked inside. She laughed and called Charlotte again before bouncing around, turning until she saw me.

Our eyes locked and she seemed to forget that she was on a

trampoline. The buckling of her legs resulted in her ending up on her knees, staring at me. I hoped she was okay, but actually didn't check on her wellbeing as I was transfixed by her. She addressed me formally as Mr Caldwell and I responded in kind making us both laugh. My eyes moved from hers, skimming down her body; her breasts that fitted my hands perfectly and currently overflowed her clothing, including the black lace bra I could see the top of, her pinched in waist, the fuller swell of her hips and down to her legs that were bare, the full length of them on show, finally I smiled at her feet, complete with pretty painted toe nails in a shimmery pink.

She clambered to her feet and as awkward and clumsy as she looked, it was endearing. God, she was gorgeous. I walked over to the opening in the net so that once she was there, I could help her to get out. She accepted the outstretched hand I offered.

I was clueless what to say next, maybe nothing would have been better than my lame offering of, "Bouncing suits you." We both knew that translated to I want to fuck you and bounce you all over my bed and all over me.

"You should join me some time...bouncing," she said. At that point I'd have sold a kidney to bounce with her.

I managed a hmmm and if she didn't fucking nibble her lip. The things I wanted to do to her, dirty things, really, really dirty things...and then the sound of Let It Go erupted behind us. We turned and found Charlotte in the doorway, dressed in one of her many costumes as she sang her heart out.

Carrie and I both laughed and applauded my daughter, even joining in with some of the singing. I couldn't keep the smile off my face as I watched Charlotte; happy, laughing, carefree and loving the addition of Carrie, a young woman, to her role models. My smile wavered ever so slightly with my daughter's suggestion that we could act out the film and my role appeared to be that of a snowman.

The loud ripple of laughter that belonged to Carrie at that particular suggestion rang around us and I am not ashamed to admit that it warmed me...warmed me and stiffened me if I was completely honest.

"Carrie, will you stay and have dinner with me? Daddy

sometimes has his later."

I wasn't sure how to handle this. Did I want Carrie to join us for dinner? Did Carrie want to join us for dinner? And where did I fit in with these dinner plans?

"Daddy's back now," Carrie replied, looking across at me a little uncertainly.

"Yes, he is, and I am starving," I called, already chasing Charlotte indoors and making out as if I was a hungry monster ready to eat my daughter.

Carrie laughed again at the scene before her, and fuck, if it wasn't her I imagined eating.

"I'll just unpack Charlotte's bag from stay and play and tidy the toys away and then I'll be on my way," Carrie said from her position standing in the kitchen doorway.

"Okay." I wasn't sure if she wanted to do that or not, or if she'd rather head for her own area of the house straight away. "If you want to, or I can do it…whatever." Fuck! This was proving weirder than it needed to be. Under normal circumstances I'd have waved off her attempts to sort Charlotte's things, choosing to do it myself and yet, now, I didn't want Carrie to think I was dismissing her. On the other hand, I didn't want her to think we could now play happy families.

Looking slightly less awkward, Carrie entered the room fully and began to unpack my daughter's bag. She gave Charlotte the soft toy from it and some leaflets they'd picked up at the coffee shop then handed me a couple of consent forms for things from stay and play.

"Will I still go and see my friends at play and stay?" asked Charlotte, confusing the order of the words.

Neither Carrie nor I corrected her, in fact, I thought I might prefer my daughter's version of the group she attended.

"Erm, I suppose if you wanted to. On the days you're not at nursery," I told her and was rewarded with a huge cheesy grin.

I rummaged around the cupboards and fridge, finding the ingredients for a cheesy pasta bake thing we regularly had.

Carrie finished what she was doing and with a ruffle of

Charlotte's hair she prepared to leave. "I'll see you in the morning. Have a lovely evening, both of you."

She turned to look at me and I was taken aback, not only by just how attractive I found her, but more so by how much I wanted her to stay. I didn't say any of that. I did, however, smile, and wish her a good evening too.

****

"And they all lived happily ever after," I said, closing the book Charlotte had chosen for tonight's bedtime story. I leaned down and kissed her head. "Night-night princess."

Gently, I closed the door behind me and paused on the landing. I looked towards the floor above and debated whether I should ascend them. No. I shouldn't. If I went up there now anything could happen and I didn't think I could cope with another close call or interruption, so for tonight I would go back downstairs, pour a glass of something and watch some TV.

With a glass of wine, I surfed the TV channels for the fourth or fifth time and still couldn't find anything to watch. I called my mum, checked on my gran and was relieved to hear that both were fine. My mum was reassured that the hospital were planning on releasing her own mother the following day. The nursing home where she lived were more than happy to be having her back. She was a very popular lady, my gran, and although slightly biased, I could see why because she was wonderful; funny, sarcastic, loving and everything you could ever wish for in a mother or grandmother, even with the advancing dementia. My mind kept wondering but never got any farther than Carrie a couple of floors above, initially thinking how much my gran would like her.

With my gran on the mend and my mum more settled and happier again I began to think of my date with Carrie. My mum had already mentioned taking Charlotte overnight but had suggested Friday rather than Saturday, which was fine by me because it meant I'd be able to get to date night a day sooner. I knew now that date night was on my mind, I would never shake Carrie from it tonight. I wondered what she was doing; was she awake? Had she thought of me? Was she thinking about me now? What was she wearing? Had she eaten?

"Shit!" I cursed myself and then laughed at the level of pathetic I had sunk to.

I hit standby on the TV and reached for my phone. Should I message her? What should I say? Was she expecting me to contact her, hoping I might?

What the fuck was happening to me? I was not an adolescent with his first girlfriend and somehow, I was behaving as though I was precisely that. Pathetic.

More pathetic than I'd given myself credit for I realised when I found myself, phone in hand texting Carrie. What harm could it do?

<Hey…was wondering if Anna would be free for a date on Friday night? Olaf is free >

Chapter Twenty-One

Carrie

<Hey...was wondering if Anna would be free for a date on Friday night? Olaf is free >

I literally laughed out loud when I read the message on my phone. Charlotte and her Frozen obsession was rubbing off.

<Why? Do you want to build a snowman?>

I had just opened a packet of biscuits and was dunking them in my tea as I waited for Gabriel's response. I was unsure just what type of response I'd get; jokey, serious, sexy, maybe even another Frozen related one.

<Not especially. I would like to fuck you senseless though>

"Bollocks!" I laughed, although I still felt shocked by the bluntness of his response. He'd obviously tired of the Frozen references. "Serious and sexy response it is then."

<And they say romance is dead! Is that your idea of date night then?>

<Could be, but I would also like to take you to dinner, talk to you, get to know you and then fuck you senseless.

Better? I am a romantic fool, I know>

With a low giggle I realised how little we knew about each other. I wanted to get to know Gabriel better. To know more about him. I'd love that.

<In that case I am definitely free on Friday>

The reply came back in an instant.

<I will pick you up at 7.30>

I was giggling like a fool. Pick me up? Did he really intend to collect me from the top floor of his house for our date? Where were we going? What should I wear?

<What and where did you have in mind? What about clothes?>

My packet of malted milk biscuits was now down to half a packet. I needed to stop eating them. One more wouldn't matter though, would it? Apparently not, if the biscuit I had just rammed in my mouth in two bites was anything to go by. I almost choked when I jumped at the sound of a message arriving.

<I'm now imagining you naked>

<Is that the romantic fool in you speaking?>

<Either that or the man who wished he had a time machine so it could already be Friday night. I can't wait to take you on our first date>

I didn't know what to say to that. I wasn't expecting that and suddenly his claims of being a romantic fool didn't seem that ridiculous anymore. Before I had chance to reply another message landed.

<I'm thinking dinner, good wine, music, maybe a little dancing and then whatever else happens...>

<Sounds perfect>

<Just like me!>

And like that, the banter was back and the earlier seriousness, maybe even romanticism was gone leaving me feeling a little calmer and relaxed.

<Obviously>

<You should go to sleep. You're likely to be busy tomorrow, playing Anna and bouncing>

<Can't wait>

<And you have a big night out Friday, so rest up!>

Another biscuit was already in my mouth making at least three since I'd vowed to stop eating them. After a hard swallow I wondered if I should go on a health kick before my date, but figured it might be a bit late, plus, Gabriel had already seen me naked.

I tidied around; put the biscuits away and vowed not to buy anymore, washed up, put my ironing away and threw my dirty washing into the basket before brushing my teeth and climbing into bed. The book I'd been reading sat on my bedside table but before I picked it up, my phone sounded another message, then another, and another.

I glanced down and groaned. Toby.

<Hi. Hope you're okay. I missed you on Sunday night. It was good but would have been better with you. X>

<Let me know when you're free. We'll go out, alone x>

I had no clue what to say to him. Toby was okay, friendly, but I was beginning to believe that he might like me properly and it wasn't a mutual thing. Maybe if I ignored him, he'd get tired and move on to someone else. The girls had said in the pub that he'd been quite keen on Nic and then suddenly wasn't. I closed Toby's messages and opened the third one that was from Gabriel.

<Goodnight, Miss Webber>

Such a simple message and it had me grinning and bouncing on my bed like an idiot.

<Goodnight, Mr Caldwell>

I snuggled down under the covers and with the biggest of smirks that I couldn't control, I closed my eyes and went to sleep, impatient for the morning to come and for date night to be a day closer.

****

The following day, Christine was still a no show, which was understandable under the circumstances and in some ways, I was enjoying spending time with Charlotte, just the two of us.

Our morning had been fun. We went to another playgroup, a sensory one this time where we'd enjoyed playing instruments and singing. On the way home we'd stopped off at the park to have a go on the slide and the swings. It was while I was pushing Charlotte on the swing to calls of *higher, higher* that I was startled to see Toby watching us, watching me from the other side of the playground and he didn't look happy. Charlotte moved onto the climbing frame.

Uncertainty rippled through my stomach, making me feel nervous and a little queasy. What should I do? Call to him? Wave? Smile? I had no clue. He stood near the exit Charlotte and I would leave by meaning if he remained there, he would be unavoidable. Maybe that was the best way to play it—leave when we were done and if he was there, say hi. Simple.

"I'm hungry," called Charlotte, coming to a standstill before me after getting down from the climbing frame. "Can I have jam on my sandwich for lunch? Strawberry jam is my favourite. And cake and crisps and—"

I laughed at her rambling that was beginning to resemble a menu. "If you have jam on your sandwich you can't really have cake and crisps. What about a jam sandwich, some fruit and a yoghurt?"

"Okay?" she said without even a hint of an objection. She really was a good girl.

"Fine. Let's go then, Miss Charlotte," I said, already offering my hand to take which I found something of a comfort as we headed towards the heavy metal gate we'd leave by. The same gate Toby stood next to.

"Hi." I thought it was a simple greeting and couldn't be considered anything less than friendly. I was wrong.

"Hi! You ignore me for days and that's it, hi?"

I resisted the temptation to point out that I hadn't been ignoring him and if I had, it hadn't been for days.

"I've been busy."

"Oh." He suddenly looked sad and hurt, leaving me feeling guilty. "I'm sorry to have troubled you." His tone was quieter and calmer.

"No, Toby, please," I called to him, but he was already leaving the park.

****

Charlotte didn't mention anything about my encounter with Toby and for that I was very grateful because I had no desire to try and explain his churlishness or my own guilty feelings to a three-year-old.

We sat at the table, drawing, writing and colouring. Charlotte was designing what felt like the hundredth butterfly of the afternoon. She took her time and showed patience and care as she strived to match all the markings on each of the butterfly's wings. She was totally engrossed in her task and I was equally as engrossed by her, so much so that neither of us heard Gabriel enter the house, not until he shouted *boo* from his position behind us. Charlotte squealed and then leapt into his arms. I

104

clutched my chest and envied the little girl's ability and right to be in his embrace.

"Is it that time already?" I asked, still holding a hand to my chest that contained my hammering heart.

"It is," Gabriel confirmed. He reached forward and put a hand over the one on my chest. "Sorry. I didn't mean to startle you quite so much. I was hoping my arrival might prove to be a pleasant surprise rather than a heart attack inducing shock."

We exchanged a smile before he withdrew his hand and returned his attention to his daughter who had already launched into her recount of the day. I tidied away the things from the table and prepared to leave as Charlotte discussed her lunch.

"How very sensible you are, Miss Webber," he teased as Charlotte explained that she hadn't been able to have cake, jam and crisps.

"And that is my cue to leave, Mr Caldwell."

He held my gaze and winked. "Enjoy your evening. You never know, you might hear from a friend later."

I assumed this was code for *I'll text you later*, or at least I hoped it was.

"That would be nice."

"Nice?" He arched a brow.

"Very nice."

"Hmmm. I'm sure your friend can do better than nice, even very nice."

"Can he?"

"I guarantee he can."

"How nice?" I asked, the rising tension between us palpable, but I swear he wore a smug smirk.

"Goodnight, Miss Webber."

Chapter Twenty-Two

Gabriel

Thursday night. Carrie and I had remained playful in our banter and texts, but there had been no more than that. We'd both been busy in the day and at night I'd had Charlotte as my mum had been doing extra visits to my gran. I had suggested to my mum that she shouldn't take care of my daughter on Friday night, not that I didn't want date night, I did, but I appreciated that my mum might need some time to herself. Fortunately, she insisted that she had been looking forward to it all week, so date night was on.

The doorbell rang, sending Charlotte rushing for the door, squealing as she went. "Uncle Seb," she screamed when she saw him standing there.

"How's my favourite lady in the whole world?" he asked, already kissing her and throwing her around.

I followed them through to the lounge, taking the beer from Seb, allowing him to throw Charlotte around a little more.

We had just opened the beer as Charlotte told us all about her day. Technically, I'd already heard her recount, but Seb hadn't. She had just got to the bit about the trip to the park and feeding the ducks when she suddenly paused, drawing our attention to her fully.

"You okay, sweetheart?" Seb asked my frowning daughter.

She seemed to think for a moment before responding. "Hmmm. You and Daddy are bestest friends, aren't you?"

We both nodded.

"Yes, and we have known each other a really long time too," I replied.

"If somebody was mean to Uncle Seb, would it make you sad?" Her chin quivered a little making me panic slightly.

"Of course. If your friend is sad it makes you sad too, doesn't it?"

"And the same for me," agreed Seb.

"I love you, Daddy." She paused. "And Uncle Seb and Grandma and Grandad too, but Carrie...she is my bestest friend."

I frowned across at Seb and understanding my confusion he chipped in. "It's good to have a best friend, isn't it?"

She nodded.

"Was Carrie sad and it made you sad?" My friend's question got a teary-eyed nod from my daughter.

"Oh, baby." I pulled her into my lap and held her tight. "Maybe Carrie wasn't really sad." To the best of my knowledge Carrie had been and still was absolutely fine. No signs of sadness, not since we'd cleared the air.

"But in the park..." she trailed off.

"Today?" Seb asked.

Her reply was a shake of her head.

"Before...another day...there was a man. Do you know him, Daddy?" I loved her innocence and her belief that I knew everything and everyone.

"I don't know, baby. Maybe. Who was it?"

"He was mad at Carrie."

Seb and I exchanged a concerned glance, but I was becoming angry and wasn't entirely sure I wouldn't be marching up the bloody stairs and giving Miss fucking Webber a good talking to. Who the fuck was she mixing with and exposing my daughter too? This was not what I wanted or expected from my child's nanny. I tuned back into Charlotte's words on a single word, a name. Toby. Fucking great, fuckboy.

"Toby?"

She nodded.

"Yes, Daddy knows Toby."

Fuckboy? Seb mouthed across to me. I nodded.

"He was in the park—"

I interrupted. "He was in the park with you? With you and Carrie? Was he playing with you?"

Seb shot me a warning glance not to lose it in front of my little girl. I was determined not to, and yet, I couldn't guarantee I wouldn't if he'd been hanging out with Carrie, Carrie and my fucking child!

Charlotte shook her head. "He was in the park playing on his own," she said, her simple wording of the situation making me smile and calm slightly.

Seb and I smirked at each other...I bet he was playing on his own, or playing with himself, wanker. My smirk broadened as my daughter continued.

"But I was hungry and when we were by the gate, he was angry with Carrie and she looked sad."

"Was Nanny sad today?" Seb asked, insisting on keeping up that ridiculous fucking Nanny thing. He really was a twat, but I loved him anyway.

Charlotte shook her head. "And she didn't cry, so she can't have been really sad."

Suddenly, my daughter was happy again, and seemingly no longer concerned about Carrie's sadness because of Toby. That in turn meant that she didn't need to be sad either.

"Uncle Seb, can I brush your hair, please?"

"Sure you can. Anything you want my beautiful girl."

She scurried off. Presumably to get brushes and clips and shit and I didn't doubt there'd be enough for us both.

"Gabe, do not lose your shit over this. Speak to Nanny rather than having one of your hissy fits."

I flipped him off. "I do not have hissy fits."

"You do where she's concerned."

I couldn't actually deny it, so ignored it. "Stop with the fucking Nanny thing. She has a name."

"I like Nanny, it's kind of naughty in a posh, wet nurse kind of way."

I glared at him. As if I didn't have the potential to be completely pissed off tonight without him making his name for her weird.

"Wet nurse? You are imagining her fucking naked again." I growled a little.

"Not exactly…topless maybe, you know, but only in a topless, lactating kind of way."

Despite him imagining her tits, I laughed. "You have serious fucking issues, my friend."

"You're welcome," he replied as my girl returned with several bags making me think we were both getting a full makeover.

An hour later and with Charlotte in bed and most traces of mine and Seb's makeover removed, we opened another bottle of beer each. We hadn't discussed Charlotte's revelations or anything beyond whatever my daughter wanted to, which was mainly how lovely Uncle Seb's hair was, soft, something he encouraged each time she said it—dickhead, how handsome I was and how much she loved us both.

But now, with little ears closed along with her eyes, all bets were off.

"What's happening with you and Nanny then?"

I shook my head at Seb but decided that the Nanny thing was going nowhere so I might as well give up on challenging it further.

I ran a hand through my hair, then quickly dropped my hand from my head as I recalled the feel of Carrie's hands being there and gripping my hair.

Seb smirked at my discomfort if nothing else.

"We're going on a date tomorrow night."

An arched brow was his response, allowing me to continue.

"I have no clue where I'm going to fucking take her." I took a swig of my beer. "And that Toby thing has pissed me off."

"So apart from the date, how are things with you and Nanny?"

I frowned at his question but quickly figured that my friend hadn't considered his question answered.

"Good." I smiled while Seb rolled his eyes. "You asked," I retorted.

He shrugged his acknowledgement.

"We keep things professional here, with Charlotte and because she is off duty when I'm here at night we haven't spent much time together, but we message and text. It's easy banter and some flirtatious repartee."

Seb nodded.

"I like her, a lot." I sounded irritated.

He openly laughed at me. "And you don't want to like her?"

"It would be easier if I didn't. I am not looking for a girlfriend. Charlotte is and always will be my priority meaning her nanny should be off limits. Fuck! I vowed to keep her that way…"

"And here we are."

"Yeah."

"You're not backing out of tomorrow, are you? You'll kick yourself if you do and let's not forget fuckboy waiting in the wings."

"He was the final straw for me, fucking touching her in that club."

"Mate, just go with it. Enjoy whatever happens and if it goes tits up deal with it, but it might not."

"With my track record—"

"Don't you dare make this about her! You did nothing wrong. It wasn't your fault."

We'd had this conversation so many times and this was always Seb's answer.

"Right, date night. Nanny doesn't need 5* or exclusive, in fact, I think she'd be uncomfortable if you went luxury with eight courses and as many knives and forks to get confused over. Simple, classy, intimate, romantic, special, thoughtful, that's what Nanny needs for a first date."

"Well, what Nanny wants…"

We both laughed at the sound of Nanny leaving my lips and Seb's thoughts about it.

"I don't know if I feel jealous of you stealing my name for her. Especially as you've seen her naked and are likely to again."

"You're imagining her naked again," I accused.

"I am. I hope my imagination does her justice."

"I guarantee it doesn't. She is beyond your wildest dreams, beyond mine."

My smug smirk caused a deep frown and a pout to mar Seb's

face.

I laughed again, unlike Seb who appeared to be sulking, causing me to laugh longer and louder.

Chapter Twenty-Three

Carrie

Nervous didn't quite convey how I felt. *Shitting bricks* might have been closer to the mark. So much so that I had just made my fourth trip of the evening to the bathroom. Gabriel was picking me up in about an hour and as I had just watched Christine drive away with Charlotte, date night was definitely on.

He met with Seb last night and other than telling me that the two of them had endured a makeover at the hands of a three-year-old, he hadn't said much about it. The truth is, he hadn't said much about anything. Last night he'd text a simple goodnight and this morning he left for work within seconds of me arriving downstairs. This evening was a little better, although, it felt as though we were both nervous. I smiled as I remembered him saying *see you later, Carrie.* How ridiculous am I, that a see you later made me giddy and grinning from ear to ear? It also made me need one last trip to the bathroom.

Almost an hour later I fastened the strap on my shoe and stood to my full height. I drew in a couple of very deep breaths, attempting to calm my nerves. A final touch up of my lipstick and a glance in the mirror showed me that I was good to go. My outfit was the third of the night, but after casting aside fitted black trousers with a slinky top and jeans with a sheer blouse, I had settled on the dress I had bought earlier in the week. It was a classic little black dress but in no way boring; it had a just above the knee solid, black shape, with a lace overlay that benefited from three-quarter length sleeves and scalloped bottom. The back offered a small split and a cut out back that fastened with a single diamante button that made it daring yet sophisticated. The sandals gave me a four-inch height boost but with the ankle strap they were comfortable and safe to walk in, even with their thin, diamante strap across the front.

I checked the clock again. Seven twenty-nine. I felt sick or did I need the bathroom again? I was hot, but my subtly made up face showed no signs of it and for that I was grateful, especially when there was a tap at my door. I grabbed my small sparkly clutch and rushed to open it.

Nothing could have prepared me for just how handsome Gabriel would look. He was dressed more casually than me in straight, dark-wash, almost black jeans and a grey sweater with a slightly rolled neck. He wore no jacket but had leather boots on. He looked fucking gorgeous and for tonight he was all mine. My mouth dried and I had no idea what to say or do next.

"Wow! You look beautiful, better than beautiful. Wow!" he repeated, making me smile. He really did seem awfully impressed by how I looked. "Your hair looks different, lovely," he added, raising his hand as if was considering running his fingers through my rough-dried hair that fell in natural waves. He pulled his hand back and dropped it to his side.

"You don't look half bad yourself." I immediately regretted that I hadn't managed to come up with something more complimentary than half bad.

He grinned, maybe half bad was good.

"For you." He reached out with his other hand, offering me a simple, hand-tied bunch of flowers.

"Thank you. They're beautiful," I told him, feeling myself flush at his romantic gesture of flowers. Maybe he was a romantic fool after all.

With the flowers placed in a jug in the kitchen I returned to the open doorway where Gabriel stood.

"Shall we?" He reached out and took my hand in his.

He led me downstairs.

"You could have come inside while I put the flowers in water," I told him, wondering if he hadn't crossed the threshold because he hadn't been invited to. Although, that hadn't bothered him previously.

"No, I couldn't," he replied as we passed his bedroom and continued our descent of the stairs.

"Why?" I was clueless as to why he'd been unable to come inside my home.

He stopped and turned to face me, him on the stair below me, leaving us eye to eye. I gazed into his eyes that flickered with warmth and attraction.

"Why do you think? You know why. If I'd followed you in there we'd still be there, kissing and touching."

"Oh." I had no more words, not a single one.

"Exactly. And I'd be calling you Carrie, a lot."

"Oh," I repeated making him laugh.

"Come on or dinner will be ruined."

With my hand still safely held in his, he led me to the ground floor, but rather than taking me towards the front door to exit the house we headed farther into it, stopping at the dining room door. The dining room I didn't think I'd ever known Gabriel to use. He turned and smiled at me before turning the door handle with his free hand to reveal the table set for two, complete with candles and soft music.

"We're eating here?" I couldn't keep the surprise from my voice.

He gave me a little frown and looked nervous. I hoped my surprise at the location of our dinner date hadn't come across as disappointment because I wasn't, not at all. If anything, I was pleased, relieved to be somewhere secluded, just the two of us together. A fancy restaurant would have only given me something else to be nervous about and the last thing I wanted was to be caught short and end up having a nervous poo in the toilet of a posh restaurant.

I needed to stop thinking of toilets and nervous poo.

"We can go out if you'd rather."

Clearly my surprise had come across as disappointment.

"No. I love the idea of us having dinner here, just the two of us." We exchanged a smile. "Unless you're expecting me to cook and then I am totally down for going out to dinner."

114

He laughed, taking me into the room until we reached the table where he pulled my chair out for me to sit down. "I've got the cooking under control, so it looks as though we've found our table and the wine is here, so..."

"What about dancing?" I smiled as he poured me a glass of wine and returned to the topic of dancing. "You said when we discussed our date; dinner, talking, dancing..."

"We can dance in here or in the lounge, the hall, anywhere you like. And if you remember, I also said whatever else happens."

His eyes held mine. I nodded and opened my mouth to speak but no words came out. A tiny curl of his lips and flicker of his eyes suggested he was enjoying this, my flustered arousal and desire for him.

"And not forgetting my wish to fuck you senseless, Carrie."

I was hot and clammy. Desperate for him already. I didn't know whether I should stand or remain seated. I wanted him to kiss me, hold me, anything, everything. The colour was rising up my neck, burning my face, drying my mouth again until I felt I might gasp for my next breath. The pulse in my neck and everywhere else began to increase, all of them hammering away until I thought I might have a stroke or something.

He pulled my hand to his lips and gently kissed the back of it. I was unsure just how much of this I could take before I'd throw myself at him and beg him to fuck me senseless, If I was honest, I wasn't entirely sure that he hadn't just kissed me senseless. He ever so gently nipped my thumb, his eyes never leaving mine. Fuck, I was going to come from this alone if he kept it up and this wasn't even foreplay, not really.

"Dinner." He smirked. Then smirked a little more when my expression morphed into disappointment at the loss of his touch. "First, dinner first."

Dinner was easier than I might have imagined, even with the persistent drying of my mouth and throbbing between my legs— an ache that really showed no signs of going away. The nerves I'd felt earlier had abated and we chatted, casual, friendly conversation with the occasional bit of flirty banter thrown in. He'd asked about my life up until this point and my responses had been a little formulaic, but honest, which was unusual for me when talking about my past. He spoke about his childhood and shared stories of his and Seb's escapades. I roared with laughter at some of the scrapes they'd got into and out of.

I had no idea if Gabriel had cooked dinner himself, but either way it was delicious. When we were eating dessert, I tried to broach the subject of Charlotte's mother, but Gabe shut it down every time, so I gave up, moving onto his work instead. It turned out that both Gabe and Seb worked in the field of psychiatry or psychology...I couldn't quite figure out the difference between them.

Once we'd finished eating, I let out a loud and long breath at the sensation of a very full belly and satisfied palate.

Gabriel laughed. "I haven't overfed you, have I?"

"I think a little dancing will resolve that if you have."

"You're not going to do that arm, legs and spinning dancing are you?" He was laughing at me now, but it was warm, plus I laughed back, laughing at myself and my baby giraffe dance.

"And if I am?" The sexual tension was thickening again. I was almost choking on it and still I pushed a little more. "How do you plan on containing my enthusiastic dancing, Mr Caldwell?"

"Let me show you, Carrie."

Chapter Twenty-Four

Gabriel

I reached forward and took Carrie's hand in mine then pulled her to her feet. Her eyes were fixed on mine, glowing with the promise of what was to come, eager for me to hold her, touch her and kiss her. The truth was that I must have had the same glint lighting my eyes too because I wanted all the things she did, and more.

With her hand in mine, I began to move back to the lounge where the stripped back and polished wooden boards made a perfect dancefloor.

"May I have this dance, please?" I even threw in a small bow like a dickhead, and her smile, slight flush to her cheeks and nibble of her lip made my own feelings of stupidity completely worth it.

"I'll have to check my card," she replied, as if we were in a royal court of the 1700's.

"Let me rephrase that. Dance with me, now." I didn't wait for anything resembling a reply as I pulled her to me, wrapping one arm around her waist while the other continued to hold her hand.

I shouted over to the virtual assistant and asked it to play the playlist I'd put together. I had no clue what music Carrie listened to or liked, although she was young and could often be found singing and dancing along to the radio with Charlotte.

The sounds of Slow Hands by one of the geezers from One Direction sounded around us. She smiled. I'd judged it well and as Carrie began to move to the music whilst in my embrace, I congratulated myself. The way she moved and the way she felt was fucking divine. I couldn't have hidden the grin on my face if I'd wanted to and I didn't.

By the time the second verse had started, my hands had moved up her face until I was cupping it and then I leaned in to kiss her. I swear she gasped as my lips got closer and once my lips covered hers, I swallowed the final gasp. Our lips and tongues moved in unison, neither of us needed to think about this, our minds and bodies worked instinctively.

It felt like forever since I'd held her and kissed her. It had been much too long and as our tongues stroked against their counterpart, I vowed not to allow us to go a day without kissing. God, I was well and truly fucked with this woman. My hands continued to hold her face, positioning it to receive the adoration of my kisses while hers had wrapped around me, stroking my neck and fingering the ends of my hair. A little reluctantly, I broke our kiss. Carrie's eyes that were an amber and brown mix seemed to be alight and her lips were pink and swollen from the kissing.

"That's our song now," she said, laughing.

The next song came on, James Blunt, You're Beautiful, and fuck if she wasn't the most beautiful woman in the world, ever.

"This is your song," I told her, not even caring how cheesy it sounded.

She laughed again. "Isn't it about a break-up?"

"Miss Webber?"

She arched a brow at my formal address.

"Shut the fuck up when I'm being romantic."

She smiled and pulled my lips back to hers. "Sorry, you romantic fool."

I grinned as my lips found hers again and like that we were back to kissing and moving to music that had changed again to Snow Patrol, Chasing Cars.

"And this, this might be our song too. Any song we dance to, kiss to."

She looked up at me, clearly loving the romantic words leaving my mouth, but then I knew it wasn't only my romantic words she enjoyed, and I was going to give her everything she wanted and more.

"And then there'll be all the songs we fuck to, Carrie."

"Gabe."

My name was like a breathy cry that somehow came out but also caught in her throat. I was hard before that sound, but fuck, if I wasn't all but bursting out of my jeans at the sound of her obvious desire for me.

I had no clue how much time had passed and had long since stopped declaring every song we danced to as *our song*. We were on the sofa, Carrie beneath me, one hand still on her face or in her hair, but the other one was currently beneath her dress and holding her arse cheek that was exposed completely meaning she was wearing one of her tiny scraps of underwear. Fuck! If that thought alone didn't almost see me coming undone right there. And still we kissed. I had no idea kissing could feel this good, making me wonder if I'd been doing it wrong up until this point or maybe I'd just been doing it with the wrong person. The feel of Carrie's legs wrapping around my hips made me forget everything other than just how good that felt. How good she felt.

"Gabe," she groaned against my lips. "Touch me."

"I am touching you." I laughed at the little growl she gave me. We both knew exactly what she meant and what she wanted.

"More, please."

Fuck, could she be any sexier?

I heard something loud and turned to see one of Carrie's shoes on the floor and then watched as the second one joined it.

She was undressing, starting at the bottom. So, yes, she could be sexier. She wanted me and wasn't afraid to ask for it.

"Take me to bed," she whispered, a blush crept up her already flushed face, but I knew the additional colour was down to a little embarrassment now, and if that didn't make me want her more.

What was it Seb had said about her, having an innocent side, others would want to pervert? The truth was, I was more than happy to pervert her myself. I mean, I had thought of her being the perfect combination of nervous and innocent mixed with confident and hot as fuck already and I was still of that opinion.

I got to my feet and took in the sight of her spread out on the sofa, beautifully dishevelled and reconsidered moving from here, but she deserved better than being taken on the lounge furniture like we were both fifteen.

Dropping my hand, I waited. "Nothing would give me greater pleasure."

With a mega-watt smile she took my hand and got to her feet, struggling to straighten her clothes and put her shoes back on as she did so.

She was seriously cute, but the sooner those clothes came off, the better.

When we got to my bedroom door she paused, seemingly uncertain whether we were going to be going into my room or hers. It pissed me off a little but once she spoke a single word, *Charlotte*, I got what her confusion was. I would never allow Charlotte to be exposed to women in my room, leaving my room the morning after the night before. Anyway, this wasn't women, this was one woman, Carrie, and whilst her concerns were valid, Charlotte wasn't here.

Entering the bedroom had been like one of those scenes from a movie where the couple kissed and fumbled with clothes as they went. Unwilling to entirely unhand each other, even for a second. After I banged her head on my elbow and kicked my toe up on the corner of a chest we laughed and decided we might need to let go of one another if we were ever going to make it to the actual sex without injury.

I kicked my boots off while her shoes flew across the room to join them. Then I pulled my jumper off over my head. Carrie paused, carefully watching me. I smiled a slightly cocky smirk when I saw the look of appreciation register on her face. I was in no way perfect, but I did try to keep myself in decent shape. Her gaze dropped to my waist when my hand flipped the buttons of my jeans and lowered them past my thighs, eventually removing them along with my socks.

Suddenly aware of my near nakedness compared to her being dressed, Carrie reached behind and attempted to undo her dress. She tried for a few seconds before dropping her arms and turning back to me fully.

"Could you do it, please? Undress me?"

Well fuck me! She hadn't just asked me to unfasten the zip or button or whatever it was keeping that dress on. No. She'd asked me to undress her. I was unsure which she meant though, so clarified as I stepped closer, turning her so her back was towards me. I rested my hands on her shoulders, then dragged them to the diamond-like button.

I leaned in closer, my breath on her neck bringing her skin up in goosebumps and then I whispered to her. "Is that what you want, Angel?" I had no idea where angel had come from and it wasn't an endearment I could ever remember using, but here, for Carrie, it seemed perfect. She seemed perfect. "Do you want me to remove your dress? To undress you and leave you standing before me, almost naked? Then, do you want me to remove your sexy underwear until you are completely bare? Waiting for me to touch you and pleasure you? Is that what you're asking for, Carrie?"

"Yes, please."

Jeez, those two words were almost my undoing there and then.

Chapter Twenty-Five

Carrie

I couldn't believe that I'd just asked him that. When the words first left my mouth, I really had just wanted some help with my button, but when he had moved closer, stood behind me and I'd felt his breath on my neck, I was putty in his hands. The words he'd used to clarify my meaning, including the use of the name *Angel* had made me desperate for all he'd suggested and everything he hadn't. My ever so polite, *yes, please*, confirmed it.

His deft fingers made easy work of the button fastening then he pulled the dress up, slowly revealing inch after inch of my legs, hips, behind, back and then, with my arms held aloft, it came off over my head.

He spun me to face him and drank in my appearance, every single inch of me, up and down his gaze swept, heating and eating me up with every breath, approving glance and lick of his lips.

"Oh, Angel."

And there it was again, *Angel*. Not that standing almost naked or the thoughts in my mind seemed like anything remotely angelic.

"You really are beautiful." As the last word left his mouth, he pulled me to him and prepared to kiss me again.

His lips claimed mine. He kept one hand on my face, my jaw or my neck, but the other one had dropped lower until it found my breast, one and then the other through the black lace of my bra. His thumb skimmed my nipple, then he rolled it between his finger and thumb, over and over, his touch becoming firmer and firmer until I was gasping. The sensation in my nipple was pain that warmed and turned into pleasure. A dark, needy pleasure that saw me grabbing for him, pulling him closer and pushing him away all at the same time. The whole time I groaned and moaned in some garbled voice I barely recognised.

"You like a firm touch do you, Angel?"

He stared down at me, his grip on my breast loosened until he removed it completely, leaving me a little cold for its loss.

"Gabriel," I began. Taking his hand, I tried to pull it back to my chest.

He shook his head. "I'll take that as a yes to whether you like a firm touch."

I lowered my gaze, unsure if what I suddenly felt was guilt or shame.

"Hey." Gabe tilted my face back up. His voice was soft, as were his lips that gently caressed mine, reassuring me.

His kisses travelled along my jaw, until his mouth reached my ear. That was around the same time that his hand came to rest on my behind, pulling me in to feel the hard length of him. A hand moved back up my body until it found the fastening of my bra the was quickly cast aside.

Before I could register anything else, I realised he'd walked me back until I was standing at the side of his bed. My legs rested against the mattress and then he dropped to my feet and slowly slid my tiny, black, lace thong down my legs. I stepped out of my underwear and with one smooth movement he was supporting my descent until I was fully reclined on his bed.

"I really had planned to take my time with you, to devour you slowly and yet all I can think about is sliding into you, being nestled between your thighs…"

I had no idea what came over me with Gabriel, but like this, when we were close and intimate, I grew in confidence. He allowed me to grow and feel confident because of his desire and want for me. When he told me I was beautiful, I believed him. When he told me he wanted me, I believed him. And now, when he told me of his thoughts, I believed them, and they were all for me.

Lying there I observed him and wondered what was so wrong in him wanting to slide into me and being nestled between my thighs. I wanted that too; to feel the weight of him on me, the scent of him filling my senses, tasting him as we kissed and most of all, feeling his hard length stretch and fill me.

If I wanted him and he wanted me, why were we waiting?

"Take me, now." I immediately drew my feet up and spread my legs, showing myself to him, inviting him in.

Everything froze in that second. Gabriel couldn't take his eyes off me and he seemed rooted to the spot. Nerves fluttered in my chest, my breathing became a little erratic and my pulse began to hammer in my ears. Maybe he didn't want this. Didn't want me like this. I tried to think of something to say, to somehow make this better, but nothing was forthcoming.

My concerns evaporated at the second Gabriel moved. He pushed his boxers down, revealing his erection that was large and already leaking pre-cum.

"You could not be any more perfect, Angel." And then he was with me on the bed. Positioned between my thighs, his hard arousal already nudging my sex.

"Now, please." My legs closed around his hips, encouraging him in.

"You are seriously demanding," he told me, but still smiled. "I was hoping to make this last."

"Sorry." My apology caused a frown to fix to his brow.

"No, don't. I love that you want me as much as I want you. Are you sure?"

I nodded and tightened the grip of my legs on him.

"As you wish...shit, condom!"

"I'm on the pill," I told him, not sure if I should insist on a condom anyway.

"When were you last sexually active?"

Shit! He was weighing up my risk factor and as much as I wanted to be offended, the fact that I was lying naked beneath him and begging him to fuck me might actually suggest he was right to ask.

"A while...months, maybe a year or so."

His eyes widened, leaving me nervously doubting whether he believed what I'd said.

"We can talk later, but for tonight, let me get a condom."

My face morphed into an offended pout.

"Hey, for you, if it's been a while you might appreciate the condom."

"Oh."

He leaned in and kissed me gently on the lips before moving my legs from around him. I watched his back disappear into the bathroom and quickly return with a condom. Once back between my still splayed thighs he leaned in and kissed me, distracting me slightly as his fingers found my sex. He allowed a single digit to slip inside me, gently gathering the moisture there, rimming my entrance before adding a second finger that stretched me slightly, preparing me for him. His fingers traced their way up to my clit that he circled, gently at first and then firmer. I moaned, reached up and grabbed for him, wanting to pull him closer, needing to feel his lips on me.

"You like that, Carrie? You like my fingers inside you and touching you?"

I didn't answer. I assumed my clawing at his shoulders and increasingly loud groans were all the confirmation he needed. His fingers continued to stroke and rub until I was no more than a mass of sensation and then as his lips crashed against mine my orgasm hit me like a brick wall. Gabriel caught my moans in his mouth and on his tongue while I convulsed beneath him as he wrung every last ounce of pleasure from me.

With me having barely come back down, he knelt up and tore open the condom between his teeth and in an instant, he had rolled it down his length. He repositioned himself so that he was lined up, the very tip of him nudging my entrance and then, he began to enter me. Slowly he moved, gently pushing farther in. The feeling of him stretching me was strange, it was uncomfortable and yet wonderful at the same time. By the time he was almost all the way in I was beginning to pant.

"You okay?"

"Yes, don't stop." I pleaded, making him smile.

"I couldn't stop if I wanted to." He grinned. "It should be

125

easier as you're so wet for me."

I flushed, unsure if that was good or bad. Not that I was wet, but because of how wet I was. Like I always was when I was with Gabriel, with every look, word or touch.

"You feel amazing."

He began to move, withdrawing slightly before sliding back in, building his pace with each thrust.

My moans grew louder and quicker with every move he made. My legs tightened around his middle before he pulled one from around him and placed it on his shoulder. It allowed me to feel him more deeply with every movement he made, and the new position facilitated a stroke of his body across my clit with each thrust forward.

"Oh God!" My garbled cries were barely audible over the sound of his breathing and slapping of our flesh.

"I'm almost there, Carrie. Come on. Angel, come for me."

With another thrust I completely fell apart while his eyes bore into me. His face contorted in torturous pleasure as he froze in time and came with a deep groan as his fingers painfully dug into my hips. His grip had been tight enough to leave bruises and I couldn't help but smile at the idea of bearing his mark.

Chapter Twenty-Six

Gabriel

What the fuck had happened last night? I woke early and smiled at the sight of Carrie lying next to me. Her hands were curled up in the pillow beneath her face that I couldn't take my eyes off. She was beautiful, although that adjective was becoming more and more inadequate with every second I spent with her. I had never been one of those people that needed to touch or cuddle in sleep, but I really did have a near overwhelming urge to pull her to me and hold her tightly against me.

The previous night had been different to how I'd imagined it. In my mind it was going to be dinner, slow dancing with my playlist. I smiled at the playlist. I'd thought it was a bit pathetic and cheesy, but Carrie had loved it and for that reason alone I loved it too. Then, after the slow dancing I had imagined us kissing and touching before ending up in bed together. The exact details hadn't been fully formed in my mind. I had no set formula in my mind, but I never expected us to get straight into fucking once we entered the bedroom. I thought we'd take our time a little more. I'd also anticipated more in terms of foreplay and pleasuring Carrie, but that's not what she'd wanted.

A big grin spread across my face. Carrie had got exactly what she'd wanted for the first time. The second and third time, not so much.

She made a little whimpering sound and rolled over, turning her back on me. I moved down the bed, pressed my front to her back and threw my arm over her middle, content to be here, with her, holding her and despite considering myself to be wide awake I fell back to sleep.

The sensation of Carrie's body fidgeting next to me broke me from my slumber. My nose was in her hair and as I inhaled the scent of her, something fruity and floral at the same time; whatever it was it was divine. She was divine.

I moved my face until my lips rested on the back of her neck. I gently kissed the skin there, then littered tiny kisses all the way to her shoulder while my hand that was still around her middle moved up. It found her full breast, cupped it and then with a sweep of my thumb I brought her nipple up into a tight peak.

A tiny gasp was her only response.

"You like that?"

"Hmmm." She arched into my touch as her hand reached back to pull me closer, her hand on my hip. "Best good morning ever."

I laughed against her ear that my mouth kissed and teased. "Oh, we can do so much better for good morning."

"Yeah?"

My reply was a squeeze of her nipple.

"Fuck!" She hissed through gritted teeth.

"Eventually, I am going to fuck you raw. You'll be lucky if you can stand, never mind walk."

"Yes," she moaned, moving her leg so that it was draped over mine, opening herself up for me.

As if she thought I might need some kind of encouragement she wiggled her arse against my dick that was hard and beginning to throb.

"You are a naughty angel." The mock outrage in my voice caused her to wiggle again. I pinched her nipple more firmly, inciting a little yelp from her.

"Sorry," she whispered and like that, I wasn't sure that I wouldn't be giving her exactly what she wanted, how she wanted for that single worded apology alone.

A little reluctantly, I released her nipple, slid my hand down her body and slipped it between her thighs where I found her hot, open and wet.

"Kiss me," I demanded and smiled a smug, content smile when she turned immediately. Her compliance was sublime and made me want her even more.

It felt as though I consumed her in that kiss. Although, the fact that I had slid inside her whilst kissing her may have added to the moment and sensations coursing through my whole body, from my toes that flexed to my hair that I could have sworn was standing on end.

I fully intended to make this last and my stamina was never better than first thing in the morning. My thrusts were slower and more drawn out than she needed to come from that alone, so I slid two fingers between her sex and found her clit. With my leisurely pace of circling and stroking her button of nerves she had no choice but to let go and how she let go...she shouted, cried and called to me while thrusting her hips against me, faster and faster, riding my dick and her own pleasure.

Just the sight of her basking in the aftermath of her release blew all my ideas about making this last out of the water. I bit her lip and ended our kiss.

"Fucking hell, could you be more gorgeous?"

My hand was still between her thighs, manipulating her nub again, wanting her to come again, needing her to. Her hand came to rest over my fingers, then attempted to move them away.

"No more," she groaned, but I was unsure if she really meant it, whether she wanted another orgasm or not.

"More."

"It's too much. I'm too sensitive."

She attempted to move away from me, but with my hand lying over her and my dick inside her, she was going nowhere.

"Come with me, Angel. All over my dick."

Immediately, she removed her hand, allowing me to bring her to the brink again, quickly and just as she was heading to the point of no return my thrusts sped up while I kissed her and in a storm of thrashing limbs, lips, tongues and absorbed cries, we came, together.

****

Somehow, we managed to sleep for a while longer before

showering together where we partook in a little more kissing and touching, but no more actual sex.

Once dry and dressed, me in track bottoms and a t-shirt, Carrie in a pair of shortie pyjama bottoms and a vest, we sat in the kitchen and ate a breakfast of poached eggs on toast. We chatted, about safe, regular topics...at one point we even discussed the fucking weather, meaning this had the potential to be awkward and I didn't want that. Before last night I did wonder if last night would be just that—one night and then nothing. Obviously, last night then became this morning and now we were still here, together, so the awkwardness needed to go because this was not the end. There would be more nights like last night.

"Do you have any plans for the weekend?" I laughed at my lame question. "I swear, that made me sound like your hairdresser."

Carrie laughed and my dick started to twitch.

"I might give Bea a call and see if she fancies meeting up or going shopping. I need to put some food in my cupboards..."

Her voice trailed off when she realised she was rambling.

"Bea, just Bea?" I couldn't keep the annoyance out of my voice at the idea of her meeting up with that whole group. With her meeting up with fucking Toby the fuckboy. I really didn't like him, and it was not simple jealousy. I didn't like him, but more than that, I didn't trust him.

"Yeah, just Bea." She furrowed her brow. She clearly picked up on my annoyance but chose not to rise to it. "Unless she has already made plans with the others and invites me along."

I stared across the top of my mug and briefly imagined telling her that she wouldn't be going anywhere with *the others*, aka Toby. She'd most likely kick off and strop off and meet up with the others, especially fuckboy. So, as much as it went against the grain, I said nothing. I simply pulled a very tight expression.

"What are your plans?" she asked, allowing the conversation to remain calm.

"I'll collect Charlotte in a while and then it will be a night of princess movies and makeovers."

She laughed.

"Not even joking."

She laughed even louder. God, I loved that sound and the way her face radiated warmth was like nothing I'd known.

"You are fucking beautiful."

The air thickened and we froze in time.

"Gabe, what are we doing here? You're my boss and I don't expect you to play along with this…"

"Carrie, I can't answer that because I don't know, not really. This was never in my plan, you and me. I found you attractive from day one and although I told myself I shouldn't offer you the job, I did. I haven't been able to stop thinking about you. I like you, a lot, and I wasn't sure if last night would be just that, but now, well, I'd kind of like last night not to be the end."

"Oh."

She looked stunned.

"But I can't promise you more than this. Charlotte is my priority and always will be. She needs stability and not to be confused by seeing us and imagining things that aren't real."

Her face dropped and I felt guilty, but I couldn't mislead her. I wouldn't mislead her.

"I would be disappointed if Charlotte wasn't your priority. So, we make this up as we go along?"

"I think we might need to."

She nodded.

"When you are done, promise me you'll tell me."

It was my turn to nod now.

"And if you meet someone else—"

I cut her off. "No! I won't cheat on you and I won't be looking for someone else and I expect the same from you."

She looked absolutely furious at what she perceived to be my inference.

"I'm just laying it out there, not accusing."

"Okay."

"Come on, let's watch a movie or something before I go to collect Charlotte if you want to…"

"I'd love to."

Chapter Twenty-Seven

Carrie

The hands of the clock seemed to be moving in slow motion. I was sitting home alone while Gabriel was downstairs with Charlotte. I didn't know how I was going to do this; remain alone and isolated while he was just a couple of hundred metres from me, two floors below.

Before he went to collect Charlotte, we lay together on the sofa and watched a film. I couldn't even tell you what it was called or what it was about. It took forever for us to agree on one and then we pretty much ignored it as we began to kiss and touch again. I wasn't entirely sure I was capable of having sex or coming again, but I was, although, everything was softer, gentler rather than frantic as it had been earlier and last night.

Afterwards he headed out to collect Charlotte from Christine and I came back upstairs. I haven't text Bea yet. I'm not sure if I really wanted to meet up with her or if I'd be happier staying here and wallowing in my misery at being away from Gabriel. With my head in my hands I couldn't help but wonder how the hell I was going to manage to do this. I mean, what would our relationship going forward look like?

I grabbed my phone again, hoping to see a text from Gabriel that I'd somehow not heard—nothing. My mood dropped a little more. I needed to get out and do something before I went mad or cried.

Subconsciously I found I'd wondered to my window that overlooked the garden below, maybe hoping for a glimpse of

Gabriel. My disappointment was quite ridiculous when he was nowhere to be seen. God, I had it bad and I wasn't sure I liked it so fired off a text to Bea. Her reply was quick, but unfortunately, she had plans so wasn't able to meet up. She suggested I could meet up with the others who were going out later. I replied a *maybe* but wasn't sure if I fancied that either. There was only one thing I wanted to spend my time doing and that was a person rather than an activity or place. That one thing was Gabriel.

I mooched around for another hour, and then, irritated with myself, decided to go for a walk, or maybe a run. With a quick change into some more appropriate clothes, I headed out and rounded the house where I came face to face with Gabriel.

"Hi," he said, sounding a little unprepared for my appearance, but his look was dark and intense.

"Hi," I replied, shrinking slightly under his boring gaze that seemed to intensify with every second we looked at each other. "I should go…"

"Where? Where are you going?"

I stared at him and his question. Why did he want or need to know where I was going? Wasn't it obvious with how I was dressed that I was going to do some kind of exercise?

"The park and maybe down by the canal."

"You'll be back though?"

I frowned at him. Where did he think I was going to go in workout gear? Take in a nightclub or something? But still, I answered his questions.

"Yes, probably in about an hour or so."

"Okay. Be careful and have a good jog or whatever."

I nodded and with a little wave I moved on, throwing in some kind of run as I got past the front of the house, my back to him. I could feel his eyes still on me as I got farther away and just before I disappeared out of sight, I risked a glance back over my shoulder only to find he was still there, watching me, but this time with Charlotte in his arms and for a split second I envied the little girl. I'd been in those arms and I missed them. I wanted to be back there, now.

****

I had just got out of the shower when my phone vibrated across the kitchen countertop. Bea had clearly spoken to Nicole, because the latter was now inviting me to join her and some of the others for a night at the cinema and then a trip to the pub. I wasn't sure who would be there. I wasn't sure if Toby would be there and after his weirdness at the park, I wasn't sure I wanted to run into him any time soon. I mean, we were barely acquaintances and he'd seriously overreacted to me not calling him. Why had he even been in the park? Maybe he was passing or lived near there. I replied with a quick, *maybe, I'll let you know* type of message. Nicole's response was a thumbs up so at least I didn't feel pressured to go regardless.

After my run I'd been to the supermarket so at least I had food in my cupboards and fridge now. I threw together a few vegetables with some rice and had just sat down to eat a late lunch, as late as half past five, although, the afternoon and evening were seriously dragging. Maybe I would go out, if only to stop my own impending insanity, especially if I had a Sunday alone to contend with.

It was harder than I'd imagined, the morning after, as it were, although, technically it was the evening after. If I was totally honest with myself, I hadn't really considered this. I had imagined us being together several times but not the reality of crossing that line. Had I been naïve or possibly plain stupid in not considering this as the aftermath? I was mooning around like a lovestruck teenager with her first crush and I wasn't used to it. More than that, I didn't like it.

The honesty Gabriel had shown me in discussing what happened next and where he stood on things was appreciated, albeit a little unexpected, so why was I struggling here? Why did every minute feel like an hour? Why did it feel like forever since I'd seen him and why the bloody hell did I miss him as much as I did? Was it the sex? Was it that basic? I shook my head. No. No it wasn't because apart from anything else I didn't think I could have had sex again so soon. I was still tender. But then, why wouldn't I be? I had consumed everything that man had given me as if I was starving and had no clue when or from where my next meal would be coming.

I needed to go out and fill my mind with something that wasn't the man currently two floors below me and memories of mind-blowing orgasms.

I picked my phone up to text Nicole when I received a text from Gabriel.

<Hi>

I laughed at the brevity of it and replied with an identical message.

<I didn't know you ran>

What was a suitable response to that? It wasn't exactly a question, was it? Another message arrived.

<You looked amazing this afternoon. Your arse in those pants made me want to drag you back inside. Your arse in those pants made me hard >

Well, fuck me! What the hell should I say to that? The grin on my face broadened as I reread it.

<Good>

<Thanks for the sympathy>

<After last night and this morning the run was a little uncomfortable>

<Good>

<Thanks for the sympathy>

<What are you doing?>

<Nothing really. Have just had something to eat and am considering going out this evening. You?>

<I have no plans beyond dinner, bathing Charlotte and putting her to bed. Who are you going out with?>

<Bea is busy but the others are going out so I might join them. Movies and the pub. Nothing special>

No reply came back this time. Initially, I reasoned that he was busy, maybe making some food for him and Charlotte or just playing with his daughter. After the first hour I decided he was ignoring me, and I had no idea why. We hadn't argued and our conversation had been friendly chatter, so what the hell was his problem? I didn't play mind fuck games and I had a horrible feeling in the pit of my stomach that this is exactly what he was doing. I threw my phone down onto the sofa.

"Fuck you, Mr Caldwell." It looked like I was going out after all.

Chapter Twenty-Eight

Gabriel

<Bea is busy but the others are going out so I might join them. Movies and the pub. Nothing special>

The others. Who the fuck were the others? The same group she was out with last week? The group that included that fucking idiot, Toby? I typed out my reply several times only to delete each and every one. What should I say? More importantly, what could I say? I had told her that I had no clue what would happen between us moving forward, and that was the truth, so did I have the right to tell her I didn't want her to go out, especially not if the others included fuckboy?

I wasn't a chest thumping, alpha kind of guy, I really wasn't, and yet with her I had a feeling I could be. I wanted to be. I had no right to tell her what she could and couldn't do, but if I replied to her now then that is exactly what I would do. So, I refused to reply. For her, not me.

"Daddy, shall we play babies?"

"Hmmm, okay." I was seriously distracted and right now Charlotte could have asked for anything and I would have agreed to it.

"What day is it?" she asked, startling me slightly with the apparently random question.

"Saturday, baby."

"Wednesday, Friday, Saturday, Monday."

I smiled across at her. We might need to work on the order of the days of the week. "Tomorrow's Sunday. It comes after Saturday."

"Do you go to work on Sunday?"

"Not on Sunday," I replied, wondering where this was going and what was on my daughter's mind.

She looked sad and I couldn't imagine that my correction on what came after Saturday had come across as abrupt or as though I was telling her off. "Don't you like Daddy being at home with you?" I braced myself for all possible answers.

"I do, but I only see Carrie on work days."

"Ah."

"I miss Carrie."

She looked as though she might cry. I hadn't realised that this might happen. That Charlotte would have forged such a strong bond with Carrie in such a short time that she would miss her when she wasn't here. Although, the truth was I was missing her too and I had seen her just a few hours before.

"She'll be back on Monday...she has friends she wants to spend time with." I almost choked on the word friends when I considered how good a friend Toby wanted to be. God! Why did I dislike him as much as I did? Was it simple jealousy? The sight of him dancing with her might haunt me forever and I couldn't let my mind go to him being in the park with her and Charlotte. I needed to ask Carrie about that.

"But she's my friend too..." her voice trailed off.

"I know sweetheart and you're her friend."

Charlotte offered a very small, weak smile. "Is she your friend too, Daddy?"

Oh, fucking hell! She was my friend, my very, very, good friend. "Yes, I suppose she is." I smiled, but honestly, this smile was not suitable for my daughter's eyes, it really wasn't. Not that she noticed.

"Does Carrie want to spend time with us then?"

I had nothing to offer in response to my daughter's question, so, she continued.

"If she is my friend and your friend..."

If only life were that simple. "Fuck," I found myself muttering, clearly, not quietly enough.

"Yes, Daddy, fuck!"

I was a terrible father and next week I was going to be called into the nursery to be told that my daughter had a mouth like a sailor.

"Sorry. That's a bad word, Charlotte. Don't say it, please."

"Okay." She came up to me and climbed into my lap. "I love you, Daddy." She pulled my face to hers by cupping each of my cheeks in her hands and kissed me gently.

"I love you too, baby."

"Carrie—"

This time I cut her off. I couldn't do this. I wouldn't keep talking about Carrie. It was bad enough that she was in my head constantly without me having to have a permanent discussion about her with my three-year-old daughter.

"What about you have a bath and then we can have some snacks while we watch a movie, any one you like?"

"Yes!" Charlotte leapt from my lap, already running for the stairs, talking herself through all the movie options.

Charlotte was bathed and in clean pyjamas. She had narrowed her movie choice down to six films and was still deliberating her final choice while I took care of snacks. I checked my phone to see if Carrie had contacted me. She hadn't, but then, should that have been a surprise, considering the fact that I hadn't replied to her last message?

"What are you doing?" I asked myself. I was being ridiculous by not messaging her and somehow wanting to speak to her still. "Man, or mouse?" My second question didn't take much answering. "Fuck it!" I picked up my phone and rather than text, I phoned her.

The phone rang and rang, annoying me that she might have been choosing to ignore me now. The irony of that, along with my hypocrisy didn't bypass me.

"Hello."

I was so stunned by her replying rather than her voicemail kicking in that I was silent for a second or two.

"Sorry. Hi." Two words, that's all I managed to utter.

"Are you okay?"

I felt a bigger dick after she'd asked that question than when I was mute. I should have replied to her sooner and still she was the one concerned for my wellbeing.

"Yeah. I'm sorry about not replying before. What are you doing?"

"Just about to get dressed to go out."

My stomach became a ball of knots in the knowledge that she was going out, but more so that she was currently naked or at least partially dressed.

"Don't." I really needed to work on building something resembling coherent sentences if I wanted her to pay any attention to me.

She laughed. A rich and deep laugh that had my dick stiffening and my balls tightening. "You want me to go out undressed?" The tease in her voice was unmistakable.

"No. I don't want you to go out at all."

It was her turn to be silent now. She was probably wondering who the fuck I thought I was and what right I had to make any demands on her or of her personal time.

"Carrie, don't go out, please.

"Why?"

"I don't want you to." I must have sounded like a complete dick now.

"Why? What do you want me to do? Stay in and what? You made your feelings very clear on what was and wasn't going to be part of this thing with us and Charlotte and your time with her was all your own. And that was fine. That is fine. I respect it, but in the meantime what should I do? Wait for you to call me or message? What?"

Her points were all valid and her questions were reasonable and deserved a response.

"Maybe after Charlotte has gone to bed—" Judging by how quickly she cut me off that was the wrong response and certainly not the one she deserved.

"I am not your dirty little secret, or maybe I am!" She fumed down the line. "I support your decision to prioritise Charlotte, but the idea that you expect me to wait in until it is convenient and appropriate for you to deem me worthy of your time or conversation pisses me off. I don't need nor expect you to put time with or talking to me above Charlotte, but the idea that once she's in bed I should be available to you is offensive."

"That's not what I me—"

She cut me off again. "Well that's certainly how it sounded. Look, I have to go or I'll be late. Maybe we both need to think about what we each want, need and expect, but if you expect me to be permanently at your convenience…"

Her voice trailed off; her ultimatum clear despite her not finishing it.

"Goodnight, Gabe."

Maybe her annoyance was on the wane with her use of Gabe.

"Night, Angel." I hung up and stared down at the phone in my hand. "Well done. Perfect." So, while her anger with me was reducing, mine was on a steady increase. "You fucking idiot."

"Daddy?"

It seemed my daughter may have finally decided on her movie choice.

Chapter Twenty-Nine

Carrie

"Oh bugger." I dropped onto my bed and looked at the outfit I'd picked out for the night; a white vest and matching jersey shorts or as I called them, pyjamas.

Why had I lied about going out? Was it simply to prove the point that Gabriel had no right to ask me, or maybe tell me not to go out? If he wanted to place restrictions on the thing between us, then he needed to accept that there were consequences to that. Plus, with restrictions in place it was even more necessary for me not to put all my eggs or my heart into one basket, into Gabriel. Whatever the reason, it was done now, and he'd never know.

With a cup of tea and a packet of biscuits I climbed into bed and reached for my book. With my head full of someone else's words and romance, I managed to pass the next couple of hours easily.

It was as I was going to brush my teeth that my phone pinged. I was unsure who it would be or who I wanted it to be. That was a lie. I wanted it to be Gabriel. It was Christine, inviting me for Sunday lunch. She said she'd missed me and our chats and would love me to meet her husband and her mother and for us to catch up. Well, even if I wanted to, how could I refuse an invitation like that? My reply confirmed that I'd love to join them. She sent me her address and suddenly I had Sunday plans and for that I was incredibly grateful.

With my teeth brushed, I snuggled down under the covers and

returned to my book when my phone alert sounded again. I assumed it was Christine with a polite *see you tomorrow* or some such courtesy. I was wrong. It was Gabriel.

<Sorry about earlier. I didn't mean to sound as though I was telling you what to do. Please let me know that you get home safely>

Why did he have to be so bloody considerate? It would be so much easier to remain cross with him if he didn't do nice things like this. But now I was having a bit of a dilemma; should I message him a reply and tell him I was home...had never been out, or, reply a, no problem and then message again later when I would have been back had I really gone out?

I reminded myself that I was not a fan of games, especially of the mind fuck variety and if I was anything other than completely honest it made me the game player, not him.

<It did sound like you were telling me what to do, and in case you were wondering I didn't appreciate it. I am already home...I didn't go out in the end. Bet you can't disguise your pleasure at that>

Nothing. Not a word. This man, as considerate and attractive as he was, and I couldn't even consider his ability to give me breath-taking orgasms, but all of that aside, he was pissing me off with his, 'we can't be together in front of Charlotte so enjoy your weekend to don't go out, stay home alone' and then there was the whole, ignoring my messages routine. I was quickly tiring of being cast aside and ignored.

I stared at my phone for minutes. Seven minutes and forty-two seconds to be precise before I threw it onto the table next to my bed, snapped the lamp off and rolled over in a huff.

I tossed and turned for several minutes, although, it felt much longer and then I jumped as I heard a noise, a knocking. Knocking on my door.

"Bloody hell," I muttered as I threw back the covers and stomped to the door. There was only really one person who could be standing on the other side of it, so why was it such a surprise when I came face to face with Gabriel? I think I managed to mutter his name.

His eyes travelled down and back up my body before settling on my eyes.

"Hi."

I stared, slightly bemused by his presence and his greeting.

"Hi."

"I thought I'd come and say goodnight." He had the decency to look uncomfortable at his own excuse for being there.

I raised a questioning eyebrow.

"And to apologise."

"Apology accepted and goodnight," I said, ready to shut the door.

"Angel…"

And like that I was putty in his hands. "What do you want?"

"To see you. I've missed you. I really did want to apologise and say goodnight."

"Do you want to come in?" I waved inside, as if he needed directions.

"Can we leave the door open…Charlotte…"

"Of course." His love and consideration for his daughter was incredibly attractive.

"We should talk, about us and how this will work."

I stared up at him as he took a step closer. "I agree."

"Maybe tomorrow, after Charlotte goes to bed, we could have a glass of wine and a conversation."

I nodded, unsure if there was anything to say. "You can't tell me what to do," I said. Apparently, I had something to say.

"I know. We'll talk about it. It's late. You should go to sleep. I would like to kiss you goodnight though."

"I'd like that." I offered a small, coy smile as my cheeks flushed.

Gabriel reached for my arm, pulled me closer and lowered his lips to mine. Gently, he manoeuvred my head and moulded my lips so they fitted his perfectly. His tongue made its way into my mouth and I let out a tiny mewl. It spurred him on to deepen the kiss. I had no idea how long our kiss lasted but when he ended it, I was disappointed and a big ball of arousal and desire. He reached down, took my hand in his and landed a single kiss to the back of it.

"Night, Angel."

I was barely able to breathe, never mind speak and then he was gone. I closed the door, looked around my living space and actually questioned if I had just imagined all of that. The swelling of my lips and the moisture and pulsing between my thighs confirmed that Gabriel coming to kiss me goodnight had indeed happened.

****

The grin I wore was beginning to make my face ache and nobody should have been this happy when cleaning the bathroom on a Sunday morning, but then, not everyone had been visited by Gabriel or been kissed goodnight by him the previous night.

With my cleaning finished I pulled a simple tea dress from my wardrobe, black with a delicate yellow flower print. I grabbed some black wedge sandals and was happy that I was dressed appropriately for a friendly Sunday lunch. I gave my hair a final ruffle and prepared to leave when my phone buzzed. Looking down expectantly, my grin was reinstated in the extreme when I saw a message from Gabriel. Just the sight of his name lighting up my phone filled my chest with happiness and my stomach with butterflies.

<Good morning. I was thinking…would you like to join me and Charlotte this afternoon/evening? We could watch a movie or play a boardgame and later we could talk. Just the two of us>

<Hi. I would love to watch a movie or play a boardgame with you and Charlotte. And yes to talking too. I have to go. Am out for lunch but will be back in plenty of time for our plans>

I waited for a few seconds and without a reply appearing I reread my message and decided Gabriel might be peeved about

Single Dad

my plans for lunch if he assumed my friends, Toby, was part of those plans. Without any further thought I sent another message.

<My lunch plans do not include Toby...just in case you were wondering>

He clearly was wondering.

<Good. Thank you. See you later>
****

"Is there anything I can do to help?" I looked across at the feast Christine seemed to be preparing and thought it was the least I could do as she had gone to so much trouble.

"No, it's all under control." She smiled as she waved off my offers of help. "Noel," she called to Gabriel's dad who was already entering the kitchen. "Can you mash please, darling?"

"How could I say no to an offer like that?" He teased her with a laugh, looking and sounding like Gabriel as he did so.

"Carrie, would you mind just checking on Mum for me, please?"

I nodded and was already leaving the kitchen to find Christine's mother, Margaret.

"Oh, hello, dear," she called as I entered the large lounge that led to the well-tended and sunny garden.

"Hi. Would you like some company?" I asked her, unsure what I would do if she said no.

"That would be nice. Are you my nurse today?"

I smiled as I took the seat next to her, remembering Gabriel mentioning her dementia.

"No, just a friendly face."

She smiled. "And a very pretty face it is too. Are you married?"

"No," I replied wiggling my bare ring finger in her direction.

"I see. What about a special man?"

I laughed at the cheeky wink she gave me as I shook my head and laughed even more when she continued to speak.

"My Christopher is a handsome man...he'll be here soon. He works so hard, but then he plays hard too, if you know what I

146

mean."

This time she gave me a very dirty smirk along with another wink that had me howling with laughter. I really did think I could become very fond of this lady with her cheeky comments and questions.

"Well, if you find yourself a special man and you need some pointers you know where to find me."

I opened my mouth to speak but no words came out. I, mean, in fairness what the hell could I say to that? Not much.

"Ah, Christopher, here he is. Hello, lover," she called, and I swear she wore an expression of pure lust and seduction.

I turned around, knowing she was a widow, only to see Gabriel making his way to her.

"Here you are, you sexy minx."

I stared at Gabriel and saw the look of adoration on her face for her husband, even if it was her grandson in reality, I swear I melted a little that he would play the part she'd cast him in.

"Miss Webber," he said, facing me with an arched brow.

"Mr Caldwell," I replied and whilst I didn't know why, I actually blushed.

"Carrie!" squealed Charlotte as she bolted across the room, not stopping until she was on my lap and hugging me.

Chapter Thirty

Gabriel

When I'd walked into my parent's house, I hadn't expected to come face to face with Carrie. When she'd told me she was going out to lunch and it wasn't as part of a group that included Toby, it hadn't entered my head that she might be heading to the same place as me. My father had looked a little uncomfortable, presumably he knew I was in the dark about the extra guest at the table. My mother, by contrast looked like the cat who'd got the cream. So, when I entered the sun filled lounge to the sound of my grandmother's chatter, I was stunned to find Carrie listening to her every word, speaking to her with warmth and kindness.

When my grandmother spotted me, her confusion had cast me in the role of my grandfather. This wasn't anything unusual, she often did it and I had grown up my whole life being told how like him I was. Her words confirmed it as did her highly inappropriate lust filled expression.

With Charlotte settled on Carrie's lap I couldn't help but wonder if involving her in mine and Charlotte's life was the right decision? I had no idea but the sight of them together melted my heart and my resolve to keep them separate.

Lunch was easy considering I was playing it cool and treating Carrie with detachment. I wasn't being an arsehole, but I didn't want my family speculating on me and Carrie, and that was without considering Charlotte. From my position between my daughter and Carrie, opposite my grandmother who was still calling me Christopher, I was comfortable.

Charlotte was chatting to everyone at the same time, mainly about our night in together the previous evening. Carrie smiled across at me as Charlotte told everyone how we, me and her, loved princesses. I shrugged, not prepared to shatter my daughter's illusions by denying it. Carrie's smile broadened into a grin and I had never been happier to be responsible for putting that beautiful expression on that gorgeous face.

After lunch, Charlotte played outside, in the garden that was equipped with all the toys and equipment a little girl could want. She ran around while we all sat watching her, Carrie being the first one to join her, both of them laughing and squealing, making my heart soar.

My parents watched them and then, when they thought I was unaware, they watched me taking in every word and movement between my little girl and her nanny. Even with my sunglasses on, I felt sure they could see the desire and intensity of my stare, and why wouldn't they, I'd put money on my eyes scorching through Carrie's clothes as I undressed her in my mind.

I watched as Charlotte hid. Really badly behind a shrub that she was clearly visible *behind*. My whole family smirked as Carrie sought her out, checking everywhere other than the shrub. With each unsuccessful seek Charlotte giggled more until her shoulders were shaking.

"She's a natural," my mother said, but I was unsure who she was speaking to. "Charlotte adores her," she added, a hint of surprise in her voice which was understandable, because as much as Charlotte was sociable and friendly, she didn't really embrace new people into her life as she had Carrie.

"She's not the only one," muttered my dad who got a sly dig from my mother.

I said nothing. My attention was fully on my girls. I immediately began to correct that statement in my head. To change it to my girl, Charlotte, but I didn't because they were my girls, both of them. My attention was broken by my grandmother, who with absolutely no filter made a more *basic* observation.

"She's a pretty girl. Nice tits."

My parents looked aghast. Me? I laughed loudly and whilst I passed no comment, I couldn't help but agree. I'd have gone so far as to say they were the best tits I'd ever seen, touched or tasted. This wasn't helping my need for Carrie and as we were watching a movie or playing boardgames with Charlotte I knew I was in for a long, hard evening.

Carrie finally *found* my daughter behind her shrub and they both squealed and giggled as Carrie hoisted Charlotte up into her arms. I did nothing to hide my huge, soppy grin at their interaction as I watched them getting closer to us.

"Carrie?" Charlotte looked up lovingly and a little hopefully. "Can you bounce with me?"

Fucking hell! I was going to explode if she agreed to this and I had to watch.

"Erm..." Carrie looked awkward as Charlotte pointed towards the trampoline in my parent's garden. "I'm not really dressed for it." She pointed down at her dress that came to just above her knee and looked amazing.

Charlotte looked totally perplexed at the notion of not being dressed appropriately for trampolining. With a glance down at Carrie and then herself she shook her head. "Why?"

Carrie blushed but with a very girly giggle for my daughter said, "I don't want to flash my pants, do I?"

Charlotte giggled, my parents laughed, and my grandmother muttered something about having flashed her own knickers on more than one occasion.

Carrie placed Charlotte on her feet and then asked for directions to the bathroom. I watched her enter the house and was desperate to follow her but needed an excuse so as not to appear suspicious, or maybe the excuse would be more suspicious.

I drained my glass of lemonade and entered the house without saying a word. With no plan, I made my way into the hall and upstairs where I found Carrie coming out of the bathroom. She jumped when she saw me but smiled a little nervously.

"I didn't know you'd be here when your mum invited me over. I hope you don't mind."

I didn't mind at all. I couldn't remember when I'd enjoyed a

Sunday lunch quite so much. I didn't say any of that, wasn't sure I was capable of speech. Instead I shook my head and stepped closer until she was backed up against the wall. Then, I placed one hand either side of her head, caging her.

She swallowed, hard, and that hint of uncertainty mixed with the fire of desire lighting up her eyes saw me using every ounce of self-control to stop myself from fucking her right there and then, in my parent's home, with my parents, grandmother and daughter close by, not caring if we were heard or discovered by any or all of them.

"Tonight, once Charlotte has gone to bed you and I are going to talk, about this, about us. After we have talked, I am going to fuck you until you are hoarse from calling my name and then I will fuck you some more until you can't breathe or think."

She released a moan, then arched against the wall. That had me all but coming in my trousers, but I loved getting her all worked up. The idea that she wanted me as much as I wanted her was the best feeling ever and knowing she was wet, that my words and her want for me had her creaming in her pants drove me fucking wild.

"And tomorrow when you walk, run, or simply sit or stand you will feel where I have been."

She stared up at me, her eyes like saucers, but she didn't deny any of it, couldn't.

"Gabriel?"

"Yes, Angel."

"Touch me, please."

I leaned in closer, my lips barely a hairs breadth from hers. "Why?"

"Because I can't go a second longer without it."

I dropped one hand so that it rested on her hip. Her hand covered it before she guided it under her dress, up her thigh until it came to rest against the barrier of her underwear, something silky, damp and warm.

"Fuck! I can feel how much you want me."

With her hand still over mine she slid it along her sex, trying to coax my fingers inside her underwear.

"Please, Gabriel, touch me, kiss me. Anything."

Her last word was a plead and if that wasn't even more of a turn on. I leaned in to kiss her and after gently applying a little pressure against her nub of nerve endings, somehow pulled my hand away.

"Later. Later, you'll get everything."

With a single, gentle kiss I returned downstairs, unsure how I had managed not to be fucking her against the wall, but this really wasn't the time or place...definitely not the place.

Chapter Thirty-One

Carrie

I could barely catch my breath when Gabriel left me standing on the landing, still pressed against the wall that may have actually been the one thing keeping me upright. God, the things that man did to me. The idea of *everything* both thrilled me and scared me shitless at the same time. I wasn't even sure how I was going to get through the rest of the day and get to *later* without combusting or having some kind of episode.

Everyone looked in my direction as I re-joined them outside. I was certain they knew where I had been and what Gabriel and I had done. I looked down at my watch and seeing it was after four decided it was time to leave.

"Thank you for lunch, but I should probably make a move."

Christine and Noel stood, while Margaret looked up at me and with her filter still absent said, "You really do have amazing tits."

I laughed, as did Gabriel until Charlotte repeated it, several times. "Tits, tits, tits," she sang as her father put his hands over her ears.

"Don't have children, no matter how good the sex is or you'll be tucking those tits into your pants by the time you're forty."

Christine looked embarrassed while Noel shook his head.

"Thank you," I said to Margaret. "I'll be sure to remember that."

Gabriel smirked across at me and shrugged as if apologising for his grandmother, but it felt as if there was more to it than

153

that.

"Can I give you a ride?" Gabriel asked, releasing Charlotte's ears. A little quirk of his eyebrow suggested the double entendre of his words had been fully intended.

Well, two could play that game. "No, thank you. Another time. Maybe."

The tension between us was palpable, thickening with every second we stood there, staring at one another.

I kissed each of Gabriel's parents and Charlotte, then with a goodbye for Margaret I began to head for the front door.

The distance between Christine's house and Gabriel's was only about a fifteen-minute walk which I hadn't realised until I'd got a taxi there earlier. I had only got about halfway home when a car slowed at the kerbside, Toby.

"Can I give you a lift?"

I didn't need a lift, but with how offhand he'd been in the park, I didn't want Toby to think I was holding a grudge nor to make things awkward between me, him and our group of mutual friends.

"Thanks."

I got into his car and gave him my address and directions. Directions he seemed to go out of his way to do the opposite of meaning my trip home took almost half an hour. It had also included several suggestions to go back to his, to the pub, or for a late lunch, all offers I had to decline quite forcefully.

When he pulled up a few doors down from the house I attempted to get out of the car, but he pulled me back, and made to kiss me. Not like a snog type of kiss, but a kiss nevertheless. An unwanted kiss. I pulled back, got out of the car with a short but polite, *see you around* and turned to face where I was going.

"Shit!"

Staring back down the road at me was Gabriel and he looked furious. Goodness knows what he had seen or thought he had seen, but he didn't look as though he was in any mood to hear my explanation about what had happened.

Charlotte appeared at his side. "Carrie," she squealed. "Daddy said you're coming to play and watch TV."

Despite her father's face, I laughed at Charlotte's excitement and enthusiasm.

"I am and I can't wait," I told her before risking a glance at Gabriel. "About half an hour?"

He shook his head, making my heart sink and tears rise as I assumed he was cancelling our plans and whatever else we had together.

"No. Why wait? Come in now."

I nervously made my way to the door and entered behind Charlotte. We went into the kitchen, followed by Gabriel who immediately sent his daughter to find a game or something for us all to enjoy. She had barely made it out of the room when he cornered me.

"What the fuck is going on here?" He didn't even wait for me to attempt a reply before he launched into another question. "Do you want this? Are you playing me, here?"

I opened my mouth, preparing my denial when he cut back in.

"I offered you a lift. You didn't want one or was that just with me? Had you already arranged your alternative ride?"

The last word was completely loaded and no matter how angry he was, he had no right and I was done with standing there while he hurled accusations, inferences and questions my way.

"Am I allowed to speak now?"

He didn't reply but gave me a reluctant half nod and a pout.

"I would have loved to have come home with you, but this is all new and a bit crazy. Plus, I don't want to do or say anything to make you uncomfortable in front of your family. Your parents are lovely people and I was grateful for the invitation so even more reason to avoid drawing opinions on my role in all of this. And don't even get me started on what your grandmother might have said had she suspected something between me and her Christopher."

He smiled at my reference to his grandmother. "Okay."

Presumably that was my cue to continue.

"I walked home and was about halfway here when he pulled up and offered me a lift. I didn't want to come across as a bitch or make it weird for our other friends—"

"What? That was fuckboy?"

He was pacing, a picture of fury.

"Yes."

"You kissed him." He sighed and ran a hand through his hair, then let both arms drop to his side, his fists clenching tightly. It was as if he was doing everything in his power not to lose it completely.

"I did not kiss him. I went to get out of the car and he stopped me and he leaned in to kiss me. I did not, would not kiss him." To my own ears I sounded convincing, and why wouldn't I? It was true. "You're the only one I want to kiss."

His expression and whole body softened slightly. "Promise me there's nobody else."

"I swear."

He nodded. "We need to have a conversation about him—" He looked around before continuing. "—fuckboy. What was he even doing there, exactly where you were, and the park with Charlotte, but later."

I opened my mouth to reply but Charlotte reappeared at that very second with a selection of games for us to play.

****

"And now that we're finally alone, let's talk."

Gabriel dropped onto the sofa next to me having just returned from reading Charlotte her bedtime story.

"What do you want to talk about?" I asked and earned myself a cut of his eyes and a twist of his lips.

"What do you think? Or should that be, who do you think?"

"Toby is nothing and no one to me. I know you think he fancies me, but he really doesn't."

"Then why did he try to kiss you?"

I had no response for that.

"Just as I thought. There's something about him I don't like. I don't trust him, and this is the second time he has popped up where you were."

"I think it's a coincidence." I wasn't sure if that's what I thought or not. I hadn't really given it much in the way of thought, not really.

Gabriel shook his head as he topped up our wine glasses and I remembered his reference to the park. "How did you know about the park?"

"Charlotte. She mentioned it and asked if I knew him. That was when she told me that you're her best friend."

"Aww. That kid melts my heart." And she did.

Gabriel smiled, pride and love for his little girl poured from him.

"Back to fuckboy."

I rolled my eyes at his name for Toby.

"Roll your eyes all you like, that's what he is. Please, be careful. I understand you and he are part of the same circle of friends, but there is something about him I don't like...there's something that just doesn't sit right. Don't be alone with him if he wants to kiss you and tries to stop you leaving his car in his attempts to do that, even when you have no interest in him. I didn't like the idea of him being near you or Charlotte."

"Okay. I get it." I did think he was going a little over the top, but I didn't want to continue to debate all things Toby or to argue.

"Good."

Gabriel seemed happier, lighter almost as he pulled me to him.

"I am going to need to kiss you now."

"Kiss me? Just kiss me?" I asked with a nibble of my lip.

"To start with, Angel."

I giggled as he tugged me more firmly until my chest was pressed to his and his hand began to stroke my hair and roam my back while mine cupped his face and gripped his shoulders.

"Then kiss me, lover," I replied, using the name his grandmother had. I laughed at his horrified expression and then he kissed me, and my laughter was stemmed.

Chapter Thirty-Two

Gabriel

I could have laughed at her imitation of my grandmother's *lover.* Maybe I should have laughed at it, like she had, but I didn't. Instead I kissed her and in that instant her laughter ended.

Kissing seemed a totally inadequate description of how it felt; my mouth on hers, my tongue against hers, our breathing becoming more laboured as our hands became as fraught as our kisses while we tried to remove the barrier of clothes, desperate to get more skin on skin.

By the time our kiss was broken, I was unsure just who broke it first. Carrie was straddling my hips. Her dress had ridden up so it sat around her thighs making her underwear just visible. She looked absolutely gorgeous; her hair was ruffled from where I'd run my fingers through it, her eyes sparkled with lust and desire while her kiss swollen lips were a deeper shade of pink than usual.

My hands came to rest on her knees, almost instinctively.

"You are fucking gorgeous." I stared up at her, unable to look away. I wanted to watch her for as long as possible and I also wanted to see her reaction to my compliment.

She smiled and flushed at my words that were entirely genuine. Without any verbal response she leaned back in, as if to kiss me again but I— with one hand finding her chin— paused her movement.

"You are, Angel, beautiful. More beautiful than anyone I have ever seen."

She looked uncomfortable.

"You are," I repeated.

"I'm glad you think so," she muttered with an awkward shrug.

"I do." My hand left her chin, returned to her knee and allowed both hands to skate up her legs, my thumbs caressing her skin as they moved higher. Carrie's breath hitched with every movement I made. "Kiss me, you sexy minx."

She giggled when she recognised the words I'd earlier uttered to my grandmother. "With pleasure," she said with a little grin then moved closer until our lips melded together as one once more.

****

The sight of her sprawled on her back in the middle of my bed might just have been the best thing ever. Her eyes were fixed on mine, never once looking away as I removed my clothes. She was naked, having been stripped by me as soon as the bedroom door closed behind us.

I'd already pulled my t-shirt off over my head and had just reached for the waistband of my jeans when Carrie spoke.

"Gabriel, do you want to go upstairs, to my bedroom?"

I had no idea where this had come from or why and I didn't want to go anywhere else, why would I?

"Charlotte..." Her reasoning began to dawn in that one word. "What if she wakes up in the night, or—"

"Ah. She's unlikely to wake, she rarely does, unless she's unwell and I think after she scuppered things before with her vomiting, we might be safe." I smiled. I wanted to reassure her that her being here in my bedroom, on my bed wasn't an issue, and it wasn't, and yet it was. I didn't want Charlotte to find Carrie in my bed or to see her leaving here in last night's dress or less than last night's dress. I was in turmoil because if she stayed here now, I would need to send her back to her own bed before morning and if we went to her room, I would be the one leaving. I was unsure which was best, or worse.

Before I could say anything to indicate my choice, Carrie was beginning to get up. She didn't look upset or angry. The truth was, she didn't look anything at all. She just looked passive, resigned almost and that made my choice for me. She knew how things were and I knew she might be disappointed at having to leave before Charlotte woke, but she'd get that and support it. Me taking her upstairs to her bed and then leaving her almost as soon as things ended would make her feel like shit. Used. The truth was that would make me feel like shit too.

"No. Stay just where you are. I have plans for you."

She lay back down and flashed me a sexy as hell little grin. "Plans?"

"Oh yes. Dirty fucking plans that are going to have you calling my name and leaving scratch marks down my back."

She flushed leaving me in no doubt that I'd made the right decision.

I quickly cast my jeans aside then my underwear and set about making my pledge to her good. I blanketed her body with mine and kissed her. I devoured her mouth before I littered a delicate path of kisses along her jaw to her ear and neck. Slowly I moved down her body, kissing, licking and nipping as I journeyed along the track of her body; chest, breasts, nipples that were hard and sensitive to every touch from my mouth and fingers that pinched and caressed them. Then lower, across her ribs, abdomen and lower still. Bypassing her sex I kissed the length of her leg, down to her foot and back up the other one until I was kneeling on the floor between her spread thighs where I watched her literally open and blossom before my eyes.

She was wet, although wet barely described just how wet she was. She was drenched, her pussy wept for my touch and if her succession of mewls and moans as I worked her body into a frenzy of want and need hadn't told me that, the sight of her arousal leaking from her core certainly would have. With no preamble I used my thumbs to open her to me fully and licked along her whole length.

"Oh God!" she cried as I returned to her core and gently dipped my tongue in to lap her sweet nectar.

From there I traced my way back to her nub of nerve endings that was already standing to attention, demanding my consideration. As I licked against it, she convulsed beneath me, barely keeping control. With the tip of my tongue I circled her clit and flicked against it.

"Gabe, baby, please," she begged.

My cockiness was soaring, between her pleads, her response and her calling me baby, I was unsure I would ever come down from this. My response to her was to do it again, but also to insert my thumb inside her.

"Yes," she moaned as my thumb began to move in time with my tongue.

She rocked against my face, desperate for her release and whilst one half of me wanted to make her wait for it another part, a greater part wanted her to come apart for me. To come apart because of me and when she did, I was going to consume every ounce of it so I might never lose or forget the sweetest taste in the world.

I could feel just how close she was and still I wanted more. I wanted to give her more but to also take more from her. I removed my thumb and her disappointed sigh made me smile. She'd get it back soon enough and even more besides. I quickly inserted two fingers that I rotated and curled, finding her G-spot that had her writhing and cursing beneath her breath.

"Not yet, Angel. You're going to come all over my face really soon."

She made no reply besides another groan.

Once my fingers were fully coated in her arousal, I removed them and pulled her closer to the edge of the bed so her behind almost hung off it. I placed her legs over my shoulders and returned my thumb to her sex and my tongue to her clit. With our earlier rhythm restored and her riding my thumb and face, I spread her cheeks with my free hand and inserted one of my moistened fingers into her tiny, puckered hole.

She paused briefly, but once I was past the ring of resistance, she relaxed into it and began to enjoy the sensations. I added the second and began to move my digits in and out of her while my tongue continued to adore her.

It felt as though only seconds had passed before she was reaching down for my hair, pulling me closer and pushing me away at the same time, not quite sure which she wanted most and then her whole body tensed, her fingers tightly gripped my hair and her nails clawed my scalp as she cried out, called my name and mumbled words and sentiments that made no sense.

My hand and tongue worked her through her release until every last ounce of pleasure had been wrung from her and then I crawled up her body and kissed her. No words were needed, our kisses and our bodies said all either of us needed to say or hear. I easily slid into her and with her tasting herself on my lips and tongue I began to move, sliding in and out of her, gently at first, then with more urgency until we came together, my own climax being almost painful in its intensity and then, sated, we fell into a deep sleep wrapped around and within each other.

Chapter Thirty-Three

Carrie

I woke a little after five in the morning, still cocooned within Gabriel's embrace. I couldn't believe how gentle and intense last night had been. When he'd told me, I'd be getting everything, I wasn't entirely sure what that meant, but now I was in no doubt. We had snoozed for a few hours and then woke almost together and as I'd prepared to leave for my own bed. Gabriel had stopped me, instead running us a bath to share and once clean and relaxed, I again prepared for my departure, but instead we returned to his bed where we kissed and cuddled before going back to sleep.

I was tired and yet wide awake as I climbed the stairs to my room. Tired and sore, having had the workout of my life. Sore seemed an underestimation of how I ached and hurt. Every muscle in my body throbbed, courtesy of the stretching and tensing it had been subjected to, and then there were my delicate folds that felt bruised and chafed. I couldn't even allow myself to think about where his fingers had been, the tissue they'd stretched. I flushed red at the memories I was refusing to recall completely.

First stop was to put the kettle on, then with a cup of hot tea I sat on the sofa knowing I needed not to go back to bed or I'd never wake up in time to be downstairs for work. A big grin was already spreading across my face at the idea of seeing Gabriel in less than two hours.

A text alert sounded, startling me.

<I already miss you being next to me>

My grin broadened and I was fairly certain I swooned when I reread it.

<Me too, but any longer and we'd have been cutting it fine>

<I know. Maybe I should come to you next time, that might buy us an extra hour>

<I'd like that>

<It's a date then. I have a later start this morning...would you like to have breakfast together, me, you and Charlotte?>

My heart skipped a beat at that offer, the extension of it and the meaning I perceived as being behind it.

<It's a yes for the date and breakfast>

I laughed at myself, bouncing on the sofa with happiness and excitement and then paused to give myself a pep talk about not getting carried away or reading more into this than there was.

An hour later Gabriel was already in the kitchen, making drinks and setting breakfast things on the table, ready for breakfast.

"Hello, lover," I called as I entered behind him.

He turned and gave me a disapproving frown that wasn't very convincing. "I am going to ban you from seeing my grandmother ever again if you keep this up."

I laughed. "I love that in her mind she still has your grandfather."

"Yeah, me too. They were quite devoted."

I smiled at that idea and made an aww sound. "And they were clearly very passionate if her comments yesterday were anything to go by."

"Or that could just be the dementia," Gabriel offered.

I shook my head at him. "Nah. The dementia has simply allowed her to share the details of what they had together."

"Maybe." Gabriel looked slightly uncomfortable at the notion.

"Definitely. I reckon they banged like a barn door in a storm at every opportunity."

He looked shocked at the words I'd chosen. I was shocked at them, but I think that had been my intention when I'd chosen them, to shock Gabriel, yet more than that I wanted to convey his grandparents love and passion for each other. Maybe I wanted ours to be like theirs.

"Do I need to stop you talking again, Miss Webber?" His eyebrow quirked, knowing how much I liked him stopping me speaking.

"You might."

I hadn't imagined adding more words to those two but even if I had they'd have been cut off because it was at that second that he reached for my arm and pulled me to him. His hands cupped my face while his lips lowered until they covered mine. My mouth immediately opened, inviting him in. Begging him in. He accepted the invitation and quickly tamed my tongue until I was hot and desperate all over again, willing to give him just about anything he wanted. He pushed his hips closer and I immediately knew he wanted me.

"Angel," he panted as we each pulled away. "Fuck, I might need to change your name to demon."

I dropped my gaze and nibbled my lip, unsure what to say.

"You're a witch," he told me, already pulling me closer again.

"Careful or I might put a spell on you." I light-heartedly made as if to wave a magic wand, not necessarily expecting or needing a reply, but nothing could have prepared me for his response.

"You already have."

"Daddy." Charlotte's voice sounded around us, interrupting the moment, but then maybe that was for the best.

As soon as the little girl appeared in the doorway Gabriel greeted her, picking her up and kissing her before putting the final touches to breakfast.

Charlotte and I were due at her regular stay and play session which meant we would probably leave the house before Gabriel. He went upstairs with his daughter to get her washed and dressed while I went to my own room to get myself ready.

I dressed in a summery, pink floral skirt that almost finished at my knees and teamed it with a plain white t-shirt and pair of white slip-on plimsolls. I had just left my accommodation when Gabriel appeared at the bottom of the stairs holding Charlotte's hand.

"Well, don't you look beautiful my potty Lottie?" I asked a giggling Charlotte.

"As do you, Miss Webber."

I offered him a small curtsey, causing another giggle to leave the little girl's lips while her father simply cocked his head and winked at me. I was the one to giggle now.

"Why don't I drop you beautiful ladies off on my way into work?"

Charlotte cheered at the offer of driving rather than walking. She moaned every morning as we walked anywhere, although she was always happy to walk home so maybe she just needed to wake up a little before the onslaught of a walk. I shrugged, unbothered either way.

"That's decided then. Oh, and Wednesday, I can take Charlotte to nursery for her first day."

I nodded, having given no thought to who would be on hand to take Charlotte. Although, as it was her first day, I suppose it was expected for a parent to take her and make sure she was settled. I chided myself for feeling slightly irked by my dismissal and my thoughts about the expectation when in reality, I knew Gabriel would take his daughter to nursery for one reason and one reason alone, because he loved her.

Charlotte immediately began to chatter excitedly about her new school and how she was going to learn lots of new things and make lots and lots of friends.

As the car came to a standstill at stay and play, I undid my seatbelt and prepared to get out of the car, but Gabriel reached across and with a hand on my knee paused my movements.

"Would you like to have dinner on Wednesday, with us, me and Charlotte, and Seb?" He raised an eyebrow at the utterance of his friend's name while his daughter began to chant 'Uncle Seb' to my amusement.

"If you'd like me to." I wasn't being awkward or fishing for compliments, I just didn't want to intrude, and I was unsure if I would be.

"Carrie, it's a yes or no choice and it's if you want to, not if I want you too." He sounded irritated with me but seeing my uncertainty he softened. "I have no issues if you'd rather not. However, if you'd like to, I'd love for you to join us."

"Thank you, yes."

"Good." He smiled. "And I should probably apologise for my friend's behaviour and most likely his lame jokes and immature use of the name Nanny for you."

I smiled across at him while he remained serious.

"Henry!" Charlotte squealed seeing her friend from the window.

Gabriel looked confused until I explained.

"I thought boys wouldn't be around for many more years," he muttered while I laughed at his expression.

"Henry is very popular," I explained. "And his mother regularly asks about you."

"Does she?" he asked, teasing me, I hoped.

"Yes," I snapped, irrational fear raising its ugly head. I got out of the car and opened the back door to retrieve Charlotte and her bag.

"Bye, Daddy. I love you," she called.

"Bye," I said too, sticking to that single word as I wondered if Gabriel knew who Henry's mum was and if he'd be interested in her.

My phone vibrated in my pocket as we entered the community centre filled with sounds of children. I pulled it out and couldn't hide the huge smirk on my face when I read the message waiting for me.

<Keep my baby safe from that boy, all boys, and if his

mother or anyone's mother asks after me today, say I have no interest in anyone…except for my sexy little angel/demon/witch. And assuming you don't back out of dinner with Seb, I'd also be free for a sleepover with you>

With a smile so broad it hurt my jaw, I replied.

<I will be telling all the mums that, and I can't wait for a sleepover with you>

Chapter Thirty-Four

Gabriel

I'd watched Carrie and Charlotte wander, hand in hand into the community centre where they attended stay and play and smiled. I was happy. Really happy for the first time in a long time.

I drove off with a sense of contentment, only slightly tinged with apprehension of what we were doing and what would happen if it all went wrong. I called Seb to let him know Carrie would be joining us for dinner and that he needed to be on his best behaviour. He laughed at the notion of that, as did I. Even on his best behaviour, Seb was a loose cannon, but that was one of the many reasons we were friends.

****

It was Tuesday night before Carrie and I got a chance to spend any time together. Monday had been busy and when I'd returned home from work, she had gone upstairs almost immediately and seemed preoccupied with words about ironing, a headache and an early night leaving her lips. I wasn't sure if they were reasons or excuses, but didn't pursue that, instead I spent the evening with Charlotte and after a bath and bedtime I set about a little washing and ironing of my own.

Tuesday had seen Carrie disappear upstairs too, but with an invitation to come back down later, our plan was made.

Charlotte had been in bed just over an hour when Carrie appeared wearing the tightest fitting, black leggings I had ever seen and a white fitted t-shirt. She looked amazing and as she got closer. She smelled amazing too; freshly showered, her soap, shampoo, perfume and the smell that was uniquely hers mingled to assault my senses in the best way possible.

"Good evening," I said as I looked up and greeted her in the doorway to my office where I was just finishing off a few things.

"I can come back later if you're busy."

I shook my head. "No need. I'm done." I was already on my feet and heading for her. "Do you want a drink? I have a very nice bottle of red wine in the kitchen.

She nodded and turned towards the kitchen giving me the sight of her arse in those very tight leggings. I drank her in from head to toe. Her feet were bare, and I even found those something of a turn on. Everything about her turned me on, not that I had planned on us having sex tonight, but if it happened, I wouldn't be turning her down. I couldn't imagine ever turning her down. Right now all I could think of was peeling those pants from her and devouring her. My dick was already hard, had been from the second her scent infused my senses and now it was lurching at the ideas forming in my mind.

With our glasses full and the remainder of the bottle on the coffee table, we settled together on the sofa. The TV was on in the background...some programme about the Greek Islands. We chatted about travel, places we'd been and wanted to go. Carrie's travels had been limited, but then, she was young. Our bodies relaxed and melded into one another as we became more comfortable in our position together on the sofa. My arm had instinctively moved so that it was draped around Carrie until she was leaning against my front, both of our legs lying along the sofa, her body positioned between mine.

I leaned down and landed a single, gentle kiss to the top of her head. "So, how's things?" I asked her, still feeling she was preoccupied.

"Fine," she replied a little too quickly and not with any certainty.

"You don't sound convinced. You can talk to me, you know. If something is worrying you or you're having second thoughts —"

"No!" her desperate reply cut off my own words. "I'm really

not, but…"

She allowed her own words to trail off meaning there was something about us that was causing her some disconcertion.

"Angel, what is it? You can talk to me. Talk it through, whatever it is."

She turned to face me and offered a nervous nod before putting her glass down. Facing me and positioned between my own spread thighs, she crossed her legs and looked as though she was about to start a class at the gym. I needed to block all images of Carrie stretching and bending if I hoped to actually listen to whatever was on her mind.

"You remember Henry, Charlotte's friend?"

I nodded.

"And his mother?"

I nodded again.

"She saw us in your car."

"Okay." I was unsure what the issue was there. I had simply dropped my daughter and her nanny off and whatever else there was wasn't common knowledge and even if it was, neither Carrie nor I were doing anything wrong.

"She said the mums don't like me."

I frowned at the sad expression on Carrie's face. Was she really that bothered by whether the local mums liked her or not?

"They don't trust me," she added and that seemed a more likely cause of her upset. "Some of them were out the same night you took me home from the club and they saw us kiss outside. She said they all see me as no more than a live-in whore and when I no longer work for you no other family will employ me for that reason."

My blood was boiling that these bitches thought they had any right to judge us, to judge Carrie. I didn't know what to say to her though, because I imagined Henry's mum was probably right about her being employed locally as a nanny. But then she didn't need to be employed by any of them. She was employed by me.

"They might have a point…"

Her scowl suggested she'd thought I meant about her being a live-in whore.

"That you'd struggle to be employed locally, but as far as I'm aware, you're happy with your current employment." I brushed a thumb across her cheek and with a half-smile she leaned into my touch.

"I wouldn't want to work for her or anyone else as judgemental as her, but it wasn't nice to hear it."

"So..."

"Bea was there with the children she looks after."

I nodded. I knew of the family Bea worked for and also knew this was where she and Bea had met.

"Bea agreed with her, not the whore bit," she clarified for my disapproving frown. "She warned me that this was a bad idea. At best I was playing a part in a cliché and at worst I was going to end up unemployed, homeless and hurt."

I pinched the bridge of my nose, again unsure what to say. "I can't promise you won't end up as the latter any more than I can guarantee you will. If you want to put the brakes on this, you can."

She shook her head vehemently, got up on her knees and shuffled closer until her forehead rested against mine. "No."

"Good."

"I asked Bea about Toby."

I bristled, pushed her back to observe her, but more for her to see my pissed off expression. What the fuck had she asked about him and why? "And why would you do that?" I sounded sulky and petulant but really didn't give a single fuck at that point.

"Because of what you said about being careful and not trusting him."

"Oh." I relaxed again. "What did Bea say?"

She looked worried again. "Not much and an awful lot at the same time. Sorry," she said when she took in my confused expression. "She didn't say anything specific but said he gets very attached very quickly and once he likes someone, he can find it tough to take a rejection. He hasn't had a girlfriend in like forever but has shown an interest in lots of girls but quickly loses interest."

She could have been describing someone who was an arsehole or just a bit of a player, but there was something else that didn't sit well with me. I still didn't like him, and it went beyond simple jealousy, and I really, really didn't trust him.

"Is that all she said?"

"Hmmm, although she looked a bit weirded out when I told her about him turning up at the park and then trying to kiss me."

"She's not the only one who was weirded out by that."

She smiled and looked relieved and relaxed again so presumably the local mums and her friend's words about fuckboy had caused her to be unsettled.

I reached for her, cupped her face and pulled her closer and kissed her; a slow, delicate, gentle kiss that saw her climbing into my lap, her legs curling around my hips, her hands wrapping around my neck.

"Angel," I whispered, having broken the kiss. "We'll be bringing our sleepover forward if you continue like this and don't get me started on how fucking amazing your arse looks in these." I ran my hand across the lycra stretched over her arse and detected no lines from her underwear. "Are you wearing anything beneath these?"

She giggled but made her way back into her original position between my spread thighs, resting against my chest. Reaching for the remote control she flicked the TV channel until some reality show with half naked people looking for love appeared.

"You're going to love this," she told me.

I wasn't. She knew it. I knew it, but I kissed the top of her head again. "Angel, you definitely need a change of name, you little witch."

She giggled and my heart overflowed.

"Wear your sexy ass workout pants tomorrow and the same type of underwear you're currently wearing."

She laughed rather than giggled now. "Whatever you want, lover."

"For fuck's sake," I muttered at her insistence on using my grandmother's term of endearment while she laughed some more, knowing exactly what she was doing.

Chapter Thirty-Five

Carrie

I can't remember when I'd had such a nice night as last night. Gabriel and I spent the evening together after I joined him downstairs. We chatted about the local mothers, Bea's views on my position and finally her comments about Toby. Gabriel still didn't like Toby or his habit of turning up where I was, but I thought that was probably down to jealousy more than anything. We had watched some TV, drank some wine and kissed and cuddled. The fact we didn't have sex made me feel as though there was more to us than just our physical interactions and that was good, wasn't it?

I was already showered and dressed, even though I knew I had nowhere to go. It was Charlotte's first day at nursery and like the good father he was, Gabriel was going to take her. The sound of Charlotte giggling from the floor below made me smile. I headed out of my door and looked down to see her skipping back downstairs with her hand firmly tucked in her father's. She was chattering away about all the things she planned to do once she got to school as she called nursery, which it was. It was a class for three-year-olds based in a local private school.

"Good morning, schoolgirl," I called from behind them.

Charlotte spun back and ran towards me until she stood at my feet, her arms held aloft for me to pick her up, which I was more than happy to do.

"Still excited I see."

She giggled. "I have new clothes, special school clothes I have to wear because I am a big girl now," she began to tell me with infectious enthusiasm.

"You really are," I replied.

"I have a tie and a special bloater hat." She was at risk of tripping over her own words.

I laughed.

"Or a boater as the rest of the world calls it." Gabriel corrected the name of her mispronounced hat and waited for us to join him.

"You know you're going to look beautiful in your uniform," I told her as she jumped ship and took up her place in her father's arms.

Charlotte looked at her father. "Carrie tells me I look beautiful whatever I wear."

"And Carrie's right, baby, you always look beautiful."

"And Carrie, Daddy. Carrie is beautiful, too."

"Yes, she is," Gabriel replied, putting his daughter down as we reached the bottom of the stairs and gently rested a hand on my hip.

He looked as though he was about to say something else, or at least something more when the front door burst open revealing Christine's arrival.

"Good morning," she called in a very cheery voice until her eyes landed on me and her son who had backed off somewhat. "You both okay?"

"Yes, thank you," I said while Gabriel nodded and muttered something about being 'just fine'.

Once breakfast was over, Gabriel took Charlotte upstairs to help her dress in her uniform. I pottered around the kitchen, tidying and loading the dishwasher while Christine seemed to just watch me, making me nervous. I felt the need to speak, to fill the silence that was unwelcome and unusual between us.

"Thank you for lunch yesterday," I said, breaking the silence if not the tension.

"You're very welcome. Charlotte loved having you there, and Gabriel." The last word, her son's name, hung between us. "We all did," she added with a smile.

175

"Well, thanks anyway. It was lovely."

"Anytime."

The silence returned.

"Carrie," she began and there was no doubt in my mind that she was going to start a serious conversation.

"Ta-da," cried Gabriel, returning to the kitchen with Charlotte who looked wonderful.

She looked like a little girl still, but somehow older, more grown up in her very formal uniform, complete with her tie, blazer and boater hat that I might forever call a bloater.

"Wow! Look at you," I called while Christine rushed towards her granddaughter to hug and kiss her.

I could see that both Gabriel and Christine were emotional at the sight of the little girl and whilst I couldn't possibly understand how they felt or why, I also found myself sniffing back a few tears and emotions pressing down on my chest.

"Is it time to go?" Charlotte asked, reaching for her bag.

"Soon, baby."

The little girl smiled then turned to take in my appearance in jeans and a t-shirt. "Put your shoes on, Carrie. We don't want to be late."

I looked around, confused as to why she thought I needed shoes, although it was obvious that she thought I was taking her to school too.

"You're going with Daddy," I told her, but I was sure she already knew that.

"And you and Grandma," she replied.

With a shake of my head I looked between Christine and Gabriel.

"Daddy and Grandma are taking you today and Carrie can take you tomorrow," Gabriel explained.

"And Carrie," the little girl persisted.

Gabriel sighed as he looked between me and his mother. I felt awkward, not because I especially wanted to go or felt I should, but because Charlotte's persistence was drawing even more of Christine's attention and it was only a matter of time before she became suspicious of mine and her son's relationship.

"Charlotte," I called to her, wondering if I should say or do anything to diffuse this situation. "I can't come with you this morning, and Daddy has taken the time off work so he and Grandma could take you and share your special day. I will take you another day, lots of other days."

The little girl nodded but looked a little sad.

"How about if Carrie comes with me to collect you later and when we get home you can help make dinner for Uncle Seb?" Gabriel was already picking his daughter up again.

"Yes," she squealed. "Can we do makeovers again?"

"Maybe, but maybe not. Can we decide later?" Gabriel asked while I laughed, gaining his attention. "Carrie is having dinner with us and I bet she would love you to give her a makeover."

I stopped laughing when I realised that the little girl's gaze had honed in on me, a plan for my makeover already forming in her mind. A gaze passed from Christine to Gabriel, not that the latter seemed to notice.

"Let's go." Gabriel rounded everyone up and once he'd ushered them through the door he dashed back. "I'm working from home today, so I'll see you soon." With a brief dip down, he landed a single chaste kiss to my cheek and then he was gone.

****

We were approaching the school via the long driveway and I felt nervous. I had no idea why, not really, but the nerves I felt were very real and fluttering in my chest.

"I hope she's had a good day," Gabriel said, sounding nervous himself, but his nerves were for Charlotte.

"I'm sure she has. Why wouldn't she? She's funny, friendly, smart and sassy as hell. I bet she's already the most popular girl in her class."

Gabriel looked across and smiled at me as he parked the car. "Thank you. Come on. I'm sorry about this morning."

I waved away his apology that was unnecessary. It wasn't my place to take her to school for her first day, however it was Gabriel's and Christine's. Gabriel had returned home with his mother but by mid-morning Christine had left. He had worked from home and apart from about half an hour at lunchtime he had been enclosed in his office. It was just after half past one and I had missed Charlotte so was glad to be collecting her.

"I didn't expect to come with you this morning but thank you for now."

"The staff need to meet you anyway, but if my mum hadn't been coming with us, you'd have been welcome this morning."

"Thank you, but it really is fine. Come on, let's get her." I was already out of the car, preparing to make the short walk to the nursery entrance.

Gabriel introduced me to the staff as Charlotte's nanny, which is what I was and yet it cut a little. I wasn't entirely sure what or who I expected him to introduce me as, but nanny seemed so formal and professional and he and I were very much informal and unprofessional.

Charlotte came rushing out and looked a little dishevelled compared to how she'd left the house that morning, but judging by her garbled and excited tales of all she'd been up to with her new friends she'd had fun and that had to be the main thing, didn't it?

As we headed for the car, she took my hand in one of hers and Gabriel's in the other. She sang and skipped making me and Gabe laugh, but mine was short-lived when I saw another parent arrive.

"Oh no," I muttered, hoping we might avoid the other woman. No such luck.

"Hi Charlotte," she called, causing Gabriel to stand still.

"Hi," Charlotte replied. "I've been playing with Henry today."

"How lovely. Aren't you a sweetie?" she cooed with a sickly-sweet smile. "I bet you get that from Daddy."

I actually rolled my eyes at that before turning a glare her way.

"No, afraid not. We all have Carrie to thank for her sweetness. She has to be the best nanny in the world."

The other woman looked as though she was sucking a lemon and Gabriel wasn't done.

"In fact, I reckon I'll be beating off my competitors to hang onto her once word gets out about just how fantastic she is at *her job*."

He stared at her, knowing exactly who she was. That she was

one of the bitchy mums, the main one. Without another word he turned and led us away and I wore the biggest of grins.

"Thank you. I'll be sure to show my appreciation later, lover," I said with a cheeky wink.

"I look forward to it, Angel," he replied with a wink of his own that made me quietly quiver with anticipation.

Chapter Thirty-Six

Gabriel

Charlotte had an amazing first day and had barely stopped speaking about it all afternoon into the evening. Carrie and I had both given her our undivided attention during her regaled stories of her day. She'd made new friends and still had old friends, including Henry, whose mother I set straight earlier today.

I didn't know the woman all that well, but I knew of her and I didn't like her, never had. Carrie said very little after thanking me for defending her, but it really was unnecessary. She had just left me and Charlotte alone for a couple of hours. A couple of hours that would see me preparing dinner before Carrie returned and Seb arrived.

Carrie was nervous about dinner with my friend, not him personally, but the significance of me inviting her into my small and exclusive circle of friends. I couldn't deny that it was significant, it was, very.

Dinner was a simple pasta bake and salad with a couple of garlic baguettes on the side that my daughter was desperately trying to crack into every time I turned my back.

"I'm starving," she moaned as I moved it out of her reach.

"Baby, you're really not, but we'll be eating soon enough."

Her silent reply was a pout and a frown until there a gentle knock on the frame of the kitchen door. Carrie.

"I'm not too early, am I?"

"No, not at all," I told her, fighting the temptation to cross the room to pull her into my arms and kiss her.

Charlotte, on the other hand had no problem fighting her compulsions. She had already made her way to the doorway and was stretching up to hug her nanny.

"I'm starving," she began, hoping to get Carrie on side in her mission to consume the bread.

"Go and wash your hands, and we'll start without Uncle Seb if he doesn't arrive soon."

Charlotte let out a squeal and rushed off for the bathroom, giving me the perfect opportunity to go to Carrie and hold her. In a matter of seconds, I'd pulled her into my arms and covered her lips with mine. Our lips had barely made contact when there was a loud knock at the door. Seb.

"Later, Angel," I told Carrie who was wearing a pair of skin-tight leggings and a very form fitting t-shirt. "Me, you and those tights, pants, trousers, whatever the fuck they are, have a date."

She giggled as the door knocked again.

"I'm coming," I shouted to the door where I found Seb already entering my home.

"I was wondering," he quipped, a large grin on his face.

"You, my friend, are a dickhead."

"And you, my friend, look ridiculously happy, so you're welcome. Where's Nanny?"

I walked back towards the kitchen, ignoring his Nanny comment as Charlotte appeared and threw herself towards Seb.

****

We ate in the kitchen and while Charlotte gave Seb a blow by blow account of her day, Carrie said little, just offering little reminders of any details my daughter had forgotten. I didn't say much either, happy for Charlotte to take centre stage, after all, today was her day.

Charlotte had negotiated an extra half an hour downstairs and was beginning to try for a little longer when I got to my feet.

"Bath time first and then ten more minutes before story time."

She looked at me from her position nestled on Seb's lap, obviously considering her options, although, she had none aside from this one. I reached for her as her protests started and with a quick look back at Carrie and Seb I threw a token, 'be back soon' their way, and left them alone. As I climbed the stairs with

Charlotte still attempting to negotiate more time downstairs, I hoped Seb wouldn't wind Carrie up or reveal any of my darkest secrets.

****

Seb

Gabe left me alone with an incredibly nervous looking Nanny so he could go and bath Charlotte who was as charming as ever.

"Seems like the whole school thing is a winner then?"

Carrie looked up as I spoke and with a broad smile, nodded. "She loved it, and as you heard, she has made lots of new friends."

I laughed at Nanny's summing up but more than that I was happy that the nearest thing I had to a child of my own had settled into school life.

"I mean, it's early days, but fingers crossed she continues to enjoy it."

"I'll cross everything for you," I told her. "Especially as you'll be the one dragging her there every morning if she doesn't."

"And on that thought I might just make a start on clearing up."

I followed her, carrying plates and glasses. We worked in unison, clearing the table, loading the dishwasher and tidying until the kitchen was restored to its former spotless state. Conversation was pretty easy, not that it was much of a surprise as we stuck to safe subjects such as the weather, dinner, music, movies and Charlotte.

She moved around the kitchen with ease. She looked as if she belonged in this space. In Gabe's space. I loved Gabe, he was my best friend, a brother from another mother, if you like, and all I had ever wanted for him since he and Charlotte went solo was for him to be happy. Whenever he spoke about Carrie, he was happy, even when she messed with his head, not that I believed that was deliberate on her part. Having seen them here tonight, together, sharing space and hanging onto Charlotte's every word, it left me in no doubt that she was good for him. He liked her, a lot, and it was totally reciprocal.

She bent down, putting Charlotte's lunchbox away and I couldn't help but stare at her arse. It was divine. No wonder Gabe was gaga for her. The way she filled her trousers was pornographic.

She straightened and turned, then looked at me with a half-smile. "Top up?"

I nodded, already getting our glasses. "Shall we?" I gestured to the sofa at the far end of the room where Gabe and I usually sat.

She headed in the direction of the sofa, showing me her behind again. I needed to keep my eyes on her face or else Gabe would notice when he returned and as much as he took my Nanny jokes and comments about her being fit, I didn't doubt he'd object to me ogling her arse.

"You and Gabe go back a long way then?"

I nodded, wondering where she was taking this. Was she about to try and get the inside track on my friend?

She laughed. "Don't look so nervous. I'm not looking for dirt on you, or him."

I laughed back and felt more comfortable in answering. "We met at school. We were eleven, in the same class, and had similar interests."

She laughed again and her whole face lit up. She really was beautiful.

"Similar interests? Would that be blondes, brunettes or redheads? Or maybe you weren't inclined to rule any of them out."

I laughed a loud, raucous laugh and shook my head. "I'm not sure I'm not still disinclined to rule any of them out."

Her arched brow was her only response.

"Do you have children? Charlotte adores you. You often fill our afternoons," she told me with a smirk and crinkle of her nose that left me unsure if she was telling the truth or not.

"No children. None that I'm aware of, anyway."

She rolled her eyes.

"And aren't you lucky to have such wonderful afternoons, filled with me and Charlotte's adoration?"

"Hmmm. So, no children. Wife?"

"God, you're bloody nosey, aren't you?"

She shrugged, not denying my accusation but still expected a reply.

"No wife, no children, no significant other, no girlfriend, nor boyfriend. Happy now?"

She looked embarrassed by my extensive reply. Maybe it had come across as being abrupt or irritated, neither things intended.

"And in case you're a fixer upper, Nanny, don't. I am happy being single and have no shortage of friends."

She laughed a little and immediately her eyes twinkled. She looked even prettier than before. I could certainly see why Gabe was so taken with her, but whether he realised it or not he had always been a one woman guy, a settle down kind of guy, he'd just had bad luck up until now, but maybe Nanny was going to change that.

"Fortunately for you, I don't know too many people, so unless you're interested in a nanny, a snooty, stuck up local mum, or Gabe's mum, you're out of luck in the fixing up stakes."

I laughed at her options for me and whilst the idea of a nanny appealed, well, if they all looked like her it did, her description of the local mums didn't. I considered her suggestion of Christine and laughed harder. "Christine is a fine-looking woman and I love her dearly, but I don't think Noel would approve, never mind Gabe."

She joined in with my laughter. "What about Margaret?"

I almost choked on my wine at the suggestion of Gabe's grandmother who had always been lovely but was out of it most of the time now courtesy of her dementia. "Really? You want to set me up with Margaret? Christine would wear my balls as earrings at the suggestion alone."

She shrugged and offered me a little wink.

"You, Nanny, are trouble with a capital T."

She said nothing, meaning she knew it and was winding me up. "Margaret only has eyes for Gabriel anyway, so she probably wouldn't be impressed by you."

I opened and closed my mouth several times, as if genuinely outraged, but the truth was, I was amused, by Nanny, but also at

Margaret and her love for Gabe who she mistook for her late husband. "Have you seen photos of Christopher?"

"No. Other than Charlotte, there aren't all that many photographs around here. And none of Charlotte with her mum."

She was right. Photos of Charlotte were in every room. Some of Gabe and his daughter, a few of us in his office and his parents, but that was about it. I was unsure if my face gave away my panic at her bringing up Charlotte's mother. This was not a conversation I was getting into. Gabe rarely spoke about it, as in never, so I wasn't going there, but I might have to tip my friend off that his nanny was becoming curious.

"Ask Christine. You'll see why Margaret is so smitten…"

"And ten minutes before bedtime," Gabe said, returning with a freshly bathed Charlotte who was now dressed in pyjamas covered in unicorns. "You both been on your best behaviour?" he asked, dropping down to sit between me and Carrie who had a lap full of Charlotte who was already yawning.

Chapter Thirty-Seven

Carrie

I hadn't intended to raise the subject of Charlotte's mother and hoped that when Seb told Gabe I had, and I was pretty certain he would report back, that Gabriel wouldn't be angry with me. He could quite easily assume I was using his friend to gain information, and if I was, it had been no way deliberate.

Charlotte sat in my lap, stroking my hair, gently tugging it between her fingers when she suddenly sprang to her feet. "Makeovers!" She squealed excitedly and disappeared from the room.

"I thought we'd escaped it." Gabriel laughed.

"I quite like a bit of self-care, a pamper and some manscaping," Seb said, making Gabriel frown and me laugh.

"Manscaping," Gabe muttered while his friend made some comment about *nothing worse than a rogue hair.*

We all laughed, knowing exactly what he meant.

"Who's first?" Charlotte asked, returning to the room.

"Uncle Seb," Gabriel and I both said in unison.

Charlotte climbed onto the sofa, ready to get to work on Uncle Seb while Gabriel moved to give her more space. He smiled before heading into the kitchen to refresh drinks. With Seb and Charlotte in a full and exclusive conversation I followed Gabe into the kitchen.

"You okay?" he asked, discreetly slipping an arm around my waist to hold me closer.

"Yeah." My reply sounded hesitant.

"You sure?"

"I asked Seb about Charlotte's mum," I blurted out.

Gabriel released me immediately and spun me to face him.

He looked angry, disappointed and very suspicious.

"It wasn't like that. I wasn't pumping for information. I don't even know how it came to that, but I wanted you to know. To hear it from me first."

He nodded and passed me a fresh glass of wine. "Thank you."

I wasn't quite sure what he was thanking me for but hoped it was my honesty.

"Are you trying to get me drunk?" I took a sip from my glass.

"Maybe." He grinned.

"On a school night?"

"I hadn't thought of that. We now have school nights. Although I could still be getting you drunk. Maybe I am planning on taking advantage of you?" He smiled and quickly his face dropped into a deep frown. "I wouldn't. Take advantage. In fact, that might be your last glass for the night."

I stared at him, unsure where this was all coming from, but he sounded so serious and desperate for me to know and believe that his intentions were good, I felt compelled to reassure him.

"If I stop drinking now, I'm going to need a guarantee of your intentions to take advantage of me." I threw in a wink for good measure.

He arched a brow, but smiled before stepping closer, close enough to whisper in my ear. "I'd like to take advantage of you right now. I can't stop thinking about you and when I look at you, I imagine each and every one of your curves curling into my touch. I almost hear your breaths and pants as you get closer to the edge and don't get me started on how I taste you on my tongue."

I was panting already. Squeezing my thighs together in a useless attempt to dampen my arousal or at least find some relief.

He smiled as he straightened and reached for the wine bottle again. "Yes, definitely your last glass, Angel."

"Daddy, Carrie, come and look at Uncle Seb, he's so pretty,"

Charlotte squealed, excited by her own handiwork.

"Very metrosexual," Gabe muttered but I had to admit that Uncle Seb looked good.

His hair had been pushed into a spiky, knotty mess and he wore a little shimmery blusher along with a gloss to his lips, but it was the smile he wore and the glint of unmistakable love in his eyes for Charlotte that made him look happy and attractive.

"Beautiful." I grinned while Charlotte beamed with pride.

"Don't you go flirting with me, Nanny," Seb replied, both of us laughing.

"No, don't," chipped in Gabriel, dryly.

"Who's next?" Charlotte cried, already grabbing her brushes and little bag of make-up.

"Nanny!" cheered Seb.

I dutifully took the seat Charlotte indicated.

"There's no improving perfection," said Gabe while Seb fanned himself.

"I might feel a bit sick with such sweetness." Seb smiled as he spoke.

"This might have to be the last makeover of the night, baby." Gabriel was looking at the time as he spoke to his daughter. "It's past bedtime."

Reluctantly she nodded as I squealed at the force with which the little girl brushed my hair.

By the time my makeover was complete, my hair had been plaited, which translated to being in knots and my made-up face resembled something between a clown and an Aunt Sally doll.

"Carrie is beautiful now," Charlotte said as she leaned in and kissed my cheek before leaping into Seb's lap.

"She's okay," Seb told her with a wink. "Not a patch on you though." He littered dozens of kisses on her face as she giggled loudly.

Gabe rolled his eyes at them but had the biggest of smiles plastered on his face then looked to me. *Beautiful* he mouthed and then louder, said, "Always was."

"Daddy, can I paint my nails?"

We all stared at Charlotte, but Gabe answered. "No baby, tonight, now, you need to go to bed. Maybe tomorrow."

The little girl pouted and was already preparing her objections.

"What if we do them tomorrow, after school? We could have a pamper afternoon," I suggested, thinking a pamper session could be fun for us both.

"Yes, please. Thank you, Carrie."

Charlotte was already up on her feet and kissing us all goodnight.

"I'll be back—" began Gabriel, but I interrupted.

"Or I could, if you two want to chat?" I hoped I wasn't overstepping some mark or treading on Gabriel's toes

Before either man could reply, Charlotte was already telling them goodnight and taking my hand to take me upstairs.

"Thank you," Gabriel called after us, reassuring me that I hadn't done wrong by offering to do bedtime with Charlotte.

****

Seb

Nanny had barely left the room when I turned to Gabe. "Fuck, you have it bad."

Gabe looked at me and said nothing, causing a huge smirk to crack my face. At least he didn't try and deny it.

"I mean, she is hot, like seriously hot, scorching, volcanic lava like hot. In fact, she gets hotter every time I see her. And those legging things, well her arse in them—"

Gabe cut me off. "Shut the fuck up, mate."

I laughed at his discomfort at my observations.

"What have I told you about thinking of her naked?"

I shrugged. There was no point denying it because I would defy any red-blooded man not to think of Nanny naked.

"And those leggings are on at my request, but my reaction to them previously was much the same as yours."

We both grinned.

"So, Christine invited her for Sunday lunch, knowing you and Charlotte would be there?" I admired my friend's mother and her tenacity in facilitating a Sunday rendezvous.

"Yes. It was quite nice, although, old Mags was on good form."

I laughed, having been on the receiving end of Gabe's grandmother and her confused ramblings. "Yeah, Nanny mentioned that she'd confused you for Gramps again."

"More than that. She also told Carrie not to have kids if she didn't want to end up tucking her tits in her pants by the time she was forty."

We both roared at that; me imagining it and Gabe remembering it. I was unsure what I should say, if anything. Not about Nanny's tits, that might tip my friend over the edge, but about her having kids.

"Well, it would be an awful shame if they ended up in her pants..." Yeah, I'd been right, by friend's scowl confirmed I was on rocky ground so moved onto the subject of babies. "Does she see herself having children?"

Gabe looked shocked by my question and the possibility of it. Clearly, he hadn't considered what Nanny might want in the future, from a relationship and as she was currently involved with him...

"I don't know. We haven't discussed that." He looked pensive and quickly seemed to go on the defensive. "But then why would we? I mean we barely know each other, do we? And we're very casual."

I said nothing, didn't know what to say. I was unsure if Gabe believed all his own lines, but I for one wasn't convinced by his protests. They may not have known each other long, but they seemed to know each other pretty well from where I was sitting. And I couldn't risk speaking up on his claim of casual. Maybe he'd forgotten that I saw him in the club when the creepy guy was dancing with her and whispering in her ear. His reaction, his anger and him dragging her off home could have been described as many things, none of them casual.

"Nanny asked about *she who shall not be named*." I hoped it didn't sound like I was telling tales, I wasn't. But Gabe deserved to know what was on Nanny's mind so he could prepare for it.

I waited for his reaction and had expected surprise followed by annoyance and then maybe some apprehension or nervousness. None of it happened. His face remained passive as he uttered five words I hadn't expected.

"I know. She told me."

Nanny really was full of surprises and assuming she'd told him out of a sense of rightness and honesty, he might not be the only one not considering things casual.

"And will you stop calling her Nanny. You make it sound fucking pervy. Her name is Carrie."

"I know what her name is." Unable to resist one final wind-up, I continued, "But she'll always be Nanny to me."

I laughed as my friend flicked me the bird while we waited for Nanny to return.

Chapter Thirty-Eight

Gabriel

"And now, I get you all to myself." I'd just shut the front door after seeing Seb out, Charlotte was fast asleep and that just left me and Carrie. Alone.

"You do," she replied with a crinkle of her nose and a little wink before turning her back on me.

In just a couple of strides I reached her. With my hand on her wrist I pulled her back and spun her to face me. "Angel." One word, her name, my name for her, was all I had to give her, and she took it with a smile and a gentle stroke of her fingers across my cheek then down to my jaw.

I reached up and pulled her hand down, releasing it so I could cup her face and pull it towards mine. Her lips were almost on mine, but not quite.

"Gabe," she whispered.

"Yes?"

Her only reply was to close the final distance so her lips crashed against mine, tasting and teasing them until I retaliated. Quickly and easily I took control of the kiss, accepting the invitation of her open mouth. She grabbed at my arms, her nails beginning to rake the skin of my shoulders before her fingers made their way into my hair. I'm unsure who broke the kiss, but when they did, we were both breathing heavily and noisily.

"Upstairs, now. I need you naked and writhing beneath me." She stared at me for a second; her eyes widened, her pupils dilated and her thighs clenched.

She said nothing but simply turned and began to climb the stairs. I stood and watched her ascent, still unsure whether she had underwear on beneath her ridiculously tight leggings. Seb had been right about how good her arse looked in them and as much as I'd bollocked him for commenting, I had no problem with him noticing. I'd have been seriously concerned for him if he hadn't noticed how fucking amazing my angel looked.

Once at the landing where my room was, Carrie stopped, uncertain as to where we were going. My room. I was going to have her in my bed once more and fall asleep with her there before she went back to her own room later. Much later. The final thought, of her going back to her own room, bothered me. Maybe we should go upstairs to her place and then I would be the one to leave, but somehow that made me feel even worse.

"Gabe," she all but whispered hesitantly.

"In here."

She opened the door and with one hand coming to rest on her hip she walked in ahead of me. There was a single lamp on, illuminating the bed. Before Carrie could say or ask anything else, I was behind her, wrapping my arms around her, skating them up her body until my hands were teasing her gorgeous tits. My lips dropped to her neck that I began to kiss, nip and devour, just like I was going to devour the rest of her.

I had no idea how long we remained that way, but eventually we were on the bed together, her topless and me in just boxers. Her sexy trousers remained on, as I wanted them.

"Baby," she moaned from beneath me.

"What is it, Angel? What do you want?" I was tormenting her. Had been since we got in this room. I wanted her desperation as much as she drove me to mine.

"Please, Gabe, baby," she cried, pressing down against my leg that was wedged between her thighs.

I hadn't touched her beneath her trousers. I was saving it, knowing that if she was naked beneath them that touching her would result in fucking her and I'd wanted this to last. I pulled my knee away and replaced it with my hand that pressed firmly against her. The heat and moisture I felt made my dick twitch and stiffen a little more.

"I can feel you." I allowed my hand to gently move against her, causing her to arch her back off the bed. "You like that?" Her groan was the only response I needed. "What about this?" With two fingers stroking their way back along her length she spread her legs further, allowing me greater access to her. My fingers came to settle where I knew her clit was and pressed against it and then, slowly, too slowly, began to rub her there.

"Fuck, fuck, fuck, Gabe, baby, please, now, anything, please."

I loved when she was stoned on desire like this; her hips thrust, her eyes rolled and her voice became hoarse.

"Anything?" I asked, unsure what I had in mind.

"Yes, anything."

I removed my hands entirely and watched the disappointed expression spread across her face. My grip moved to her waistband. "Let's see what you're hiding under these, then."

Her hips lifted as I slid her final item of clothing down her body and thighs, revealing nothing that wasn't her.

I arched a brow and smiled. "I was right then, naked."

She offered a little shrug that was as cheeky as it was tantalising. Once they were down her legs, I pulled them off completely and threw them behind me. With the tiniest amount of pressure and no words, she spread her legs, revealing her moist, pink folds that glistened.

"You are fucking beautiful, Angel."

She blushed. Lying there, naked with her legs spread and my eyes on her leaking core didn't cause a blush but the accurate description of her being beautiful, that made her blush.

"Touch yourself." I didn't know who was most shocked by that, me or her because I hadn't planned on saying that.

Carrie looked startled initially, but as I gazed down at her hands and then the space between her thighs, she settled, moving one hand down her body until it found her own heat. She first pressed a finger inside her sex, then a second. She gasped as she moved them in and out a few times before dragging them as far as her clit that she circled. Her rhythm picked up and she was close; her breathing, the rise and fall of her chest indicated it as did her eyes that glistened. She gently bit down into her bottom lip, but the shaking and trembling of her inner thighs while her sex contracted around emptiness confirmed it.

"You want a hand?"

I'd already cast my underwear aside and was stroking along the length of my own arousal that was leaking my desire. She nodded and with my free hand I inserted two fingers inside her, two fingers that pumped in and out.

Her pants and breaths became louder and ragged.

"More," she hissed through gritted teeth.

I wasn't entirely sure what more she wanted.

"More, more, like before."

I was still none the wiser and she was dangerously close to coming, we both were, and I wanted to give her everything she wanted and needed.

"Use your thumb," she said, slowing her movements, presumably trying to delay her release.

"My thumb?"

"Put your thumb inside me."

I did exactly as she asked and then what she really wanted became clear.

"Now your fingers…" She panted and let out a little yelp at the end. "Inside, but not there."

Fuck me! She wanted my fingers in her arse while my thumb filled her pussy at the same time that she played with her own clit. I'd done this before and she'd come, had enjoyed it and now there was no doubt just how much she'd enjoyed it.

I said nothing, but I did reach around until I found her puckered hole. With my fingers still moist from her arousal, the first went in easily, the second caused more of a stretch, but she clearly liked that too.

"Take your thumb out. I want you, to feel you." She reached for my dick and held her hand over mine that still had my dick encased within it.

I didn't need telling twice. I eased my thumb out, being careful not to remove my fingers from her behind and thrust inside her, pausing to acclimatise myself before moving. With every thrust I made, she matched me move for move. We worked in perfect synchronicity so that we each aroused the other's body with our own until we were both seconds from release.

"You like this?" I phrased it as a question but the way she squeezed my dick and clenched around my fingers left no room for doubt. "It feels good, doesn't it? Makes you so fucking wet. I can feel how wet you are, Carrie. Fuck."

My words were intended to drive her closer and hopefully lose her mind a little too, but it was having the same effect on me.

Carrie groaned against my ear as I gently bit into the soft flesh of her neck.

"Oh, yeah. You want me to fuck you here?" I flexed my fingers, leaving her in no doubt what I was saying more than asking.

"Yes, fuck, yes, baby, Gabe."

Her words were halted with a scream as she came hard, taking me with her in a series of hisses and gritted teeth that ended with me biting down into her neck far harder than I'd have ever imagined doing.

Chapter Thirty-Nine

Carrie

It was already light when I woke and found Gabriel lying next to me, watching me.

"Morning, Angel." He leaned in and kissed my head.

"Morning." I smiled up at him and stretched, something I regretted as I felt everything ache; muscles, tendons and possibly bones too. "What time is it?" Neither of us put an alarm on having collapsed into an exhausted slumber after the amazing sex we'd shared.

"Six. Just." Gabriel pulled me closer.

"I should go…"

"Yeah, but five more minutes."

I relaxed into his hold, happy for just five more minutes. "Just five though. I'd planned on being back upstairs by now."

"Shhh," he whispered against my hair.

"Last night—" I began but was cut off by Gabriel who finished my sentence for me.

"Was amazing."

"Yeah?" I hated myself for the neediness of the question and yet had asked it anyway. I needed to know that it had been as intense for him as me and I didn't mean physically.

"Yeah. Amazing. Phenomenal. Like nothing I have ever known. Happy now?"

"Sorry. I didn't mean to sound pathetic, but it was a lot, wasn't it?"

He laughed. "It was a lot, yes, but I did say you'd get

everything I'm sure. I blame those legging things of yours."

It was my turn to laugh now. "You really liked them, didn't you?"

"I more than bloody liked them, not that you should wear them outdoors ever again."

I laughed again, he didn't, but I knew he was joking.

"Seb liked them."

I flipped over, startled by Seb's name coming up, especially in relation to my leggings. "What do you mean, Seb liked them? How do you know? What did he say?"

"Calm down. He's a man, he noticed them, noticed you in them and he told me he appreciated them. Or at least appreciated your arse in them."

"Oh my God! I should never have worn them last night. I wore them for you."

I rolled onto my back and threw an arm across my face, hoping to hide my red hue and mortification.

Gabriel laughed as he peeled my arm from over my face. I gazed up at his gorgeous face that smiled down at me.

"I like that you wore them for me."

He leaned in as if he was about to kiss me and as much as I knew I'd respond to him and his kiss, I was sure my five more minutes were up meaning I should get up and return to my own room. If I didn't say or do something to stop him in the next couple of seconds we'd be kissing and touching, and Charlotte would be out of her bed well before I left her father's.

"What the fuck!" Gabriel leapt back and turned my head to the side, unable to take his eyes of my neck. "Sorry..." he began but his voice trailed off.

"What?" I grabbed at my neck where his gaze had been fixed and it felt tender, but as everything else did it wasn't anything out of the ordinary.

I was already leaping from the bed and heading for the bathroom mirror to see what he'd seen. As I gazed at my reflection, Gabriel appeared behind me.

"Sorry," he repeated and looked absolutely horrified at my reflection looking back at us both.

I laughed at his face and the reason for it adding confusion to his horror.

"You've marked me."

"I'm sor—"

I cut him off, neither wanting nor needing yet another apology. "Do not apologise again, please. It's okay, really. It's like being fifteen again with a love bite."

He laughed a little himself now. "I kind of remember biting you, but I never thought it would do that."

"I have no recollection of it, but I'm guessing I was riding the wave of an amazing orgasm at the time."

He nodded, his face morphing into a grin.

"Then thank you." I turned and stretched up, preparing to kiss him, somehow forgetting my need to leave.

"Then you're welcome. Come on, shower," he said, giving me the briefest kiss on the cheek before leading me to the shower.

I got in first while Gabriel grabbed some towels. He was poised to join me when we heard Charlotte's voice call him. She was in the bedroom.

"Hold on, baby," he called back and with a towel wrapped around his waist he went to her. As he reached the door, he looked over his shoulder and mouthed, *sorry*.

I wasn't sure what to do initially, but as I was already in the shower and wet, I quickly got clean, then wrapped in a towel I gathered my things and dashed back up to my own accommodation.

****

By the time I got downstairs, Gabriel had already left for work, leaving Charlotte eating her breakfast while Christine sat opposite her chatting about our night with Uncle Seb.

The little girl was full of how pretty she'd made me and Uncle Seb but had run out of time to do her father's makeover.

"I bet Daddy was disappointed," Christine said, her voice laced with sarcasm.

"Gutted," I added, making us both laugh.

"Maybe Daddy gets the first makeover next time." Christine's suggestion was met with enthusiastic nodding from Charlotte who had just finished her breakfast. "Now let's get you ready for school and then I think Carrie is dropping you off this morning."

"Okay," squealed Charlotte before running back upstairs leaving me and Christine alone.

We moved around each other in silence, a slightly awkward silence. It was unusual as well as uncomfortable because we'd previously enjoyed each other's company, with or without conversation.

Eventually, Christine spoke. "Did you enjoy your evening with Seb?"

I nodded. "He's funny. Good fun. Nice."

She laughed. "It's not a test, Carrie."

I joined in with her laughter. "Sorry. I have no idea where all that came from, but yes, it was a fun evening all round." I smiled as I remembered the evening after Seb had left.

"That's good. I'm glad you all had fun. Gabe doesn't involve and include people very often, not with Charlotte and Seb. He's private, insular, but he's let you in."

I had no clue what to say. Less clue what not to say and then there were my feelings on what my lover's mother had just said.

"He likes you."

Her statement threw me into a state of confusion.

"Seb? Seb likes me?" I shrieked my question and realised my error when Christine laughed, then replied.

"I'm sure Seb does, but I meant my son. Gabriel likes you. A lot, and I am guessing it's mutual."

My mouth dried, as did my eyes that were out on stalks. I had no clue whether I should speak or remain silent. What could I say? I didn't want to lie to her. I liked her and respected her, plus I was unsure if she'd believe any words that disagreed with what she'd said.

She laughed and waved away my inner turmoil and silence. "Carrie, I wasn't asking questions, simply stating what I had observed. Why don't we both take Charlotte to school and on the way back we can stop off for a chat."

I felt my face morph into a horrified expression at the prospect of dissecting everything about me and Gabe with his mother.

Christine laughed again. "I didn't mean we had to chat about anything you didn't want to. Just a chat, a friendly chat, no more."

I laughed myself, slightly embarrassed by my misunderstanding. "Thank you. I'd like that."

"I can't find my shoe," cried Charlotte, appearing in the doorway holding a single school shoe.

****

We sat in a coffee shop about halfway home and having succumb to the temptation of cake, Christine went back to the counter to order more coffee to wash it down.

My phone that was in my pocket, vibrated against me. I pulled it out to find a message from Gabriel.

<Hi, Angel. Sorry I didn't see you before I left this morning, but between keeping Charlotte occupied and keeping my hands off you it seemed like a good idea to head out as soon as I could>

I grinned down at the screen and attempted to compose a reply. On my third attempt I was happy with it.

<Sorry I missed you too. I like the idea of you not keeping your hands off me. Charlotte is safely at school and I am about to have coffee and a huge slice of carrot cake with your mum>

<Are you messaging me about liking my hands on you while you're sat with my mother?!>

I stifled a giggle at his outrage, whether it was genuine or not.

<She's grabbing the coffee while I guard the cake, although she might be on a fishing mission about you, me and touching>

<Please be tactful. Tactful as in don't tell her anything. It's not her business>

I was unsure how I should feel. How I actually felt was irritated, annoyed and hurt. I knew I was a secret he was keeping, but his horror and insistence that his mother shouldn't know, suggested I was more of a dirty secret rather than just a secret.

I made no reply and slid my phone back into my pocket as Christine re-joined me.

Chapter Forty

Gabriel

My phone sat on my desk, silent of any contact from Carrie. What had I said that might have caused her to ignore me? I reasoned that the most likely cause of her silence was my mother; that they were together, and Carrie was being discreet. The last thing I needed was for my mother to become involved in my love life. I wasn't eighteen and Carrie was not the daughter of one of her friends who together with my mother had decided we'd be a good match.

I had put my phone in the drawer when a client arrived for their appointment and when they'd left my phone revealed a message from Seb.

<Thanks for last night. It was nice to get to know Nanny a little better and as always to see Charlotte, oh, and you, I guess. Am I allowed to ask if she was wearing underwear?>

I laughed. My best friend really was a dickhead.

<You're welcome, as always. Stop with the fucking Nanny! And of course you're allowed to ask, but I won't be answering>

<You're no fun. Maybe I'll ask Nanny when I next see her. Are you free for lunch? We could meet>

<Can do 1 if you're free then. But no questions on underwear!>

<See you in the café round the corner and no promises about the questions>

"Dickhead," I muttered before preparing for my next client.

****

It was exactly one o'clock when I arrived at the café, a regular lunchtime haunt for me and Seb. He hadn't yet arrived, so I used the time to contact Carrie. Considering my message remained unanswered I opted to call her.

The phone rang for what felt like forever and then went to voicemail meaning something was wrong or she was ignoring me. Either way, I wasn't happy and when I got home, I would leave her in no doubt about that.

"Am I late or are you early?" Seb's question broke my thoughts and without answering him we both knew it was him who was late, although not by much.

"Usual?" I asked, already preparing to order our usual choices.

His nod was his affirmative response as the waitress appeared at the side of our table.

We chatted for about ten minutes, friendly chat built around 'safe' topics before conversation turned to Carrie, or Nanny as Seb persisted in bloody calling her.

I sighed and ran a hand through my hair as I attempted to put my thoughts into words.

"That bad?" My friend frowned across at me.

"No—yes—maybe."

He laughed and despite myself I joined in.

"Glad we've cleared that up then."

"I don't really know what's happening."

My admission wasn't met with amusement or a smart-arse reply which threw me slightly, but it did make me want to continue and expand.

"I like her, a lot." I released a long breath as I considered what that meant. "She is everything I could want and more, but we don't know each other, do we?"

Seb shook his head. "And yet you do."

"Exactly. It confuses me to feel this comfortable with someone so soon. She's great and I love the time we spend together…"

"But? That sounds like a definite but there."

"I don't know that I am ready for a relationship yet." I shook my head, wondering what to do for the best. Maybe I should never have hired Carrie or maybe just kept things professional. "What if I never am?"

"Fuck, Gabe. Do you want me to be totally honest with you?"

I nodded. Seb and I had always been honest with each other, never pulled punches.

"You have two choices…maybe three. One, call the whole thing off, end it. Two, talk to Carrie and tell her all you can offer is sex and maybe a friendship of sorts, no more. Or, three, you try and make this work. Let things progress and see where you both end up."

He was right. I knew he was and when he lay the options out like that it seemed so simple, an easy choice. It wasn't. Quite the opposite.

"I doubt she'll go with two and I'm not sure I want that either. It seems a bit cold and calculated. She's not a fuck buddy kind of girl."

"Fair enough. You know her better than me, although, if you're going to bag yourself a fuck buddy, they probably don't come any hotter."

I glared across at Seb, for the fuck buddy comment and because he was thinking of Carrie naked. Fucking.

"Calm your tits, Gabe."

He laughed, as did I, and for some reason, I opened up.

"It's confusing me. She's confusing me. I like her a lot. She likes me. Charlotte adores her, but I am scared of fucking it up. Your option number three seems like the best and worst idea in the world at the same time because if I go for it and it doesn't work out…"

"You both end up hurt, as does Charlotte and presumably neither of you could revert back to a strictly professional arrangement, assuming it ever was."

His final comment pulled me up short. He was right. We, Carrie and I had never had a professional relationship. From the day she turned up for her interview I had wanted to strip her bare and fuck her senseless and her attraction had been present all along too. Seb was right, we could never go back to something we never were.

"It could be the best decision ever though."

I stared across at my friend. "Are you counselling me right now?"

He shrugged which was as good as a nod of the head.

"I'm not paying you for it."

He laughed. "You'd do the same for me. You have done the same for me. Now stop stalling. It could be the best decision," he repeated.

"It could. But is it worth the risk? Is it worth risking my daughter's happiness on a chance?"

"You're using Charlotte as a human shield." His words along with his serious expression were an accusation and not one I could deny.

"Well, I can't pretend she isn't a part of this can I? A huge part."

"Of course not. I'd be kicking your arse even harder if you tried. Gabe, I want you to be happy, you and my little princess, but you have to want it for yourself or it won't happen. You also need to be honest with yourself about what and who make you happy."

I nodded, unsure what to say.

"You can't let your past dictate what you do now or for it to shape your future."

I laughed at him now. "That's rich, coming from you."

"I know I'm fucked up, possibly beyond repair, but you're not."

"Maybe." I slumped back in my seat, more confused than ever.

"And if neither of those options float your boat, you're left with number one...call the whole thing off."

That was my least favourite of all my friend's options. My

mind went back to Carrie; from her interview, to her moving in, her pants. I smiled remembering those that were still in my own underwear drawer. How close we'd become, the tension and sexual chemistry that roared between us before we finally gave into it and since. Then there was now, although now involved her ignoring me for no reason I really knew. That had pissed me off. Still was. Despite my reservations, I didn't play games and those who did, riled me. Plus, we'd parted on good terms, even if I did end up missing shower time this morning. Last night had been amazing, better than amazing. I replayed every second of it in my head.

"Fuck!"

Seb looked concerned at my sudden panic.

"Last night, me and Carrie…I don't need to go into details."

His disappointed look made me laugh, briefly, as I went back to my panic.

"It was the best, ever. All I wanted was her. Her and me together in my bed. We were very nearly busted by Charlotte this morning."

"So, you're losing your mind. What did Carrie think about last night?"

"She was pre-occupied and wasn't thinking at all."

My friend grinned now and actually reached over the table to high five me. Not for us almost getting busted by my three-year-old daughter, but for Carrie's inability to think.

"Looks like you have some decisions to make, both of you."

"Yes, it does, doesn't it?"

Chapter Forty-One

Carrie

Apart from ignoring Gabriel's messages and calls, the day had been good. Christine and I had chatted about lots of things including her first meeting with Noel, their courtship and their early family life. Her stories of Gabe as a young boy painted a wonderful picture of a happy, carefree, and sweet little boy who looked a lot like his daughter did now.

There were several attempts by Christine to discuss my past, my life before coming to work for her son. I managed to shut her down at every turn, to move conversation back to topics of my choice. She then began to fish, looking for information on me and Gabe. His words about discretion and us not being any of her business swam around in my head in the worst way possible. As far as I was concerned what he was really saying was, *don't tell her about us because there is nothing to tell. You are nothing.* The inference of his words made me angry, but more than that they'd hurt me.

Charlotte was running around the garden, racing, like she had done that morning at school during her P.E. session. The difference this afternoon was that I was the nearest she had to an opponent. Having run several races, I opted for a break. Christine and I drank tea while Charlotte had milk and cookies.

"Grandma, where's Granny?"

Christine looked up from her phone that she seemed quite preoccupied by.

"She's gone home, sweetheart. Do you remember when we

visited her, and she lived with lots of other people and had all the people to help her?"

Charlotte nodded.

"She stayed with Grandma and Gramps for a while when she was unwell, but now that she's a little better, she's gone home."

Charlotte nodded again while Christine looked as though she'd had a lightbulb moment.

"Would you like to visit Granny?"

"Yes. She's funny." Charlotte giggled, covering her mouth, knowing exactly how naughty Granny was in her funniness.

"Why don't we go this afternoon, later? We could visit Granny and then meet Gramps for some dinner before we bring you home."

"Yes!" She squealed with excitement before rushing to start another race with a call of *Carrie* over her shoulder.

I dutifully followed and raced another race, then another and with the offer of a final lap of the garden and Christine shouting that she was almost ready to go, we set off. Charlotte made the best start but with my legs being longer I could easily have caught her. I did that thing of making it look like a close-run thing by being close on her heels, spurring her on to maintain her lead. She laughed as I got closer and called to her that I was going to win this one. As we neared the end of the lap and approached the open conservatory door something caught my eye. I lost focus and looked up to see Gabriel standing there, watching us with a smile and then my life flashed before my eyes as I tripped over a brick near the edge of the wall that was rushing towards my face. Some kind of self-preservation kicked in as I manoeuvred myself in mid-fall to avoid a lip splitting, nose breaking, black eye inducing collision with the wall, but at the expense of landing on my knees and elbows; the latter grazing along the grass while the former hit a solid piece of ground causing an excruciating crunch that literally knocked me sick.

The next couple of minutes passed in a blur; Charlotte looked worried to death and began to cry, causing Christine to rush from the house. The little girl's tears were the only thing that stopped me from crying. Gabriel was at my side in an instant,

Single Dad

checking me over, trying to help me to my feet. His eyes looked worried and concerned, but his touch was soothing and more assured. Once standing, everything hurt. Glancing down, I was covered in dirt and my trousers were torn at the knees, revealing blood.

"Come on, let's get you cleaned up."

Gabriel led me as far as the conservatory where Christine was ready to leave.

"Is there anything I can do?" she asked.

I shook my head, still determined not to cry.

"It's fine, Mum. I can clean up grazed knees and apply plasters," said Gabriel.

I remembered my earlier irritation with him and thought it might be on the rise again at his attempts to downplay my injuries and the pain I was in, not to mention the damage to my clothing. I was in bloody agony and he had the audacity to make light of it.

"If you're sure?" Christine looked down at Charlotte. "Come on then, sweetheart. Granny is waiting for us to visit and Gramps is already thinking about dinner."

Charlotte laughed but looked at me with concern.

"I'm fine, my little Potty Lottie."

She smiled at my use of her pet name.

"And your dad is going to get me a plaster."

"Okay." She still didn't sound or look sure about leaving.

"Granny will be waiting, and you need to tell her how you won the races at school and home."

She giggled before leaning in to kiss me and Gabe then took her grandma's hand for them both to leave us alone.

The sound of the front door closing signalled that it was just the two of us and in an instant the tension rose between us.

"Take your trousers off."

Gabriel's command threw me. This was not the time for sex. I needed to tell him how pissed off I was with him and why if he hadn't figured that out yet. I watched his back disappear from the room, confusing me even more as I tried to figure out why he was leaving if he wanted sex, not that we would be. Unless he expected me to simply follow him. Well, if he did, he had

210

another thing coming. If he was embarrassed to admit what we had done, that we were kind of involved, then that was fine. It actually wasn't, but if that's what he felt I couldn't argue with it, but that didn't mean I was going to follow him around like a well-trained pet, to be used by him.

I remained seated with no intention of moving or removing clothing.

His reappearance startled me more than his departure, as did the realisation that he had gone to fetch the first aid box and that is why he wanted me to remove my trousers. I flushed at my own inaccurate and judgemental thoughts.

"Angel, take your trousers off. I can't clean you up and make it better whilst you're still dressed."

I flushed crimson now. The idea of him making it better with me undressed caused a sense of arousal that had my nipples stiffening to peaks and the soft folds between my legs moistening.

"Angel—"

His repeated pet name for me was cut off as I leapt to my feet and immediately undid my trousers, regretting the speedy movement that forced my bleeding and grazed knees to straighten. Gabriel's hands came to rest on mine at the waistband and in the most erotic sensation ever, we began to slide my trousers down my legs.

By the time they were past my thighs I let go and allowed my lover to continue undressing me alone. He lowered to his knees, putting his face directly in front of my groin that was covered by a simple white satin brief. With my trousers bunched in his hands, he pushed them as far as my knees.

"This might sting a little," he warned as he continued forcing the fabric down.

I winced and let out a short hiss when the fabric pulled against my abraded skin.

"Good girl."

His commendation sounded as though it could have been directed at Charlotte, but rather than being offended it warmed me, the sentiment and the warmth of it.

"Sit down."

I sat and watched as he pulled my trousers off completely along with my shoes and socks.

"We'll soon have you fixed up and as good as new," he told me, again sounding like the kind and caring father he was.

"Gabe," I whispered, unsure what I intended to say, but knowing this was becoming highly charged with the sexual tension ready to implode in this less than sexy moment.

"Ssh," he said as he opened the first aid box.

"We should talk." The sensation of a cleaning wipe, cold and painful on my knee halted my words.

"I know. We will, that's why I came home a little early. That is why Charlotte is on her way to visit Granny."

That explained the way things had panned out and why Christine had been preoccupied by her phone earlier; Gabe had been making plans. He reached for a plaster to cover my knee.

"So, we can talk, properly, about us and what we're doing here?"

"Yes, but I should warn you, I have no clue what we're doing or what we should do."

I nodded, as clueless as him, although, I knew what I wanted, but without the same responsibilities as him I feared we may be on very different pages.

"Ouch," I cried as he brushed his thumb over the most badly injured of my knees.

He smiled. "You're such a baby."

"Am not." I pouted, making him laugh. "It really hurts."

"I know. It's quite a nasty cut but you'll live."

He covered the injury with the plaster making me squirm and wince before releasing a few moans of pain.

This time he didn't laugh, but with his eyes fixed on mine and somehow darkening he asked, "Do you need me to kiss it better?"

"Yes." My voice was low and husky, needy and desperate suddenly as he lowered his lips to my knee, his eyes still firmly fixed on mine.

The sensation of his lips, gently pressing to my knee sent shudders through my body.

"Better?" His question wasn't as innocent as it first appeared.

We both knew this was my get out or my jump in with both feet.

My response was always going to be the latter. I shook my head. "Here, it hurts here," I told him pointing to the space just above my knee.

He smiled, a wolfish kind of grin as he landed a single kiss to where I'd indicated then stopped. "We should talk, first."

I had a feeling I knew what this talk would involve and I wasn't ready for it, didn't know if I ever would be, so did the opposite of what I should do, as usual, and let out another *ouch* and pointed to the skin a little higher than before.

"And here, it hurts here."

"You want me to kiss it better? Before we talk?"

"Yes, baby."

The final word was barely out before his lips landed again. We both knew in that instant what was going to happen and that talking would be waiting. However, we both also knew that the talking was necessary and would only wait until what we were about to share was over.

Chapter Forty-Two

Gabriel

My kisses had just reached the top of Carrie's inner thigh and any thoughts I had of talking or thoughts she had of her sore knees were gone.

"Better?" I asked and had no way of hiding the grin splitting my face as her hand dropped to her satin underwear that I could already see was moist from her arousal. "Gosh, you really did hurt yourself, didn't you?"

She looked momentarily embarrassed by my words or their meaning that she was feigning the degree of her injury, which she was, but this was now a game that would see her writhing beneath me and calling me baby as she came against my mouth, coating my lips in her sweet nectar.

"I'd better kiss it better then."

"You had," she told me in a whisper as her eyes glazed over.

I planted a single, gentle kiss against her underwear and felt her heat whilst smelling her desire.

"Better?" I asked, my lips still against her underwear, breathing against her, warming her and then I allowed the chill to filter through.

The feel of her shudders made me want to strip her off and fuck her like a wild animal, but that wasn't happening, not yet.

"No."

"No?" I smirked to myself, knowing there was no way a single kiss was going to be enough.

I kissed her again and again before making the kisses longer, involving the use of my tongue to lick across her outer lips. Her groans and moans got louder and louder. I introduced a hand, spreading her lips, opening her for me, but still I left her underwear in place.

"More, more," she chanted.

I was unable to do anything but what she asked for, what she needed. I allowed the fingers of one hand to slip beneath her underwear and stroke along her sodden length. My other hand pulled her underwear to one side so I might kiss her more intimately. My fingers slid inside her and she bucked in response. Her fingers grabbed for my head and tugged on my hair as I drove her to release. The point of my tongue circled her clit at the same time that my fingers found her G-spot. With several strokes inside and out she was riding my hand and falling apart. My eyes moved to her face and if it wasn't the most beautiful sight in the world, I didn't know what was.

We never got any farther than the sofa in the conservatory, potentially giving the neighbours over the back of my house a live action porno to enjoy. Although, they'd need binoculars or a telescope to get a decent view. We'd lay together for some time and as the breeze coming through the still open door caused a chill to wash over our naked bodies we got up and redressed. Me into my trousers and shirt that I left the top couple of buttons undone on and Carrie opted for her pants and t-shirt only as her trousers were probably only good for the bin.

We sat opposite each other, both nursing our own cup of tea, avoiding the discussion we knew was coming.

"You wanted to talk?" Carrie said. She was clearly taking the bull by the horns.

"I think we ought to."

She stared across at me, studied me, possibly believing my words to be pedantic in their insistence that the talk was something I needed rather than wanted. Carrie didn't comment, she simply leaned back into her chair and allowed me to continue.

"This thing between us…it's kind of getting complicated and confusing. I'm getting confused. I like you, a lot, but I don't know what we're doing or where we're going with this."

"I see."

Two words, that was it. No screaming or shouting, just two words spoken with an unnerving flatness. Those two words suggested she saw nothing.

"We could call the whole thing off and revert to how we were originally."

We both laughed at that because the sexual tension and sizzling chemistry had been there since day one and having had her, there was no way I could simply go back to that, as if turning a switch.

"Okay, maybe not. We could agree to no strings attached fun."

She scowled at that suggestion but did at least speak. "As in, you fuck me when it's convenient but beyond that there is nothing?"

Not how I would have put it and yet I couldn't exactly dispute it. "Okay, maybe not." I repeated my previous answer. "That leaves us with the option to explore this and see where it goes, but I don't know that I'm ready for that—"

Carrie cut me off and I don't think I have ever seen anyone look quite so angry or indeed hurt.

"Well, let's just forget about it then. You are not the only one in this and yet this is all on your terms; your options, what you are ready for or not. I would have been happy to test the waters and still kept it under wraps a little because believe it or not, I am not ready for the full exploration of it. You clearly have some baggage to work through and before you remind me that Charlotte is your priority, I should warn you that she is mine too and I also carry my own baggage. So, let me make this clear for you; we are doing none of your options. I am putting the brakes on this and we should both take some time to think about what we do want. If you decide you don't want any more than a bit on the side then you should find yourself one, but it won't be me. Oh, and you made me feel more of a whore this morning by telling me not to say anything to your mother than those bitchy mums ever could have. I don't mind us keeping secrets from the world until we know what this is, but I refuse to be treated or made to feel I'm dirty."

She got to her feet in something of a stagger and winced as she straightened her knees.

"Carrie, Angel—"

She cut me off again.

"No. I am not Angel. I deserve to be more than your paid whore."

Her voice broke a little and I felt a stab to my heart as tears began to fill her eyes.

"I liked you Gabe, really liked you, like maybe kind of loved you and that's not easy for me to admit to and you made me feel shitty about that and myself. Maybe that's the problem when someone makes you feel so amazing, they also have the ability to make you feel like nothing too. I'm going upstairs. I will see you in the morning."

I nodded. "Carrie, I like you too and I never meant to make you feel bad about anything, never."

She made no reply but gave me the tiniest of nods.

"How long do you want to think about things? Overnight? A couple of days?"

A shrug was her response now. "I don't know. Let's give it a couple of weeks and see how things are then."

She turned to walk away.

"I'm sorry, but there are things about me you don't know."

She spun sharply. "Well, we never did much talking, did we? In a couple of weeks we might need to think about talking some more. Goodnight, Mr Caldwell."

Fuck, we were back to formal titles. Or at least she was. "Goodnight, Miss Webber." No, we both were.

Chapter Forty-Three

Carrie

The following morning, I was barely able to function. I was tired. Beyond tired having slept very little after my discussion with Gabriel. Mr Caldwell. This was all a big mess and proof that shagging your boss, who also provided a roof over your head, was a really bad idea.

I stared in the bathroom mirror. My eyes glistened with yet more tears that for now were unshed. How many tears could I cry for this man? Another tear breached the dam and I realised I wasn't all cried out yet. My nose looked like I was going for a Rudolf the Red Nosed Reindeer look. I briefly wondered why snot accompanied tears. It was unnecessary in terms of making one more unattractive because the eyes and sad expression were more than enough to convey that emotion.

I dragged a brush through my hair and tied it back as a song came on the radio that played in my bedroom. And why did that happen when you were sad? All the songs you heard were sad or seemed to sum up the shit you were going through. This one was no different. There were lines about needing to hate you to love me and losing you to find me. Shit! I really hoped that was the case and once I'd found myself and loved me, I might find a way back to having and loving Gabriel Caldwell too. I shook my head and laughed at my own foolishness. This was over and I just needed to get on with my life.

Nothing and nobody was capable of sorting this mess.

Dressed in baggy jeans, to avoid any pressure on my

throbbing knee, and a t-shirt, I headed downstairs to find Christine and Charlotte sharing a laugh.

"Morning." I called as cheerily as I could muster.

Charlotte ran towards me, as happy and excited as ever. Christine, however, looked across at me with a frown and a glint of concern in her eyes.

"Tea?" she asked, already grabbing a cup and switching the kettle on.

"I probably don't have time." I glanced at the clock and saw that by the time Charlotte was dressed and her belongings had been got together we'd need to leave.

"Of course, you do. Look, why don't you stay here. I'll take Charlotte in the car and when I come back, we can have a chat."

I rather rudely rolled my eyes. Christine couldn't miss it but chose to ignore it.

"I can bring cake back, if you fancy it?"

"Thanks." I had no clue what else, if anything, I could say.

"Carrie, I'm offering cake, coffee and a chat, no more. You look distracted as did Gabriel before he went to work and I'd guess that neither of you have slept much, if at all."

I nodded and repeated my earlier thanks. She was being nice, and she had done nothing for me to reject her friendship, even if I was sure I was all chatted out.

****

I picked at my cake and sipped my coffee slowly while Christine chatted away. I had no clue what she thought was wrong with me. Did she suspect that things were going on between me and her son? Had she figured that things had soured between me and Gabriel and there no longer was a me and him? Maybe she had no inclination that anything had ever been between us and she was edging towards me having boyfriend troubles with someone else or even family problems.

"Carrie, I'm worried about you." She had finally tired of skirting around things.

"There's no need." I wanted to reassure her but without coming straight out and lying to her face.

"I disagree." She held my eyes with a stern expression that reminded me of Gabriel.

Immediately, with thoughts of him in my head and a reminder of him looking straight at me, I struggled to contain my tears.

"It appears that my worry was well placed, as it is where my son is concerned. I don't know what has happened between you and I don't need to, unless you need to talk, but I can see that you're both hurting."

"I don't know what to say to you." My admission was honest and if we were going to talk, I'd feel much better with her driving it.

"What if I wasn't Gabriel's mother?"

"But you are."

She smiled and gave a little shrug. "Guilty as charged. He likes you, Carrie. There has been nobody serious since Charlotte's mother."

I didn't point out that we hadn't been serious, not really. We'd been serious enough to have lots of hot sex, but not serious enough to come out as a couple and certainly not serious enough for him to tell her about us.

"What did he tell you?"

"Nothing. Absolutely nothing, but I have eyes and he's my son and I know my boy."

"Oh." My lack of words seemed to amuse Christine. Her laugh confirmed it.

"Shall I tell you what I see, as you seem to be struggling for vocabulary right now?"

I smiled a weak and nervous smile at what she might see.

"My boy loves you and you love him, that much is clear. But it's not that simple, is it?"

I prepared to answer, but to say what? I did love Gabe, although I was less certain that it was mutual. It seemed her question was rhetorical as she continued.

"He has Charlotte to consider and the fact your job is to take care of her complicates things, as does the fact that she adores you. Her and the rest of the family, including Seb. Hmmm…"

She seems to ponder the part about Seb. Still I remain silent.

"He could be a great ally in this."

I was clueless as to what *this* was.

"Gabriel is stubborn. He gets that from me, and I got it from my father, so I'll apologise in advance. He is also scared. Charlotte's mother hurt him badly…I can't, I won't go into that. Gabriel needs to tell you that, not me. He closed off after her as far as women and relationships, until you." She smiled. "I saw it from that first day when you came for your interview. Anyway, he has fallen for you hard and now he is flailing and making a pig's ear of it. So, we need to help him see what is in front of him and give him the push to take the final leap of faith with you."

"I don't know…this could backfire. I don't want to force him to want me and not be ashamed of me. I want him to want me and to do this because it's what he wants."

Christine shook her head. "He does want you and he isn't ashamed of you, Carrie. He's scared. And then there's you."

I stared at her and then, a little outraged at the inference that I could be in the wrong here, I responded in a slightly high-pitched voice. "Me?"

"Yes, you. You're as closed as he is. Apart from the friends you've made here you don't appear to have anyone, family, friends, former colleagues. I can count on one hand the number of times you've answered your phone. You have no active social media either. I've looked. Now, you could make my son incredibly happy and vice versa, but not if we all keep pissing around, so, are we doing this or not? Do you want to be with Gabriel and accept my help? Oh, stubbornness comes from my dad, the language from my mother."

I stared at the woman before me and laughed. She really was something else and seemed to think she had all the answers here. Maybe she did. I had no room to judge or criticise because me, well, I had zero answers.

"Okay, what did you have in mind."

Her response to that was the biggest grin I had ever seen and suddenly I realised her son was a lot like her, so maybe, just maybe this would work out for the best and if not I had nothing to lose, did I?

Chapter Forty-Four

Gabriel

I was like a bear with a sore head and by two o'clock I had no clue how I was feeling; sad, lost, angry, frustrated…all of the above?

My last appointment for the day was a couple who had been going through a rough patch. They'd each lost a parent and then one of their children had died from leukaemia, leaving them heartbroken. Maybe just broken. They had two other children they were trying to support through the loss of a sibling whilst dealing with their own loss and grief. They seemed, on the face of it, to be managing and they were, kind of, but at the expense of their relationship with each other.

I welcomed them in and could immediately sense that they hadn't had a good week.

By the end of their visit I felt like shit. They were going through the toughest of times and although they had my undivided attention and professional advice and guidance all I had in my head was Carrie.

I gave them a couple of targets and goals to work on over the next week, including spending ten minutes each day talking about themselves; their thoughts, feelings, memories, aspirations, anything that allowed them to connect on a level that wasn't connected to their children, but just them.

They looked relieved when they left my office and a little lighter, whereas I felt a little heavier.

I wrote up some notes and just as I finished, I got a message off Seb, who had also finished for the day.

With a couple of texts back and forth we agreed to meet for coffee rather than beer.

I entered the coffee shop near his office and found him chatting up one of the waitresses. Unable to resist scuppering his plans for the pretty little blonde, I leaned in and kissed him on the cheek.

"Sorry, sweetheart. Things took a little longer to wrap up than I was expecting."

My friend glared at me as I took the seat opposite him and reached across to take his hand in mine. The waitress took my order for coffee and scurried away while Seb pulled his hand free of mine.

"You bastard! You really are an absolute tool." He fumed, making me laugh.

"She was too young for you anyway. You'd have broken her heart."

He knew I was right. "Hmmm, maybe. You're still a dickhead though."

"You're welcome."

"What's up then?" he asked, cocking his head to the side as he watched my expression drop.

"Three fucking guesses."

"Nanny."

"Give the man a prize."

"Tell Uncle Seb."

I did. I told him everything there was to know. All that had happened since we'd last spoken and how I had somehow fucked it all up and lost Carrie.

"I'm guessing me telling you that you're an idiot is unnecessary?"

"Yup."

"Is now a good time to ask if you'd be pissed if I asked her out?"

"You make one move in her direction and I will fucking kill you." I was seething, not that I believed he ever would ever ask her out, but still.

"It's too soon then."

"Seb." His name was a warning.

"Okay." He held his hands up. "I don't need to ask if you want her back."

"It's a fucking mess. A mess I have made. I don't blame her for sacking me off. In fact, I respect it."

"So, what are you going to do to get Nanny back?"

"Nothing," I replied to a stunned looking Seb.

"What the fuck is the matter with you? You like her. You hate that you're not together and you're going to do sweet FA to get her back."

"She deserves better. She wants someone who will put her first, take her out on dates, to call her his girlfriend and maybe even get married and have babies. That's not me."

"Isn't it?"

"You know it's not," I snapped angrily, knowing my friend was deliberately trying to goad me.

"It used to be." He was like a dog with a fucking bone.

"And look where that got me."

I got to my feet and prepared to leave. Before I could bid him any kind of goodbye his phone rang. Seb looked down at it and smiled.

"Ooh, my favourite beautiful, older woman."

He winked, like the dick he was, but it did make me smile.

I gave him a wave as I turned to leave and laughed as I heard him answer the call with the words, "And to what do I owe this pleasure you sexy little vixen?"

****

My arrival home startled both my mother and Carrie, Charlotte not so much. While my daughter leapt into my arms, my mother welcomed me with a warm smile, but Carrie, she looked sad and uncomfortable.

"You're back early, darling," my mother said before speculating aloud as to the possible reason for that. "Are you unwell? You don't look yourself, does he, Carrie? Gabriel looks out of sorts—"

I cut her off. "Mum, I am fine, but was done for the day. You can go home if you want."

My mother shook her head. "I had said I would stay and

cover for Carrie. She's out with friends tonight."

I glared at my daughter's nanny who at least had the decency to hang her head at my mother's revelation.

"Well, unfortunately, Mother, it is Miss Webber I pay until five thirty, not you, so she'll need to make her social life plans for outside of her working hours."

With no further words exchanged, I stormed from the room, heading for my office, glaring at Carrie as I passed her. I slammed the office door behind me.

"Fuck! Bastard! Bollocks!" I kicked my desk for good measure.

How the fuck was I going to do this if the idea of her going out with friends sent me into a fucking furious meltdown? My brain was pulsing inside my skull, I was certain of it. My head throbbed and I swear my eyes were bulging. Who was she meeting and where were they going? Was it a date? Was fuckboy, Toby, going to be there? He'd better not be, or my brain would be exploding before the night was out, although, how was I going to know where she was or who with?

"Shit, shit, fucking shit!" I snarled, slumping into my chair. "And this is why she should have remained off limits." I wasn't even convincing myself of my ability to have stayed away from her.

A text landed in my inbox, Seb.

<Sorry about earlier, mate. You know I only want to help. Maybe this is for the best, you and Nanny ending it now if you don't really want her to be yours and to commit to all of the things she needs>

His message made me feel sick, the reality of her not being mine. The nightmare of her being someone else's was a bigger worry. It wasn't that I didn't want her, I did, but I couldn't give her what she needed, could I?

I quickly text back a 'thanks' then threw my head onto the desktop with a hard thud and lay there like a teenager nursing his first broken heart. But I wasn't a teenager and I wasn't nursing a broken heart. I refused to. I just needed to get back to normal. Back to who I was before Miss Webber arrived and rocked my world. If only it were that easy.

Chapter Forty-Five

Carrie

I went back upstairs at exactly five thirty, having made a point of telling Mr Caldwell what time it was. Arsehole.

This would have been so much easier if I could truly hate him, but I couldn't. Even when I was mad at him, I remembered the person behind the arsehole, the one I really, really liked... loved.

"Fuck it!" I snapped at my reflection.

What was I doing? This was potentially a crazy game I was playing. One I was almost guaranteed to be on the losing end of. Christine knew her son better than anyone, I accepted that. However, she knew him as a boy, young man and then an adult, but still in his role as her son, not as a man, a boyfriend, lover and that is where this might go completely pear-shaped. If I followed her advice and did what she suggested, and my former lover didn't react as her son was supposed to, I was fucked in all the wrong ways.

I was dressed casually in jeans, heeled boots, but had dressed the outfit up with a flowing, flowery blouse. Before I backed out completely, I grabbed my bag and jacket, then headed for the door.

It felt as though I was sneaking out as I scurried around the side of the house and made my way down the road. Part of me hoped Gabe wouldn't see me and yet I needed him to, to know, or at least to believe that I wasn't shutting myself away, moping and nursing my broken heart. He needed to think I had taken his words seriously and was moving on with my life, without him.

When I turned the corner into the next street I waved and offered a small relieved smile to Christine who was waiting for me.

"Seb is meeting us there," she told me as I got in beside her.

"Christine—" I began, nerves kicking in and turning my stomach over and over until I thought I might be sick.

Christine was in full flow and cut me off in an instant. "Carrie, do you love Gabriel?"

"I, erm…"

"Simple question. Yes or no."

She was seriously fucking determined and at that second reminded me a lot of her son and just like with him I had no option but to be honest. "I do, yes."

"Then this is what we need to do. You have nothing to lose here."

"Yeah, except my home and job and any chance of finding a way forward with him."

She frowned across at me and shook her head. "Trust me. He needs a shove and if we play this right you will keep all the things you fear losing and more besides.

I nodded, still uncertain about her plan or the possible outcomes from going along with it.

"If this goes wrong and he thinks I don't care." I sniffed back tears at the mere thought of it.

"Carrie, he knows you care, he knows he cares, but he's not ready to admit it yet, so, we need to give him a little push."

I nodded, not that I was convinced, but I wasn't exactly overrun with my own ideas, was I?

****

Christine spotted Seb as we entered the bar and almost leaving me behind, she made a beeline for him. He stood to greet her warmly then leaned in to hug me.

"Nanny," he said with a cheeky smile that did make me laugh.

"Are you ever letting that go?"

"God, no, if nothing else, it pisses Gabe off." He laughed loudly as we ordered drinks.

Seb and Christine chatted until our drinks arrived and then it was Seb who took the bull by the horns.

"Right, ladies, tell me what you're thinking."

"I'm thinking this is madness," I said, earning a smack on the wrist from Christine.

"Nonsense. Seb, you know Gabe better than anyone and you and I know how much Carrie means to him."

He nodded.

"And that he's stubborn and scared and is flailing."

Seb nodded again.

"And that without some help he stands a good chance of screwing this all up."

Seb nodded, yet again.

"And we're his best chance at being able to help him."

"Agreed." At least Seb had moved on from simply nodding now. "But I don't know that your idea on how to help him and mine will match."

I hadn't yet been involved in this conversation. I hadn't even been sure of the wisdom of this, but now, I was desperate for Seb to agree to help us. To help me get Gabe to reconsider his future with me.

"Ladies, tell me what you're thinking, and we can take it from there."

Christine immediately swung into action, discussing her plans for me being seen to be moving on and ensuring that Gabe became aware of it via her friendship with me.

Seb listened to everything; her ideas, plans and thoughts, and then he paused, leaving silence hanging over us.

We looked at each other, then to Seb and back at each other before he spoke.

"Making Gabe jealous could be risky. He has issues with opening up and trusting so if you appear to be moving on too soon…"

"Let's just abandon this. I don't want to hurt him."

Seb looked across and smiled at me while Christine was already muttering her objections.

"I didn't say it couldn't work and the fact you want to love him not hurt him reassures me."

"So, you're in?" asked Christine, already applauding.

Seb and I both laughed at her clapping.

"I need to think about this. The best way to make it work, without hurting either of you any further."

"Thank you, both. I might just pop to the ladies."

I was already on my feet and heading for the bathroom.

The bathroom was empty, giving me a few seconds of silence to really question if this was the best thing to do, attempting to manipulate a relationship with Gabe. I had no answer, but then I also knew that I couldn't carry on as if we'd never happened.

I was standing at the sink, washing my hands when the door opened, revealing Henry's mum.

"Well, well, well, if it isn't little Miss Gold-Digger."

"So says Mrs Desperate."

I made to move past her, but she sidestepped, blocking my path. "Watch your back because you will fuck up, and when you do? I will be there to ensure the good doctor knows every dirty, stinking detail."

She openly sneered at me before unblocking my path.

"Off you go then. Happy whoring."

"Send my regards to Mr Unfortunate, sorry, I mean, your husband."

I walked away, refusing to be drawn into a slanging match or to defend myself against this awful fucking woman. This plan, whatever it ended up looking like needed to work or else this bitch would certainly witness my heartbreak and if she had her way, she'd contribute to it too.

Chapter Forty-Six

Gabriel

Charlotte was chattering away as I ate breakfast opposite her, but my mind was all over the place and all those places had the common link of Carrie.

I saw her leave the house last night and although dressed casually in jeans, she looked amazing, as she always did. I wanted to march out of the house and stop her, to drag her back inside with me. I didn't. I had no right to want such things, never mind do them. I knew I'd hurt her. My suggestions for how to conduct our relationship had hurt her. Fuck! They'd hurt me too, but maybe I deserved it. She didn't and I had no doubt that long term I would have hurt her worse than I already had, so this was for the best. At least that's what I told myself. I just hoped I might start to believe it and soon.

The scent filling my nose told me Carrie was near. My mouth dried, my skin prickled and every hair on my body raised with awareness of her. She entered and I may have forgotten to breathe. She looked amazing, although, as I'd already told myself, she always did. Her body was covered in a modest, but close-fitting grey t-shirt and those skin-tight fucking legging things.

"I thought we might pop to mini-me yoga later, if that's okay, Mr Caldwell."

I stared at her, my mouth hung open like a horny dog or a teenage boy with a crush. Her words registered and I couldn't stop myself from thinking of her in those positions, bent and open, subtle and flexible. My thoughts were pure filth but me and now my stiffening dick were incapable of thinking of anything else until she spoke again.

"Mr Caldwell." She repeated her formal address and my heart sank at the same second my dick became flaccid. I didn't want her to call me Mr Caldwell unless she was teasing. I wanted her to still call me Gabriel, Gabe, baby, but she didn't, was unlikely to ever again and it was all my own fault for being a fool, for fucking it up and for being scared.

"Of course," I replied, trying to keep any hint of emotion from my voice but I probably just came across as curt. "I'm sure you'll have a lovely time, both of you."

Carrie stared across at me while Charlotte promised to tell me all about it later. My daughter rushed from the room leaving us alone with an increasingly thickening atmosphere.

"Could we be friends?" I had no idea those words would leave my mouth, but they had.

She looked dumbstruck but managed a shrug.

"I miss you." More words I hadn't planned on uttering.

Her eyes filled with tears and I knew I was being unfair. She didn't want me as her friend, and I was somehow trying to hang onto her in any capacity I could. Any capacity that would allow me to know what she was doing, when and who with, like last night.

I prepared to backtrack, to offer her a get out and apologise when her phone sprang into life. She looked down at it and smiled. Her smile infuriated me more than I ever imagined it might. She neither wanted nor needed me as a friend, she'd moved on and while half of me was incensed, the other half, maybe the bigger half was heartbroken.

Grabbing my things for work, I looked at her again. "I'm glad you enjoyed your night out last night."

With a slam of the door I was gone, acting like the injured party, which I knew I wasn't, and like a dick I got into my car, slammed the door to that too and punched the steering wheel. I had been so devastated and blinded by my fury that I hadn't even kissed my daughter goodbye. Never mind that, I hadn't even said goodbye.

I pulled my phone out. I was a prick, an arsehole and a lot more besides. I knew that, but the one thing I wasn't was a bad father. I composed a quick message.

<Could you please tell Charlotte I had to leave in a hurry and that I am sorry I didn't say goodbye and kiss her before I left? Tell her to have a lovely time at mini-me yoga and that I will see her later. Please tell her I love her and that I sent a kiss x>

Her reply came as I was about to pull away.

<Of course. She sends her love and many kisses back xxxxxxxxx She can't wait to tell you all about yoga and says to have a good day>

I smiled at that, albeit briefly. I would be a good father, always, and would not let my baby girl down, not ever. I considered the mini-me yoga and thought that all the other children were likely to be there with their mothers. I wondered if the people there would assume Carrie was Charlotte's mother. There was no doubt that she could be, was old enough to be and they had similar colouring I supposed. There was an occasion where a girl Seb was seeing had been mistaken for Charlotte's mother at a friend's wedding and I had been bothered by it because my daughter didn't have a mother, and yet, the idea of people seeing Carrie and Charlotte together…it didn't bother me in the slightest, quite the opposite.

****

At almost one o'clock I was considering lunch plans when there was a knock at my door. With a summons to enter I was surprised to find Seb filling the doorway. He was carrying a bag from a nearby takeaway.

"I phoned earlier and was told you were busy until now so I thought we could have an unhealthy lunch together."

I viewed him with suspicion. We didn't really do this kind of thing.

"Is this an intervention you're staging?"

He laughed, entered and sat opposite me. "Do you think you need an intervention?"

"I need something," I admitted, but wasn't ready to admit what that was.

He spread the food out and then added dips, sauces and drinks. "How are things at home?"

I was startled by that question. I had expected him to probe my admission of needing something.

"Weird."

He leaned back and gave me his best, 'go on' expression. I laughed. "Psychologists, counsellors, therapists, analysts and psychiatrists should never be friends with each other."

"And yet here we are." He repeated his 'go on' expression.

I told him about my morning at home and how Carrie had clearly moved on already. For the first time I thought that maybe what we'd had might not have meant as much to her as me if she'd moved on so quickly, but I knew it had.

"Yoga?"

I stared, maybe more glared at him. "Really? Is that what you're focusing on here?"

"Sorry. It's those pants. Did she say she'd moved on?"

"No, but she smiled at her phone."

"Clearly she's ready to accept a proposal then."

It sounded ridiculous when he put it like that. I sounded ridiculous.

"Maybe she's making the most of her time, not wanting to stay home alone and brood so is seeing her group of friends."

That sounded more plausible.

"Maybe."

"If she is going to live in your house and work for you, you'll need to find a way to make this work."

"What do you suggest?" I wasn't sure if Seb was going to respond, if he had anything in terms of an idea or plan.

"Be her friend. Strip it back to Carrie and Gabe again, talk and laugh and maybe get to know each other."

"I know her," I said, thinking that I really did know every inch of her.

"Not what I meant. Where is she from, what groups does she

like, has she got siblings, food likes and dislikes, the normal stuff. Maybe you rushed things."

He might have a point, although… "Wasn't it you who encouraged me to drag her out of the club that night?"

"Yes, and that worked for a while, didn't it? But those stupid feelings got involved…soppy, happy, endorphin fuelled feelings and fear, too, for you both I'd guess. So, remove those and maybe all is not lost."

"I can't do a serious relationship with her, with anyone. This isn't going to be romance, love, paint charts and picking out soft furnishings."

"Maybe not, but then you were never going to fuck her either."

I threw a handful of fries at him then flipped him off, refusing to acknowledge that his idea might be a good one, so long as I could keep my desire under control and contain my jealousy.

Chapter Forty-Seven

Carrie

My day was proving to be surprisingly pleasant. After dropping Charlotte at school, I walked home via the park and was thrilled to find Bea with the children she worked with. I grabbed us coffee from the nearby café and together we watched the children playing while chatting.

"How have you been? You haven't been around much."

I nodded, unable to dispute her words. "I'm okay. Things are just a bit complicated."

"You boyfr— boss?"

She looked awkward as she stammered between Gabriel's titles. It wasn't funny and yet it was. I laughed and nodded my head.

"Sorry."

I laughed again, at her apology this time. "No need. It's complicated, as I say…we're okay, I think." I had no idea if we were okay or if we ever would be again, but she didn't need to know that or anything else, including Seb and Christine's involvement in patching things up, if that was possible.

"We could go out if you fancy?"

"I'd love to. I've missed you."

She grinned. "Me too." She leapt up, rushing to where the children were attempting to go down the slide standing.

"I'll leave you to it," I called and waved as I left the play area. "Text me when you know what you're up to."

I went home and tidied the house of Charlotte's mess before

dashing upstairs to tidy my own.

With a cup of tea made I settled in front of the TV with a gossip magazine. I was halfway through an article I didn't believe about a married couple who presented together being on the verge of divorce when my phone rang. Seb.

I threw the magazine aside and answered on the second ring.

"Good morning, Nanny. I just wanted to check in and see how things are."

I explained about mine and Gabriel's morning and how it had ended and then told him I was planning to see Bea, maybe in a group and most likely at the weekend. He in turn told me that he was going to lunch with Gabe, although he didn't know that yet and once he had spoken to his friend he would make a final decision on whether he wanted and was willing to be involved with mine and Christine's plan.

"Okay," I told him and then with concern for his friendship expressed some reservations. "Seb, I don't want to cause a problem for you, nor you and Gabe so will completely understand if you want no part of this, or if you tell him what's going on."

"Oh, Nanny, you are going to make this impossible for me to say no to if you keep showing me how much you want to protect my friend. I will call you later or drop you a text and we can take it from there. Sorry, I have to go, Christine is calling me, again."

He hung up and I laughed at Christine's tenacity in her mission to get me and Gabe together again.

****

With Charlotte changed into her leggings and vest top we made our way to the sports centre for mini-me yoga. She chatted excitedly as we got our mats and lined up our water bottles. I took my shoes off and placed them behind me, laughing as one of Charlotte's flew past my ear.

"Someone's excited," laughed the instructor.

I turned and nodded. "First timer," I told him. "Charlotte, not me."

I didn't know this instructor. The session I came to was run by a lovely lady called Karen. She was well over fifty but had a body and the flexibility of someone thirty years younger. She inspired me to do yoga more frequently.

"Well, Charlotte, it's always lovely to welcome a newbie. I hope you and Mummy have fun."

He left us before either of us could correct his error. Charlotte looked at me and giggled, causing a peal of laughter to rise in me.

For the next thirty minutes or so I had the best or times; Charlotte and I worked individually and together, bending ourselves into all kinds of positions, some more easily than others. I had a fairly decent downward facing dog on me, but as Charlotte perfected her own, I couldn't help but be impressed by it.

I was just about to commend her on it when the loudest and longest fart rang around us. We both laughed, as did many others, but my own laughter and that of Charlotte saw us shedding tears as I realised the breaking of wind had come from her.

After lunch Charlotte flaked out on the sofa. This school life was beginning to take its toll. I wondered if it was too much too soon, but despite the yoga instructor, Rowan, mistaking my role in her life, it wasn't my place to decide that. I watched her sleeping peacefully and noticed a similarity between her and her father, reminding me that I missed him. Not just the sex, but being with him, talking and laughing with him, seeing him.

My phone's text alert made me jump, but I quickly smiled when I saw a message from Seb.

<Okay, I'll help, but we do this my way or I am out>

<Thank you. I appreciate it>

<Don't thank me yet, Nanny. This could still go horribly wrong>

I knew he was right, but I still couldn't hide the grin splitting my face. I wanted Gabe back in my life and this might be the only chance to do it.

****

"But can we?"

"Charlotte," I began but the little girl was already cutting me off.

"Not all of it, just a bit."

"Now?" I asked, knowing Charlotte was like any other three-year-old and now was the only timeframe she worked to.

"Yes, please." She giggled, confirming that now was her only reference of time.

"Will I get any peace until I say yes?"

"Hell, no!"

I stared at her use of that phrase.

"Is that naughty, like fuc—"

"Yes, no!" I cut her off before she added the final letter of her curse. "Maybe hell no isn't naughty like the other bad words but it's kind of rude."

She nodded. "Sorry. So, can we?"

"Fine."

Charlotte didn't have her own yoga mat, but she did have some non-slip foam pieces that fitted together like a jigsaw. We put enough together that it worked as a mat for us both and side by side we began to do some stretches. After about ten minutes, Charlotte wanted to try downward facing dog. We both assumed the position and held it for a little while. I demonstrated the breathing and Charlotte copied. As we remained in the pose, I remembered Charlotte's earlier and quite common problem for yoga participants of wind.

I blew the loudest and longest raspberry I could until we both fell over laughing. She lay on her back in the middle of the mat. I got up onto all fours and leaned over her, my face hovering over her bared belly courtesy of her t-shirt that had ridden up and proceeded to blow raspberries all over her belly. She squealed and screamed and roared with laughter until she could barely breathe.

"Carrie, Carrie," she cried, pleading for me to stop. I prepared to pull away when she continued to call to me. "No more. Mummy."

The world stopped, for me at least.

I leaned back, unsure what to say or do and then we both heard a voice behind us. "And what is going on here?"

Never mind Mummy, Daddy was home, and I was shitting myself.

Chapter Forty-Eight

Gabriel

The sight that greeted me when I got home was one I would never forget. It was the glorious sight of Carrie bent over in those positively pornographic leggings that clung to everything and yet showed nothing. They were bewitchment at its best. She held the pose she was in, one I knew was a downward facing dog, and fuck me if the word doggy wasn't screaming in my head. The idea of standing behind her, pulling her tight pants down to reveal her glorious arse before sliding inside her and fucking her hard was in my head and wouldn't be shifted anytime soon. Maybe not until me, my hand, her underwear and my shower had a date tonight. Even then, I doubted I would ever free myself of this image.

I glanced from Carrie and turned my attention to my daughter which was a great diversion tactic from my arousal and desire. They looked amazing together and the way Charlotte mirrored Carrie's breathing and pose tugged at my heart strings.

Carrie was proving, along with my mother, to be my daughter's greatest female role models. Her nanny was proving to be a greater one in terms of impact she was having. Possibly because of her younger years and the fact that her whole role here with Charlotte was as a caregiver. A surrogate mother. Fuck! All the lines were blurring here.

My deep and potentially disturbing thoughts were shattered when Carrie began to make the loudest raspberry I have ever heard. That was followed by my favourite sound in the world,

Charlotte roaring with laughter. Carrie's laughter merged with my daughter's and they fell into a heap together.

My heart swelled at that sound and the sight of the two of them together. Carrie got up onto all fours...I would not make this an X-rated moment. With her face hovering over Charlotte's belly that was visible I watched on as she began to blow dozens and dozens of raspberries over the surface of my little girl's belly. Her laughter got deeper and more raucous until she was begging and pleading for Carrie to stop her raspberry blowing assault.

I could see that she was already slowing down and retreating when Charlotte called out to her.

"Carrie, Carrie," she pleaded between squeals.

Carrie seemed to be going in for maybe one final blow when my daughter implored her with two more words. "No more."

I prepared to interrupt right there and then. I may have even had the words *and what is going on here* in my head when Charlotte added one more word that blew the wind from my sails.

"Mummy."

The words I'd thought may have been in my head left my mouth while Carrie looked like she wanted to be sick and I didn't know whether my heart broke a little more or if it was somehow being mended.

Charlotte breathlessly sprang from the floor and ran towards me.

"Daddy. I do yoga now."

"I saw and you are brilliant. I don't think I've ever seen a better downward facing dog."

My daughter giggled and leaned in for a kiss.

"Carrie is really good and very bendy," she told me.

I laughed.

Carrie blushed when I risked a look at her with one eyebrow raised, both of us knowing my first-hand knowledge of just how bendy she was.

"The man said she's fucksable."

I could only imagine what the man, whoever the man was had said about my...about Carrie.

She finally found her voice. "Flexible. He, the yoga instructor, said I was flexible."

"Ah." The relief I felt was immense.

"I'll tidy this away and then I'll be off," Carrie said, gesturing to the foam floor tiles.

I nodded and placed Charlotte on the floor so she might help to tidy the makeshift mat they'd both been using. "I'll go and get changed."

I closed my bedroom door and grabbed some clothes; track bottoms and a t-shirt would do. Quickly I stripped down and put on my trousers. There was a knock on the door and thinking it was probably Charlotte I called for her to come in.

The door opened to reveal Carrie. She stood on the threshold to my bedroom and with us remembering the times she'd been here before and all that had happened during those times, the atmosphere and air between us thickened until I thought I might choke on it.

"Sorry. Charlotte is next door, getting some pencils and a colouring book."

I nodded.

"I should go." She flicked her thumb behind her as if hitching a lift.

I nodded again while her eyes ran across my naked chest.

"I—erm—if you heard—I—erm—"

"Carrie." She looked shocked that I was using a more familial term of address. "Now, with little ears nearby is probably not the time."

"Okay. Sorry."

"Don't." She had nothing to be sorry for, did she? Unless adoring my daughter and earning her love and friendship were things that necessitated an apology. "Would you like to talk later? Once Charlotte has gone to sleep."

She looked shocked.

"Unless you're busy." I was already retreating and second guessing everything Seb and I had discussed and all the other things I'd decided in my own mind.

"No, no, no plans tonight. Thank you."

Charlotte suddenly appeared with enough pens and pencils to

open her own stationary shop, ending the conversation and interaction, for now.

****

I had just tucked my daughter into bed and was reading her a bedtime story when she brought up the subject of Carrie.

"Daddy, you know Carrie?"

"Yes."

"I like her. She's my best friend."

I gazed down at her and stroked her head. "I know, baby."

"I love her. Is that okay?"

She looked up at me with big enquiring and nervous eyes that beseeched me to reassure her.

"Of course, why wouldn't it be?"

She smiled, relieved. "She is funny and takes care of me and she makes me laugh and is kind and very pretty."

My daughter's wide-eyed stare warmed me more than anything ever could.

"She is all of those things, baby and she cares for you very much."

She grinned. "Does she love me?"

"I'm sure she does."

Charlotte nodded. "Daddy?"

"Yes, baby."

"The man at yoga called Carrie my mummy."

"I guess you must look like you're out with your mummy. Did it upset you when he said it?"

"No. I liked it," she admitted and suddenly looked sad. "I feel a little bit sad because I don't have a mummy, do I?"

"Oh, sweetheart."

I pulled her from beneath the covers and held her to me tightly. How the fuck was I going to make this right?

"No, you don't, but you have me and Uncle Seb and Grandma and Granddad and Granny."

She laughed when I mentioned my grandmother.

"And Carrie. I have Carrie too, don't I?"

Even if I'd wanted to, I couldn't take Carrie away from her and I didn't want that, so somehow, I needed to make this fucked up mess work.

244

"Can I have a mummy one day."

Well, fuck me if this kid didn't slaughter me. What could I say to that? I had no clue because I never wanted to lie to her and yet she needed some comfort and reassurance.

"Maybe. One day. Perhaps, in the future, Daddy might meet someone really special that we both love and who love us and they'll join our family and although she won't be the mummy whose belly you grew in, she will be your mummy that loves you and cares for you."

"Oh, Daddy." Her eyes filled with tears as she squeezed me tighter and kissed me. "What if Carrie—"

I really couldn't offer her that reassurance. "—And now it's time for bed."

I read her story to her and watched as she lost the battle with sleep.

"Night, baby." I leaned down and kissed her forehead.

She had everything she needed and wanted, or so I thought until she'd dropped the mummy bombshell on me. I'd never lied to her, not about anything, least of all her mother, but I had tried to give her the information on a need to know basis and in child friendly language she understood. She knew her mother wasn't here, never would be and that she hadn't always been a good person. She also knew that she was loved and wanted by all the people in her life. I had guarded her. Refused to allow people to pass through. I insisted that the only people who could get close to her were the ones who'd always be there for her; me, my parents and grandmother, Seb, and that was kind of it, until Carrie. That had been my biggest objection to a paid nanny and now look where we were; me having fucked her and fucked it up, my family adoring her and my daughter harbouring designs on her being her new mummy.

Chapter Forty-Nine

Carrie

There was a gentle tap on my door. I jumped as if the bailiffs had just rocked up and pounded on it.

I opened it and was in no way surprised to find Gabe there, only because there was nobody else it could be.

"Hello," he said and looked awkward, adorably so.

I needed to stop thinking about him being adorable.

"Hello," I replied.

"Charlotte's in bed and as I was so close…"

"Would you like to come in?" This was really awkward in a way it had never been before. He sensed it too.

"Or you could come down."

I didn't know if he was concerned that if he came in, he might never leave or if it was for Charlotte's wellbeing, in case she woke up. Either way, I was happy to go downstairs to him and nodded my confirmation of that.

"Five minutes?" I didn't know why I needed five minutes, but I did.

He nodded and headed downstairs.

It was probably only a couple of minutes later when I joined him in the conservatory where he was tidying Charlotte's remaining toys away.

"She is like a tornado, isn't she?" I laughed and he joined in with it.

"And that's on a good day."

With the toys away he gestured to the sofa for me to sit. We both stared at the space where just a few days before he'd tended to my injured knees and so much more besides. I swear I flushed and not just because of embarrassment. We both chose to ignore the thickening atmosphere as we sat down and I accepted the glass of wine I was offered.

"I'm sorry about this morning…I would like us to be friends, on better terms."

I nodded and without being an arsehole about it, asked, "Would you? Friends?"

Gabe ran a hand through his hair and let out a long, deep breath. "I miss you, I told you that. Maybe we jumped in before, not that I regret it, but could we talk, be friends."

I looked at him and couldn't hide my confusion and maybe some cynicism too.

He laughed. "I'm not looking for a fuck buddy, not in you and I don't mean because I don't want to fuck you, but even if you agreed to it, I know it's not what you want."

I should have been pissed off at him telling me what I did and didn't want, but he wasn't exactly wrong.

"So, we make friends and talk?"

"Exactly."

"We could try," I agreed.

"Good." He smiled and looked relieved by my agreement. "Charlotte was still raving about yoga when she went to bed."

I grinned a broad, toothy grin at the little girl herself, then remembering our first yoga session I smiled more. That led me to the moment she called me Mummy and my grin fell from my face.

"She enjoyed it," I said, hoping to hide my inner turmoil.

"She loved it," he said, ignoring any negative feelings he'd detected. "She loves you."

I stared, open mouthed. "I, erm…"

"Hey, she does. She told me. I heard her call you Mummy, and it broke my heart a little, almost as much as her desire to have a mummy. She did lots of talking before bed."

I offered him a small smile of support but had no clue what to say so went with an apology. "Sorry."

He shook his head and waved my apology away. "No need,

really. She wants a mummy and she has chosen well."

I opened my mouth, but no words came out. What the hell could I say to that?

"I don't expect you to become her other parent and that is not what this is about. I had planned on trying to build bridges with you before Charlotte…"

I nodded, still unsure what to say or even what was happening between us.

"I must admit I nearly died on the fucking spot when she told me the man had said you were fucksable."

We both laughed. Loud and genuine laughter sounded around us.

"You and me both. She had me doubting what he had said for a moment."

We laughed again.

"He had a point though because nobody is bendy quite like you."

In that one sentence the air crackled and all air seemed to leave the room. I jumped when my text alert sounded. Gabe got to his feet and paced the room a little. This friends without benefits was going to be hard, harder than hard when we both wanted to jump each other at every other word uttered.

I glanced down and saw a message from Seb as another landed from Bea. I smiled at Seb's.

<Can you meet me for lunch tomorrow? Maybe the riverside café?>

<If it's an early lunch…12>

He replied with a thumbs up and then I moved on to Bea's message.

<Saturday night drinks and dinner at the tapas bar, about half 7?>

<Works for me, see you then>

"Everything okay?" Gabe asked, both of us knowing that what he was really asking was who had messaged me and why?

"Yeah, fine...Bea...weekend plans."

His face dropped but I needed to hang onto the few friends I had.

"How was your day?" I asked to a frowning Gabe. "It seems only fair as you know so much about mine."

His smile returned as he began to talk about his day. He'd been chatting for a few minutes and had got as far as lunch with Seb when he looked sad. I have a couple...they lost a child and they're finding it tough. Life is tough."

I nodded, feeling sad for the couple he spoke of. "How awful."

"Yeah."

"Can you help them to make it through?"

He shrugged. "I hope so, but there are no guarantees, are there?" He continued without much of a pause. "They made me think about us."

"Really?"

"Yes. I advised them to talk. To make a little time each day to talk to each other about each other. Not the kids or gripes or hassles, but each other."

I nodded again. His idea seemed so simplistic and obvious and yet they'd needed someone outside of things to see that.

"They need to connect with each other and find positives in this sea of sadness if they have any chance of moving forward together."

"Is this what we're doing, Gabe, moving forward together?"

My question gave him pause for thought.

"I hope so, Carrie, I really do."

We chatted for another half an hour or so, but without really doing the discuss and talk about each other to each other, but it felt comfortable and natural.

I let out a long yawn that was accompanied by a stretch. Gabe's eyes lit up as his gaze passed over my body, head to toe and back again, settling on my eyes.

"That stretching takes it out of a girl." As soon as the words were out of my mouth, I heard the possible connotations of them. I was not flirting. I really wasn't, not intentionally.

"I bet."

"I should go to bed, alone, sorry."

Gabe laughed at my rambling and stammering.

"I've enjoyed tonight, thank you."

"Me too. Night."

I had barely got into bed when my text alert sounded.

<I really did enjoy tonight. Night, Angel>

The grin I wore almost cracked my face. *Angel.*

<*So did I. Goodnight, Gabe*>

I resisted the temptation to respond with a babe in response to his Angel, just.

Chapter Fifty

Gabriel

As much as I hated to admit it, Seb's advice and in turn, my own had been good. A couple of weeks had passed since Charlotte's declaration of love and desire to have Carrie as her mummy, and those weeks had been good, great. We chatted every day. Sometimes over breakfast, sometimes over dinner. Other times we'd have an after-hours meet up, once Charlotte was in bed. It was during those times that things became fraught and charged with the obvious attraction and desire we still had for one another. Those times were also the most difficult and the easiest at the same time. Somehow, we had managed not to jump on each other, ripping clothes off as we went.

Charlotte was thriving in her relationship with Carrie and was still loving their mini-me yoga sessions and repeatedly told her she loved her, a sentiment her nanny returned. Truthfully, I had taken a leaf out of my daughter's book in speaking openly and honestly with Carrie, hoping we could build something real or at least reduce the chances of one of us, me, panicking and fucking it up again when conversations or feelings got real.

Carrie was enjoying a more active social life, often with Bea alone, and other times with the rest of the gang, although, there had been no mention of fuckboy. I managed to contain my jealousy, or at least hide it from Carrie, but that was proving trickier as the days went by and our friendship developed.

I stirred the beef stroganoff and quickly glanced at the clock. I had just enough time to put Charlotte to bed, shower and change before Carrie was due. Tonight, was different. I was nervous because although we now knew each other's favourite food, drink, TV shows, music, movie and even colour, the big stuff not so much so, meaning tonight, I was going in for the big stuff, hers and mine.

****

"Daddy?"

"Charlotte?"

She giggled at me answering her question with my own enquiring tone.

"You know when you have dinner with Carrie?"

"Yes."

"Is it a date?"

I didn't know what to say because I had no clue if she classed it as a date. I knew in my mind they were dates; we arranged the details, agreed them and followed through with them, just the two of us. They were dates.

"Kind of, like friend dates, baby."

"Hmmm," she whispered.

"What?" I asked, wondering what the hell was going through my daughter's mind.

"My teacher went on a date. I heard her telling the other teacher and Miss Peal asked Miss Maine if they'd kissed."

My daughter began to giggle at the idea of kissing in general, I think, but also at the idea of her teacher kissing. I wasn't sure if I approved of my daughter being privy to this type of conversation between her teachers, especially not when I was paying for the privilege, but I also knew that Charlotte always managed to be in the wrong place when these types of conversations were happening, at home as much as anywhere else.

Between giggles that I couldn't help but smile at, Charlotte said, "And Miss Maine said yes...lots!"

She literally rolled in her bed now and my smile had turned into a laugh.

"Do you and Carrie kiss?"

I stared down at her and with a quick shake of my head and a silent refusal to be drawn into this I bent down and kissed my little girl. "Goodnight, baby. Sweet dreams. I love you."

"I love you too, Daddy. Tell Carrie I love her too."

Freshly showered and dressed in jeans and a t-shirt I waited for Carrie to arrive. I had laid the table and was just putting the food on it when she arrived. She stood in the doorway, which she usually did. Turning and seeing her there took my breath away. She wore a floral sundress and sandals. Her hair was down, in soft, natural looking curls and she looked amazing.

"It smells good."

I nodded, it did, but while she was referring to dinner, all I could smell was her.

"Good enough to eat." She smiled, indicating that her words were a joke but all I could think of was her, eating her, tasting her unique flavour, devouring and savouring every last drop of her.

My thoughts were obvious I imagined when I saw the flush creep up her face.

We ate in a comfortable near silence, as we often did after discussing our day. I was distracted by the moans leaving Carrie's lips as she ate. I reminded myself that we were going to talk, share, serious details and not end up shagging on the table, although I couldn't deny how much that idea appealed to me.

"That was beautiful, thank you." She pushed her plate away and relaxed into her chair.

"You're welcome. I'm glad you enjoyed it."

This was becoming awkward, as if we both knew that tonight's conversations might prove to be a turning point so that we were somehow putting off having it with this strained, polite interaction.

"Wine." I held the bottle towards her.

"Thanks. It will be my third, so I might have to make it my last one."

"Come on, we'll take it with us."

I stood and reached for her hand. She took it without hesitation, and I swear my heart skipped a beat. I led her into the lounge where we sat on the sofa, one of us at each end of it. She placed her wine glass on the coffee table and stretched her legs along the sofa so that her feet reached my legs. I held my own wine glass in one hand and allowed the other one to drop to her feet that I stroked.

"I'm assuming you have wondered about Charlotte's mother."

She nodded and I could tell she was startled by me raising the subject.

"Well, yes, but—"

"It's okay. I get that I haven't exactly been open about things before you came here."

"No, but then neither have I."

"No." I agreed. "I'd like to right that now. So, Charlotte's mother." I honestly didn't know where to start so I just let the words come out. "We met at uni and got along famously. She was great, perfect; beautiful, funny and smart. Seb was never entirely on board with us but I thought he was jealous. Maybe he was, but that wasn't the real cause of his concern...that's a whole other story. Anyway, we started dating, things got serious and when we left uni we moved in together. Everything was going great. Both of our careers were going well and I asked her to marry me a couple of years later, she agreed and about eighteen months after that we got married. Everything was great and then she got pregnant with Charlotte. I had never been happier."

I looked up and saw Carrie smiling at me, happy that I had been happy, thrilled at the news of Charlotte's existence.

"She found pregnancy difficult and was very stressed. She continued to work as a pharmacist, and as the pregnancy progressed, she settled into it. I thought things would get even better once she started maternity leave and then when Charlotte was born. They didn't. If anything, they got worse. I thought it might be post-natal depression and got her all the help that was available. The doctor's she saw weren't convinced it was depression. One even went as far as to suggest her issues were deeper seated than that and Seb tactfully brokered that too. Things settled into a pattern and although there was tension, it was okay."

Carrie moved down a little, resting her feet in my lap and although that was quite possibly the least reassuring touch ever, it was strangely comforting.

"She went back to work, and things seemed to improve. Charlotte was a dream." I did nothing to fight the smile on my face. "She ate well, slept for twelve hours a night and was generally content. She was like the most laidback baby ever. My mother and mother-in-law helped care for her. She had me and Seb wrapped around her little finger."

Carrie laughed, clearly already knowing that's where Seb and I belonged. "And her mother?"

I shook my head. "She cared for Charlotte and loved her." I had no clue how she felt about our baby with hindsight, but I had to believe that she had loved her.

"What happened?" Carrie had moved down and with her legs crossed, sat next to me, facing the back of the sofa.

I sniffed and realised I was crying. I brushed the tears I was unashamed of shedding from my face and allowed Carrie to pull my hand into hers.

"She had a sister who had a baby a few weeks younger than Charlotte. Her sister asked if Alice, my wife, would watch the baby one night. She agreed. I was out with Seb."

A sob caught in my throat and although Carrie could have no idea where this was leading, she looked close to tears herself.

"I came home, a little the worse for wear, but fuck, if I didn't sober up when I got there, well, we, me and Seb. We got in and heard crying, a baby. We assumed one of the babies wasn't settling but the crying sounded distressed. Seb and I followed the cries, expecting to find Alice with a fraught baby. Fuck!"

I downed the glass of wine I had.

"It was the worst moment of my life. There was no sign of Alice, but Charlotte was in the bath, alone, cold, naked and crying. Alice was nowhere to be found, but her niece lay next to Charlotte in the bath, face down, floating in the water."

I sobbed as I remembered that moment, a moment I had tried to block out as much as I could and I hadn't shared this with anyone since it happened.

"Oh, fucking hell," Carrie cried, moving even closer until she straddled my lap. She wrapped her arms around me and held me tight. "Baby," she whispered against my hair and nothing had ever felt this right, ever.

Chapter Fifty-One

Carrie

I didn't know what to say. I was still unsure whether Gabriel was a widower, a divorcee or still married. He sobbed as I held him, offering comfort of some sort, I hoped. His wife, who was most likely suffering some kind of mental illness, had killed her own niece by negligence at least and at the same time had left Charlotte in a vulnerable position. No wonder Gabe had closed off somewhat and was overprotective of his daughter.

"Baby," I whispered for what felt like the twentieth time.

This time he looked up with sad, almost empty eyes.

"I'm so sorry," I told him, and I was. Sorry that he had gone through that. There were dozens of other questions I wanted answers to, but I was also nervous of pushing him too far too soon.

I instinctively lowered my lips to his and he allowed me to kiss him and to take control of his pain and sadness, if only for a few seconds. Quickly, his sadness was pushed back and he was the aggressor in our kiss and before I could register it we were lying together on the sofa, lips and hands everywhere like a couple of teenagers who'd been left home together.

Eventually, with me offering no objections to anything that this might lead to we came up for breath.

"That was not supposed to happen," Gabe said. "I was talking, telling you about things."

"I know there's clearly more, but you don't have to."

He nodded and seemed to be preparing to sit up.

"And just so you know, I enjoyed kissing you whether it was supposed to happen or not."

He smiled a tiny half-smile and remained lying next to me.

"As you can imagine the shit hit the fan big style. The police, social services and every man and his dog became involved. Alice had disappeared. Her family were devastated, the baby, that poor baby."

I reached up and gently stroked his hair. "You really don't have to."

He pulled my hand from his head and kissed the back of it. "I want to. I want to tell you. If this is going to go anywhere, you need to know. The thinking was that she had put the babies into the bath and left them. Charlotte, being a little bigger and older had managed to keep her head above water, maybe been able to move around independently. The younger baby had somehow ended up on her front and had been unable to right her position."

I nodded, that seemed to make sense.

"The post-mortem contradicted that."

I swallowed, hard. "There were drugs in the baby's system. Fuck! That's why her sister had asked Alice to take her because the baby was fraught and cried, a lot and she was getting to the end of her tether and just needed a break."

"They thought Alice had given her something?"

"Yeah. They tested Charlotte and there were traces of sedatives...no wonder she slept for twelve hours a night."

"Fuck, Gabe. What happened?"

"The police found Alice a few days later, in a real state. She was admitted to hospital and subsequently charged with murder and negligence in Charlotte's case. Social services went through everything with a fine toothcomb and Charlotte became my sole responsibility."

"Where is Alice now?" I was almost as scared of the question as I was of the answer.

"Everyone disowned her, her family disowned us all. I wanted to help, but Charlotte was my priority and the authorities left me in doubt that there could be no contact with Alice. The police refused to accept that she wasn't fit to be charged."

He sighed a long and loud sigh that made my heart ache for

him.

"The police made their case and in doing so investigated Alice's background. It turned out that as a child, ten, eleven, one of her friend's had died, a tragic accident in a brook near to where she'd lived."

"Fuck!"

"Yeah. They put two and two together and they added to four. Other details came out about pets that had suffered strange deaths. The police put together a strong case, so strong that nobody who was around at the time doubted her guilt. We, Charlotte and I, moved here after that. My parents were happy to move with us and as my grandmother needed care, they bought a house big enough for them all. It was far enough away that it's not common knowledge and Alice had kept her maiden name so there wasn't a direct link. Even Seb moved his life to be with us. It's amazing that moving a couple of hours away can give you a fresh start."

I nodded. I knew that better than anyone.

"What happened to Alice?"

"She was held on remand. She self-harmed a couple of times and when that didn't get her anywhere, she goaded a woman in there. This woman had lost a child herself and was serving time for killing the person she deemed responsible. By all accounts, Alice sat and laughed and joked about what she'd done. The woman flipped, eventually forcing the end of a mop through Alice's groin. She hit a main artery and she bled out."

"Oh my God!"

"So, you see why my circle is small and closed and why I was reluctant and fought against a nanny. Against anyone having access to my child because if her own mother didn't care for her as she should have and if I couldn't see that things were wrong…"

"This wasn't your fault, none of it."

"I do know that. I didn't always believe it, but I do know."

"What does Charlotte know?"

"Very little. She knows that she had a mummy whose tummy she grew inside of and that she loved her but was unable to love her properly, like she needed. She knows she died, but not the circumstances."

I smiled. I was unable to do anything else. My beautiful man, despite all this woman had done, he told their child that her mother had loved her, but was unable to love her properly, and although that might be the truth, I was amazed that he had done that, been able to do that.

"You are a very special man and Charlotte is lucky to have you."

He looked uncomfortable at my complimentary words, amusing me. Neither of us said anything for ten minutes, maybe more. We held each other close, appreciating the comfort that brought.

The sound of us each yawning at the same time made us laugh.

"Bedtime," Gabe said getting to his feet and helping me to mine.

We walked upstairs together, still quiet. When we reached Gabe's door we paused.

"Thank you, for sharing that with me and for trusting me."

"I really am trying here, Angel."

"I know and I'll try too, I promise."

"Night." He leaned in and landed a single, delicate kiss to my cheek.

"Gabe, let me stay with you, please."

He said nothing, but opened the door, held it open and allowed me to enter before him.

Chapter Fifty-Two

Gabriel

I had no clue what would happen once the door closed. In the past the door would have barely closed before clothes would have flown and skin to skin contact would have ensued, but this was different. Tonight was different. We were different.

Carrie took my hand and led me to the bed. We stood, gazing upon each other. I cupped her face while her hands came to rest on my chest.

"Let's go to bed."

I looked down at her and as much as I wanted to be with her tonight, I didn't want her to feel taken advantage of.

"We don't have to do anything, Carrie—"

She cut me off. "I know, baby." She pulled the bottom of my t-shirt, moving it up my body. "Let's get undressed, climb into bed. Let me hold you, please." Her thumb rubbed across my lips.

I nodded. Slowly and with care and attention we each undressed the other until we were both naked. She was beautiful. More beautiful than I remembered. I wanted to kiss her and hold her, maybe even make love to her but I didn't want to fuck her. There was more to this than passion and sex.

She climbed into bed and held the covers back for me, waited for me. I slid in next to her and pulled her into my arms and held her like she was my life raft, maybe she was. We remained together as one for long, silent minutes. Her head rested against my chest. I was unsure if I'd fallen asleep or had been nodding off when I felt the sensation of her mouth littering kisses against my chest.

"Angel," I whispered, one hand moving so my fingers could lace through her hair.

She continued to kiss me, moving from side to side, then higher until her mouth was against my neck, jaw, lips.

We kissed. That was a serious understatement for what we were sharing. She was on top of me, straddling my body. I grabbed her hair and held her face close to mine, slowly taking control of what we were doing. I rolled us over so she lay beneath me and I was between her thighs. The kiss remained unbroken. My dick was ramrod hard, had been from the second she'd lay down next to me. Still we kissed as I slid inside her. Her body arched, meeting mine. We moved in time with each other perfectly. This was heaven, perfection, home. Her arms wrapped around me and quickly her fingers began to flex into my shoulders and then as her nails clawed at me and I absorbed her cries of pleasure she pushed me over the edge of release so that we both fell together.

After relaxing, still coupled for minutes, I rolled over. In silence we lay in the dark, arms and legs entwined and fell asleep.

****

It was still dark, just, when I woke to find Carrie watching me.

"You okay?" I asked her, hoping she hadn't thought of all I'd told her and was about to tell me she was leaving.

"Yeah, kind of."

"Kind of?" My breath hitched with dreaded anticipation.

"Can we talk?"

My heart sank and my face must have given that away based on her response. She leaned in and kissed my chest.

"About me. You were so open and honest last night that I think I should show you the same trust and faith."

"Okay."

"I don't know where to start, Gabe."

I squeezed her hand, hoping to give her the reassurance she had shown me. "I know how that feels. Just take your time and tell me whatever you want or need to."

She nodded and squeezed my hand a little tighter.

"I've lied to you."

She looked close to tears and it honestly felt as though she'd just dropped a bomb on me. She'd lied to me. About what? I hated dishonesty and had trust issues so this could be a game changer for me.

"When I applied for the job here…I may have exaggerated some points…like exam results and the extent of my experience."

I watched her carefully, she looked devastated to be confessing this. I hadn't checked her qualifications. Everyone lied or exaggerated on C.V.s and job applications. I had checked her references and done a credit search, all of which had come back fine. Her references were excellent and the other searches, including social media were not causes for concern.

"Explain."

"I'm not a qualified nanny."

"Oh." I was telling my inner rage that even if she wasn't qualified, she was amazing. I also screamed at myself for taking such risks with my daughter's safety, not that Carrie posed a risk, I knew that for sure. But what if she had. What if she was like Alice? I shuddered.

"I saw the advert for the job here and it sounded perfect. It offered me a chance to start again and I love children. I always wanted to train as a nanny or nursery nurse, but things happened. When I came here you scared me, petrified me and also turned me on like you wouldn't believe, but Charlotte was a dream and I thought if I got the job you'd see how good I was and then even if you found out you'd keep me on."

"And now?" My irritation was on the rise because so far all she'd done was to try and save her job.

"And now." Her voice broke. "It's so much more. I love being here with you and Charlotte and if you sacked me I would accept it, understand it, but if you abandoned me, left me, well, made me leave, that would break me."

She was going to cry, her voice, the tears in her eyes and the wobble of her chin confirmed that.

I took a deep breath. "You are going nowhere, and neither am I, but I can't have you lying to me. I need to be able to trust you and I don't trust easily so if you lie to me, you're going to break that trust and if you do, there's unlikely to be any coming back."

She nodded and replied with a remarkably heartfelt sorry. She humbled me with the sincerity of her apology.

"So, why don't you tell me everything, and then we can try and move forward, together."

With a firm nod, she spoke. "When I was born."

I stared at her, unsure if I needed her life story. Had she misunderstood when I'd said everything? I didn't know, but maybe I needed to give her the chance to get things out in the open, the same chance she'd given me.

Chapter Fifty-Three

Carrie

"When I was born..." I began and immediately saw the look of shock on Gabe's face. I almost laughed when I realised he thought I was going to tell him my whole life story from the day I hatched. "Just stay with me here."

He nodded and we both adjusted our positions so that we each lay on our sides, propped up on an elbow, able to see the other.

"I never knew my dad. My mum was young and in a bad place. She drank and used drugs."

I watched Gabe's expression sadden. He leaned in and brushed the hair back off my face.

"When I was born, I was taken straight to intensive care as I was already addicted to drugs and needed to withdraw safely."

"Oh, Angel."

"It's okay." I smiled as I tried to reassure him. "I don't remember it and I made a good recovery. My mum should never have been allowed to keep me, but she was. Social services were supposed to monitor and keep a close eye on me and the situation."

"And?" He looked concerned.

"They didn't."

Gabe leaned in closer and ran a thumb over my cheek.

"I lived in pretty dire conditions for probably six or seven years. She was still on drugs and drinking. We lived in a one bedroom flat in a rough part of town. I don't remember a time when she wasn't a prostitute. She had a pimp and he was a fucking pig. He scared the crap out of me. He would come round and always seemed angry; he shouted and broke things. He used to hit my mum..." a sob caught in my throat at the memories I'd spent years supressing.

Gabe leaned in even closer, resting his forehead against mine. "Did he hit you?"

I nodded, a single tear rolling down my cheek. Gabe brushed it away.

"He hated me. I think I represented an obstacle in his complete control of her, although he managed to control most things she did. When she had clients, I had to watch TV while they were in the bedroom. I never knew any different so assumed this was how everyone lived."

"What about school? Did nobody express concerns?" Gabe's desperate tone almost implored me to tell him that someone had been there, that someone had cared, but they hadn't been, and they didn't.

"I didn't go, had never been at that point."

He nodded but I doubted he understood much of what I was saying beyond being able to comprehend the words.

"Anyway, one day she was in the bedroom with a client and I watched TV. The guy came out after lots of noises and shouting and he gave me some money. I watched the TV until it was dark and went in the bedroom where I slept with her."

Gabe looked like he was going to be sick at the notion of me sleeping in that bed that had seen so much. He tried to hide it, but I saw it. When I thought of Charlotte and her beautiful room full of toys, books and clothes and this house filled with care and love I could understand his difficulty in hiding his expression that betrayed his thoughts. This man had put his daughter first at every turn, regardless of the consequences to his other relationships.

"I found her lying in blood. Her face was a mess and I didn't know what to do. I had found her when she'd overdosed a couple of times and her pimp had dealt with that, but this was something new. Don't get me wrong, she had been knocked about on many occasions, but this was something different. I tried to wake her, but she wouldn't wake up. I made her a cup of tea and tucked her into bed, but she still didn't wake up. I climbed in next to her and hugged her."

"Carrie. You really don't need to tell me this."

"I do and I want to." I really wanted him to know this about me, to know everything about me. "When I woke up the next day, she was cold, really, really cold. We didn't always have heating, but I put extra blankets on her. She didn't wake up and she didn't get warm. It was probably a couple of days later when her pimp turned up and found us. For the first time ever, he was kind and gave me some money before running off. I guess he must have called for an ambulance because they came a short time after he left and took her away. Social services took me into care, and I remained there for a few years. I had a couple of foster homes and then I got adopted."

"Please tell me that your adoptive family treated you well."

I leaned across and kissed him gently. He needed me to have been looked after more than I had. If they hadn't, I think I'd have said they had just to make Gabe happy.

"Yeah. They were good people. A little older and childless. They sent me to school and loved me. My dad died in an accident when I was about twelve and it was just me and mum then. She got sick when I was about fifteen, hence the less than perfect exam results and my inability to go to college and become a nanny. I took care of her and got part-time jobs. She was unwell for about seven years in total and about a year ago she died."

"Oh, Carrie." He pulled me closer until I felt I was struggling to breathe.

His embrace was comforting but also constricting. I wasn't used to such displays of emotion and my natural instinct, when laid so bare was to withdraw but he needed this from me, to hold and comfort me and I wanted to give him whatever he needed. And I wanted what he was offering me.

"It's okay, baby."

He held me to him.

"That's why when I saw your advertisement to be Charlotte's nanny I applied. I had nothing keeping me where I was and I had never really been in a family, a proper family with only love and warmth. When I came for the interview, that's what I felt here, between you, your mum and Charlotte, love and warmth. A bond that could never be broken. I never thought you'd offer me the job." I laughed causing him to frown at my apparent amusement. "I thought you were a scary arsehole who hated me, but when you offered me the job, taking care of Charlotte, it was the best day of my life along with being adopted."

With the final word out, my emotions of a lifetime were unleashed; the baby who'd been born addicted to fuck knows what, the child who had been exposed to the worst life had to offer, the girl who had gone through the care system several times over, the adoptive daughter who thought she'd struck gold just by being wanted to the grief stricken daughter who'd lost the father she'd been robbed of knowing for long enough before becoming the daughter who had nursed an ailing mother to the bitter end to find herself where she'd started off…alone, unloved and unwanted.

Sobs sounded around me, louder and louder until I shook uncontrollably from head to toe. Gabe held me, pulled me closer, rocked me, whispered to me, soothing me through it all.

Chapter Fifty-Four

Gabriel

I'd barely been able to think of anything that wasn't Carrie since we'd spent the night together and shared our deepest secrets. We'd continued to make time for each other, and things were going well. Charlotte was happy and settled but unaware of anything going on between me and Carrie and that is what we agreed to maintain for now, just in case it didn't work out. My mother definitely suspected and her soppy, knowing smile was a testament to that. Seb also knew, although that was because I'd told him, but then he knew me well enough to take one look at me and know.

"Where do you think you're going?" I pulled Carrie back down into her bed where we'd been all afternoon.

"I need to get showered if I'm meeting Bea."

"Five more minutes."

She shook her head and laughed but did lie back down with me.

"Five minutes," she said, softening against me as I held her.

"Is it just you and Bea tonight?"

I hoped it was. Her nights out in a group always caused me concern and when she returned home from them, she seemed distracted and not as relaxed as when it was just her and Bea. Maybe I was imagining it. Maybe it was me that was more relaxed when it was just the two of them and no fuckboys with them, although, the main fuckboy had been quiet of late, having only popped up on one night out she'd had. I still didn't like him, and I definitely didn't trust him.

"Yes, just the two of us as far as I know."

"Hmmm."

"Hmmm, what?" She leaned up so she was looking at me.

"As far as I know does not convince me that it's just the two of you." I had a pout on my lips and the sulk was mere seconds away.

With a frown, Carrie leaned in closer. "Baby," she whispered against my lips. "Are you jealous in case there are boys joining us?" Her face cracked into a big grin but even without it she was laughing at me and I didn't like it.

"Do I need to be jealous, Angel?" I placed a hand on her hip and pulled her closer so she could feel how much I wanted her again.

"Never."

The conviction with which she spoke floored me. She meant it. She wanted me, only me and had no interest in anyone else. I wondered how she managed to trust anyone when those she should have been able to trust without question had only ever let her down.

"There really was no need for you, my mother and Seb to try and make me jealous then, was there?"

The day after we'd revealed the truth about ourselves, Carrie had confessed to being in cahoots with my mother and best friend, plotting to win me back, not that she'd ever really lost me.

"That wasn't the plan." Her protests were half-hearted.

"Only because Seb knew better than that."

"Sorry." Her repeated apology was sincere. "But I missed you so much..."

"I know and without Seb we might not have spoken openly and with honesty so it's good that you and my mother drew him into your coven, kind of, but no more."

She stared at me, her mouth agape. "Did you just inadvertently call me a witch?"

I laughed at her outrage but made no effort to deny it. "I believe I've told you before that your angel title may need revising...devil, witch...temptress."

"Temptress?" She bit down into her lip, and allowed one hand to slip between us, stroking across my hardness then squeezed it. Never taking her eyes off me, her hand came to rest on my arse cheek.

"You know you might need to let Bea know you're running late, temptress."

I pulled her even closer and placed a gentle kiss to her lips then traced a path lower until I had captured her nipple between my lips. She inhaled deeply as I drew it into the warmth and heat of my mouth. With a little gasp she threw one leg over my hip.

"I'm not running late."

I sucked harder on her nipple and then released it, grazing it with my teeth. "You're going to be."

"Am I?" She grinned knowing that she was. "And why is that?"

"Because I intend to work my way down your body until you're coming on my tongue and then I'm going to fuck you until you can't think of anything other than how it feels to have me inside you."

"Oh." A flush crept up her face making me laugh.

"Any objections?"

"Nope, none, not a single one." With one hand she reached for her phone while her other began pushing my head down towards her open thighs.

****

Seb laughed at my inability to sit still or leave my phone unattended for more than a few minutes.

"Fuck off."

He laughed louder at my two-word response.

"Where has she gone?"

"Not a clue because when I asked, I equally as quickly told her not to tell me."

Seb frowned. "Why would you do that?"

"Because...I don't know. Maybe I would have followed her if I'd known and that is desperate and stalkerish."

He shook his head. "Dickhead. Because this is so much better than that, isn't it? Now I can sit and watch you flap like a mother bloody hen that she is out, and you don't know where or who with. I haven't even got my princess, Charlotte, here to help me out with keeping you sane."

"Sorry." I should have let her tell me where she was going just in case there was a problem and I needed to contact her.

My friend waved my apology away, but I was killing the mood here and with Charlotte staying with my parents I was ruining the opportunity for a fun evening with Seb.

"Come on."

Seb looked startled. "Where?"

"Out. The pub, a bar, anywhere. I can't spend the evening wearing a groove in the floor and I know I'm putting a downer on things."

Seb was already on his feet and grabbing his jacket. "You gonna be my wingman?"

"Depends; if by wingman you mean will I tell a pretty girl how great you are and not be offended at being ditched, of course. If you mean taking her mate off your hands, regardless of how she looks or her personality, not a bloody chance because if Carrie got wind of me giving anyone else the impression I was interested she would have my balls."

Seb laughed, but I knew he didn't need a wingman, not really. "I think I might prefer you as a mother hen rather than hen pecked."

"Fuck you." I flipped him off as I grabbed my wallet and keys.

"Nanny really does have you pussy whipped, doesn't she?"

"I'm not talking to you," I told him as I reached the front door.

"We both know that's not true so let's get some drinks down you and then you can tell me exactly how she's managed it."

"You're thinking about her naked again, aren't you?"

He slapped my back and passed by me, so I looked down at him at the roadside. "Naked and shagging if I'm being honest."

I shook my head yet couldn't quite hide a small smile. "You need a woman of your own so you can forget about mine."

He smiled, not at getting his own woman, I didn't think, but at me claiming Carrie as mine, something I vowed never to do again after Alice.

Chapter Fifty-Five

Carrie

The sound of my own cackle rang around us. My laughter only got worse when I saw actual tears rolling down Bea's face. Fighting hysteria, I managed to get our order out to the barman who laughed with us.

"Would you like to share the joke?" He winked at me and I flushed crimson.

"You don't want to know," Bea told him, and with a flick in my direction, added, "She's being very rude."

"You should definitely share it then." He grinned as he presented our drinks to us.

We scurried off together like a couple of schoolgirls, giggling as we went.

"He was cute, and he liked you."

I shook my head. "The barman was just being a barman. Flirting is part of the job."

"Maybe, but checking out your boobs isn't."

I ignored Bea's insistence that the barman had any real interest in me. "Let's sit down and you can tell me what's new, especially after last week."

We took our seats and Bea shook her head, looking beyond apologetic.

"I had no idea that was all going to kick off. I had no idea they'd turn up."

"They?"

"Yes, they," she insisted. "I thought it was going to be just the two of us. I don't even remember saying we were meeting up, but I must have."

I nodded. I believed what she said. "Nic and Sasha are good fun."

"They are but I wasn't expecting them."

"Bea, please don't worry about it. It wasn't your fault, really."

"Thanks," Bea said and sounded genuinely grateful. "But the way Toby behaved—"

I cut her off. "Was not your fault. He was a dick, to all of us. I didn't get where all the angst and anger came from, and how fucking drunk was he?"

"Yeah, he was pretty wasted." She suddenly looked nervous, sheepish which I took to be guilt.

"Gabriel doesn't like him."

Bea looked uncomfortable as she fiddled with her glass. "Did you tell him about last week?"

I shook my head. There was nothing to be gained by causing Gabe to dislike fuckboy any more than he already did. Maybe I should change the subject because Toby being an arsehole last week was beginning to put a downer on this week's night out.

Last week had started off well. Bea and I had met about halfway between her home and mine and from there we'd walked to the pub. The plan had been for a catch-up, just the two of us. We'd had a couple of drinks and brought each other up to speed on our lives when Nicole and Sasha appeared. We shuffled along the bench seats we were sat on and invited them to join us. A couple of the lads we knew appeared a few minutes later and seemed no way surprised to find us there. It turned out they'd spoken to Nic, or Sasha, maybe both, and that is how they knew where we were. The lads had barely sat down when Toby appeared, and he didn't look happy.

He forced his way onto the edge of the bench on the opposite side of the table to me and glared across at me. Everyone was tense and a little on edge, more so when Toby began to berate everyone in turn. After he'd finished telling Bea her shortcomings he got to his feet, staggered slightly, then pointed at me.

"And you…" He seemed beyond angry as he glowered at me.

His phone rang and glancing down at it he smiled before returning his attention to me. "Later." With that one word uttered I had no clue whether I should have felt relieved or afraid.

I returned my attention to Bea. "What is Toby's issue?"

Bea blew through her softly closed lips making a pfft sound. "Too many to name. He isn't good in social situations and he often speaks without thinking. Nic really liked him and he seemed to like her, but then once they got close and seemed to be on the same page he flaked and friend zoned her."

I remembered Sasha telling me that story. "Yeah, when she got drunk and he took care of her."

"Hmmm."

"What?" I was missing something here.

"Shit. Look, this is suspicion on my part. I have no proof or even anything resembling facts, but your man, Gabe, might be right to mistrust Toby."

I shuffled to the edge of my seat, wanting, no, needing Bea to continue with her thoughts on Toby. I did allow myself a small smile at her phrasing of *your man, Gabe.*

"I have never known him to have a girlfriend, nor a boyfriend. He seems to like girls and he goes all out when he gets a crush or whatever, but then he goes cold, like suddenly, overnight. Often, he friend zones them, like Nic."

"Okay, but I don't understand how this has anything to do with suspicion…"

"There was a girl…about a year ago. She worked behind the bar in a pub we used to go to. Toby liked her, a lot. She used to say he was weird and full on. He kind of is, but that's who he is. Plus, she was a bit outrageous and dramatic, so we never really knew which one of them was the weird one."

I nodded, it all sounded straightforward and normal for drama enjoying men and women. "I'm still not getting where your suspicion comes from or why."

"One night we went to the pub and she wasn't there. Wasn't there for a few visits and then she was, but Toby wasn't, and she made some fairly wild statements—"

"Well look who we have here, Nanny!"

I jarred my neck, I spun with such speed at the familiar sound of Seb's voice. Looking up he stood at the end of the table, grinning down at me.

"Why aren't you at home with Gabe?"

He flicked his thumb over his shoulder towards the bar. "I was, and now I am out with Gabe."

I looked past him to see Gabe waving at me. My glance flicked back to Seb who seemed to pick up on my unasked questions.

"We had no idea where you were, and we got bored at home. I got bored of watching Gabe pacing the floor waiting for you to come home and here we are."

I laughed at his honest and blunt explanation.

"Would you lovely ladies have any objections to me and my scaredy-cat friend joining you?"

I shook my head at Seb. He was so cheesy and yet, when I looked across at Bea, she seemed to be hanging on his every word with a doe-eyed expression. I needed to call or text her tomorrow and warn her about Seb who was amazing in every way but was also a confirmed bachelor.

"If Carrie doesn't mind," my friend said, and without further input Seb was summoning Gabe over while Bea simply stared at Seb who was already taking the seat next to her.

Chapter Fifty-Six

Gabriel

I stood at the bar and ordered drinks. Seb was talking and suddenly stopped when he began laughing.

I turned to see the cause of his amusement. "What?" I followed his gaze. "Shit. Maybe we should go."

He looked at me and frowned. "You've been pining for Nanny all night and now we've found her, albeit accidentally, you want to sneak off again? Am I understanding this right?"

"I don't want her to think I've followed her or that I'm checking up on her."

"You are such a pussy."

I was coming up with a retort but there was no point as my dickhead friend was walking away and heading for the table where Carrie and Bea sat. Seconds passed and then Carrie looked over at me. I waved. I could have kicked myself. She didn't wave back but returned her attention back to Seb. He turned his attention to Bea and then I was being summoned over.

Carrying the drinks from the bar I headed for the table and sat next to Carrie.

"Hi," I whispered against her ear as I leaned in and kissed her cheek.

"Hi," she said back, turning to smile at me. "Fancy meeting you here."

We both laughed, as did Seb and Bea, the latter saying, "Quite the coincidink."

I looked at Bea with a frown then to Carrie, to translate.

"Coincidence."

"Ah, yeah. We had no idea where you were…"

"Seb mentioned that," said Bea, looking at my friend with innocence, as if she had been hanging onto every word my friend had uttered.

"I bet he did," I muttered making Carrie giggle.

"Didn't want Nanny to think Gabe was stalking her, did we?" Seb looked down at Bea and his look was anything but innocent. He looked like he planned on devouring her to within an inch of her life.

Carrie and I chatted for a little while, including discussing my plans for collecting Charlotte the following day. We laughed at the messages we'd each received from my daughter via my mother.

I picked up my drink and took a sip, using the opportunity to glance across at my friend who was laughing loudly at something Bea had said. Seb was clearly at his most charming, meaning that if my friend decided he liked Bea, even for just tonight, she was going to be completely powerless to resist his charms. He was a dickhead, but I had never met anyone as charming and smooth in my life and I had never seen him fail in his pursuit of a woman.

Bea laughed and flushed at whatever he'd said. Yeah, she was fucked, probably literally. I wondered if I could or should warn him off because if he ended up hurting Carrie's friend then she may end up stuck between them and if she ended up in that position, I would too. I decided I probably couldn't and really shouldn't, they were adults after all.

"Seb said you'd missed me." Carrie's teasing words gained my attention. I liked her teasing me, although I didn't doubt Seb had been a twat in the way he'd told Carrie I'd missed her.

"Always, Angel."

She watched me closely, maybe looking for any sign that I might be joking about it, I wasn't.

She reached up and stroked my cheek before leaning in and kissing me gently on the lips. "Aww, baby."

We both remembered that we were not alone when Seb coughed. Looking across at him sitting next to Bea they both looked equally horrified by our open display of affection.

"Sorry," said Carrie, irking me slightly.

"No, she's not, and neither am I," I said defiantly before the sound of music from the nearby DJ filtered through from the dancefloor. I had no clue what the song was, but I recognised it as one Carrie and Charlotte had danced to a few days before. "Let's dance."

I wasn't much of a dancer, never had been really and yet the idea of dancing with Carrie again, like we had at dinner that night, at home with my playlist, well, I couldn't wait to have her in my arms. Plus, it got us away from Seb and his fucking arsehole comments.

We stepped onto the floor and I pulled her to me, holding her close.

"You okay?" she asked sounding concerned for me.

"Yes. I'm just enjoying holding you."

She smiled up at me and stepped further into my grip. "And I am enjoying being held by you. It might be my favourite place to be."

"Bloody hell, it's a good job Seb and Bea aren't close enough to hear us or they might just vomit."

She laughed. "Not everyone can be romantic like us, can they?"

"They can't and not everyone can be loved up like us, can they?"

"They can't." She smirked. "Nor can they claim to have been shagged eight ways to Sunday and enjoyed multiple orgasms all afternoon."

"No, they fucking can't and that might be the only way we will ever spend a childless afternoon at home from this point on."

"Sounds perfect, baby."

I watched her chest, neck and cheeks flush while her pupils dilated, and she licked her lips. "It does. It was."

We continued to move together when Carrie nervously asked, "Do you think we are quite sickly though?"

I paused our movements and cupped her face, gazing down at her. "If we are then I love being sickly with you."

A small smile tugged at her lips until she grinned up at me.

"I love being anywhere, doing anything with you."

She began to lower her glance, but with my fingers moving to her chin, I tilted her face back up leaving her with no choice but to look at me. See me.

"And, Carrie, Angel, I love you."

Chapter Fifty-Seven

Carrie

Was I dreaming? Had he just said what I thought he had or was I mishearing things? The fact that he was staring down at me expectantly suggested I had heard correctly and was wide awake.

"You love me? Me?" I could hear the disbelief in my own voice and the quirk of Gabe's eyebrow suggested it was clear to him too. "Are you sure?"

He laughed, loudly and pulled my body closer to his, still ensuring my eyes remained on his. "Never been surer of anything."

Tears pricked the back of my eyes and my jaw began to burn with emotion I was reluctant to release. With a sob and tears escaping my eyes it seemed my no emotion plan was seriously flawed.

"I—love—you—too—" I managed to say, the words broken by gasps and sobs.

Before I could think or say anything else, Gabe's mouth was covering mine. The rest of the world ceased to exist; there was just the two of us in our own world, our own little bubble that nobody else could penetrate. A couple of people bumped into us as we stood perfectly still except for our mouths and tongues that worked together, perfectly matched and working in totally synchronised movements.

Eventually, Gabe broke our kiss, revealing the biggest smile I'd ever seen on his face. "Let's go home."

"What about Bea and Seb?" I asked, not wanting to be anywhere other than home and with nobody other than Gabe.

Gabe glanced around, searching for our friends. "Ah."

I followed his gaze until I found what he was looking at… Seb and Bea on the other side of the dancefloor, moving together to the music, holding each other, gazing at each other and looking totally content in each other's company.

"Seb and Bea?" I wasn't sure what else to say.

"So it would seem."

"I hope he won't hurt her or mess her around." I was genuinely concerned for my friend because although I didn't know all the details of her past, I did know she had previously been hurt and taken advantage of.

"Angel, you can't do this. Seb is not looking for serious right now, so if she is then you might want to warn her off, but beyond that you need to butt out."

I stared up at him, trying to process his words and come up with an objection. "But Seb helped us…" My voice trailed off at his expression that was telling me he meant what he'd said.

"He did, with advice to me and an offer to manipulate situations for you, but he didn't need to do that because we worked things out by being honest with each other."

"But—"

"No buts, Carrie." Suddenly Gabe sounded like the Mr Caldwell I'd first met, the one who had interviewed me and scared me shitless. "I mean what I am saying; warn Bea that Seb is most likely to hurt her if she wants serious and happy ever after, and I will speak to Seb about being clear about what he wants and what he will give, but beyond that we keep out of it."

I nodded but knew that action was in complete contrast to the frown I was wearing.

He turned me towards our friends and spanked my behind. "Go get her."

I felt slightly awkward when I came to a stop before Seb and Bea.

Gabriel had no such problem. "Well, you two seem to have hit it off."

Seb smirked while Bea laughed but flushed too.

I clumsily announced my need for the bathroom. "I might just go for a wee."

The others looked at me.

"Do you need to go too?" I asked Bea who looked startled.

"You've been mixing with three-year-olds for too long if you're checking on the status of everyone's bladder when you're in company," she replied.

Gabe laughed, as did Seb who also high fived my friend.

"I think, what Nanny is trying to say is that she needs you to go to the loo with her so she can warn you about me. She's going to tell you how incredibly funny and handsome I am, but she'll also tell you that I'm a commitment phobe who is going to break your heart."

I stared between the others. Seb had spoken with a flatness to his voice but his lips quirked into the tiniest of smiles. Bea shook her head. I was relieved when she smiled at me. Gabe rolled his eyes at his friend who was now opening his mouth to continue speaking.

"Rest assured though, Princess, it will be the most fun you've ever had having your heart broken."

"Yeah?" Bea was playing along. Playing with fire, batting her eyelids and nibbling her lip.

"Yeah, and then some. Toe curling, sheet gripping, screaming my name fun."

I dunno about Bea but I was flushing crimson. Heat rushed through me, a combination of embarrassment and goodness knows what else. I had never seen this side of Seb before and it was no surprise that he could charm the pants off any lady he wanted and now it seemed he wanted Bea.

Watching on as he stepped closer, I couldn't take my eyes off them. "Go with Nanny and let her give you some words of warning and then..."

"Then?" Bea asked and I was sure she was panting.

"Then I reckon Gabe is going to whisk her off for some sheet gripping, screaming his name fun, so then it will be just the two of us."

Bea looked momentarily rooted to the spot. Well, me and her both.

"Angel," Gabe's voice, whispering against my ear sent chills through my whole body. "Go and take Bea to the ladies and then you and I are going home."

By the time Bea and I entered the ladies, one look at her face told me that no amount of warning was going to do any good. She was already smitten and who wouldn't be? I might have swooned at Seb myself, even with Gabe there. He was charming in the extreme, in a very direct make your pants wet kind of way.

"Why didn't you introduce me to that God of a man before tonight?"

I laughed at Bea's wide-eyed expression.

"I mean he is gorgeous and funny and sexy as fuck."

"He's my boyfriend's best friend so I probably shouldn't comment."

With a point in my direction and a loud laugh, Bea shook her head. "You probably shouldn't but if you did you wouldn't be able to deny it."

A shrug was the only response I offered. She was right, I wouldn't have been able to deny any of her claims, Seb appeared to be all she'd said and more.

"Seb is lovely, and I don't know him that well beyond him being Gabe's friend, but he doesn't seem to do serious, love you forever kind of relationships."

Bea nodded and looked in no way surprised at my words. "Seb is very honest and open, even on a first meeting."

"Oh." I was surprised. Not that he was honest, but that she was okay about it. Maybe Bea wasn't looking for her Prince Charming.

"Hang on!"

I jumped at her startled cry.

"You called Gabe your boyfriend. I know you're shagging him, but boyfriend?"

I felt a huge, smug grin spread across my face and I did nothing to disguise it. "He told me he loved me."

"Fucking hell! That is huge," my friend cried, a smile that matched my own plastered on her face. "Have you told him you love him too?"

I nodded and suddenly, like schoolgirls again we leapt up and down waving our hands and giggled.

Chapter Fifty-Eight

Gabriel

I woke to the sight of Carrie exiting the bathroom naked.

"Good morning to you." I stretched so that I virtually filled the bed.

"Morning, just." She glanced at the clock that showed it was after eleven.

"Hmmm, well, it was a late night."

She grinned down at me. "I dunno, we were home for midnight."

I shook my head, that was not the kind of late night I'd referred to. "It was a late night."

A mischievous glint appeared in her eyes as she scrunched up her nose and bit gently into her lip.

I arched a brow. "I can accept that our late didn't start until we got home."

She giggled and it might have been my favourite sound ever.

"Now, are you bringing your arse back to bed?"

She looked down, her eyes roaming my body that was uncovered to the pelvis and spread across most of the bed still.

"I might if there was any room for me."

"Oh, Angel, there is always room for you. In fact, I have saved the best seat in the house for you."

"You have?"

"Well, you actually have a choice of two." I threw the covers back, revealing my erection that was good to go again, despite the action it had seen the previous night, into this morning.

"It's a tempting offer of a seat."

"Or," I said, taking her hand, pulling her onto the bed until she had no choice but to kneel next to me.

"Or?"

"Or…" I licked my lips as if I was a starving man, starving for a single taste of her.

Her eyes widened and from my position, the squeezing of her thighs was unmistakeable.

"I do like both seating plans."

"How about this then. You climb on my face and let me devour you until you come over my face and on my tongue."

She gasped and moaned as her thighs tightened again.

"And I can guarantee that once I have tasted you, I will need to fuck you, so maybe you get both seating plans."

She giggled at my use of her seating plan reference but was already moving towards me, one leg lifting over my face so she was perfectly positioned above my mouth. I raised my hands and arms, cupping her hips and behind and then I pulled her closer so that my mouth was on her. Fuck, she was beyond wet already. I loved that she wanted me as much as I wanted her. She immediately began to release little mewls as she began rocking against my face. I tightened my grip on her and she stopped her movement, knowing I wanted to do this my way. I felt her relax her whole body before she stretched out, forward and then I felt her lick along my length before her hand cupped my balls and she drew me into her mouth. Fuck! This was not going to last long if she carried on like this. So much for doing it my way.

****

"Did you want to come with me to collect Charlotte?"

Carrie looked startled by my question. I wasn't entirely sure why, though. She knew I needed to collect my daughter from my parents and my mother had suggested having a late lunch together. I assumed the invitation had included Carrie, in fact, I'd be amazed if it hadn't.

"Angel, I think you might be overthinking it."

"Sorry. What will they say? What about Charlotte? What will we tell her?"

"Yes, you're definitely overthinking things now."

I pulled her into my lap from the stool at the breakfast bar next to mine. With an extremely late breakfast of French toast and crispy bacon finished after we'd finally moved from the bed as far as the shower where we both got dirty again, I pushed our plates away.

"What if Charlotte or your family don't approve?"

"Carrie, stop and breathe. There's nothing for them to approve or disapprove of."

Her face dropped and I immediately knew her overthinking had kicked in again.

"Let me finish. My mother is already on board so there's no need for you to worry on that score. Charlotte doesn't need to be explicitly told anything, does she? She loves me, she loves you and she'll spend time with us together and individually. Beyond that I don't think she needs to be told anything, do you?"

"No, of course not, sorry. This is all getting real and scary and I don't want to fuck it up or for it to go wrong—"

I cut her off before she rambled herself into oblivion. "Carrie, sweetheart, let's take it one day at a time. Is there any rush for you?"

Carrie shook her head firmly. "No rush at all. I love being with you and Charlotte."

I grinned at her, pushing her still damp hair back off her face and leaned in to kiss her lips gently. "I love being with you and Charlotte, too."

Her face splitting grin matched my own. "I love you, baby."

I had no words for how broad and bright my face was at her declaration of love for me. As my smile continued to grow hers did the same until we both laughed.

"I had no idea I could ever be this happy."

My heart sank at her sad expression and I made a silent pledge there and then that Carrie would only ever know love and happiness from that point. That I would show her love and happiness, whatever it took.

"Yeah, well, get used to it and in case there was any doubt, I love you too. Now, let's get moving and go and see our girl."

Chapter Fifty-Nine

Carrie

We entered Christine's house together and immediately she saw us and smiled.

"Hello, you two. Good night last night?"

I swear my face was burning with embarrassment at just how good a night we'd had.

"How's Bea?"

I felt a little awkward because as far as she was aware, I was out with Bea and Gabe stayed home with Seb.

"She's well and we had a lovely night," I replied. "It really had been too long."

"And was last seen dancing with Seb," Gabe told his mother who laughed. "We met up with the girls," he explained to her as if we were a regular couple who frequently met up on individual nights out.

"Oh dear, the poor unsuspecting girl." Noel's voice joined us in the kitchen.

Christine smacked her husband's arm. "Seb is a good boy really, underneath everything."

Gabe and his father smiled as the sound of Margaret's calling interrupted. "Christopher, is that you, lover?"

I laughed loudly and shooed Gabe away with my hands. "Go on then, lover."

I was dumbstruck when he leaned in towards me and kissed my cheek. "On my way, you sexy little minx," he called to his grandmother then turned to me. "See you shortly, Angel."

I was crimson now. The look exchanged between Gabe's parents meant they had seen it, not that they could have missed it.

"Where's Charlotte." The absence of the little girl dawned on me and gave me an ideal diversion from myself.

"We went swimming earlier and she wiped herself out, so she is currently snoring her head off on the sofa," Noel replied, his face glowing with love and pride for his granddaughter.

"Do you mind if I go and check on her?" I had no idea what I would do if either of them said they objected because I was desperate not to be under their scrutiny, never mind their questioning if that's how the mood took them.

"Of course not." Christine smiled across at me. "I'm sure there's no other face she'd rather wake-up to."

Relieved, I scurried away and waited for Charlotte to wake-up and take her rightful place in the limelight.

****

Lunch was easier once I'd got used to everyone knowing about me and Gabe. The looks and nudges between Noel and Christine had decreased and the atmosphere felt somewhat natural and relaxed.

I sat next to Charlotte who was opposite Gabe. Margaret sat across from me while Noel and Christine sat at the ends of the table.

We all chatted about everything and nothing, all except Margaret who only had eyes for Gabe, Christopher.

I watched with interest the way Margaret interacted with Gabe. When she looked at him she smiled and seemed genuinely happy, but it was more than that; her eyes were alight when she gazed at him, when he looked at her, when he spoke to her, smiled or took her hand in his. When she was with Gabriel, or Christopher as he was for her, she came to life in a way she didn't at any other time.

Is that how I looked when in Gabriel's company? When he bestowed his gaze, words and love upon me? Probably. A smile curled my lips. I had no ideas these feelings existed, certainly not within me, nor for me and yet they did, Gabe had shown me that and now I'd experienced it I would fight tooth and nail to hold onto it.

"When are you taking me to Paris then, lover?"

Margaret's question gained everyone's attention.

"Dad used to take Mum to Paris for their anniversary," Christine explained. "They honeymooned there, and it became a bit of a tradition."

I smiled at the sentiment behind it and felt sad that Margaret no longer had Christopher in her life.

"I'll book it soon," Gabriel replied and leaned in to kiss his grandmother's cheek.

Could my boyfriend be any more perfect? I didn't think so.

Margaret giggled like a giddy girl in love, which I suppose she was.

Charlotte giggled too and looked up at me. "Granny is funny, isn't she? She really, really loves Daddy a lot."

I smiled down at her.

"Like you do."

I opened and closed my mouth three or four times, but no words passed my lips and the truth was that I had no clue what I should or shouldn't say to that comment.

She continued before I had the chance to commit to words. "She gets sad sometimes because Grandpa is dead, and she misses him."

I nodded and squeezed her hand. Everyone around the table was aware of the conversation I was a near silent partner to, all except Margaret. She seemed unaware of anyone there other than her and Christopher. She was already reminiscing about their last trip to Paris.

"It makes me sad too because I miss Daddy when he goes to work and I miss you at weekends and I sometimes miss having a mummy, but I have you and Grandma, don't I?"

I was running on empty here in terms of what to say back so stuck with a simple and honest, "Yes. Yes, you do."

Charlotte's mouth opened, but before any words left it, Margaret spoke to Gabe again, this time in a very loud and clear voice.

"Do you remember Paris in '78?"

Gabe said nothing, but then he didn't need to because this trip down Memory Lane was all his grandmother's.

"What a time we had, lover. You tied me to the bed…"

Margaret got a far-off glance in her eyes that suggested she was back in that moment. Everyone else looked horrified while I fought a laugh that I feared would only be held back for so long.

"Mother—" Christine was desperate to steer the conversation in any direction that wasn't this, her mother had other ideas.

"Christopher, do you remember that night? I will never forget it, lover, not least because that was the first time we did anal."

Gabe laughed, as did I. Noel looked startled and Christine, well, speaking of anal, she looked like she wanted to crawl up her own arse at the revelations of her parent's sex life.

The laughter seemed to halt Margaret in her tracks. She gazed up at Gabe and had more than a twinkle in her eyes. "Book Paris, lover."

Noel began clearing the table and escorted Margaret back to a comfy chair while Christine topped up her own wine glass.

"Carrie?"

I looked down at Charlotte who I'd almost forgotten was sitting next to me.

"What's anal?"

I heard Christine whisper under her breath and then watched as she took another slug of wine while Gabe muttered something that sounded a lot like *fucking anal*.

He stared across at his daughter who was pursuing her thoughts about anal. "Is it an animal?"

"No, baby, it's not an animal," Gabe replied firmly, as desperate as his mother to shut this down.

"Is it—"

"Probably not," I cut in. "It's one of those things that is a little bit rude."

"Is it like the naughty words Daddy doesn't like me to say?" she asked innocently and realising it probably was, she looked slightly guilty.

"It is, but Granny doesn't really know that she shouldn't say those things in front of you."

Charlotte nodded and climbed onto my lap. "Sorry, Carrie." She looked across at her father. "Sorry, Daddy."

"That's okay," we said in stereo before the little girl climbed down to follow Noel into the kitchen.

"Bet you're glad you agreed to come with me now," Gabe said.

"I wish I hadn't witnessed that," chipped in Christine, eyeing up the last of the wine in the bottle.

I laughed at them both then with a sympathetic smile for Christine, I nodded. Gabe, I looked at more intently. "I'd go anywhere with you," I told him.

He stared across at me darkly. "I believe Paris is nice this time of the year."

Chapter Sixty

Gabriel

Charlotte had requested that Carrie bath her and as I was going out and meeting Seb, that worked for me. When I passed by the open bedroom door, I could hear them chatting between pages of the book my daughter had chosen.

"Carrie," I heard Charlotte say. "Do you like princesses?"

I smiled at my little girl's obsession with all things princess.

"Yeah, I suppose."

"And Prince Charming?"

I swear I heard Carrie sigh and roll her eyes. I was instantly reminded of the time I heard her thoughts on happily ever afters. I really hoped her opinion may have changed, even just a little in the short time we'd been together.

"Not like a real Prince Charming who saves the princess and takes her back to his kingdom."

It wasn't an outright no.

"How then?" My daughter sounded beyond confused by Carrie's vague answer.

"I believe that you can have your own Prince Charming who will love you and treat you well, but I don't think us girls have to have a man to save us. We can save ourselves."

"Can we?"

"Of course, look at you. You're funny and smart and amazing and strong and brave. You can do and be anything you want."

My heart swelled. Carrie was right in everything she said about my daughter, but the truth was I was more touched by the fact that as another female she could be the most amazing role model my girl could ever wish for.

"Carrie."

That one word was loaded with possibilities and expectation.

"Yes." I smiled at Carrie's response...she knew it was loaded too.

"Is Daddy going to be your Prince Charming?"

I should have moved away in case I heard something I didn't want to. I should have but didn't.

"Maybe," Carrie began. "I think I'd like him to be."

With a very big smile on my face, I headed into my own room and jumped in the shower.

****

"You are looking beyond smug this evening." Seb raised his glass in toast.

I met his glass with my own and smiled, unable and unwilling to hide my smug happiness.

"I take it I have Nanny to thank for your stupid smiling face."

"Maybe."

My friend laughed. "That's a yes then, and I can only imagine how she paints that on your face."

I laughed back. "I'd rather you didn't imagine it if it's all the same."

"You really need to get over your objections to my naked Nanny thoughts."

I flipped him off with another smile.

"I am pleased that things are going well between you. She's good for you, and Charlotte."

"She is, and thank you. How are things going with your own nanny?" We hadn't spoken about him and Bea yet, but now seemed as good a time as any.

His own face broke into a smile. "I don't know if she is mine as such, but I like her, she's fun."

"Fun?"

"Yes, fun." Seb quirked a brow at me. "Go on, give me your pep talk, Dad."

I shook my head, possibly more at me than my friend. Seb loved ladies, the more the better. He always maintained he was looking for fun and nothing more serious. He hadn't always been like that, but this had been the Seb I'd known and loved for more years than I could remember. The problem he had with it was other people's insistence that he wasn't happy with his life. I was not one of them; I wasn't of the mindset that he couldn't be happy in a serious relationship but I did accept and had seen that he was happy in his own skin and with his life as it was.

"Come on, let's have it."

"Fine," I muttered, knowing he was going to rip the piss out of me once I'd finished speaking. "Is she on board with your plans and commitment, or lack thereof?"

"Is this you or Nanny speaking?" He barely paused before answering his own question. "Of course, it's Nanny. I get it, Bea is her friend, but I need her not to be planting ideas in her head. Bea knows exactly where I stand and she is fine with that, we're both more than fine with it, but if Nanny starts pecking in her ear about love and forever…"

His voice trailed off and I was surprised at just how uncomfortable Seb looked.

"Mate, I get it. If you and Bea are okay with whatever is happening between you then nobody else should interfere."

He didn't look convinced by my words. I laughed until his expression morphed into one of genuine worry.

"Seb, this isn't my business and I apologise for opening the conversation. Carrie is worried for Bea because she is her friend. She loves you and wants you to be happy too, however, I have told her she is not to get involved or try and influence things."

"Really?"

"Yes, really and although she's unlikely to adhere to it entirely, I don't think she'll push her nose in too much so long as her friend doesn't fall head over heels for you and you kick her to the kerb and break her heart."

His smile was reinstated. "No chance. You know me, the first sign of emotion and I am gone."

I did know him and that was his usual method of operation.

"Hang on, did you say that Nanny loves me?"

I laughed at where I knew he was going to take this. "I did."

"Wow. You need to watch your back, buddy. Your girl is mine

for the taking." He laughed heartily. "I might not have to imagine her naked for much longer."

Okay, enough was enough. "I will fucking knock you out if you continue with this, buddy."

He howled at me as I landed a hard punch to his arm. "Thanks, Gabe, and thank Nanny too, I appreciate the concern, but me and Bea, we're not like you two. We're casual and know what we're doing."

I nodded, there was no more to say and as for Carrie, I would remind her again that Seb and Bea's relationship was out of bounds.

"Now, let me fill you in on Margaret's latest pearl of wisdom as shared over lunch."

Chapter Sixty-One

Carrie

I couldn't believe how amazing things were between me and Gabe. It had been a couple of weeks since that night in the bar where we both admitted our love. Gabe was right about his family, who sussed us almost immediately, and Charlotte who seemed happy to take things as they came. We'd been spending more time together as a trio now and it was better than I imagined it being.

Charlotte had been doing just three half days at nursery after Gabe and I chatted about the impact of it on her. She seemed less tired and happier with a slower transition into the school system. I loved having time with the little girl who really had become the light of my life. The evenings had been starting with me going upstairs to allow Gabe and Charlotte some valuable father and daughter time. Sometimes I joined them for dinner and a little family time, other nights it was after Charlotte's bedtime before I joined Gabe. Christine visited regularly, but she seemed to have taken a step back in her role as a primary carer for Charlotte.

Bea and I met up a couple of times since our last night out, but with children around it had been hard to discuss her and Seb beyond him escorting her home that night and knowing they had been messaging and talking.

Waiting for Charlotte outside of school, I noticed Henry's mother a few feet away, sneering at me. Rumour had it that she used to have a nanny and her husband cheated on her with the nanny, which kind of explained why she was so suspicious of me and my role in Gabe's life, but I was not her nanny and Gabe wasn't married.

My phone vibrated in my pocket. I pulled it out to see a message from Bea.

<Are you free tonight? We need a catch up!>

I laughed out loud, assuming her need for a catch up was Seb related. Briefly, very briefly, I wondered if getting the lowdown on her and Seb was a good idea because I knew that no matter what else happened, I was going to have to spend time with him and probably didn't need images of them in my head when I did so.

<Yeah, I have no plans and Charlotte is at home tonight so Gabe won't have any either. About 8 o'clock at the pub?>

<See you then>

I put my phone away, ignoring Henry's mother's continued glare, just in time to find Charlotte rushing towards me.

"Can we do some yoga today?" she asked and before I had chance to reply she continued, loud enough for everyone present to hear. "Daddy says I'm getting super bendy now, nearly as bendy as you."

I laughed and heard several other sniggers at the little girl's innocent comment. I made no comment on her father's love of my bendiness. "Of course we can. Lunch first, then we can chill for a while and then yoga."

Charlotte gripped my hand tightly, happily swinging arms with me as we walked away.

****

"I still think you should stay at home with me."

I laughed at Gabe's faked pout as I sat with him and Charlotte eating dinner before getting ready to go out.

"Can I come, too?" asked Charlotte, gaining our immediate

attention.

"No," we replied in stereo.

"But Carrie said it's a girl's night and I am a girl."

"A big girl's night out," Gabe explained.

"So, when I'm a big girl I can?"

"Yes, a very big girl," her father agreed.

"Can I help you to get ready?" Charlotte asked now, somehow determined to be a part of my night out.

I looked across at Gabe, hoping for an indication of which way I should jump on this. He shrugged and I took that to be confirmation that he had no objections his daughter's plan.

"Of course."

Gabe and I both laughed at her squeal of delighted excitement.

Charlotte sat on my bed, propped up on pillows, watching me get ready. She asked countless questions about my hair, make-up, my clothes, even my underwear! I answered her questions as best I could.

"Can I have some make-up on?" she asked, causing me to wonder if she could.

I had no idea what Gabe's stand was on this. Did he even have a stand on his daughter wearing make-up? I remembered her own make-up collection that she very often applied to her father and Uncle Seb.

"Maybe a little," I agreed.

Forgetting my own getting ready routine I began to apply a little of everything to the little girl's face. By the time I was done she didn't look that different but was slightly bronzed and sparkly.

"I look so pretty," she cried as I passed her my mirror.

"You look pretty all the time," I told her seriously. She really was one gorgeous little girl.

I spritzed her with my favourite perfume.

"Shall we show Daddy how pretty we are?" she asked, bouncing around on my bed now.

Before I could answer, an answer that would have involved me needing to get dressed as I was still wearing just a robe, Gabe's voice called from the next room.

"Hey, where are my girls at?"

Charlotte giggled, whereas my breath caught, and my heart skipped a beat.

Gabe appeared and kissed, first Charlotte and then me. "You two smell nice."

"Daddy, look at my sparkly face."

Charlotte stood on my bed and bounced as her father scooped her into his arms. He kissed her face all over, making her giggle.

"It's a beautiful face whether it's sparkly or not. It's my favourite face in the world and I love it."

I laughed at the scene before me. It was truly beautiful and I felt privileged to be allowed to share it with them both.

"I can make you beautiful later." I wasn't sure whether Charlotte was issuing some kind of threat.

"Whatever you want, baby."

Charlotte scooted away, leaving me and Gabe alone.

"Angel, you seem a little underdressed for a night out." He pulled me to my feet and held me against him as one hand skimmed beneath the robe I wore and cupped my behind. "Shit! Definitely underdressed, but this is the perfect outfit for when you get home."

I reached up and pulled his head down to mine where I landed a brief kiss to his lips. Before either of us could deepen it, Charlotte called to him and like that, he was gone. Grabbing my clothes, I put on underwear, jeans, a t-shirt, boots and a denim jacket then left to meet Bea.

Chapter Sixty-Two

Gabriel

Carrie looked amazing when she left the house and I couldn't wait for her to come back. The sight of her with my daughter, putting make-up and perfume on her, treating her like mums normally treat their little girls made my heart swell and something deep and pure to blossom in my chest.

"Daddy." Charlotte was snuggled under the bed covers and after a story we decided to chat.

"Yes, baby."

"Carrie said she will paint my nails tomorrow, if I'm allowed."

I smiled down at her with not a single objection to this plan. Carrie's own toenails were usually painted and often her fingernails too.

"Do you think Carrie will have pink nail varnish?"

I knew Carrie was currently wearing pink on her toes so answered with certainty. "Yes."

"Daddy."

"Yes, baby," I repeated to her repeated Daddy.

"Will Carrie be home soon?"

"Not for a while. It will be really late so you will see her in the morning."

She nodded as my phone sounded with a message. I glanced down at it on the floor where it showed a message from Seb.

<Are you in? Will pop round if you are>

<Yeah, just putting Charlotte to bed so let yourself in>

I returned my attention to my daughter who was back with another, "Daddy."

"Yes, baby."

She smiled up at me, recognising my own repeated response if not her own repeated opener. "When Carrie comes home, where will she sleep?"

"In bed." My response was immediate and almost instinctive. I wasn't being an arse or flippant.

My daughter shook her head, disapproving, almost. "Whose bed? Her bed or your bed?"

I stared down at my three-year-old going on twenty-three-year-old daughter and wondered how I found myself in this position.

"Carrie sleeps in your bed sometimes, doesn't she?" Charlotte barely paused for breath. "I know when I have a bad dream or if I'm poorly I sleep in your bed, don't I?" Again, she hardly paused between the questions she apparently needed no answer to. "Carrie must be really poorly or have lots of bad dreams because she sleeps in your bed, a lot."

"I—erm—" Apparently, my input was not required.

"I see her in the morning sometimes and other times I hear her cry in the night and then she goes quiet because you take care of her, don't you?"

What the fuck was happening to my life that I was having this conversation with my child? Well, it was more that I was being subjected to this one-sided conversation. It suddenly dawned on me that Carrie's crying could only be us having sex, her coming. Fucking hell, I couldn't have my child waking up to that on a regular basis.

"My friend at school says her daddy sleeps with a lady sometimes." She giggled. "She's his girlfriend. Daddy, is Carrie really your girlfriend?"

Where the fuck were Carrie or Seb when I needed a wingman to field these conversations and questions?

Ah fuck it. I decided honesty was the way to go.

"Yes, baby, Carrie is my girlfriend and she sometimes does sleep in Daddy's bed, but not because she's poorly or scared, not like you. We like to spend time together." I impressed myself with my honest, simple and concise explanation.

"And kiss?"

Just when I thought I'd done so well!

"I see you kiss Carrie. You kissed us on Carrie's bed but sometimes I see you kiss her in the kitchen or in the morning when I go to get my things for school."

"Yes, and kiss." I swear I was as red as beetroot, blushing more as a grown man to be under this scrutiny from my daughter than I was as a teenager being grilled by my parents.

"I love you, Daddy."

"I love you too, my beautiful baby girl."

"I love Carrie too."

Fuck it! In for a penny, in for a pound. "So do I."

My little girl looked up and grinned at me. "Can Carrie really be my mummy?"

I didn't see that coming, although with hindsight I should have. I needed to handle this with care. "I don't know, baby. Maybe one day."

She smiled now, snuggled further beneath the covers and closed her eyes. Clearly interrogation time was over.

"Night-night, my beautiful girl." I kissed her forehead and left her to what I hoped would be the sweetest of dreams.

I headed downstairs, unsure if I should go over my conversation with Charlotte or at least share it with Seb. It was no surprise to hear Seb moving around before I reached the bottom of the stairs; he had a spare key and often let himself in, especially like tonight when I was indisposed with Charlotte, not least because if she had any inclination that Uncle Seb was in the house she would have refused to stay in bed without seeing him.

What was a surprise was the sound of Seb's voice. He was known to occasionally talk, or moan to himself, but this was different. It sounded as though he was speaking to another person...probably on the phone and then I heard another voice. A woman's voice.

"Promise," she said.

"Really?" Seb laughed. "If it means that much to you."

"It does," she replied.

"Okay, pinky promise it is."

I turned the corner and came to a dead stop when greeted by the sight of Seb, linking his little finger with Bea's and shaking on their pinky promise, for what I didn't need to know. What I did need to know was what the hell Bea was doing here when she was meeting Carrie tonight, and if she was here, where was my girlfriend?

"What are you doing here?"

They both turned.

"I text," said Seb with a laugh.

"Yeah, sorry, I meant Bea. What are you doing here?"

Seb frowned at me. "I didn't realise it would be a problem for us both to drop in on you and Nanny."

Bea rolled her eyes at his *Nanny*.

"It's not, except she's not here, Carrie. She's meeting you tonight in the pub."

Bea stared at my finger that pointed at her, almost with accusation.

"We talked about meeting up earlier in the week, but we made no plans."

"You text her." I was beginning to panic now; why were Bea's plans and Carrie's poles apart? Was Carrie lying to me about her plans? Had she misunderstood Bea's message? Or was it something else?

"I lost my phone."

Those four words made my heart sink to the pit of my stomach. If Bea didn't have her phone, who did? And why would they text Carrie?

"Shit!" Bea's startled cry caused me and Seb to turn our full attention to her.

"What?" I was beginning to panic and raised my voice at the woman before me. "What?" I repeated.

"Gabe, calm down." He looked at Bea again. "What's going on?"

"I don't know, not for sure, but, I think, maybe...Toby."

Chapter Sixty-Three

Carrie

Bea was usually punctual, but tonight, I arrived first. I milled around the bar in case she was sitting out of view. She wasn't. I found a quiet corner to stand in where I could see the door so as not to miss her when she arrived. I wondered if she'd seen Seb before leaving to meet me. That could certainly explain her delay. With a giggle I thought how Gabe usually made me late.

I was about to text Bea when my phone vibrated in my bag with what I saw was a message from my friend.

<Sorry, something has come up so will have to rearrange. Will check in tomorrow and arrange something. Sorry>

Immediately, I wondered if Seb was the reason for her change of plans. I might need to check if Gabe knew anything. With my phone still in my hand I prepared to call Gabe and let him know that I'd be on my way home in the next couple of minutes. I wondered if I should tell him to get my robe ready for me. I giggled at that thought and all thoughts of what the rest of the night might look like.

I had just selected Gabe's number when I felt eyes on me. Looking up I found Toby a few feet away, heading straight for me, but at least he was smiling.

"Hi, it's been a while. How are you?"

I stared at him, unsure what to say as he was being so friendly, unlike our last meeting.

"I owe you an apology. The other week, I was out of order. Sorry."

I nodded, unwilling to tell him it was okay. It wasn't.

"Can I get you a drink? Unless you're meeting someone, as a peace offering."

"I was meeting Bea, but something came up."

"That's a shame. Come on, Carrie, one drink. Let me make amends for being a dick."

I laughed and nodded my agreement.

We chatted and laughed as we had our one drink. As I drained my glass I attempted to get up, to go to the bathroom where I would call Gabe and tell him I was coming home. I'd also tell him I'd met Toby, even though I knew he wouldn't like it. Me and fuckboy. I sniggered.

"Hey, that one glass of wine has gone to your head."

I fell back onto the bench I sat on and laughed as the world began to spin.

"I should call Gabe."

"Your boss?" Toby didn't sound thrilled at the introduction of my boss' name.

"Yeah, but, he's erm, also my boyfriend." I giggled at the last word then felt awkward revealing the fact to Toby, especially when his face contorted, just briefly, with contempt for Gabe who I still believed he mistrusted.

"Come on, I've got my car, I'll drop you off."

This time when I attempted to get to my feet, Toby caught me and with his arm around my waist he almost carried me out of the pub. I was certain I heard him shout to someone, something about me being a lightweight.

When the cold air hit me, I became even more incapable. I felt ill, disorientated, like I was having some kind of out of body experience. I was hot, dizzy and suddenly emotional. I wanted to go home. I wanted Gabe, but he wasn't there, Toby was.

Suddenly the sounds around me became echoey, distorted and my vision began to blur. I felt sick and my legs became heavy, like they were going to buckle beneath me at any second.

We were now standing next to Toby's car. I remembered it from when he gave me a lift home after I'd been to Christine's the first time.

In no time at all he opened the car and was picking me up to put me in the passenger seat. He got in next to me and reached over to fasten my seatbelt. I felt his hand touch me, a little more than fleetingly as he pulled the seatbelt and allowed his fingers to brush across one of my breasts. My hand came up in an attempt to brush him away from me, far away, but I was unsure if I managed to make contact.

The engine started and we drove away from the pub. The lights outside flashed as we passed them and they hurt my eyes, dazzled me. I closed my eyes, the lids so heavy I had no choice. They were just too heavy. I had no idea how much time passed but what felt like a short time afterwards the car quieted and then fell silent.

Still my eyes remained closed and my head and brain felt foggy, as if they were finding it difficult to remain switched on. The feel of the seatbelt losing tension was my next thought. It slid slowly across my body and as when it had been fastened, I felt a touch to my breasts, both of them now. My nipples beaded at the fleeting contact and then fingers gripped my knee, pulling my legs apart. The same hand moved up my inner thigh until it pressed against me and then I felt my jeans opening.

I don't know how, but this felt wrong, so wrong. The fingers were alien, the touch rough and in no way loving. I felt sick and the more I fought to open my eyes and gather my bearings the more difficult it became. I was fighting emotionally, mentally and physically now. I could feel my limbs flailing but I had no idea why or how I thought I could fight anything without seeing what was happening.

Loud sobs sounded around me, my sobs and cries as I felt cold air across my skin.

"No, no, no," I screamed as I realised my clothes were being moved if not removed.

"You little bitch!"

Toby's voice. I was with Toby. This made no sense, except it did.

"Oh God! No, please."

"Keep fucking fighting me, bitch, and I will tie you up and

fuck every hole you have."

My screams sounded more like howls now, like a frightened and hurt animal, which was probably the best way to describe me.

"And the best bit about it? Tomorrow morning you will wake up with the mother of all hangovers and won't remember anything about it." He laughed. "Even if you do, think you do, you won't quite know if it was real and if it was you won't remember if you consented or not." He laughed again as I felt cold air move up my belly.

Chapter Sixty-Four

Gabriel

"What do you mean, Toby?" I could feel the anger rising and my tone did nothing to hide it.

"I saw him the other day. He was sorry about how he treated us—"

I cut her off there. "What do you mean, how he treated you?"

"He saw us in the pub before and was an arsehole to us. He had a go at us all and then turned on Carrie but stopped...it was weird."

"I don't have time for this. What does he have to do with you being here while my girlfriend thinks she is meeting you?"

"He apologised and was friendly and I lost my phone that day too. I just thought it was lost until now...what if..."

She didn't need to say anymore, by the look on Seb's face, he and I were on the same page here.

"I need to find her."

"I'll come too," said Seb, already pulling his car keys from his pocket.

"There's more."

When I turned back to Bea I could have cried. She had a shit scared look on her face and tears welling in her eyes. "What?" I really didn't have time for this and yet I knew I needed to hear what she was going to say.

"Toby. There have been rumours. He doesn't have real girlfriends but chases a girl and then when it seems things are going well, he loses interest."

I looked between her and Seb because ironically, she could have been describing my friend.

"He often rescues them or looks after them. One girl worked in a pub we used to go to, and she made wild claims…"

"Bea, what claims?" Seb held her hand as if to encourage her to go on.

"She said the night he'd been with her, they'd had sex. She didn't remember it and hadn't had much to drink, but she knew they had, she felt it the next day. She said she'd been drugged and raped."

"Fucking hell! And you didn't think to mention this before. My girlfriend is probably with this psycho!" I was raging with anger and fear.

"Does Carrie know this?" Seb was the voice of calm and reason.

Bea shook her head and released a cry. "I started to tell her and then you two arrived in the pub and we didn't believe it, not really, although…"

"What? Although what?" My grip on control and sanity was slipping more with every passing second.

"One of our friends had a drunk night, although she hadn't drunk much, and Toby took care of her, but friend zoned her the next day."

"Where will he take her?" I grabbed my phone and hit Carrie's number. It rang and rang and rang and then went to voicemail.

"I don't know. He lives with an aunt, so he never takes anyone home."

"Let's start at the pub then," Seb said. "Bea, can you stay here and take care of Charlotte and if you think of anything call?"

She nodded and Seb leaned in to kiss her cheek and then we left.

****

Seb drove, not fast enough for me, but he was at least safe. My mind raced from one awful thought to something even worse when my friend's in car handsfree picked up a call from Bea.

"I've just remembered, Toby used to talk about an old car he was fixing up and his aunt wouldn't let him do it on her drive, so he has a lock-up. I don't know where it is, except for it not being far from the pub and the park."

"Okay, that's great, thanks, babe."

I looked across at Seb who seemed a little too keen on Bea, well, by his usual standards.

"Is Charlotte okay?" I shouted down the line at her.

"Yeah, out like a light. Please find Carrie."

I found her plea a little irritating as she had to accept some responsibility for this situation. She should have told Carrie, warned her.

Seb ended the call and looked across at me. "This is not Bea's fault."

"I didn't say it was, did I?"

"You didn't need to, and if she had warned Carrie about everybody she knew who there'd been a rumour or hunch about, would that have been better?"

I frowned.

"Exactly. We both know people who have had accusations made against them and we have chosen to ignore them, disbelieve them."

I traded my frown for a huff this time.

"Hindsight is a wonderful thing, Gabe, and now is not the time to apportion blame and guilt. Let's find Carrie."

We pulled up outside the pub and nervously entered. I was desperate to see Carrie sitting at a table with a drink in her hand, even if she was with fuckboy. There was no sign of her. Seb even asked a lady entering the toilets to check for her in there. My friend spoke to a barman who recognised my description of Carrie and Toby. I felt sick. I might have actually heaved at the possible outcome of tonight.

"Yeah, she was pretty wasted when they left here. He virtually carried her out."

I stared across at the barman. "How much had she drunk?"

He shook his head. "There's a lot of customers and a lot of staff but we did comment that she'd only been here about half an hour or so and nobody remembered serving her, just him."

"Shit, fucking shit! Do you know where they went?"

The barman shook his head, but a lady serving next to him interrupted.

"Sorry, couldn't help but hear. They headed down towards the park. I was out having a smoke. She looked unwell to me rather than drunk. He was holding her up and seemed to pick her up to put her in the car. I asked if she was okay, if he needed help or an ambulance but he said they were fine and that she was a lightweight."

"Thanks." I looked across at Seb. "If they were heading towards the park and Bea said his lock-up is somewhere between here and the park."

"That has to be where he's gone."

The barman interrupted now. "The lock-ups nearest to here are on the ground near the old access road to the park, where the derelict high-rise is."

"Thank you." I was already heading for the door with Seb in pursuit.

It took only a few minutes until we reached the lock-ups I didn't know were there. We both leapt from the car and looked around.

"Which one?" Seb asked.

I shrugged, then paused and looked around using the torch on my phone to get a better look. There were a few tyre tracks and one set looked fresh. I followed them and Seb followed me. I turned my torch off and selected Carrie's number. I hit dial and from the other side of the door we stood by, I heard it ringing.

We'd found her and now I was going to kill fuckboy.

Chapter Sixty-Five

Carrie

My phone rang again. I could hear it and I knew it was my ringtone but was incapable of finding it or answering or doing anything beyond lying there.

I didn't know if I was even conscious anymore. I felt as though I was in a dream like state. There was a weight on me, preventing me from moving, although, as I tried to move my limbs, I was unable to assert any control over them. There was breath on me, on my face and I could smell beer and something else, weed. God, that smell made me sick at the best of times, but now...I was dry retching.

For what felt like the millionth time I tried to open my eyes, with little to no avail. Sleep was summoning me and as much as a small part of my brain beseeched me to fight it, I wasn't sure if or why I should.

I heard something in the distance, voices, footsteps or maybe it was just the wind blowing. The weight that had been heavy on me disappeared and then there was no mistaking the sound of a loud crash. I was being moved, pulled, into a sitting position and my skin was warming as my clothing was put back. Was I still dreaming?

The sensation of gentle tapping against my face drew my attention, especially when the taps became harder and turned into smacks.

"Ow." I tried to pull away and put some distance between me and whoever's hand was striking me.

There was a short laugh I recognised as Seb's. "Good girl. Come on, Nanny, wakey wakey."

Reluctantly my eyes opened into the tiniest of slits.

"There she is. You okay, Nanny?"

I nodded and forced my eyes to open a little more.

"I need to get your man sorted now."

I frowned, confused about everything including his words until I heard more noise; grunts, heavy breathing, shouting and swearing. Something else registered; banging, grinding, crunching.

The scene beyond Seb came into view, Gabe, punching someone I barely recognised as Toby.

Seb was on his phone, speaking to someone, telling them someone had been drugged and somebody else was attempting to commit rape. Seb hung up and approached Gabe, pulling him off Toby who lay in a heap, a limp, bloody mess.

"I will fucking kill him." Gabe was raging.

I didn't think I had ever heard someone so angry, but as he turned, allowing me to see him in profile, I saw something else, sadness.

He took a step closer to Toby, who was beginning to move, possibly preparing to get to his feet.

"You need to stay the fuck down or I will punch you myself," Seb warned him, but I sensed his motivation in warning the other man was to protect his friend, my boyfriend who looked to be shaking with emotion.

Suddenly, I found my voice. "Gabe, baby."

He spun and faced me, sadness completely taking over from anger.

"Go get your girl. She looks like she could do with a hug." Seb patted Gabe on the back as he approached me.

Gabe dropped to his haunches and carefully, as if preparing to handle the most precious and valuable of artefacts, he reached out and stroked a finger across my cheek then used his whole hand to cup the back of my head. He pulled me in so that my face was safely tucked into his neck.

"Angel, you gave me a fucking fright. If you ever do that to me again…"

I sobbed, loudly, wrapping my arms around Gabe's neck, pulling him closer and closer as his free arm wrapped around my waist, holding me tighter than I thought I had ever been held, making me feel safer than I ever had for certain.

"I don't really know what happened. Bea couldn't come..." I was rambling as more tears of confusion and disorientation flowed.

"I know." Gabe rocked me gently. "I'll explain it all."

"I'll message Bea," said Seb and then pointed towards the back of the building. "Gabe, police are here."

****

I woke up, unsure of where I was and then it all came back to me.

"Hey, Angel."

Gabe's face came into view. He took my hand and kissed my knuckles from his position in the chair next to my hospital bed.

"Ow, my head hurts."

"Yeah, the doctors said it would. Let me get a nurse."

"Not yet, don't leave me."

"I'm going nowhere."

"What happened?"

"What do you remember?"

"I left the house to meet Bea, but she wasn't there. Toby came in and we had a drink. It's all a bit fuzzy after that. I was scared and tired." A little cry left my lips as the foggy memories of the previous night flooded back, the confusion, emotional state and lack of control.

For the next twenty minutes or so, after a dose of painkillers, Gabe went over everything from the previous night. I was shocked but it all made sense, the sounds and thoughts I recalled and some I thought I'd imagined.

A doctor joined us shortly afterwards and went on to tell me that all my test results were back. I was still confused because I was struggling to follow the conversation. He told me that I had drugs in my system...date rape drugs. I felt sick. I had once considered Toby a friend of sorts and he had deliberately done this to me. The next thing I tuned into was confirmation that I hadn't been raped or sexually assaulted, well, not in a penetrative way. The police had been made aware of the results and Toby remained in police custody.

I heard Gabe mutter something involving thanking God and being relieved. I cried loudly, knowing I should be relieved too, and yet I wasn't. I was angry, with Toby for doing it at all, and myself for having been in that position, for not listening to Gabe's warnings about fuckboy.

Gabe got up onto the bed next to me and held me close until I fell asleep again, hoping that when I woke this would prove to have been a bad dream, a nightmare, no more.

Chapter Sixty-Six

Gabriel

It had been a couple of weeks since I'd found Carrie in that lock-up with that fucking animal touching her. I swear I will never get that image out of my head. Carrie was beginning to come to terms with what happened and what could have, but fortunately hadn't happened. We were both relieved that most of it remained foggy and didn't seem entirely real like a memory would normally be. She was virtually my prisoner as I barely let her out of my sight, but knew I'd have to at some point, sooner rather than later as she was desperate to get back to normal.

Fuckboy was still under lock and key, undergoing assessment. I hoped to God they never let him out because I couldn't guarantee I wouldn't go back for another go at him. The police had built a pretty solid case against him and had several more girls go forward to claim he'd done the same to them. When the police went to his home, they found more drugs, the same one that was found in Carrie's system and others. They'd also found photos of girls, some who had now come forward, others unknown and lots of Carrie. He had obviously been following her for weeks and weeks. Some of the photos were taken when she was with Charlotte which made me want to punch the creep all over again, but harder.

The sound of my girls laughing pulled me back into the room. They were sitting on the sofa, with their feet up on a footstool and a blanket over them. They had a huge bowl of popcorn balanced between them while they watched Mary Poppins.

Carrie began singing along while Charlotte watched her, looking up in awe.

I swear my heart skipped a beat at my daughter's look of pure love and adoration for the woman I loved.

Charlotte attempted to join in with the singing and I might be biased but she did a damned fine job of it. Carrie pulled her closer and kissed the top of her head.

"Hey, you two, are you saving any popcorn for Daddy?"

Carrie held the bowl aloft for me to grab a handful, but I took the bowl making them both shout out at me. Carrie threw the blanket back, inviting me to take the space next to her. An invitation I didn't hesitate to accept.

I leaned in and kissed her on the cheek. "How you doing, Angel?"

"Good." She smiled across at me then reached up to kiss my lips gently. "Never better."

Charlotte began to chuckle at something on the screen and in turn we laughed at and with her.

We stayed like that, wrapped together, cocooned in our little family for the next couple of hours. Charlotte fell asleep shortly after Carrie and somehow, they ended up lying together. I was considering carrying each of them upstairs to my bed then joining them when my phone sounded. Seb.

<Hi. How's things today? How's Nanny doing? I thought I might pop in, with Bea>

I scratched my head and pinched the bridge of my nose, warding off an impending headache. Bea was a bit of a sore spot for me. I knew that Toby was the one responsible for what happened to Carrie and that without Bea we wouldn't have found her, saved her, but I still felt she should have warned Carrie about him. Seb understood my point but reminded me that Bea did what she thought was right at the time and could have been way off the mark about Toby whilst spreading rumours.

Carrie held nobody responsible, except herself. We talked for several days about that and I think she could now see that her naivety and good nature were not flaws, but were taken advantage of by fuckboy, and that none of this was her fault.

I re-read my friend's message and after a stern word with myself about my slightly irrational thoughts I did what I knew Carrie would want me to do.

<Yeah, all good. We're all in so come round whenever you're ready>

Within the hour, Seb and Bea arrived. The latter looked nervous, but once she sat with Carrie and Charlotte, she relaxed, and I realised how unfairly I'd treated her.

Seb and I went to the kitchen to make drinks while the girls chatted.

"How's Bea?"

Seb spun and stared at me, startled by my question. "Okay. She feels shit about not warning Carrie, but as I've pointed out to you and her, this is not her fault."

I nodded and he arched a brow. "I know. I was angry and just needed someone to blame."

"I do understand," he said with conviction.

"I know and I will apologise to her for being arsy and obstructive in her seeing Carrie."

My friend smiled at me, looking genuinely happy and relieved.

"So, you and Bea?"

His laugh cut me off. "Are having fun. Now, tell me about you and Nanny."

I almost snarled at him which only served to amuse him.

"Not like that. Not naked Nanny. I was checking if everything was okay and if you've moved her downstairs yet."

"Ah. We're good, better than good all things considered, and she has slept in my bed every night since last week, but we haven't discussed her moving downstairs officially, but she will."

Seb laughed. "I am glad you're happy and the fact that Charlotte loves Carrie makes me even happier.

I nodded because I was happy, too. Happier than I had ever

been or dreamed of being and that was all down to one person, Carrie Webber and she was mine, mine and Charlotte's.

Chapter Sixty-Seven

Carrie

"Good morning, Angel."

The feel of Gabe's breath on my shoulder made me smile. I stretched like a recently woken cat, flexing all my muscles.

"Morning, baby."

He kissed my shoulder as his arm that was around my middle scooted up until his hand cupped my breast and thumbed my nipple. I hissed as sensation began to course through me.

"I missed you last night," I told him as his back blanketed mine more closely. So close that there was no mistaking the erection digging into my behind.

"You're the one who fell asleep before I got here." His chuckle rattled against my neck.

"Yeah, well, I managed to stay awake for almost an hour."

He laughed now, the rasp of his laughter rolling and rippling across my skin. "It took just over twenty minutes to get Charlotte settled, so you didn't even last half an hour."

I rolled over to face him and leaned in to kiss his lips gently while ruffling his hair. "I'm awake now."

He arched a brow and slipped a hand to my behind. He stroked and cupped the cheek. I raised my leg, putting it over his hip. He stroked lower so that he was able to slide a finger through my arousal then slipped it inside me. I clenched around him immediately.

"You really are awake, aren't you?"

I reached between us and found his naked erection that I

palmed and pumped gently.

A screech from behind us made us both literally jump. The metaphorical cold water that had been thrown over us doused our ardour.

"It's my birthday!" squealed Charlotte, already leaping on the bed between us. "I am four." She clapped and giggled.

"Yes, you are." I laughed at her excitement.

Gabe pulled her in for a kiss. "Happy birthday to the most beautiful girl ever."

She clapped again, making me laugh louder. "And you have a party and cake, and, ooh, I wonder," I whispered, "could there be presents for you?"

She beamed with delight and bounced on the bed again. "Can we be awake now? Is it proper morning time now?"

"I'd say so," Gabe said, already passing me his discarded t-shirt to put on.

Once I'd slipped it on, in one fluid movement, I got up, dashed to the bathroom then returned to collect Charlotte while Gabe put some clothes on. We waited at the top of the stairs for him and then, the three of us together descended the stairs.

Within an hour the living room looked like an explosion of pink. I was still collecting wrapping paper while Gabe tidied all the toys, and tidy translated as piling up in a corner. There were banners and balloons everywhere.

"I swear this is what the land of unicorns must look like when there's a tummy bug doing the rounds," Gabe said seriously and then laughed with me.

"And this is only round one, baby."

"Mum and Dad will be here in about an hour and Seb and Bea, then the party guests should start arriving. So, about ten hours before it's just the three of us again and twelve hours before I can take you to bed and make up for last night and this morning."

"Can't wait." I bit down into my lip and crinkled my nose.

"Oh yeah, you won't be able to walk tomorrow if I get my way."

"Can't wait," I repeated with another bite into my lip and crinkle of my nose.

"Well, you'll have to." He stepped closer, pulled me to him and leaned in to give me a single peck to the cheek.

"You're kissing, again!" cried Charlotte as she re-entered the room.

"Yup, waiting," I said, already stepping back and turning my attention to Charlotte. "Right then, birthday girl, shall we go and find our best party outfits?"

Charlotte's party was at a local trampoline centre, Bounce Around. Gabe made countless references to me and him doing some private bouncing later. I laughed each time but couldn't deny how appealing it was. I was more than happy to join the children on the trampolines with Bea and was surprised when Gabe joined us, Seb less so.

Gabe and Seb were like naughty schoolboys, bouncing into each other, trying to make the other fall and then giggling when they noticed mine and Bea's boobs bouncing.

Charlotte seemed to be in her element with her friends, family and me and Gabe all together with her. We bounced around, the three of us and then joined some other children who were attempting somersaults.

"Is that your daddy?" one of the children asked.

With adoration and pride Charlotte nodded.

Another child looked at me. "Is that your mummy?"

Charlotte looked awkward, embarrassed and sad as she glanced between her friend, me and then Gabe.

"Not yet," she replied. "She's Carrie and she does all the things a mummy does and she's Daddy's girlfriend."

Gabe and I exchanged a glance that was loaded with emotion, so many emotions I wasn't sure what they all were.

Gabe reached for Charlotte, threw her up and caught her before taking my hand in his. "Cake time!" he cheered and led us both towards the giant unicorn cake we'd chosen together for his daughter.

Everyone stood and sang happy birthday while Charlotte beamed and then she blew out her candles and smiled at the applause.

"Make a wish," called Christine.

I watched on as the little girl tightly squeezed her eyes closed and I could swear I heard the determination of her wish.

****

By the time we got home and were alone, Charlotte was almost ready to pass out. If I was honest, I was too. She lay on the sofa, her eyelids losing the battle for consciousness while Gabe piled up the presents from her party and I washed up and tidied around a little.

He crept up behind me and wrapped his arms around my middle. "So, when are you moving all of your things downstairs?"

We'd talked about this several times and each time I made a non-committal response. Not because I didn't want to live with Gabe properly, but because I didn't want it to be rushed or for him to regret it or resent my presence. After everything with Toby, who was currently being held on remand, some six or eight weeks before, Gabe had turned ultra-protective and I was unsure whether that was because he finally saw me as his or because he wanted to take care of me. That also nagged in the back of my mind when I considered the option of moving in properly.

I drew a deep breath in and considered what to say. Eventually, after a few seconds that seemed longer, I spoke. "Are you sure that's what you want? That I am what you want, properly want, not just to be responsible for?"

"I'm sure." I heard nothing but total conviction in those two words.

"You don't just want to save me? Be my Prince Charming?"

"I've already saved you, Angel."

Tears welled in my eyes. He had saved me and despite all my objections to needing to be saved, to finding my prince and living happily ever after, I wanted them all and I wanted Gabe.

I felt his hands move from me and suddenly bereft and panic struck that he might have taken my words and questions as objections and was now having second thoughts. I spun to look for him. He wasn't there. I was confused.

I looked around where I found Gabe, down on one knee holding something beautiful and sparkly.

Chapter Sixty-Eight

Gabriel

I stared up at her as she turned around, unable to hide my smile as she searched for me. Her breathing itched when she finally looked down and saw me. Recognition flickered in her eyes as realisation dawned about where I was, what I was about to do, what I was holding.

"Now, I am somewhat of an expert in fairy tales, so, having saved you, I now need to take you back to my castle as my bride." I let out a low, shaky breath and blinked my eyes shut for a second and then, with my full attention on her, I spoke. "Carrie Webber, my very own princess, Angel, would you do me the very great honour of marrying me?"

Her mouth opened but no words came out. There was a noise, a sob, a garbled release of sound and then tears breached the dam of her eyes, but still no coherent words. Seconds followed, as did snot, which was the least romantic thing to be greeted by in these circumstances, but even then, she was beautiful.

And then, like the sun breaking on the dreariest and darkest of days, she lit up the room, the world, my life, with a nod and a smile and finally a single word, "Yes."

I slipped the diamond ring onto her finger and got to my feet and pulled her to me. One hand rested in the small of her back and the other gently held her neck. With nothing left between us I leaned in and kissed her. She kissed me back immediately and although there was lust and passion arcing between us, it was more, it was love and reverence, with promises of forever in

325

every touch we shared and every second that passed.

This was one of those moments that would last a lifetime and be forever burnt on my brain and soul.

"Yes!"

Carrie and I pulled apart and frowned at one another and then slowly turned to see the owner of the single word of approval.

What greeted us was the image of Charlotte, smiling, but beginning to cry. We each held out a hand to summon her to us. She rushed towards us and threw an arm around each of our hips.

"Yes," she repeated. "I wished for it." She sobbed, struggling to get her words out. "I wished for a mummy."

We both dropped to our knees, putting all three of us at similar heights.

"I wanted Carrie to be my mummy and when Grandma said to make a wish, I did."

I looked across at Carrie whose tears were flowing faster than my daughter's, our daughter's.

"And now, you're going to get married and you will be my mummy, my real mummy."

"I will," Carrie sobbed, pulling Charlotte in for a long hug and lots of kisses.

"I'll have a mummy and a daddy, just like my friends and when it's Mother's Day I can make you a card and buy you flowers, can't I, Daddy?"

My tears were now flowing as freely as both of my girls. "You can, baby, whatever you want. If that's okay with Carrie." I knew Carrie was happy to behave like my child's mother, to treat her as her own, but I suddenly wondered if she wanted the title and the expectation.

She looked across at me and then with another hug for Charlotte and a tender and loving kiss to the top of her head she spoke. "That is by far the most okay thing in the whole wide world, along with marrying you."

My longer and stronger arms opened and encompassed both of my girls, and as I closed them around my whole world, I knew that this was it, forever. There was nothing I wouldn't do to make them happy and to keep them safe.

"Can I be bridesmaid?" Charlotte suddenly asked, her head popping up from the cocoon we held her in.

"Absolutely," said Carrie with a laugh.

"When? When are we getting married?"

Her use of the word we had me fighting tears while Carrie bit her lip to stem the flow of fresh ones of her own.

"I don't know," replied Carrie.

"Soon," I said as a question for my girlfriend, fiancée.

"Soon," she repeated with a beaming smile.

"You'll have to go to the moon," Charlotte announced startling us both, but she continued with an explanation. "When Grandma's friend, Lisa, got married she went to the moon afterwards. She went somewhere really hot and Grandad said they paid through the nose for the privilege."

This girl really was something else and I loved her take on things.

"Ah," Carrie and I said in unison, understanding why we needed to go to the moon.

"Where shall we go on honeymoon then, Angel?"

"I believe Paris is nice at any time of the year."

I stared across at the beautiful woman who was mine, the one I'd had no intention of employing and still brought her to work for me, and now she was never leaving. She would be my love, my wife, my life, and I would no longer be a *Single Dad.*

The End

If you enjoyed Gabriel and Carrie's story, read on for a sneak peek at the soon to be released, Pinky Promise that tells Seb and Bea's story...

About The Author

Elle M Thomas was born in the north of England and raised near Birmingham, UK where she still lives with her family. She works in local education and writes in her spare time with dreams of becoming a full-time writer.

Whilst still at school, and with a love of writing slightly risqué tales of love and romance one of her teachers told her that she could be the next Harrold Robins. Elle didn't act on those words for many years. In February 2017, with her first book completed and a dozen others unfinished, she finally took the plunge and self-published the steamy romance, Disaster-in-Waiting.

Elle describes her books as stories filled with chemistry, sensuality, love and sex that she always wanted to read and her characters as three dimensional and flawed.

You can keep up to date with all things Elle M Thomas on social media here:

Twitter – Elle M Thomas Author

Facebook – Elle M Thomas and Elle's Belles

Instagram – authorellemthomas

Goodreads – Elle M. Thomas

Pinky Promise

Chapter One

Seb

"So, what's the plan?"

I looked across at my oldest friend, Gabe, who really did look like the cat who'd got the cream and swallowed a canary. He kind of had. He had gone from being single, widowed, with a little girl of three-years-old and then he'd hired a nanny. A nanny he hadn't wanted but had fancied the pants off, literally, and after a few bumps in the road they'd got their acts together. I did take some credit for that.

"The plan is as I told you it was last night; breakfast, shower, get dressed and marry my angel." Gabe smiled, confidence oozing from him, knowing this was the first day of the rest of his life with his perfect woman.

I wondered what that felt like, having been hurt in the past, burnt by trusting and loving, only to find the strength to try again, to trust, and to love again.

My friend stared at me as I tried to temper my own thoughts and emotions.

"You all good?" he asked with a slightly concerned frown.

"Yeah, why wouldn't I be?" I heard the snap in my voice but was incapable of stopping it.

"If that doesn't tell me you're not, I don't know what does."

"Fuck off, Gabe."

He laughed at me and then shook his head. "Me and you are

going for breakfast and we are going to talk this through, whether you want to or not because today is my wedding day. It is going to be perfect, Carrie and Charlotte deserve for it to be perfect, so the fact that we both know that it's your past relationship with the bridesmaid that's eating you, it needs resolving."

"We didn't have a relationship. We fucked, no more." I was being a dick because I was agitated and becoming more pissed off with every second that passed. I knew that every second that passed was taking me ever closer to coming face to face with Bea.

"Then there won't be a problem, will there, if you only fucked her? We both know there have been dozens, if not hundreds of women you have fucked. Women you only ever viewed as convenient and willing, and you've never had an issue with them, so Bea won't be any different, will she?"

"Fuck off, Gabe." I couldn't bring myself to say that maybe, just maybe, this was a little different.

Because it wasn't.

He laughed at me, like he could almost hear my internal monologue, and turned to pick up his wallet, phone and room key. "You need some new lines, buddy."

"Fuck you, you smug, arrogant fucker."

With a small shake of his head, he grinned.

"If today wasn't your wedding day, I would spread your nose across your face."

"Yeah, like you're man enough to do that."

I flipped him off and he shrugged it off with a smile. The truth was, I wasn't much of a fighter, I was the typically laid back one of the two of us. Gabe was the fiery one, always had been, and was the one who threw the punches. I was more likely to get punched by an angry boyfriend or husband due to the lack of relationship status I had, there wasn't a tick box for womaniser. I liked being with a woman for a good time then walking away, sometimes asking about their relationship status got lost in translation.

My mind went back to the night we'd found a guy, Toby, attempting to rape Carrie after drugging her. The sight of her being touched by him whilst clearly stoned almost to the point of unconsciousness will haunt me forever, so I could only imagine how that played on my friend's mind. He had been frantic as we tried to find her then relieved when we had. His relief was short lived. In the second he saw her, saw Toby touching her, something went off in his head and the short fuse he had been working with burnt out completely.

Gabe had grabbed for the other man who was slightly taken aback to have been discovered, so probably didn't see the first blow coming, but all the others that followed, well, he felt every one of those, even if he hadn't seen them all. Gabe rained blow after blow on him, while I took care of Nanny, trying to get her to come around a little as I covered her up. I was also the one to call the police as my friend continued his attack on Toby.

As much as I understood Gabe's need to pummel him—and why wouldn't I?—truth be told I would have happily punched the fucker myself for what he'd done to Nanny. However, I also needed my friend not to end up being arrested and charged with a serious assault or murder! So, with reasonable force still arguable, I pulled my friend clear and redirected his attention to his woman.

I allowed myself a small, ironic, internal chuckle as I recalled that fucking animal attempting to get up and possibly make a run for it. I'd even threatened him with a punch of my own at that point, and truth be told, I think I would have enjoyed it. Thank fuck he was locked up for a minimum of ten years, although in a psychiatric unit rather than prison. I briefly wondered what would happen to him if he was deemed of sound mind before the ten years. Would he be transferred to a prison to serve the remainder of that time? I had no clue and now was not the time to discuss this with my friend, this was his wedding day. This was Nanny's day. I was even more determined than ever to ensure they both, but especially Nanny, got the day she wanted and deserved. There was something truly special about her. She was funny, kind, and took no shit, not really, but there was more than that for me. I loved how she loved Gabe, but by far her most redeeming quality for me was the way she loved Charlotte. I loved that kid as much as if she was my own, and so did

Nanny. That little girl had been through far more than she knew, although one day she would know and would need to be loved by everyone in her life, even more than she did now, and to be happy, and Carrie, well she did that in the most magnificent way and I trusted her to always to do that.

Now, I was the one thinking that his bride deserved the perfect day but was still pissed off, with what, or who, I wasn't fully prepared to admit yet, not even to myself and as my friend was the only one here, well, all of my angst would be heading his way. Even as I thought that I felt bad, but I couldn't magic up a stranger or someone I didn't care about to turn my mood on. Plus, even if I could, would I? Probably not because I wasn't an arsehole, generally, and my moods were private. I only really revealed them, the negative ones to those I trusted, so basically Gabe. Yeah, he was going to have to deal with my bad mood and anger.

"I mean it, if it wasn't for the fact that I love Nanny, and it would make her sad that I'd punched you on a day where photos would haunt you for the rest of your natural life, you'd be nursing a broken nose. Although, if I did it, she might see that I was always the better looking one and she'd come away with me."

He shot me a glare that said I was getting to him. Thinking, or suggesting that I might be thinking of Nanny in naked terms always riled him. I was a man, and she was one hot nanny.

"I reckon Nanny and I would make a very attractive couple, sexy, really, really sexy."

"Seb," he warned in his firm tone.

I laughed. I was being a dick to him, and he didn't deserve it. "Fuck, you're too easy to wind up. Come on, let's get the condemned man a hearty breakfast and I promise to be on my best behaviour, unless Bea rocks up with a new guy and then all bets are off." I was deadly serious, and that was going to be a real issue.

"For fuck's sake. I have no clue if she's bringing anyone. However, I doubt she is as she only dumped your arse four months ago."

Long-term, serious relationships were not my thing. We'd

agreed in advance that we were both looking for fun, no expectations and no commitments beyond us being exclusive, which was a big thing for me. We didn't even have an argument. At the very beginning we discussed things, and both said that if either of us decided we were done, we'd say. We'd promised, pinky promised, no less. She'd called time on things when I thought everything was going well. It had bruised my ego as I was usually the one to end things, but not this time, not with Princess Bea. It wasn't even the fact that she'd ended things with *me*, it was the fact that it had ended *full stop*.

"Seb, come on. I need food."

Like a sulky teenager, I followed my friend out, shuffling my feet and huffing as I went, incapable of thinking of anything other than Bea now and whether she had brought a plus one with her.

****

Gabe was pacing the room, waiting for me to finish getting ready.

"I will go without you," he threatened.

"I am fastening my shoes and then I need to figure out how this fucking tie works."

"It's a cravat, and it fastens with a pin."

I stood up, having fastened my shoes and laughed at my friend. "Well, sorry for not knowing that, Gok Wan."

We both laughed but I was more than grateful that he knew how to fasten the bloody cravat. Who the hell wore one of these anyway?

"Isn't a cravat what posh people put wine into?" I asked.

Gabe smacked my shoulder. "That's a carafe, you bell end."

"I knew that," I protested, making my friend arch a brow disbelievingly. "Now, today is all about you and Nanny and my beautiful girl, Charlotte, so let's go and find your girls."

We exchanged matching grins. He was more than ready to find them both and nobody deserved happiness more than him and his girls.

With our jackets on, we were good to go.

"Seb," he called to me as he reached the door.

He sounded serious, so I gave him my undivided attention.

"I text Carrie earlier. Bea has come alone, no new guy."

"Thank you." I was unsure when I'd last felt that relieved. If I'd ever felt that relieved about a woman before.

Printed in Great Britain
by Amazon

41680416R00189